Casey Teel

Casey Teel

Dale Sprinkle

AuthorHouse™
1663 Liberty Drive
Bloomington, IN 47403
www.authorhouse.com
Phone: 1-800-839-8640

First published by AuthorHouse 09/26/2011

ISBN: 978-1-4670-2445-7 (sc)
ISBN: 978-1-4670-2444-0 (hc)
ISBN: 978-1-4670-2443-3 (ebk)

Library of Congress Control Number: 2011915816

Printed in the United States of America

In memory of
two special policemen, killed in action:
Leonard A. Christiansen and Gerald "Blacky" Sawyer.

CHAPTER 1

Eastern Canada, May 13, 1941

Major Peter Duncanwood was tired. It showed in his eyes that had seen more than any 31-year old should have. He slumped wearily into an over-stuffed chair in the student lounge at McGill University in Montreal.

Peter was half asleep when a soft tapping noise reached past his exhaustion. It took him several minutes to realize that he was listening to rapid Morse code. It took another minute to understand the code was being spelled out in French.

He stood up and walked toward the door leading to the dining room. A young man sitting at a table several feet away was slyly tapping out the Morse with a knife against a medal coffee pitcher. The soft taps were just audible, and not disturbingly loud.

Peter leaned against the doorjamb and lit a cigarette while mentally spelling out the Morse. The boy was in the middle of a sentence, ". . . . can not live without you".

Two tables away a strikingly beautiful young coed with long auburn hair appeared to be furtively glancing toward the fellow. Other students in the area seemed oblivious to the tapping, most being absorbed in textbooks. The girl was deep into her book too, but Peter got the strong feeling that she was aware of the message.

Developing a devilish smile the boy continued the Morse, ". . . . want to rub your tits." The young lady suddenly changed her curious expression to one of surprise. She picked up a fork and began tapping on an empty coffee cup. She was sending Morse, also using French: "Bastard".

With that she snapped closed her textbook, gathered her book and bag, and abruptly left the room, throwing a look of contempt at the boy as she departed. Peter was curious about the expression on the boy's face, one of complete and humiliating rejection.

Duncanwood walked over and sat down across from the boy. He looked into a pair of the bluest eyes he had ever seen and asked, "Mind if I join you"?

Casey smiled an easy but curious smile. "It looks like you already have. Would you like some coffee"?

"At this point in my life, coffee is as essential as breathing," the Major said smiling back. Casey reached for a clean cup stacked on the table and filled it.

Casey looked at the man with interest. Peter was of medium height and build. His smile revealed white even teeth. Casey was drawn to the Major's eyes. They were half lidded and sleepy.

Having several friends in the Army, Casey was more than interested in the uniform the man wore. It was the uniform of a major in the Royal Marines. Casey recognized the ribbons on the Major's left breast. The Military Cross with bar, the Distinguished Service Order, and the Military Medal. On his right sleeve he wore parachutist wings.

Casey suddenly realized that he had been staring. With a start he noted the Major appeared to be studying him with some interest.

The Major had a soft smile, "Too bad about the girl. Does she always turn you down so abruptly?"

Casey blushed and looked quickly around. Looking down, he replied, "I know she's fluent in French, but Morse?"

"Don't worry lad, it's not likely that anyone who understands both Morse and French is within a hundred miles of here."

Casey visibly relaxed and said, "My God I hope not. How did you learn Morse and French? You're obviously English."

"Oh, one picks up odd knowledge here and there," the Major replied vaguely.

"How is it that sweet young thing knows French?" Peter asked.

Casey explained, "Her parents are French. Her dad had worked for the French railroad or something."

"Tell me about yourself," the Major asked abruptly.

Casey seemed to sense this was not an idle question. He thought about not answering, but the military uniform seemed to prompt his response. “Well, I’m 20, just finishing my second year in Civil Engineering and plan to go back to Colorado and enlist in June. It looks like the varsity hockey team will have to wait for the end of the war to take advantage of the best forward McGill ever had.”

“You’re an American then?”

Casey nodded in affirmation. “You won’t hold that against me will you?” Casey smiled and opened his arms.

The Major smiled back. “Where did you learn your Morse and French?”

“My dad helped rebuild the French railroad system after the war to end all wars.” The Major acknowledged the irony.

Casey found himself more willing then usual to talk. “Dad was in the trenches, then in the Signal Corps. Somehow he found the time to marry my mother who grew up in a small town near Paris.”

“What town was that?”

“You probably never heard of it, it’s called St. Denis.”

The Major rolled his eyes. “Yes, I’ve heard of it.” Peter had an ugly scar on the inside of his upper left thigh. He briefly drifted into nostalgia as he recalled, “The Germans almost made me a soprano in France.”

Casey broke a brief silence by continuing that his language skills came from a schoolteacher French mother and his railroad telegrapher father had taught him Morse. The two chatted on for another hour and a half. Only three months later when Casey was taking a course on POW interrogation did he stop to realize how easily the Major had gotten his life story. That, without even revealing his own name.

After making his appointment with McGill’s leading chemistry professor, Major Duncanwood made a call to a friend in the RCMP Security Service.

“David, old boy, do you recognize my voice?”

The man on the other end of the line laughed out loud, “Of course you sod. How could I ever forget almost getting arrested for indecent exposure trying to out piss you against the wall of St.

Patrick's Cathedral? We were lucky that Bobbie had a brother in the Canadian Army!"

Peter, unable to keep from laughing, said, "Your problem, you ponce, is you can't hold your liquor."

"Holding it is not the problem. Getting rid of it while making the wager with you is the real problem. Sober, I would never believe anybody could piss as far as you can."

Peter changed the mood. "Did you hear about Charley Scott"?

"Not all the details."

"It was stupid; he trusted the wrong woman and the Gestapo got him."

"Oh shit," David slurred. "Did they torture him?" Peter didn't answer. David knew the answer.

"See here, David, I'm short on time. Can you do a little checking for me?"

`"Who and how deep?" came David's no-nonsense reply.

Thank God for the old boy network Peter thought. It certainly saves time and cuts through all the unnecessary bureaucratic nonsense. "The chap's name is Casey Teel. A male, six-one, about 180, brown hair, blue eyes. He's 20 and just finishing his second year at McGill. Civil engineering I believe. Apparently born in Colorado at a place called Durango. He talked a lot about camping off the Million-Dollar Highway. David, I need everything you can turn up, yesterday. He's going to join the Yank Army in 3 or 4 weeks."

"Where can I reach you?"

Peter thought for a moment. "You know our summer place?"

David knew Peter was referring to Camp X in Ontario where Allied spies and saboteurs were trained. "Yes I was there during the off season last year. A very rough element seems to be going there now."

"Well, old boy if you can't reach me there, try our main office." David knew the main office was SOE Headquarters, Barkley Square, London.

"Peter."

"Don't say it. You know I'm always careful."

David sighed. "Yes, of course. Actually, I was going to suggest you go play on the railroad tracks.'Course you'd probably derail the bloody train. Do be careful. I'll be in touch."

Two weeks later Casey was home in Colorado cleaning his fishing gear. He heard his black Lab bark at an approaching car. He watched in amazement as the man he only knew as the Major got out of a '38 Pontiac. The Major, dressed in a brown tweed suit, stared at the house for some seconds. Even at this late day he had doubts about his mission. Why should I recruit babies for a job like SOE? The chances of surviving spy work were slim at best. He was unsure too because he liked the boy. On the other hand his chances of surviving in the American military service were something less than optimistic. Well, at least in the SOE he'll be far better trained than anywhere else. Casey's quick wits might bring him through. You don't make McGill's hockey team by being slow, physically or mentally.

The two shook hands at the door and the Major gave his name. Casey brought Peter a scotch and soda from his folks' bar. Glancing about, the Major asked, "Are we alone?"

"Yes, my mom and dad are in town. Well, Fritz is here," added Casey, nodding toward the dog.

"Fritz, that's a German name," Peter declared with a bit of curious spite.

"Yeah, my dad likes to kick his butt." Casey then confessed, "Actually, Dad loves Fritz, he just threatens a lot; makes him feel better."

It got quiet in the house as the Major sat staring into the amber liquid in his glass. Casey sat on the edge of a hassock, as if anticipating being told a story.

Casey broke the silence, "You didn't come all this way for a drink, did you?" They both smiled.

"Casey," the Major began, "I belong to a rather rum group. We do a little bit of everything except regular soldering. I can't tell you much now but my people would like you to join us. I must tell you that the work is extraordinarily dangerous. There's not much glory in it. The chances of you coming back in one piece or even at all are not good. You would be far better off going through with your plans to attend Army Engineers Officer Candidate School".

Casey sat back and began absorbing what the Major just said. He started to speak, then stopped. He asked himself how did the Major know he was planning on going to OCS? And, what is the

Major doing here in civilian clothes? Both men sat motionless, looking straight at each other.

Casey broke the silence, "How could I refuse a gracious invitation like yours? It looks like I'll be blowing up bridges instead of building them".

Silence reigned again. Peter thought, this is too easy, he must be kidding. Casey thought, what am I saying—is he serious?

The next half-hour was taken up with back and forth conversation regarding the job the Major was offering. Casey's reaction went from, *You must be kidding*, to *That does sound exciting*, to *Why not?*

Actually, Casey did not succumb easily. The rapport they had established and the respect Casey found for the Major guided him to his decision.

Peter Duncanwood laid his head back against the chair, closed his eyes, and held the glass of iced whiskey against his throbbing right temple.

"Casey, if nothing else, you will find this job rewarding. And you will be doing more than your part to secure this War. Now, you must keep your mouth shut about this. When you leave here with me tomorrow you must tell everyone, including your parents, that you are joining the Royal Canadian Army Signal Corps. You'll be stationed in Regina. You know, your adopted Canada is calling. Any questions?"

"Would you tell me the truth if I did?"

The Major held his glass up in front of him, looking through it at Casey. Silence.

"That's what I thought."

"Welcome to the club, old boy."

CHAPTER 2

Colorado to New York, June 1941

Casey drove the Pontiac over Colorado's treacherous mountain roads toward Denver. Casey, who had driven ranch equipment and pickup trucks since he was 12 enjoyed the smooth handling Pontiac and hoped he would be able to buy something like it after the war.

Peter Duncanwood slept in the back seat for most of the five-hour trip, waking only when Casey stopped for gas and to eat. He also woke one time near the top of Wolf Creek Pass. Looking over the side of the road at the hairpin curves below, he uttered a low, "Oh, God", then rolled back down.

After the lunch stop, Peter grumbled, "Don't Americans eat anything but hamburgers and chips . . . . and why isn't there any Bovil?" Casey figured out that "chips" meant French fries. Peter only grumbled when asked for a definition of Bovil.

Arriving at Denver they drove immediately to Union Station. Following Peter's instructions, Casey parked the Pontiac in a remote corner of a parking lot. "Lock it up and lock the keys in the trunk."

Casey did as he was told and asked, "What about the car?"

Peter, a bit grumpy from his broken rest, replied tersely, "It'll be taken care of."

Peter and Casey walked into the cavernous waiting room and sat on a hard wooden bench near the tunnel to the gates.

"Our train leaves at 9:45. If I'm asleep wake me at about 9:30."

"What about the tickets?" Casey asked.

"Not to worry. Everything's laid out." Peter smiled and placed his canvas suitcase on the bench as a pillow. Peter promptly went to sleep. Casey shook his head in amazement, *how can he sleep in this busy place?*

With some time to kill, Casey walked over to the newsstand and bought copies of the Rocky Mountain News, the Saturday Evening Post, and after studying the paperback bookrack, bought a copy of Thomas Wolfe's, You Can't Go Home Again. He considered getting some air but thought better of it and sat on the bench across from the soundly sleeping Peter. He tried to read Thomas Wolfe but found it too difficult to concentrate. He glanced through the newspaper and read brief accounts about the war in Europe. Stories of the sinking of HMS Hood and the German, Bismarck were still coming in.

Generally, the news did not look good for England. He skimmed through the Saturday Evening Post and looked long and hard at an advertisement inviting young Americans to join the military service. Casey felt Uncle Sam's accusing finger was pointing directly at him.

Am I doing the right thing, he wondered? Dad said to wait until America gets into it. But then Dad hated the British for their stupid leadership in the Great War. He would never forgive the British generals for the needless slaughter in the trenches. Casey had grown up reading Joyce Kilmer's poetry and Ernest Hemmingway's *Farewell to Arms* and *The Sun Also Rises.* Casey had no illusions about war; his dad had seen to that. There were no heroes; no glory; the world kept spinning regardless of which side won. But Casey wondered about the brutality of the regimes in Germany and Japan.

Just last semester, Casey's psychology professor, a Jewish refugee from Germany, patiently explained how Germany's leading psychiatrist, Alfred Hoche, advocated killing off mental patients and those with severe physical disabilities. During the 1930s German psychiatrists murdered almost three hundred thousand people, including epileptics, mental patients, the physically disabled, and many thousands of children. Many of Casey's classmates refused to believe the professor. They attributed these stories to Jewish propaganda. Casey could not support the propaganda theory, as he could not determine a good motive for it.

As part of his "sales pitch," Peter told Casey that this wasn't just England's war. It was a fight for Western civilization and freedom.

Peter explained that Italian fascism, Nazi socialism, and Russian communism were the same thing. All advocated government control of the people and economy. Neither recognizes the human right of freedom, nor any individual rights. This had confused Casey, as he had always been taught in school that fascism, socialism, and communism were all very different political movements. Peter indulgently told Casey, "Wait until you see them side by side."

Well, I sure hope this is something worth risking my neck for, Casey thought. Like most young men throughout history, Casey's main concerns were not political issues, but things far more personal. How will I stand up in a dangerous situation? Will I run away? Will I stay and fight? Will I be so afraid that I can't do anything? Will I be able to kill another human being? And most of all, what if I piss in my pants? God, what else is there?

Casey was still puzzling over these age-old questions when the loud speaker announced their train in ten minutes. He hurriedly woke Peter and told him, "Time to go."

Peter looked at his watch; it was 9:35. "You must learn to be punctual old boy. One day somebody's balls might be forfeit, possibly your own."

Casey filed the advice away for future reference. He didn't know it yet, but his military education was starting.

The two walked down the long platform into the underground hall. They walked up the stairs and to their train. Peter stopped a porter and asked directions to their compartment, dining car, and club car.

The huge black porter had a smile that lit up the evening. "What does you want to do first? Take care of your stomach, improve your disposition, or catch up on your snoozers?"

Peter laughed and replied, "I wish I could do all three at once. Is the dinning car still open?"

"No sir, but I can rustle up a batch of sandwiches and if you want anything to drink I can get that for you now. In fact it's a good idea since Kansas is dry."

Peter mumbled to Casey, "Only Americans could dream up an insane idea like prohibition."

Keeping his gaze on Casey, Peter told the porter, "Yes, I'd be most grateful for some sandwiches and whatever you have to go with them. No hamburgers, if you please, and ah, a bottle of Johnny Walker Black Label will do just fine."

"I think I can manage that nicely," said the porter, accepting several bills from Peter. Peter was generous, and the porter quickly stashed the money and assumed a facial expression that would have suggested a completed drug deal. "My name is Mac and I'll be your porter all the way to Chicago. If you need anything just press the bell in your compartment."

Peter and Casey settled into their bedroom on wheels. The compartment had two lower and two upper beds and a small bathroom.

Casey looked expectantly at Peter, "Aren't you going to sleep again?"

Peter was looking at the cover of You Can't Go Home Again. "One learns to sleep whenever and wherever one can. I'm still playing catch up for the last four years. Have you read this?" Peter held up the book.

Casey ignored the question. "But England has only been at war since September of '39. What war were you fighting the other two years?"

"Ah yes, well, there are wars and then there are wars. Some of them go on all the time rather quietly. What we're doing now is shooting each other on a grand scale. When this war is over the battle will continue, only we won't be killing so many all at once."

Years later Casey would remember those words.

"You didn't answer my question about the book," Peter scolded.

"No, I was supposed to have read it in my English Lit. course, but didn't get to it. Gabriel wrote my book report for me. You remember Gabriel, the girl in the dinning room at McGill."

"Yes indeed I remember her. Her father would undoubtedly slit your throat if he knew about you two, or at least about you. However, don't worry, my lips are sealed."

At the same moment, following a series of light jerks, the train started pulling away from the station. As the lights of the City began to be spaced far apart, there was a loud knock at their door. "Your refreshments gentlemen," said a loud voice that could only belong to Mac.

Peter unlocked the door and instructed Casey to pull up the foldout table between the seats. Mac put down a platter of eight sandwiches, a bowl of potato salad, a jar of mustard, plates, silver ware, glasses, and a fifth of Johnny Walker in an ice bucket.

Peter looked distastefully at the ice bucket and under his breath muttered, “No wonder so many Americans have edema.” Peter shook his head when Mac offered several bills in change. Mac smiled a thank you and repeated his advice to ring if they needed anything.

They ate in silence and Peter had three large drinks of whiskey, neat. Casey declined the whiskey and drank ice water. “You'll develop this bad habit soon enough,” Peter said confidently.

After a good night's sleep and an uneventful day they arrived in Chicago. Two hours later they sped through a darkened Gary, Indiana on the New York Limited. The flat green of the Midwest slipped by rapidly. They arrived at New York's Pennsylvania Station the next day.

Peter and Casey took a cab to the Waldorf-Astoria. A bellhop walked rapidly toward them before the cab came to a full stop.

The man behind the desk beamed when he saw Peter and said, “So nice to see you again Mr. Duncanwood. Your family suite is prepared as usual.”

Casey looked over the manager who wore a silky smile, a dark blue double-breasted pin stripped suit, black hair slicked straight back, and a thin pimp's mustache. Casey didn't like him.

Casey whistled at the ornate living room in Peter's suite. Peter tipped the bellhop and quietly surveyed the living room that was full of Louis the XIV furniture that spelled money, old money.

“Been in the family for years,” said Peter vaguely. “Your room is the second door on your left. Why don't you clean up while I go make a phone call.”

Casey grew an expression that hinted he suddenly didn't know this man with him. “Go? Where do you have to go? The phone's right there on the bar.”

“Yes, it's right there on the bar, isn't it?” Peter picked up their room key, tossed it into the air, caught it, and quietly walked to the door. As he opened it he stopped, turned back toward Casey and instructed, “Be a good lad and ring the restaurant. You'll be talking to Rene'. Tell him we'll be down in an hour for two deviled beef ribs." Casey acknowledged with a shrug as Peter departed.

They immediately returned to the room after supper and Peter told Casey to be ready to leave early the next morning. Casey didn't question the instruction as Peter immediately headed for his room, no doubt under the influence of the whiskey he had consumed.

It seemed as though Casey's head had just hit the pillow when Peter was shaking him by the shoulder. "Wake up, it's time to go."

Casey came to life quickly as anticipation and curiosity seemed to spike a flow of adrenaline. He dressed rapidly and with Peter leading the way, they took the freight elevator to the basement. They walked through a damp cement passageway. After about 150 feet, Peter stopped at a large metal fire door.

"I used to sneak out this way when I was a kid. I would put a small piece of wood in the catch so I could get back in. I never got caught," Peter mused.

They walked down the alley and turned left at the first corner. They continued three blocks, and went down a ramp to an underground garage. Peter opened the rear door on a 1940 Cadillac Fleetwood, motioned Casey in, and nodded pleasantly to the driver.

"Well Charley, things are looking up. Where did you steal this fine limousine?" Charley looked pained as he handed Casey a thermos and a white paper bag full of doughnuts.

"I haven't stolen anything, sir, at least not since you had me obtain the loan of that Nazi general's Mercedes in St. Denis. You know, the place where that colonel almost shot your cock off. If I hadn't stolen the good colonel's monocle you'd be dancing in a tutu with the London Ballet." Charley was looking and talking to Casey, as if ignoring Peter's presence.

"Charley," the major said reaching out his hand, "You just keep on picking up those souvenirs. I do want to have children one day."

"By the by, this is . . . . ah . . . . Denis."

"Of course sir. It's a pleasure Mr. Ah Denis."

Casey smiled and nodded at Charley, threw a confused look toward Peter, and filled his mouth with a doughnut. Eyes open and mouth shut. Another lesson learned.

As they drove north, Peter asked Charley, "Got the stuff?"

“It’s in the spare, the trunk, and you’re sitting on some.”

Casey raised an eyebrow over his cup of strong black coffee, then looked suspiciously down at the car seat.

Peter explained, “Since you’re going to help smuggle the stuff across the border you might as well know your Yank government has put an embargo on a number of items we need desperately in England.”

“It’s nothing that will give us a hot seat, I trust,” Casey inquired with a worried tone.

Charley smiled at Peter in the rearview mirror and said, “Not unless sulfur powder will explode.” Casey visibly relaxed. He wasn’t sure, but supposed by Charley’s tone that the powder was harmless.

The almost new Cadillac hummed along the hilly New York countryside. They went north through Albany and then west through Utica and Syracuse. At Rochester Charley headed north and drove through a very old section of Irondequoit and parked the car on a long cement pier on an inlet which fed into Lake Ontario.

The trio sat in the car as though momentarily mesmerized. Peter broke the silence; “This is a round about way to get where we’re going. Two months ago we went out of a little cove near Olcott. The locals got suspicious about the heavy traffic going in and out, so we bought out a fishing company here that had seven boats. They still fish and even make money despite the odd job they do for us.”

Suddenly they all came to life. Charley tossed the keys to Peter who got out and opened the trunk. He stacked boxes marked “dry ice” next to a gangplank leading to a 40-foot fishing boat. Casey and Charley were rolling a spare tire up the gangplank while Peter retrieved more boxes of “dry ice” from under the rear seat.

Three men in work clothes came off the boat and quickly placed the boxes and the tires inside a cabin to the rear of the deckhouse. A fourth man was casting off the heavy lines that had secured the fishing craft to the pier. Charley had placed their two suitcases on the deck and was driving off. He had not said good-bye.

Casey and Peter went below to the galley where a crewman offered them coffee and oyster stew. The man was unassuming, looking down and away. The food and drinks were gratefully accepted. A man dressed in bib overalls, a very dirty once white wool sweater, and a black wool-stocking cap soon joined them. The man had penetrating black eyes and studied Casey carefully.

"Captain, this is my associate, Denis. You may be seeing him from time to time."

Peter and the captain nodded without shaking hands.

"The things I do for money," the captain moaned, sending an icy look toward Casey.

Peter smiled and sarcastically replied, "I thought it was patriotism."

"Patriotism don't feed the bulldog. If your people didn't pay me the extra dollars I think I would buy German war bonds," the captain said, smirking. "Well, enough of this stimulating conversation. Back to work. You two can bunk in my cabin while I pray for fog and blind Coast Guard lookouts."

Casey had a hard time falling asleep. Suddenly he found himself waking to the sound of the boat's diesel engine stopping. He looked out the starboard porthole; he was looking at a cement pier. A large army two-ton truck drove up cutting off his view.

Peter entered the cabin looking wide-awake. "You're home old boy; let's get cracking."

As they went on deck, four soldiers were loading the "dry ice" and the tire into the rear of the truck. The boat crewman hoisted another 20 large wooden crates out of the hold.

Casey nodded towards the crates and asked, "Bibles?"

Peter smiled and said, "However did you guess. At the seminary for our missionaries, we have great need for spiritual inspiration."

Casey and Peter threw their suitcases into the rear of the truck and followed them in. They rode with two of the soldiers who were at the dock. Casey took the cue from Peter and remained silent for the trip.

They came to a compound and drove passed a number of obviously newly constructed wooden buildings. Some were made of clapboard. Casey was amazed when they drove by what looked like a street in a European town. It took him a few seconds to realize that he was looking at buildings with false fronts.

Casey's amazement increased when they passed up a platoon of soldiers. Casey had expected to see uniforms, but not German

SS uniforms. Certainly not SS soldiers carrying submachine guns and goose-stepping in perfect order.

With a baffled look on his face, Casey looked at Peter. “Welcome to Camp X, old boy.” Peter smiled.

CHAPTER 3

Camp X, Ontario, Canada. June 1941

"Where the hell, just exactly, are we?" Casey demanded.

"Well, we're east of Toronto. It's pretty remote and hard to get to. Camp X is mostly woods. Fences, dogs, and veteran commandos protect the important places, so don't go wandering about. The south side is 40 miles of cold Lake Ontario water. The whole area is under 24-hour scrutiny, comprende'?"

Casey looked worried. "What would I be doing here?"

Peter smiled, a habit that was beginning to irritate Casey. "Among the fuzzy wuzzys and aborigines I think they call it the rites of passage."

"Oh shit!"

The corporal poked his fellow soldier in the arm, and said, "Eddie, the lad knows our national anthem."

The truck stopped in front of a large two-story wooden building. The two soldiers jumped down and the corporal handed Casey and Peter their suitcases. He looked at Casey and in a serious tone said, "Good luck, mate." Casey watched him as he walked away.

Casey followed Peter into a shingle sided building and they walked to a small office in the rear. As they walked through the hallway Casey noticed there were no names on doors, just numbers. The atmosphere was heavy, as in a fog.

Peter unlocked the office door and Casey found himself sitting in a metal folding chair in a small windowless room. The walls were unpainted pine. The wood still smelled fresh and outdoorsy. Peter sat behind a small battered wooden desk whose only adornment was a black telephone. The only other furniture in the room was a locked four-drawer cabinet.

For a long moment Peter sat with his elbows on the desk, his hands covering his face. Slowly he sat back in his chair and looked intently at Casey.

"Listen very carefully," Peter began, "You're here because you know Morse almost better than anyone in this business. Also, you speak French. You've been to France and have relatives there. Couple these factors with high intelligence and excellent health and you make an ideal candidate for this organization."

"Which is?" Casey blurted.

As if Casey had said nothing, Peter continued, "Before I hand you over to our processing unit and then our training group, I have a few words of advice." Peter paused to be sure Casey was with him. "Don't ask questions. You'll be told what you need to know. You'll be able to figure out some of it. When you write home say that you are attending a signal course. We will forward your letters from Regina and letters from home will be forwarded here. You'll have some help with the letters."

Peter paused to light a cigarette, bringing an ashtray out of a desk drawer. "Your name while you are here will be Denis. Our background people had another name picked out for you but I'll straighten that out. You are not to discuss anything about your life with anybody here. There may or may not be classmates who are counter intelligence officers who will try to get information out of you and the others."

May or may not be, my ass, thought Casey.

"You've already learned a little. Once again, eyes open, mouth shut; understood?"

Casey sighed deeply. "Understood."

Peter picked up the telephone, asked for a number, and spoke briefly. A few thoughtful, silent minutes later a soldier entered the room.

"Harry, this is Denis, take care of him will you?" Peter said.

"Certainly, sir," Harry snapped, casting a sizing up look at Casey.

Peter rose and shook hands with Casey, "You won't be seeing me for a while, but I'll be keeping track of your progress. I'm sure you'll do just fine." Peter was smiling, but the smile had a certain chill about it.

Feeling a bit like a puppy following its master, Casey joined Harry as they walked from the building. They walked across the camp, which gave Casey a chance to size up Harry. He was about 5'9" and apparently didn't know about fat. He was wearing plain British army battle dress and heavy army issue boots. His left ear was misshapen, his nose was ever so slightly off center, and there was scar tissue around his eyes. He could have been anywhere from 25 to 40. Casey almost asked him where he had boxed, but remembered Peter's advice.

They entered a T-shaped barracks where Harry told Casey to leave his bag in a room that contained three metal bunks, three metal wall lockers, and two old battered desks similar to Peter's. Casey looked over the room and dropped his bag on the only empty bunk. "Just like home," Casey said, smelling the fresh pine again. Harry smiled his little Mona Lisa smile.

In a day or two you'll think of this room as your mother's womb." Harry's smile belied the frankness of his tone of voice.

Harry then escorted Casey to a large mess hall. "We don't keep regular hours here so this place runs 24 hours a day." Casey followed Harry's lead and picked up a tray and silverware and passed quickly through the cafeteria line. Casey ate quickly in silence, as did Harry. To Casey's relief the food was surprisingly good, hot, and tasty.

Next they walked to another large wooden building constructed exactly like the one in which Peter's office was located. The first floor was almost all open space. Harry led the way to a desk manned by an imposing warrant officer who boasted three rows of ribbons on his chest.

"This is Denis," explained Harry. Ignoring the introduction, the warrant officer picked out a file folder among a small stack on his desk and told Casey to sign the first 14 copies. "Sign your real name," he specified.

Suspicious and confused, Casey was about to protest when he saw his real name typed on the first page, which was titled, <u>Official Secret Act.</u>

"Do I get to read them first?" Casey asked, not expecting an answer.

"Just sign the bloody things," the warrant officer replied in a bored tone.

Casey sighed, shrugged, and signed.

As they were walking through a large warehouse, soldiers behind a long counter were filling Casey's arms with army uniforms, boots, socks, long underwear, raincoat, overcoat, and all the paraphernalia every new soldier is issued.

"Don't I get sworn in or something?" Casey asked Harry, who was standing by.

"You did that when you told the Major yes. The paper work is just a formality. You must understand that this is far different from the regular army."

"Am I in the Army?"

"No, don't worry about it. It will all come clear in time."

The next six weeks were the toughest in Casey's life. The days started at 4:30 with an hour of calisthenics. Then came breakfast and then classes in map reading, explosives, and firearms. He learned about all kinds of German, British, and other European small arms. There were other, more sinister classes. Harry ended up being the instructor in a class called "self defense." Casey learned how to kill with a hatpin, a piano wire, and even his bare hands. He learned how to follow people and how to recognize and lose a tail. He was taught how to tell if anyone had been in his hotel room while he was out.

A former Shanghai policeman by the name of Fairburn taught Casey how to use a knife in ways that Casey never dreamed possible. Fairburn's most important lesson was that winning the fight was the ONLY option. Losing the idea of fighting "fair" was step one.

Once during a training session a student was not aggressive enough to suit Fairburn. He knocked the knife out of the student's hand, kicked his feet out from under him, kneed him in his groin as he fell, then held the kid's knife to his throat.

"You bloody stupid sod! What the hell are you going to do when some German SS man is tickling your balls with a bayonet?" Fairburn screamed into the terrified recruit's face. "Do you think you're going to ask him to wait a minute, you ignorant turd?"

Fairburn's saliva was dripping on the recruit's face but he was too terrified to wipe it. "Now little boy blue do you think you can get in there and forget being nice?"

The kid croaked out a hoarse, "Yes sir!" He couldn't nod since the knife was still pressed against his throat.

Fairburn let the kid up and put a sheath over his knife and handed it back. Fairburn noted with satisfaction that the recruit went after his opponent aggressively and without hesitation.

Some lessons were not at all violent. One day the class convened in the mess hall. While waiting for the instruction to start, Casey and the others imagined how they would be taught how to use the chairs, tables, or maybe even food as weapons. They all glanced at one another with sheepish grins as they started their lesson in table manners. They also learned about foods, particularly typical French and German fare. One whole session was devoted to identifying and serving European wines. The fact that they would be sent behind enemy lines undercover was truly beginning to seem real.

Toward the end of six weeks they had a weeklong course on interrogation. It wasn't devoted to nice quiet talk sessions trying to get information out of a POW. Rather it covered Gestapo interrogation methods. It wasn't pleasant.

The instructor carefully explained that the Gestapo preferred manual interrogation methods. This meant physical beatings that were solely to soften up the prisoner. Then came the real tests. Electrical wires attached to the testicles, fingernails pulled out, head held under water, etc. "When you see a bath tub in an interrogation room don't think they're going to give you a bath and a new suit," the instructor advised.

The next week was pure hell. Even though the students knew their interrogators were on their side, they fell easily into the role-playing. Their interrogators wore the black uniforms of the SS. While the trainees were not tortured, they were deprived of sleep; received very little food and water; and were pushed, shoved, and screamed at for the entire week. The recruits loathed their tormentors. Their view softened somewhat after the course when they learned that three of their instructors bore the physical and psychological scars of actual Gestapo interrogation. Casey wondered if this training would be useful to him. He hoped not.

When the initial "rites of passage" were over, the remainder of Casey's group, 13 out of the original 24, were given five days leave. Casey wanted to go home or at least visit friends at McGill, but he was forbidden to do so.

"Go with your mates to Toronto," Harry advised. "You'll have a good time. Find a good hotel. I'm sure a good looking lad like you can find some sweet young thing to keep you warm at night."

Casey knew that was more than advice. He was to stay away completely from his former life.

Casey, Black Jack, Ying Yang, and Marceu went to Toronto. The latter was known as the "knife" because he always carried a Fairburn special strapped inside his left sleeve. Most of the class thought he didn't have all that much to learn from Fairburn.

In Toronto, Casey did indeed pick up a girl with astonishing ease. He also experienced his first hang over, and he slept twelve hours every night. The other four had gone their own ways, but their paths crossed occasionally. Casey hated to leave when their time was up. But the young lady he was "with" each night seemed to be losing interest in him. He thought they might have had something going. But thoughts of what he was embarking on quickly pushed any regrets out of his mind.

On their way back to Camp X on the bus, Black Jack was complaining about his lack of success with the ladies. "The first night I picked up the most beautiful woman in all of Canada. She ended up being a Mother Superior. She thought fucking was a small village south of London. Little did I know but I found her soul mate two days later. I took her to dinner and she hardly spoke three words. We ended up in this little bar, see, with me trying to make conversation at least. That's when a cat done me in for good."

"How could a cat screw you up?" asked Yang, who was starting to take an interest in the story.

"Well, there was this black cat. I never thought they were bad luck, but this one made me a believer. The cat was sitting by the kitchen door scratching the back of its head with a hind leg. I poked the girl in the ribs, pointed to the cat, and asked this vestal virgin if she could do what the cat was doing. When my nun looked over, the cat was licking its balls. My little blossom picked up her purse and left me sitting there with my black cat, who was by now scratching his head again."

"What did you do then?" Yang asked, laughing.

"I went looking for a brick and a gunny sack. Without success, I might add. That damned cat is still there being the patron saint for Toronto's virgins."

Back at the camp, Casey and the others found that their short furlough was not a benevolent gift from the gods. Casey was ordered to see a Captain McDonald, who had something to do with security.

McDonald was a balding middle-aged man who greeted Casey with the word, "Sit."

"Did you enjoy your leave?" he asked with little emotion.

Casey said nothing, sensing that he was not really being asked a question.

"For a beginner you gave very little away. Our operative did figure out that you're an American, you love Dixieland jazz, you're articulate, and you speak French." McDonald looked at Casey over his steel-framed glasses, "You really shouldn't show off so much to your women companions. She told us you are in the military. You used several soldier slang terms; very tacky. Also, you like to fish in the Green River. Fortunately for you there are three Green Rivers in Canada and at least five in the States. I think that's it. Oh yes, you have a rather ugly appendix scar, and nobody really gives a shit how great your dog Bailey was."

"Did she say how many times I passed gas?" Casey asked caustically.

"Don't get smart, youngster, all in all you did rather well; much better than your companions. You won't be seeing Black Jack any more. His pursuit of the fair sex makes him inclined to talk a bit much." Casey sensed that was an understatement, but had to ask. "He didn't get the boot over a cat incident did he? That was an innocent mistake." McDonald raised his eyebrows and responded, "No, no cat involved. I think I don't want to hear about that."

Changing the subject abruptly, McDonald picked up another file and told Casey, "You are scheduled for a two month course at our radio training facility."

"Wouldn't that be a waste of time?"

"If it were basics, certainly. We understand that no one can teach you about Morse. However you do need a bit of training learning codes and some of the tricks of the trade you will need to become a good pianist."

Casey knew from the grapevine that a pianist is the radio operator for a small group of saboteurs who operate in occupied Europe. He didn't want to go into the "grapevine", so he just nodded his head and gave a slight puzzled look.

Captain McDonald leaned back in his swivel chair and said to Casey, "Actually, we're very pleased with your progress. You're a quick study. You spend time in our library. You've checked out, let's see, 18 books these last weeks. You're stronger and more physically fit than most of the people taking the course. In fact, you've received a nice compliment when you picked up the pace on your last 30-mile stroll. Sergeant St. Johns told me he would have liked to have broken your knee caps."

Casey smiled at the memory. "Is that all, sir?"

"Yes. Oh, just one more thing. Stand up and raise your right hand."

McDonald mumbled some words while reading a small file card. When he finished he held out his hand to Casey and said, "Congratulations, you are now a subaltern in His Majesty's Army. If you will, sign these papers." The words were a question; the tone a command.

"Why am I being selected for this honor?"

"Well," McDonald began, "When there's been a decision to be made, the others look to you and you instinctively take charge. Your instructors have reported that you're totally adaptable. When those rascals threw monkey wrenches into a prepared plan of action, you adjusted. You didn't let pressure bother you, which is important. In your future line of work you will work alone and receive little or no direction or supervision.

"Now, take the rest of the day off and report to the radio school tomorrow."

The next two months were the most intense Casey ever experienced. There were classes covering ciphers, radio theory, and antenna formulae. Casey also increased his speed at Morse code after learning the disquieting fact that the average life span of a pianist behind the lines was six months. The faster you send messages the less time German radio direction finders have to locate you.

Casey was so engrossed in his studies that it wasn't until the radio course was completed that he became aware that the ground at Camp X was heavy with snow. The maple leaves had long since turned gold, yellow, and red, and now the trees were barren.

Captain McDonald invited himself to a seat at Casey's table in the officers' mess. "Don't tell me," Casey said, "You're here to promote me to General."

"Not yet, you cocky twit," McDonald said jokingly, "You're off to another school."

"God, not another rapid course I hope; I dream in Morse code now."

"No, you're finished with that part of the training. Now you're off to Ringway."

Casey's stomach tightened. The camp rumors described Ringway as the parachute training school in England. Casey mumbled, "Shit."

"What was that?"

"Delighted sir, absolutely delighted," Casey answered with a grimace.

McDonald beamed at him, "That's the spirit now."

Casey traveled in civilian clothes and used his own passport. He took a flight from Toronto to New York City, where Charley, who was still driving the Cadillac, met him.

"I see you bought new tires."

"It's the eighth set, I think, since you had your boat ride." Apparently not wanting to engage in small talk, Charley quickly continued, "I'm to take you to your hotel and put you on the Pan Am Clipper for Lisbon tomorrow morning."

"Lisbon?" Casey questioned. "I thought . . ."

Charley interrupted, apparently anticipating the question: "There are many routes to England. Some are watched more closely than others."

Casey nodded approval and said, "Oh, OK;" not wanting to get too inquisitive.

Nothing more was said, as they both entered the car and drove to a small hotel in Manhattan. Charley instructed, "You have a room here; it's taken care of." Charley handed Casey a copy of the New York Times. "You might be interested in the entertainment section, but get to bed early. I'll pick you up at six sharp."

The transatlantic flight to Lisbon was uneventful. He barely had time there to get to his next flight, which was to Manchester. One theme frequently replayed in Casey's mind during the long hours of flight: How do I feel about jumping out of an airplane? He came up with no real enthusiasm, nor any sense that he didn't want to go through with it.

Casey was surprised to be met in Manchester by a white-haired man in his 60s. The man wore a dark suit and overcoat, homburg, a cavalry officer's mustache, and was wielding a gold-headed cane. The man walked right up to Casey as if they were old friends.

"Peter asked me to meet you. I am Charles Duncanwood, his father."

They shook hands and Casey said, "I just left a Charley in New York. I wouldn't imagine many people call you Charley though."

"Not for a long time," Charles Duncanwood smiled. "Collect your bags. I've cleared you through customs. We'll spend the night at my flat and someone from the firm will collect you tomorrow."

Duncanwood's "flat" proved to be an elegant 15-room townhouse in one of Manchester's most desirable districts. The two talked through dinner and well into the evening. Duncanwood found Casey to be a bright fellow with a young man's enthusiasm for life. Casey found Duncanwood to be a very worldly man, yet not at all condescending, and so easy to talk to. The traits of a truly "big man", Casey thought.

Casey learned that Charles lost his right leg above the knee in the last week of the War, but had stayed in the army "flying a desk." Charles specified that he, "Now works for the same firm with Peter."

At Ringway Casey was assigned to a small group of five men and two women. They were issued Royal Air Force coveralls, boots, and a padded helmet. They were needlessly instructed not to talk to anyone outside the unit.

The two-week parachute school was brutal. The physical training went on incessantly. The first week included some ground school. They learned everything there was to know about parachute paraphernalia, windage, and emergency procedures. They even learned to pack a chute.

True to tradition, one class member asked the emergency procedures instructor what would happen if his parachute didn't open. Over the class snickers, the instructor pointedly explained that, "We'll pick you up with a large sponge." The lack of frivolity in his abrupt answer immediately stopped the snickers, and brought somber reflective expressions to the faces of the students. For Casey, and he surmised for the rest of the class, that was the moment of realization that he was actually going to jump from an airplane, thousands of feet above the ground.

The second week they were required to make seven jumps. Two from a suspended balloon and five from airplanes. The normal course required that one jump be made at night. Casey's group made all their plane jumps at night. Surprisingly all seven made it through the course. There were no broken bones, and no one froze in the air.

Acting on an invitation from Charles Duncanwood, Casey spent another day with him before his return flight to Canada. The two talked for hours in front of a large fireplace. Charles never placed Casey in a position of violating his trust by asking questions about his training. Casey learned to appreciate 20-year-old brandy.

Upon his return to Camp X, Casey was ordered to report to Captain McDonald. Casey wondered what pleasantness McDonald had for him now.

"No broken bones I see?" was McDonald's greeting.

"No thanks to you, Mein Fuhrer."

"Diplomatic language is not your strong suit, is it?" said McDonald pretending to be severe.

Cutting through the pleasantries, Casey asked, "What gala are you inviting me to next?"

Casey found himself in the last and most interesting phase of his training. He was taught the basics of guerrilla warfare; ambushes, raids, finding drop zones, escape and evasion, assassination, agent selection, intelligence nets, local customs, forgery, false identification, explosives, and countless other tricks of the trade. He was taken on a tour of Canadian factories and utility plants and was shown the places where explosives would do the most damage. In a somewhat joking tone, one of the plant managers asked Casey if he intended to join the plant's union after the war. Casey wasn't given time to respond. The instructor abruptly told the manager that that was not the plan. The manager sheepishly backed away.

It was now Christmas Eve, and McDonald was driving Casey to the Toronto airport. They drove slowly due to the ice and snow. It was bitter cold.

"I'm glad you decided not to join the Yank army after Pearl Harbor," said McDonald, throwing a fatherly look towards Casey.

"I thought about it, but I'm already trained to do a job." Looking introspective, Casey continued, "It will take us a long time to gear up for this war." Lightening up, he added, "Besides, I don't want to ever go through another training course." McDonald threw an acknowledging nod and grin at Casey.

At the airport loading gate McDonald took a small package from his coat pocket and handed it to Casey. "Open it on the plane; just a little something."

They shook hands, and after a moment's hesitation, roughly embraced. They pulled back and McDonald looked deeply into Casey's face. For a moment he felt the fright of war, as though reading and feeling Casey's future.

McDonald snapped to, and putting on an official air instructed, "Remember what we taught you and bring it all back in one piece."

Casey wasn't sure but he thought he saw a tear in the corner of Mac's eye. As he boarded the plane Casey turned and waved goodbye to McDonald, who was standing very still in the softly falling snow.

As the C46 gained altitude Casey opened the small package. There was a note on top of the box. It read simply, "This is for after the war."

Casey opened the box and found a heavy silver I.D. bracelet with his name on the top, "Casey Randall Teel". He turned it over and found the inscription, "1941, lest we forget."

A priest looked across at the young Army lieutenant with the paratrooper wings on his shoulder and a nametag reading, "Denis". The priest thought the young man was crying.

CHAPTER 4

England. January 1942

Harry, a tall, rather large man with a big chin and Roman nose picked up Casey at the airport. Harry spoke with a heavy English, almost Cockney accent. Harry held open a rear door for Casey. As Casey entered, he was surprised to find another man sitting in the front passenger seat. The man was about Casey's age, trim, with a look of excitement in his eyes. He turned to Casey, "Hi, I'm Jacques. Appears we're going to the same place."

To Casey, Southampton was a peaceful sounding town name. Casually driving through it invoked the same emotion. Alone in the back seat, Casey nearly fell asleep, though he was rather spiked with anticipation. This was it. The training was done, now to battle.

Casey realized that the battle was going to wait awhile, as Harry turned the car into an alley, and parked snug against the wall of a three-story building. The name "Surrey" was displayed above a nearby door. This was obviously the side door of a bar. Following Harry like two puppies, Casey and Jacques entered a dimly lit pub. The trio went immediately to a booth near the door. The booth was made entirely of dark wood, with high backs. As soon as Casey and Jacques sat down, Harry leaned over and said, "I need to get a clearance here, then we'll be on our way." Harry quickly disappeared into a side room. Casey and Jacques exchanged looks of puzzlement, but neither spoke.

Three men were seated at the far end of the heavy wood bar, which stretched nearly the full length of the room. A bartender was standing with one leg up and engaged in quiet conversation with the three patrons. There were other booths, but the newcomers could not see if they were occupied. Casey got the feeling of being watched, but he could see no one looking in his direction.

Harry was gone only a few minutes when he returned and, scooting Jacques over, sat in the booth. The bartender walked from behind the bar and toward the trio. "Harry?"

"I'll just have a pint to quench me thirst."

"All right then", the bartender said, "and for your friends?"

"Them too, if they don't object." Casey and Jacques looked at each other, shrugged their shoulders, looked toward the man, and nodded their heads affirmatively.

Harry leaned forward and talked softly, "This is kind of like a border crossing station. We always stop here before going on. It'll take a bit of time for clearances to be forwarded, and then we'll be on our way." The rest of the time in the bar Harry gave his charges a verbal tour of London and Southampton.

As they pulled into the driveway of a large house, Harry announced, "This is Beaulieu, your home away from home." They pulled through a veranda and stopped next to a side door, hidden somewhat from the road by hedges.

The driver removed the key and prepared to open his door. He stopped momentarily and looked at Jacques. "So they named you after a martyr?" Jacques looked at Harry, who was now exiting the car, raised his eyebrows, and then exited the car.

Casey walked into the building looking like a kid entering a candy store. This was his first exposure to the inside of a real English manor. The manor had a large foyer that was open to the second floor. A number of rooms were off the foyer. An upstairs balcony surrounded the open area, and had numerous doorways off of it. The woodwork, ceiling sculptures, and window treatments were exquisite. People scurrying in and out of rooms, and the sounds of typewriters tapping, radios buzzing, and numerous voices going at once quickly broke Casey's spell. It was obvious; this was some type of nerve center.

A young woman quickly greeted Casey and Jacques. She was 20 something; trim, rather cute, but emanated a business-like countenance. "Hello, Denis and Jacques, my name is Sarah. I will be introducing you to your new jobs." Her French accent belied her name, Casey thought, but then he realized that "Denis" didn't exactly fit him.

Jacques couldn't contain his curiosity any longer. He asked Sarah what Harry meant by the martyr remark. Obviously not wanting to go into details, she simply replied, "You know, the first resistant executed . . . . now come with me." Following Sarah, Jacques hunched his shoulders and threw a puzzled look toward Casey, who returned the look.

They went upstairs and entered one of the few rooms that had a closed door. Several file cabinets lined the walls and papers and folders were strewn about them. A large desk was straight away against the far wall, and it too was in disarray with paperwork. A fit man, in his 40s, looked up and spoke first. "Denis and Jacques, I am Lieutenant Sumac, like the tree. You will never address me or anyone else here by their rank. This is to get military titles out of your heads, lest you slip in the wrong circles. That will be all."

Denis and Jacques turned toward the door. "Not you, Sarah. You two sit down please." Sarah left the room and closed the door.

A few moments of silence ensued while Sumac pondered two folders on his desk. "Denis you are Casey Teel, an American from Colorado. You speak fluent French and are a master at Morse. Seems your Camp X instructors had positive things to say about you." Shifting folders Sumac addressed Jacques; "You are Kevin McDonough from where . . . Quebec City?"

"A bit south of the City", Jacques explained.

"So, you're nearly a Yank too," Sumac continued, "but you speak German. Your training record was also excellent. But then, you wouldn't be here if that weren't the case." Sumac then looked intently at Jacques and wryly exclaimed, "You're a curious chap, a German speaking Irishman from French Canada."

Jacques smiled and shrugged, not knowing what to say.

Sumac took several papers from each of the folders and slid in his chair over to the side of the desk. A metal bucket was on the floor, and he held the papers over it. Striking a match, he ignited the papers, and after they were engulfed in flame, gingerly dropped them into the bucket. He did this while apparently ignoring the two curious onlookers.

Sumac slowly looked up and very deliberately addressed the two men before him. “There are two reasons I did that,” he said gesturing toward the now smoking bucket. “Casey Teel and Kevin McDonough just evaporated; those two no longer exist . . . . understand Denis and Jacques?”

Both men knew that was a question to be answered. Both quickly replied, “Yes sir.”

“And no one, no one has a last name.”

Again, “Yes sir.”

Sumac slid back behind the desk and almost sheepishly continued, “The other reason is that in case this establishment is ever compromised, there will be nothing . . . . Well let’s get you two started here.”

Sumac led Denis and Jacques back down the stairs and into an open room on the first floor. There were five people in the room, but it was apparent that one was a supervisor. That man was sitting at a desk paying attention to a woman and a man who were standing talking to him. Two other women were working over papers at other desks. Sumac walked up to the supervisor and interrupted. “Dalton, this is Denis.” Dalton nodded a greeting toward Denis and resumed his conversation. Sumac tapped Jacques on the shoulder and started for the door, “You’re with me.” The two left Denis standing there, feeling a bit awkward as all in the room essentially ignored him.

Ultimately the conversation finished and Dalton rose and came around to greet Denis. Dalton had a firm grip and a sincere greeting. He gripped Casey’s shoulder and said, “Let’s go and I’ll show you around this place.”

They exited the room and went to a small room near the front entrance. There was one desk, occupied by Sarah. Dalton offered, “You’ve met Sarah. You go to her if you need any supplies, food, or the like. If you have some information that you need to share, but you don’t know who to talk to, go to Sarah. She can guide you through this facility, and around town, as needed. Make no mistake,” he admonished, “Sarah is an agent, not a clerk. She keeps this place running and knows where everything is buried, if you get my drift.” Casey shook his head in acknowledgement and followed Dalton as he walked to another room.

In all, they visited just about every room in the Manor. The main floor was primarily clerical offices, with files, typewriters, and a lot of busy people processing papers. A fairly large dining area was connected to a butler's pantry and a rather well set up kitchen. Upstairs was the command area, with a few private offices. This floor also had two conference rooms, and two bedrooms separated by a full bathroom. The basement was the communications center. Radio operators sat in dimly lit areas with reading lights by their radio/teletypes. There were three bedrooms here that shared one bathroom.

When Dalton showed Casey the basement, some operators were simply pondering their machines. A couple were pounding out and receiving messages while one or two other people stood around them looking on. Casey got the distinct impression that he and Dalton were invisible to those working there.

Dalton turned toward the door, motioned toward it and instructed, "Let's go to the dining room and get some tea. We have a lot to talk about before you get down to work."

Jacques and another man were sitting at one of the two large tables in the dining room when Casey and Dalton entered. Dalton showed Casey how to fetch some tea, and then invited him to sit at the unoccupied table. They were basically out of earshot of the other two.

Dalton started by telling Casey that he is one of the coordinators for the information that flows through this organization. There were others, as this is a round-the-clock operation. Dalton admonished, "Everything that you get comes to me, or one of the other coordinators. We will assume that from your training you know how to handle the mechanics of this job. Obviously, there will be a lot of work-a-day procedures that you will learn. Any questions, bring them to me or to Sarah."

As though reading from a script, Dalton continued, "SOE headquarters is in London. We have some training areas near Southampton, and some of the instructors bunk here from time to time. Much of the radio communications from Western Europe Resistance people is received in our basement. The messages are relayed to Anthony Eden's office and to de Gaulle. The General has offices in London. We receive messages to relay back to Europe from London . . . . sometimes we improvise from here. You'll see what I mean."

Dalton leaned back and appeared to settle in for some long conversation. "Of course, there are Nazi spies lurking everywhere in this country. This manor absolutely has to look like an innocent commercial operation. It is a hotel/residence that caters to those Englanders who can afford a little getaway now and then, but who are not so rich or connected to be worth a spy's time to watch. So, you, as is true with all of us, will be playing a double role. Besides your radio duties, you will start out as being a workman hired for the manor. You will come every morning and leave every night. You probably have wondered about your belongings. They have been taken to an apartment a short walk from here. That will be your home for a while." Casey seemed to be staring toward the ceiling. Dalton insisted, "Are you with me?"

Casey quickly replied, "Yes, Yes. I'm paying attention, really!"

"Paying attention is essential here. I cannot emphasize that enough," insisted Dalton. "Countless lives are at stake in everything that we do. Do not forget that the chaps on the other end of your radio are constantly being hunted down, and sadly, sometimes caught and . . . your training taught you about Gestapo tactics . . . . you know what I mean. You must think on your feet. You must absolutely be on constant vigil for Englandspiel." Dalton lightened up a bit. "Englandspiel refers to Germans who have captured a Resistance radio station and are trying to continue to communicate with us. It's essential that we communicate with the Resistance. It's equally essential that we don't ruin their cover by communicating with a Gestapo stand-in." Dalton looked directly into Casey's eyes, "Nobody here is perfect. We make honest mistakes. We don't make lazy mistakes." Silently staring at Casey, Dalton drove this point home.

Dalton stood up, walked a couple of short circles, and then sat on the edge of the table in front of Casey. Looking back at Casey, Dalton continued, "You know generally about the French Resistance; some of the hows and whys. The intent is that with your talents and training, we can plug you into the Resistance generally, or most likely, for a special operation. If and until that happens you will be assigned here. Don't try to jump the gun, like Hitler accused that Negro Yank. This work is vital to the war.

"You probably don't know that the Resistance recently had some major setbacks. There were originally a lot of separate little regional Resistance groups. They were just getting organized, when Fritz captured a radio station, and apparently forced one of the operators to cooperate. Anyway, they rounded up a bunch of leaders and operators. For a while there we were not getting much contact through here. The Resistance that was still working was working mostly through other groups, like the BRAC."

"The what?" asked Casey.

"That's de Gaulle's Bureau Central de something something. Anyway, we are now pretty much back in full operation and many of the groups are back on their radios. There are movements toward organizing the various Resistance groups. Most of them seem to favor such an arrangement, except the Communists."

Dalton returned to his chair and leaned back. "Ah the Communists, now there's a bloody confused group. You may know that Hitler has referred to this war as pitting the have-nots against the haves. Well, when Russia was working with Germany to take over the world of the haves, the French Communists referred to de Gaulle as an aristocrat who had sold out to the British capitalists. 'Course, after Hitler decided he didn't need the Russki anymore and invaded Russia, these French chaps changed their tune. Now they are on our side, fighting a democratic war against fascism." Dalton concluded, "We get little information or cooperation from them, but they do reek some havoc on the Gestapo. They are a ruthless bunch. Mind, they are on our side, but don't cross them." Again, Dalton made this a special point by staring into Casey's eyes.

Recapping, Dalton stated, "The French Resistance is doing what it can to disrupt the German occupation. At such time as the Allies launch an effort to retake Western Europe, the Resistance will be of enormous help in disrupting things behind the lines to make things run smoother for the chaps in uniform." Dalton stood up and interrupted Casey who appeared to be about to ask a question. "I know this just covers the surface and you have a world of questions. You'll have to get them in as you work here. Do ask questions, but try to figure things out on your own as much as possible. We don't have the luxury of time for training sessions. This is about it." Dalton motioned toward the door. "Now, let's go and see Sarah. She'll get you settled in."

Sarah was all business as she handed Casey and Jacques empty lunch pails and gave them precise verbal directions to the apartment they would be sharing. She gave both a very meaningful look as she instructed, "Avoid talking to anyone outside who is not part of this operation; that is unless you can develop a real convincing English brogue. Remember that you are maintenance workers for the manor, who are rather anti-social. Most of the people in this town are very loyal subjects, but there can be some spies about." As the men turned to go, Jacques' eyes met Sarah's. Jacques detected a faint smile. Could that be, he thought.

Following Sarah's directions to their apartment was easy for Casey and Jacques. Jacques observed, "For a female, she has a good sense of direction."

"Don't let her hear you say that," cautioned Casey.

The narrow streets they walked gave both men a good sense of being in Europe. Jacques remarked that the area was very reminiscent of Quebec, inside the wall. Casey, who had visited Quebec, agreed. Carrying their empty lunch pails, both truly looked like men going home from work.

The third floor apartment was comfortable, albeit very small. Casey thought that fitting two bedrooms, a small bathroom, one-person kitchen, and eating/sitting area into one apartment so small was truly an architectural feat. A window looking onto the road was welcome, as the kitchen window looked toward an opposing wall.

The men found their belongings in the bedrooms. The cupboards, though limited, had some packaged food items in them. Casey looked at Jacques with a jaundiced eye, "You cook?" Jacques paused, and then replied, "You tired of living?"

"So, the company cafeteria it is," Casey concluded.

Sarah had explained that they could take most of their meals at the Manor. Casey and Jacques slept well that night. The relief of feeling settled into a somewhat permanent place overrode the anticipation of starting a new job.

Early the next morning they walked together to the Manor. Sarah had told them that they should not always travel together to and from work. But, both were anxious to get into their new jobs. They went to the side door. Entering, they were met by Dalton and another man. All four went to the basement, where Dalton took Casey into a room and up to a desk with a radio and teletype. Jacques was led away to another basement room.

Dalton instructed, "We don't currently have contact with anyone, and we have no particular messages to relay. You will monitor the equipment, and if you begin to receive anything, that's anything," Dalton emphasized, "raise your hand. At this point you become an acrobat. You did have a class in acrobatics didn't you?" Casey raised his eyebrow as he looked over at Dalton. "Thing is, you need to record every word that is transmitted. You also need to get someone over here to listen in with you. Don't stop waving your arm till someone arrives. There are several of us watching at all times, but we may be tied up here or there . . . . so, keep waving. When there is something to transmit, you will be instructed in how we do that. For now, just pay attention to your unit. If something is going on in the station next to you, go ahead and listen, but do not, do not get out of ear shot of your station."

Dalton drew back as Casey settled into his chair and looked over the equipment. Casey stated, "This all looks familiar. I'm sure I can handle it."

"Well they did say you weren't lacking confidence. Seriously, just relax and pay attention . . . this'll be by far the easiest job you will have over here."

Casey caught the remark, but didn't ask for an explanation as he was now concentrating on the equipment, looking at every knob and dial, memorizing their positions.

Most of the day Casey spent observing other stations and listening to messages. He very closely monitored his radio, but received only a brief partial message. It began with a code name, but then abruptly ended. Dalton responded to Casey's arm wave and stood by for some time while they listened for further. Ten minutes turned into twenty; still no more transmission. Dalton got up to leave; "The sender probably got spooked and had to abandon his position. That happens quite a bit. We just hope that's the worst of it."

"You mean there could be a trap set for someone going to the radio." Casey offered. "Ah, well, there could be a lot of explanations. Just stay close by."

"So Jacques, anything interesting happen with you?" Casey asked as he settled into one of the three chairs in their sitting area. "I mostly just listened to some chatter, apparently coming from Rotterdam, or there about. They said the sender is some kind of German civil worker being a mole. And you?"

"No, the F section was basically quiet . . . . just a few messages received."

"F section?" inquired Jacques.

Casey explained, "That's what they call us SOE people who deal with the French Resistance."

The next morning, Casey left the apartment a few minutes before Jacques. That was because Casey was the first home the prior evening. Casey went right to his station. He did not see Dalton, but there was another man sitting at the coordinator's table. After an hour of close attention to the radio, Casey leaned back and took a deep breath. Probably another nothing day he thought.

Casey spotted Dalton entering the room. Before he could offer a greeting, Casey swung around to face his radio. Clearly a message was coming in. Unbeknownst to Casey, Dalton took a position directly behind him. Casey began writing, "This is Hog. We have moved our location. Important troop movement information to send. First confirm your password and our prior location for identification." Casey picked up a binder labeled, "Do Not Remove From Desk". It had many pages with tabs identifying various contacts. He turned to the tab, "Hog". Casey worked fast and moved to transmit the requested information. Before he could start, Dalton's hand came down on Casey's, accompanied by a hearty, "Wow!"

Casey was startled somewhat and turned quickly to face Dalton. Dalton stepped to Casey's side and exclaimed, "My error. Big error." Dalton calmed and then added, "I failed to explain to you that right now we are using a twelfth letter error code; know what that means?"

"We did learn about that in school. The sender's identification is by code name and by an encrypted error in the message. Right?"

"That's right. The word 'have' should have been cave, mave, nave, or some such."

Dalton motioned for others in the room to gather round. The meeting was quick and to the point. "Denis here just received a message, no doubt from the Gestapo as it did not observe the twelfth letter error code. They stated that they had important information, that they had moved, and that we could properly identify ourselves by confirming where they had been located. Silly Fritz."

Dalton scanned the group. "Stay alert for this. It's easy to forget since it happens so seldom." Without further instruction, all returned to their stations.

Looking into the binder, Dalton declared, "Now, let's see if we can throw Fritz a curve, as you Yanks say. The sender would know that it would probably take us a few minutes to look up their location. So just about now we should be responding. Ok Denis, give them this: Send your code and the address: 84 Avenue de Villiers. That was an old address for Hog."

Casey did as he was told, then both men stared into space with an ear bent toward the radio. The silence was broken after a few minutes by Dalton. Shifting his feet, he instructed, "We'll give 'em three more minutes." Both men stood motionless for that time. "Bloody hell, I did hope we could have established a dialogue with them," Dalton stated.

"So what's the deal?" Casey asked.

"Right now the door at 84 Avenue de Villiers is going down under the boots of Nazi troopers. Good hunting Blokes. I do hope if someone moved in after Hog that they have a good standing with the Nazis. Keep a sharp ear out, but I don't suppose we'll hear any more from them.

"So Denis, you've been formally introduced to the Gestapo," Dalton observed as he slapped Casey on the shoulder and walked back toward his desk. He stopped half way, looked around the room and in a voice loud enough for all to hear instructed, "Hog is probably compromised. Do be alert to anything coming from him."

"Hey, Dalton, you think you might have just gotten somebody hurt?" The question came from another radio operator not known by Casey.

"Look," Dalton started while addressing all within earshot, "Nobody there is going to get hurt. Oh the Gestapo will mess things up looking for the radio. When they don't find it, they'll realize that we were on to them. If the folks living there support the Resistance, their resolve will be strengthened. If they sympathize with Petain and his collaborators, they might just rethink their love for the Nazis. Now back to work."

That evening Jacques was a bit late getting to the apartment. Casey was already settled in with a Life magazine that he managed to borrow from the manor. "You must have had something going at the office?" Casey asked, barely looking up from his reading.

"No, just talking."

Jacques went to his bedroom, and emerged a few minutes later sporting a change of clothes. Now Casey looked up and remarked, "You don't need to get all dressed up just to spend the night with me."

"No my boring room mate. I'm going out tonight."

Recalling Sarah's admonishment, Casey pointedly asked, "So, you picked up a good cockney brogue today?"

Jacques smiled. "No. Don't fret, I'm not going to mingle with the masses. I'm meeting someone from the company."

"Ah, male or female?" Casey reluctantly asked.

"Sarah," was Jacques complete answer.

"You dog. Fraternizing with the management. Hey, have a good time." Casey went back to his reading and Jacques departed with a smile and a wave.

The next six months Casey did his job without significant incident. He received and forwarded many messages with the French Resistance. Little by little he developed a good understanding of how they operated. He also developed a deep respect for their dedication. He communicated with a number of operators whom it was suspected were subsequently captured. Casey tried not to dwell on their fate.

Jacques and Sarah continued to see each other. Their latent relationship went almost unnoticed by most people around them.

Only they were aware of the growing deep feeling they were generating for each other. They did include Casey on a number of their outings. At first Casey was reluctant to tag along as a third party, but Jacques and Sarah insisted. They knew that Casey needed the distraction of at least some social life. Casey did not accompany the couple everywhere.

Casey was enjoying the warmth of a July morning as he walked to work. He had a smile on his face as he entered the basement and started toward his desk. He stopped abruptly when he saw that one of the new arrivals who had toured the facility yesterday was sitting at his desk. Casey started walking again, but Dalton stepped in front of him. "We need to go upstairs," Dalton insisted as he pointed Casey toward the stairs.

Entering Lieutenant Sumac's office, Casey noted three strangers seated in a semi-circle about the Lieutenant's desk. Casey started to greet Sumac by his rank, but stopped just as the words were forming, "Ah, Sumac, how are you."

The Lieutenant mumbled a reply and while looking through papers on his desk motioned for Casey and Dalton to sit down.

Sumac leaned back in his chair and looked at Casey. "These gents are here from London. You don't need their names. A decision has been made to put your training to use. You are going to France. We assume you knew you didn't go through all that training just to be a radio operator."

Taking that as a question, Casey answered, "No sir, I assumed I'd get into the thick of it eventually."

"That's right. I must say that we have appreciated the job you've done. You paid attention and learned quickly. You will want to do the same after you leave here. Now then."

One of the unidentified men consulted some paperwork in his lap and interjected, "We've gotten word that the German SS has begun rounding up Jewish people in Paris and shipping them to Germany. God only knows what they are doing with them, but it cannot be good. We smell Himmler here, which if true means that the Jews are probably being killed. It may be that they are being put to work in factories. Either way, well they're basically dead."

Another man turned to look at Casey and began, "We know that you are probably aware of a lot of this, but it's essential that you are fully informed." Casey realized this man was American or Canadian, or at least faking a good North American accent. "Anyway, the Resistance is quickly organizing to identify Jews and to help them escape from Paris. Problem. Being a participant in the Resistance is hazardous, to say the least. But there seems to be an inordinate number of folks in this area being fingered by the Gestapo. Enough so that we're convinced there's a mole working. The poor bastards in the Resistance have enough problems without having to contend with one of their own." The man speaking shifted in his chair and looked around the room. "In the grand scheme of things, the abduction of Jews in Paris probably isn't as big of a priority as is information as to troop movements, destruction of rail transportation, and the like. But that's not the point. Anytime the Resistance is compromised; something has to be done. Mark my words, the day will come when an effective Resistance will have a major effect on this war."

Casey sat up in his chair as the man returned his attention toward him. "Denis, we want you to go to Paris and find this mole." Time seemed to go into slow motion for Casey. He was at McGill playing hockey. The classes. Peter. Home in Durango. Training in Canada. "OK, how do I do that?"

The mystery North American got up and walked over to Casey. He leaned over in front of him and took hold of both chair armrests. Looking straight at Casey, he said, "You can decline this mission. We really don't want someone there who has doubts about his abilities. You've been trained and chances are you will complete this mission, have a great adventure, and someday tell your grandchildren about it. But of course, this is war, and you may not survive. The decision is yours. We must have someone who accepts the risks and wants to do the job."

Casey thought, *Shit! How do I say no?* The room went silent, and nobody moved, save for Casey who was panning the other men. Casey looked back directly into the face in front of him and firmly stated; "Of course I'll go."

CHAPTER 5

England to France, July 1942

Casey thought how strange it was to drive into an airport in the early evening and not see lights and people about. Harry pulled the car up in front of a Quonset hut that appeared to be near a runway. A dim light hung over the doorway. One aircraft was parked beside the building. Casey could barely make out the figure of a man poking about it. No one else appeared in the area. The hut had no windows.

"So then, that's it I suppose," Harry said as he exited the driver's seat. He opened the door for Casey, who exited slowly, looking about. "They're waiting for you inside the hut," Harry directed, "I'll take your bag to the plane." Both men stood still for a moment, Casey looking toward the hut, Harry looking at Casey. "It's been a pleasure, sir. Do come back in one piece."

Casey caught Harry's eye, which appeared to be moist. "Thanks for everything, Harry." Casey attempted a smile. "I do definitely plan on coming back in as few pieces as possible."

Casey slowly turned and walked to the hut door. He thought it strange that despite there being no visible window, a man opened the door for him just as he got to the single step.

"Come in Denis," directed the trim middle-aged fellow who was holding the door open. "My name is Clifford. That's Marie, and the big fellow is Tom." Casey entered and stopped to look around.

Clifford continued, "Marie, as you probably have guessed, is French. She works in the Resistance, but recently has come here to help train folks like you." Casey proceeded toward Marie, shook her hand, and issued a formal greeting in French. She smiled and replied that she was pleased to meet him. "Tom, well Tom has had, how do you say, a colorful past. He's kind of an artist. You know those phony documents you were given? Well they are Tom's creations." Casey walked up to Tom and shook his hand. Both men smiled and spoke each other's first name. "Tom will go over those documents with you once more. Marie will answer any questions you might have regarding the Resistance. Don't hesitate to ask any question that you might have. Better to ask now than to guess later. As soon as he's done inspecting the Lizzy, the pilot will join us. My function is to give you your final briefing," Clifford concluded then went to a table and began filling teacups from a steaming pitcher. "Tea young man?"

Casey nodded affirmatively as he sat in a chair.

Clifford motioned toward the big man, "Tom, you're up". Tom walked over to Casey and directed, "Denis, I want to see all your papers and tell me what they are."

Casey pulled out a tri-fold wallet and from it produced several documents: "This is my ID with my thumbprint, this one is my work permit, my ration card, and I'm not sure what this one is."

"So what do you think the Gestapo will have to say about, 'I don't know what this one is?' Hand me those."

Casey sheepishly handed the documents to Tom, who dropped them to the floor and lightly ground his heel into them. Picking them up, Tom handed them back to Casey, "Here, now your papers look like they've been around a bit. This card is your permit to travel near a frontier. Denis, know your papers. When you're asked for them, and make no mistake, you will be asked for them, pull them out like you are tired of being asked, but you are very willing to comply."

Casey looked at the documents in his hand, then up at Tom. "I understand; really I do."

Tom pulled his chair up next to Casey, then sitting square in front of him stated, "There are artists in the Resistance who can reproduce any documents you might lose, but it may be a while before you have access to them. You must take care to keep all your papers."

Casey cocked his head and looked straight at Tom, "Really, I'm not that careless. I'm not prone to losing things."

Tom sat back. "That's not what I mean. The Germans are people. The soldiers and Gestapo and whoever else may question you are not supposed to confiscate your papers. But Denis, piss one off, like by saying you don't know what a paper is for, and you may just lose all your ID. Then, God help you. Know your papers, and always comply with orders. It's best to do so with a sigh of disgust. If you appear happy to comply with their brutishness they will figure you're hiding something."

Casey sat back. "OK, I understand. Except, what do you mean it may be a while before I have access to the Resistance? I thought I was going to join them."

Tom looked at Clifford. "I guess you need to explain the mission." Clifford nodded then replaced Tom in the chair next to Casey.

"The original intent was that you would go to Paris and immediately hook up with the Resistance. Well, that just won't work. Since we don't know who the mole is, and your mission is to find the mole, we could just be handing you to him . . . or her. Do not think that women don't play a significant part here, on both sides. Right, Marie?"

Marie chimed in, "No. We're just soft and gentle and can always be trusted."

Clifford continued, "Anyway, the approach has changed."

The Quonset hut door opened and a man walked in. Medium size and build, he had a kind of smirky smile implanted on his face. He was dressed in some sort of non-regulation looking military garb. "Ah, here's Jack now," Clifford offered. Looking at Casey, Clifford continued, "Jack here doesn't know who he is. He's sort of English, sort of French, sort of German. But, he's a tolerable pilot, so we keep him around."

Jack approached Casey and they shook hands. Jack smiled and stated, "He's just being kind. You should hear what he says about me behind my bloody back. I just ignore him though. What have you gained when you've bested a fool?" Clifford and Jack waved at each other, and Jack helped himself to a cup of tea.

"Now then," Clifford continued. "If Jack can find France in his flying machine, you and Marie will be dropped about 20 miles outside Paris. And no, you don't have to jump out. The Lizzy will be put down in an open field."

"Lizzy?"

"The Lysander plane. You do know about the Moon Squadron?" Clifford asked.

Casey replied, "Well yes. They fly spy missions into the mainland around full-moon nights. I guess that's because it's light enough for pilots to see, and dark enough for the planes to get by unseen. Right?"

"OK then," Clifford continued, "Marie is going with you so that she can guide you into your cover. That is, you are going to Paris with the intent that you become established as a native who has no problem with Marshal Petain and the German occupiers. In fact, you will be dropping hints that you have information regarding members of the Resistance. Maybe nothing will come of this and you'll be reassigned. Hopefully though, German intelligence services will pick up on you, and they will want to find out what you know." Clifford walked about the room, as if contemplating some great theory. He stopped in front of Casey. "The point is, Denis, you must convince those chaps that you do know something. Just not enough that they pay too much attention to you. Done right, the Fritz will immediately put you in contact with their French counterintelligence, then forget about you. It follows that the mole will get involved in some fashion because his whole mission is simply to identify Resistance members."

Clifford looked almost exhausted, and sat down. Casey chimed in, "OK, so I find out who the mole is, then what?"

"Fair enough," Clifford answered. "You will communicate that information to the Resistance, and they will eliminate the problem."

"Let me get this straight," Casey replied. "I am not being introduced to the Resistance, yet when I have the ID of the mole, I magically get that information to them?"

"See that lady over there," Clifford replied, pointing to Marie. "She will be in the background, advising and guiding you through this." The room fell silent. Clifford continued, "Marie is providing the know how. You are out on the point. You are on your own interacting with the Fritz. Marie will get you to the right people and the right places. Working together, this task may just be easier than you imagine."

Another silence fell over the room. Casey leaned back and contemplated. He leaned forward and said, "It appears you have this well planned out. It does make sense." Casey looked at everybody in the room then stated, "I'm ready to go."

There were smiles around, then everybody moved toward the door. Clifford stopped abruptly and looked back directly at Casey. "Marie's with you to help with contacts and to advise. She's not a bloody crutch; the success of this mission and your very life will depend on your being able to stand on your own two feet. Got that?" Clifford didn't wait for an answer but proceed to lead the group through the dark to the plane.

As the Lysander climbed into the dark night, the three aboard the plane ceased all conversation. They appeared mesmerized as each stared out a window. The hum of the engine carried its own conversation.

Casey broke the silence about twenty minutes into the flight. "Question, Jack. I thought we were going to fly during moon light?"

"Patience my boy" Jack said. "It should be breaking moonlight shortly. That is provided the storm approaching isn't ahead of schedule."

Casey pondered a moment then asked, "So if clouds come in and block the moon light . . . ."

Jack interrupted, "We have about a two week window around the full moon. We'll just try it again tomorrow." Casey nodded and leaned back.

Marie shook Casey's shoulder. "I'm awake," Casey blurted trying to cover the fact that he was asleep. Marie smiled at him then instructed, "We'll be landing soon. We have to get out quickly. Jack has to get back up and out of here and we'll have to get to cover. The faster this goes, the less chance that someone will see what's happening."

Jack chimed in, "I'll set us down on a grass field. Denis, get your pack in hand, and when the Lizzy is about stopped, open the door and get out fast; roll out if you have to. Marie knows the drill. She'll get out at the same time. Get together and stay low. Quickly head toward the nearest row of hedges. Crouch there and be quiet. No sounds Denis. Don't ask her what's happening. Don't ask anything, just be silent." Marie smiled at Casey, who was looking back at her.

"Denis, it's OK to say something if you see Fritz aiming a rifle at us; we'll go the other direction." Casey attempted a smile.

The craft rolled slightly and inconsistently as it glided over treetops. As predicted, the moonlight illuminated the landscape. Jack was busy with the controls, when a loud pop sounded and some debris bounced around the cockpit. Another loud bang came from behind the back seat.

"Hang on!" Jack blurted as he pushed the throttle forward and headed the plane back up. Marie shouted, "I don't see 'em, I don't see 'em!"

"No matter, we have to get out of here," Jack replied, with a calming voice.

"Gun shots. Crap, was that Germans?" Casey asked, looking at the hole in the floor between his and Jack's seats.

"We really don't know, kid. Could be locals thinking they were going to bring down some Nazis. Hard to see much at night, even with the moon. They were probably lucky they hit us at all."

"What now?" Casey asked looking at Jack then Marie. "Hey, that was just a bump in the road. Better get used to using alternate plans," Jack advised, casting a fatherly glance toward Casey. "There's another field a few miles from here, if I can find it." The smirk on Jack's face gave Casey confidence that Jack knew exactly where that field is. "You'll just be a couple of miles on the other side of the town," Jack explained leaning back toward Marie. Marie acknowledged.

The next landing was without incident. Casey and Marie exited the plane before it came to a complete stop. The Lizzy was back up and out of sight by the time they reached a hedgerow and stopped to look back.

Taking Marie's lead, Casey crouched and quietly scanned the field they just came from. Casey looked at Marie, but she held silence and her position. After about twenty minutes, Marie tapped Casey on the shoulder and said, "Good job. Let's walk along these hedges to your right. We should come to a road."

Casey acknowledged and they walked quietly to the edge of a narrow paved road. Holding back against a large bush, they saw a dark house across the street about one hundred yards to the left.

Another house with a dim light inside was down the road to the right.

Marie nudged Casey and nodded her head toward a mound almost across the road. "What?" Casey asked.

Marie put her finger to her lips and said softly, "Gun emplacement." She crouched down and backwards, pulling Casey with her. A few yards back and out of sight of the mound, Marie stood back up and explained: "That's an old, ah, fort you would call it. It was part of our wonderful defense line. Soldiers with machine guns used them to watch the road. After the Nazis took over, they use them sometimes. It's probably vacant, but we'll go around it just in case."

The pair used the moonlight to find their way along the road until they approached a small town. Finding an old barn, they went inside and sat amid some usual barn rubble and hay mounds. Marie proposed an itinerary: "We should stay here till after dawn. When the town comes alive, we will stroll into it. There is a train station. We can get a ride to Paris. There's an apartment that others don't know about. It belongs to my cousin. He's not in the Resistance, but he hates the Nazis. You can work from there."

"So, just where are we now?"

"North of Paris, near Montmorency. Does that help?" Marie quipped.

"I'll need that information for my memoirs," Casey quipped back.

The night went by slowly for Casey. He spent some time reflecting on his current situation and doing some mental exercises to condition his thinking. He told himself that if he were to survive he would have to blend in. Looking about at all the new sights and activities like a tourist will have to cease. OK he thought, I've got the puck and I'm heading toward the goal. I'm going to play smart and tough. Mostly smart.

Casey woke with a start to the sound of voices. Male voices. Agitated men, coming this way. Casey peered through an opening in the barn wall. Three men coming, one was pointing toward the barn. Each man had what looked like a weapon in his hand; one looked like a rifle. Casey quickly rocked back and looked toward Marie. She was not there. He couldn't see her anywhere.

Crouching, Casey quickly ran to the other end of the barn. He hesitated just a bit as he slowly eased around a lopsided door, watching for the men to enter from the roadside. No sight of them he turned and made his way to a brushy ditch bank just a few yards behind the barn. Tucked into the brush he scanned the scene. The voices stopped.

Suddenly a large tan dog emerged from the ditch bank a few yards from Casey and ran across the back of the barn, and into a field on the far side. Suddenly the voices started again, and the three men emerged from the far side of the barn, and in full pursuit of the dog.

Casey's tense body relaxed as he knelt in position, smiling and shaking his head. He reasoned that the dog probably bothered some livestock and the vigilantes were after him. Casey's smile quickly disappeared as he searched for an explanation for Marie's disappearance.

His mental search turned into a physical one. He did not risk calling, so he carefully searched the area. There was no sign of her.

Well, they told me I'd have to learn to improvise, Case remembered. He carefully reentered the barn and retrieved his bag. He stiffened up, tucked his shirt in, stood up straight, and walked out onto the road. Casey cast a smile and assumed a jaunty pace. Inappropriate behavior for a young man in an occupied nation perhaps, Casey thought, but what the hell, this is a new adventure.

Looking ahead on the road, Casey saw a person approaching. His first real contact as a spy, but Casey felt a refreshing confidence. A fleeting confidence as he realized that his first contact was Marie. She was wearing a kind of light colored shawl that she didn't have before, but it was she.

Casey wasn't sure if he should recognize her, speak, ignore, or what. He decided to follow her lead. When Marie got within a half-dozen steps, she cocked her head and surveyed the road behind Casey, then looked back over her shoulder. Seeing no one, she smiled at Casey, and reversed her direction to walk beside him. "I'll join you, sir."

"What happened to you?" Casey asked without looking at Marie.

She calmly replied, "You were sleeping so quietly. I know you needed the rest. I checked out the town and train station. It's quiet there, and the trains are running. I trust you didn't take up with any strangers while I was gone?" Casey smiled and nodded, thinking it was strange she would leave him in the barn alone, but then the sleep was appreciated, and she wouldn't have been any help with that barn situation.

The train ride was to be less than an hour. Marie and Casey found a vacant cubicle. Just a few minutes into the ride, Casey began to squirm on the hard wood bench. Marie leaned close to him and whispered, "Why don't you take a walk through the train. Greet a few people; get a feel for them. If you run into a soldier or Gestapo looking fellow, make eye contact, but only briefly. Relax and fit in."

Casey looked at Marie for a few seconds. "Sure," he exclaimed as he rose and exited the cubicle. He slowly walked through three passenger cars. There were only a few empty seats. Casey nodded and greeted a few people who happened to look at him. He did not get a sense that he was standing out in any way. He did notice that like a cloud of cigar smoke at a poker game a real sense of futility and hopelessness permeating the cars.

Casey was lulled into a quiet feeling of sorrow and lethargy as he slowly walked. His distraction caused him to lightly bump into a man who was standing in the aisle. In every way that man fit the visual profile of a Gestapo agent. As Casey pulled up and back, he also noticed a German soldier immediately behind the man.

"What are you doing?' the man demanded. Without waiting for a reply he continued in accented French, "Who are you. Where are you going?"

Casey looked at him, then the soldier, and replied in French, "I, I, I was just going back to my seat."

"That doesn't answer my question. Where are your papers?" Casey couldn't stop looking at the men as he nervously pulled out his wallet and handed it toward them. "What am I supposed to do with that?" the Gestapo agent demanded, looking Casey straight in the eye.

"My papers, you said . . . ."

"I didn't say hand me your wallet, you idiot." Casey withdrew his wallet and started to remove his ID papers. Before he could get one out, the agent grabbed the wallet and handed it to the soldier. Looking at the soldier, he instructed, "We'll be in Paris in a few minutes. Take him to the holding cell so we can see if he wants to cooperate with us there."

Casey pleaded, "Really, I didn't mean to . . . ." The agent turned to walk away, and the soldier grabbed Casey's left arm. Casey's pleas to himself to calm down were made more difficult as he noticed another soldier walking toward them.

With one soldier in front of Casey and one in back, they walked to his cubicle. Marie was not there, nor were her things. The lead soldier picked up Casey's bag.

As they exited the train, Casey could not help but notice how the other passengers in the area seemed to purposely ignore what was going on with him. One passenger did make brief eye contact with Casey as the soldiers escorted him along the platform toward the terminal. It was Marie. Her look was brief, but Casey caught a subtle smile of positive confidence.

The soldier in front of Casey shouldered an automatic rifle. The one behind had a holstered pistol. There were other well-armed uniformed soldiers standing at intervals along the way. Casey was not handcuffed or otherwise restrained. He figured, regardless, this probably was not a good time to employ his learned escape tactics.

CHAPTER 6

Paris, July 1942

An office was near the end of a concrete tunnel under the train platform. Casey was led inside, through an area with several desks and file cabinets, and back into a corridor. That hallway was walled in concrete on one side, with a floor to ceiling heavy chain link fence making up the other wall. Behind the fence was a 12 by 20 holding cell.

Inside the cell Casey joined three other men. One was an older man, small and kind of stooped over. The other two were Casey's age. All were casually dressed, wearing very worried looks on their faces.

No one spoke. It was as if all were suspicious of the others. Casey took a seat on a bench along the back wall. He felt as though he were invisible.

About an hour passed when two men approached and opened the cage door. Casey thought how totally German they looked. Both were about six feet tall. One had short blond curly hair; the other neat brunette. One man looked at one of the younger detainees and motioned for him to approach. He gave a command in German, which Casey felt unmistakably meant that the young man should go with them.

The trio turned right out the door and continued down the corridor and through another door. Casey and the others briefly looked at each other with questioning expressions. The other two turned to look away. Casey walked up to the fence and looked down the now empty hall, holding his position for several minutes.

It seemed like an hour to Casey, but it probably was just thirty minutes later when the back door opened. One of the Germans was escorting the man they took back to the cell. The man was bent over as he walked. Blood was dripping from his nose, and saliva from his mouth. He was holding his left arm against his body as though it was in a sling. He had obvious red welts on his neck; his cheeks and lower lip were swollen and red. Fear was the obvious expression on his face.

The young man was pushed into the cell, and the German looked around. He looked straight at Casey. Casey swallowed hard. He looked down the hall, trying to appear as though he didn't catch the German's look. Casey sighed noticeably as the man exited the cell and walked back down the hall.

As if suddenly becoming best friends, the cellmates gathered around their wounded mate and consoled and inspected the damage. The other young man said a few words as he carefully assisted the wounded mate to sit down. Casey and the older man stood close by, showing looks of pity.

A German soldier and a suited man approached the cage, coming from the front office. The soldier opened the cage and looking at Casey, motioned and in broken French gave verbal instructions to Casey to approach. Casey's legs could hardly move. He knew resistance was futile, so he gathered himself, stood up straight, and walked to the door. Casey reminded himself to remember his torture training. A huge lump was in his throat.

The soldier directed Casey to the left, up to the front office. There another soldier handed him his bag and wallet. Skeptical about what was happening, Casey, looking slightly down, scanned the room. A middle-aged man approached Casey and stood directly in front of him. The man was kind of short, dressed in an impeccable suit. He had a long face, adorned by a pair of small-rimmed glasses. He had a square mustache on his upper lip. The man slowly looked Casey up and down. Casey thought: *Napoleon*. The man spoke in broken French, "A lady said she was traveling with you. She said you are not a threat to the Reich." Casey could only nod affirmatively. "Do you know her name?" Casey's heart almost stopped. He didn't want to rat her out. But, he reasoned she wouldn't given a phony name which would just cross him up. "She is Marie."

"Took you a while to remember it."

Casey replied, "I'm just a bit nervous, I've never been arrested before."

"So you are lovers? Isn't she a bit older than you?"

"No sir, we're just friends."

"Your just friend is waiting for you outside. You may go now," the man said slowly while looking intently at Casey's eyes. Casey nodded and sort of bowed as he quickly walked around the man, who stood fast, out the door and into the tunnel. All the while Casey could feel the man's glare penetrating the back of his head

Marie was standing on the top step leading to the train platform. She was leaning against the wall, and threw a smile at Casey as he approached. "So you survived," she observed.

"What was that about?" Casey asked in a huff.

As they walked out of the train station, Marie explained, "Casey, that happens once in a while. Remember that the occupiers don't need a reason to take someone in. Just play it straight. Don't try to lie your way out of it. If it happens again, which it may, just be humble. Answer their questions and don't get hostile. Remember they don't have time to jail and beat everybody in the City. Unless they think they have something specific to get out of you they won't detain you long." Marie didn't explain her role in getting him released, and Casey didn't ask.

Rue d'Argenson looked like, well like a street in Paris. Marie led the way as they walked up to a second floor apartment. She knocked on the door while Casey stood back, perusing the surroundings.

A man about Casey's age opened the door. Kind of short with short black hair, he smiled wide, opened his arms, and he and Marie embraced. Marie stood back, smiling, pointing toward Casey and said, "Peter, this is Denis. Denis, Peter." The men shook hands and all entered the apartment. The entry was into a narrow but adequately long kitchen. To the right were a living room and a small bedroom. To the left was a bedroom and bathroom.

They all proceeded toward the living room, talking all the way. "Peter you've been looking for a room mate. Denis needs a place to stay for a few months or so, and I can vouch for him."

"Another of your radical friends?" Peter asked smiling.

"Peter, all my friends are model citizens, you know that. I met Denis up north. He decided to see if he could find work in Paris, so I told him about you."

Casey observed that Peter had a kind of sneaky look in his eye. He wasn't sure why he got that impression, but vowed to himself to watch his back around Peter. "Yes, I would appreciate it if you could put me up," Casey added. "I'm reasonably neat and don't need . . . ."

Peter slowly turned his head to look at Casey. He took a moment to look Casey up and down, then smiled: "Yes of course Denis, you can stay here. You will be able to help with the rent?"

"That's my intention," Casey answered, thinking about the currency he had been fronted.

"So it's settled then," Marie offered. "Now where are your manners, Peter? Don't you usually offer your lady friends something to help them relax?"

"Yes, but that's to encourage them to stay a while. Since you're my cousin . . . . well I guess I can get out the cheap wine."

Looking indignant, Marie questioned, "You mean you have a variety of wines?"

"Hell no, I have to do some real dealing to have anything," Peter said, as he poured three glasses of wine from an unlabeled bottle.

The trio sat down and each took a healthy sip of wine. Looking at Casey but addressing Marie, Peter asked, "So, are you just passing through?"

Marie leaned back, crossed her legs, and holding her glass up to the light said, "No, I'm here for awhile. Say Peter, is there something floating in my glass?"

"You take what you can get," Peter replied, raising his eyebrows at Marie.

"Right," she replied, taking another long sip.

Looking at Peter out of the corner of her eye, Marie asked, "Joined the group yet, Peter?"

Silence prevailed for several seconds, then Peter replied, "I know what you people are doing is important. It's just not my nature to do that clandestine stuff."

"Pity," Marie replied, thus dropping the subject.

"You're still tending bar at the hotel?" Marie asked in a leading manner.

"Yes," Peter said in a suspicious voice. "So do they need any other help there?"

"What are you up to, Marie?" Peter asked.

"Not for me silly. Denis will need work."

Looking relieved, Peter answered, "As a matter of fact, the Germans have been hiring a lot of laborers for factory work. There's always a shortage of wait staff."

"See how easy that is, Denis?" Marie shot out. "You can move up in the world, serving meals and drinks to Germany's finest."

"Slow down there, cousin," Peter interjected. "I don't have anything to do with hiring. They may not be able to put anyone else on."

"Surely with your influence . . . ." Marie stopped while directing a longing smile at Peter.

"OK. I'll take him in with me tomorrow." Peter sighed. "Truth is, they really do need some more help."

Casey had little problem landing a job. In fact the manager of the Italian restaurant in the Hotel Firenze hired him with the enthusiasm he might extend to an accomplished chef. Though Casey quickly and often apologized for his inexperience, Georgio repeatedly insisted that he was right for the job and eagerly walked him through the routine of a waiter. Indeed, help that was willing to work and could follow instructions was at a premium. Being willing to work in an establishment which frequently hosted Nazi's was also a real plus.

Georgio was a bit older than Casey. He looked very European, but not particularly Latin. He was in fact a native of Florence, Italy, who migrated to Paris less than a year before it fell to the German Army. He worked as a waiter in the hotel restaurant for a few months, but was soon made the manager. Being a bit of a perfectionist, he found himself in a stressful situation. He needed to feed his desire to be perfect, while using an inadequate help staff trying to please difficult customers, the German occupiers.

Getting used to the job, Casey began losing himself. He actually found a sort of peace, working and having some fun with his co-workers, and getting to know Georgio. He even found some enjoyment in waiting on the Nazis who frequented the restaurant. Casey had a knack for diplomacy. He could always quell complaints and smooth otherwise rough situations, even with the most demanding customers. Georgio became very attached to this young energetic mystery person. Georgio was becoming increasing interested in Casey's history.

To Casey, Georgio seemed to be just another nervous restaurant manager. His other personality emerged one Tuesday night.

All other employees had finished their work and departed. Georgio and Casey completed their chores and as Casey walked toward the door to leave, Georgio called to him. Casey turned and saw Georgio just going behind the bar. He motioned for Casey to approach and invited, "Have some wine with me."

Casey said nothing as he stood facing Georgio. Casey had an inquisitive expression on his face. Georgio smiled reassuringly and again motioned for him to approach. "Come on, we should talk," he added.

Casey suddenly felt very uneasy. He always felt that Georgio was a bit effeminate. Damn, if that guy hits on me . . . . I really need this job but I'll be damned . . . . Casey slowly walked toward the bar casting a very suspicious eye toward Georgio. A glass of red wine awaited Casey as he sat on a stool on the customer side of the bar. Georgio sat back on a stool behind the bar. He took a sip from his glass while looking straight into Casey's eyes. Casey drew up a rather stern look and thought, *here it comes*.

"I've finally figured you out, Denis," Georgio offered.

"Oh really?"

"Yes, but you need to be careful of the company you keep," Georgio warned. Casey's only thought was how this was going to end up in an invitation to spend the night at his apartment.

"I suspect that your roommate Peter may be very dangerous to you." Casey thought, this is an interesting line.

"So, you don't like Peter?"

"This isn't a game you're playing," Georgio warned in a suddenly harsh voice. "Do you think you can play with the Gestapo?"

"Wow, what are you talking about?" Casey asked in a voice that took on a new seriousness.

Georgio leaned back, took a sip of his wine, and folded his arms across his chest. "Denis, you're no more a French native than I am. Oh, you could convince most people that you have a North Country accent, but come on. I've studied the language. You throw out words that could come from any part of France. But mostly, your inflections say, French American."

Casey rolled his eyes and tried to muster up a confident expression. "What are you talking about?" was the best response he could come up with.

Georgio leaned forward and looked Casey in the eye. "There probably isn't a German in Paris who could make your accent. Are you willing to risk your life on probably?"

Now it was Casey's turn to lean back, pick up his drink, and fold his arms. Looking straight at Georgio, he answered, "I have no idea what you are talking about."

"You'd be stupid to admit anything to me. There's no point in me trying to get you to confess to your real identity. So, I'll just talk and you should listen."

Casey drew a blank expression as the two men seemed to be frozen staring at each other. Georgio broke the spell as he stood up and refilled their half-empty glasses. Casey was staring at him the whole time. Georgio sat down and both men leaned back.

"There are people working here who are involved in the Resistance," Georgio began. "Personally I try to keep neutral, but I must say their cause seems to be legitimate. Anyway, they have had some problems lately with the Gestapo. Seems the Nazis learn about new recruits soon after they join the movement. Even some veterans have been arrested. Obviously, there is a mole in the organization. That probably has shut down their activities until they can find out who the mole is." Georgio adjusted his seat and took a sip of wine. Casey stayed silent, trying to figure out what he should say when Georgio is done.

Georgio looked down, then away, "Well, the arrests are public knowledge, and one can figure what effect they've had." Again, both men looked silently at each other.

"You don't need to figure out what to say," Georgio consoled. "If none of this means anything to you, well, you've enjoyed a glass of wine and caught up on the latest gossip. But if your being here has anything to do with that rodent, hear this. I believe Peter is part of the Resistance. Twice I've heard someone I suspect is in the

Resistance giving Peter the name of a new recruit. Both recruits were picked up by the Gestapo a day or two later." Georgio leaned back, tilted his head back, and looking down his face at Casey added, "Once is a coincidence . . . ."

With that, Georgio stood up and drank the remaining 1/3 glass of his wine. Casey took the cue and did likewise. Georgio walked from behind the bar and said, "I'll finish locking up. I'll see you tomorrow at five?"

Casey, a bit taken aback, recovered and said, "Yes, I'll see you tomorrow." He walked straight to the front door, as Georgio faded into the back of the restaurant.

Casey stood on the sidewalk in front of the door for several moments. He thought about Peter. It's hard to believe that he would be working for the Nazis. Sure he has resisted joining the Resistance, but he seems so sympathetic toward the cause.

Casey began to walk when the thought occurred to him that he is now in the middle of the action. I am a spy, in a hostile land, he told himself. It was as though he had an epiphany. For the first time since coming to France, Casey broadened his vision to be aware of his surroundings.

The street was dimly lighted. Casey paused just for a moment and glanced about. The street was deserted. He continued. An automobile approached from the rear. Casey turned his head around, and the headlights caused him to turn back toward his front. The car passed. Looking down and a bit back, he caught the figure of a man across the street and behind him.

Casey continued a few yards, stopped, and then turned away from the street to look into a shop window. In this position he felt he could see two images walking his way, one on each side of the street.

I don't know what this is, Casey thought, but let's find out. Walking straight ahead, Casey soon arrived at a corner. Keeping the same pace, he rounded the corner making a left turn. As soon as he cleared the edge of the corner building, he sprinted several yards, slowing as he approached a porch leading up to the front door of an apartment. The porch and apartment were dark. Just beyond the apartment was an alley. As he mounted the porch, he could see one figure walking briskly rounding the corner he just came from.

Casey moved quickly across the porch toward the alley, vaulted the porch railing, landing in the alley. Turning left, he sprinted half way down the alley and crouched behind a tall trashcan. Casey remained still there, watching the alley.

Only one man was in sight. He was slowly walking into the alley, staying very close to a building wall. He was scanning windows of the apartment which Casey faked entry. Casey was too far away to get much of a look at the man, who began cautiously peering into the apartment windows.

That man then stepped back across the alley and stood in a shadow. Within a minute, another man, who must have been checking out the front of the apartment, joined him. They seemed to converse for a few seconds, and then both looked down the alley toward Casey. Casey was confident that he was in a shadow and out of sight. Apparently that assumption was correct as both men turned around and walked back out of the alley and made a left turn onto the sidewalk. Casey stood but held his position for several minutes. The air seemed heavy and a bit rank. It was very quiet, except for the occasional muffled sound of a door closing and distant car noises. The alleyway seemed to have its own creepy presence. Several times Casey started to crouch back down as he detected some movement in the night. Composing himself, Casey reasoned, rats maybe. No, probably my imagination. Taking a step toward exiting the alley, Casey instinctively crouched down in a shadow. Two men again at the end of the alley. Probably the same two, slowly and cautiously reentered the alley and began again to examine the area of the apartment. They disappeared to the right this time back along the front of the apartment.

Slowly Casey again stood up. Damn, oldest trick in the book and I about fell for it. Turning, Casey walked out of the alley in the opposite direction, glancing behind as he walked.

Peter was up reading when Casey entered the apartment. Looking up from his book, Peter asked, "So, how was your night . . . . anything exciting happen?"

"Oh, a German soldier threw up before he made it to the men's' room."

Peter chuckled, “That’s it?”

“That’s it,” Casey replied as he walked to his room.

Casey sat on his bed and put his head in his hands. He thought that Peter was really expecting him to have more to say. Casey pondered recent events. Peter was expecting me to tell him about being followed. He was waiting up for me so he could find out what happened. Damn, and here I am living under the same roof.

Remembering his training, Casey forced himself to think. What better place to be but in the den of the enemy. Then again, don’t jump to conclusions. Peter could be innocent. Casey composed himself and went to bed.

Casey woke early the next morning. He had intended to sleep in, but his mind was racing. Since Peter was not active in the Resistance, how would he have inside information? Since he is just kind of a fellow traveler, wouldn’t he be the first to be suspected? Casey was a bit upset that he couldn’t go back to sleep. Finally he gave up and got up.

Peter was not in the kitchen sipping his tea, so Casey assumed he was not up yet. Walking past a kitchen window that looked out onto the street, movement caught his eye. Casey could see Peter standing on the sidewalk, talking with a man. The stranger was Peter’s age, medium height, with blond hair and fair complexion. Casey jolted back as Peter turned back toward the apartment and his companion turned and walked away. Casey walked over to the counter to prepare a cup of tea. Peter entered the apartment and cheerfully addressed Casey, “Good morning Denis; up early huh?”

Confident that Peter hadn’t seen him in the window; Casey smiled, turned, and greeted Peter. “So, out for a morning walk?”

“Oh, I awoke early, so thought a turn around the block would get my head working.” Casey looked at Peter, smiled and nodded affirmatively, taking note that nothing was mentioned about meeting someone.

Small talk was exchanged over tea for about an hour. The front door opened and in walked a smiling Marie. She opened her arms and presented herself. “Did you miss me?”

Peter answered drolly, “You were gone?”

With hands on hips, she said, “Up north, visiting friends.”

Casey rescued her, "Yes, Marie, we certainly did miss you . . . . Say, don't you ever knock?"

"Not when I come to Peter's. I might catch him doing something embarrassing." Peter looked at her and gave her an upward arm gesture.

You know Peter, I'm disappointed in you," Marie admonished. "Now what?" Peter asked.

"Correct me if I'm wrong. You have yet to introduce Denis to any of the lonely ladies you know?"

"I didn't know that was my job," Peter sighed.

"Well anyway," she said, "I've taken care of that," Marie offered as if it was a big task. "So, Denis are you free this afternoon?"

"I go to work at five. Otherwise, well I think I have to sweep the porch or something."

"No, no," Marie insisted, "come with me. I have someone for you to meet; it'll be fun."

It suddenly occurred to Casey that this might be more than just a casual meeting. "Sure, why not, I can go with you."

Peter mumbled, "I can tell you why not."

"What?" asked Casey. Peter did not reply as he walked from the room.

Marie explained to Casey that he was to go alone to Le Foyer, a neighborhood restaurant, and she would meet him there. Entering a bit before lunchtime, Casey was just the third patron in the square-shaped dining room. There was a bar along much of the west wall, and a fireplace in the middle of the east wall. Tables were randomly scattered about, with several booths along the walls. A waiter walking into the room looked at Casey and motioned for him to sit anywhere. He picked a booth next to the fireplace.

Casey was in the restaurant only a few minutes when the lunch crowd started to fill the place. Marie walked through the door in the middle of about six people. Marie and another lady peeled from the group. Looking around, Marie spotted Casey and waved. The ladies sat down and Marie introduced Casey to Julie. Julie was a pretty brunette, with a childlike smile. Her eyes captured a bit of sternness, which contrasted sharply with her smile. She was 5'6", average build, and a total puzzle to Casey. One profile exhibited sweet innocence, another worldliness. With rather light complexion she could pass for being of north European descent, but her French was without accent.

The three spent over two hours in the booth, with no let up in conversation, save to eat. The food and menu were decent, owing to the fact that a number of ranking German officers dined there.

Casey summarized his thoughts about Julie. He certainly was physically attracted to her, but he realized that that was as much long abstinence talking as true affection. She seemed pleasant, easy to talk to, and apparently interested in him. But what Casey noticed the most was what was going on in the booth behind Julie. A pretty dark haired young lady sitting facing Casey seemed to be looking at him whenever he glanced her way. Each time she would shyly turn her head away or down.

This meeting had to end, so Casey excused himself with the explanation that he wanted to get a little rest before going to work. Marie and Julie agreed that they had things to do as well. Casey's departing comments were to ask Julie if she would be interested in meeting for a walk in the park. She smiled a "yes", and handed him a paper with her address on it. Marie stood back and rendered a job-well-done smile. Casey's departing thoughts were that he would like to meet that other girl.

Peter was gone when Casey got back to the apartment. Casey was leisurely getting ready for work when the door opened smartly. Marie walked in and smiled a greeting to Casey. "Is Peter here?"

Casey replied, "No, he wasn't here when I got back."

Suddenly turning serious Marie continued, "You know of course that there is a purpose for you and Julie to get together?"

"I suspected as much."

"This isn't a romantic thing. Julie is new to the area. The Gestapo won't have any information on her or you. You both look like good Resistance candidates, so they will pay attention to you, particularly if now and then you appear in places they suspect Resistance people hang out."

"Makes sense," Casey observed, "so what do I do?" That had already been planned out, as Marie ran through specific instructions for Casey and Julie to follow. They involved going as a couple to a number of locations where Resistance people might appear. Marie continued, "You will always pick Julie up and drop her off at her apartment. Your conversations with her should never include the word Resistance. But use your wits to sound like, well, you know about the Resistance but think they are a bit foolish. Never ever let drinking cloud your mind. Some times though talk just a little loud, as though you've had a drink too many. Do not act drunk."

Marie stopped and looked at Casey as if waiting for the information to register. "Understand?" she asked. Casey nodded.

"Now, the best scenario is that at some point you will be quietly picked up by the Gestapo. Quietly because they won't want anyone from the Resistance knowing they have you, in case you have good information for them. Of course, the first things they will want are names. You don't have any because you recently got in town. You went to work at the Firenze and are sure the Resistance has approached you. Explain that some people have asked you about your loyalties, things like that. Explain that you are a live, let live kind of guy. They will smell weakness and start to press you for more information. Play it by ear, but when they ask you, and they will ask you, to do a little spying for them, you must agree. Do not, do not just jump on it. Think about it, then give the impression that you don't want to piss off the occupiers so yes, you will get what information you can." Marie paused again to let Casey process what she said.

Casey looked down, then slowly back up at Marie. "So what information will I feed them?"

"When you get to that stage, we'll, I'll give you some nicknames, addresses, stuff like that that you can pass. The idea is that we will be watching you, where they take you, like that. I'm sure there will be some contact made along the line that will involve someone we know in the Resistance. That'll be our mole. Your job will be done."

"Well, that's simple enough." Casey smirked.

"You'll do fine. Just be kind of cool with the Germans. They have no reason to kill you; don't give them a reason for torture. Remember, you don't know much, but can be useful in gathering information." Casey leaned his head back and with confidence concluded, "I can do that."

After a brief moment he turned back toward Marie and asked, "What about Julie? What is her role in this?"

"Denis you're a virile young man. Well I assume you are. At, at least you appear to be, and you would look very suspicious if you weren't towing a cute young thing around with you. Cover Denis, she's cover." Marie glanced upward and continued, "More than that though. Julie's sweet looking but she's been around enough to be your partner. Trust her, and make sure she knows what's going on at all times. She may see something helpful, or dangerous, that you don't, so talk about everything that you do."

Casey pursed his mouth and shook his head, "OK."

Marie rose to depart when Casey interrupted, "Marie, how well do you know Peter. I mean really know him?"

With a troubled look she turned to face him, "Why do you ask?"

"I just wonder if he can be trusted, you know, with Resistance stuff."

Marie looked Casey in the eye and said calmly and slowly, "Denis, we don't share anything with anyone outside our organization. We don't even share information with people in the group unless they have a need to know it." She paused and reestablished her gaze, "Denis, I don't trust you, and hell I'm not sure I fully trust myself."

They both smiled slightly, and Casey replied, "OK, don't trust anyone."

"That's right; you may use people, but don't needlessly share anything."

"And Peter?" he asked again.

"Peter won't hurt you, but he is not in the circle."

Casey nodded understanding.

For several weeks Casey and Julie frequented a number of meeting places. Cafés and café bars mostly. One was rather an open and visible restaurant. Others were more of hole-in-the-wall cafés, while one was like a speak-easy. The entrance for that one was off a dark alley. Casey felt this looked too much like a covert meeting place to really be one.

They mingled well, and were able to strike up conversations with a number of people. The pattern was the same though. Singles and couples were easy to talk to, but all conversations were small talk. Any time Casey or Julie would try to move conversation toward current events, the other parties would find a reason to change the subject, or just excuse themselves and mingle with others. Casey was growing impatient; this approach wasn't getting them anywhere. Periodically Marie would drop by the apartment or the restaurant to see Casey, and he would explain his frustration. Marie insisted that he be patient and keep at it.

It was a Wednesday morning that Georgio came by the apartment to see Casey. He explained that Casey was not to work that night as scheduled. "There's some German command thing going on; dinner, drinks, meeting; and they want their own wait crew there. You're not to be trusted, you see?" Georgio continued, "I wish I could still pay you for the time, but you know how it is."

Casey nodded understanding, but had to add, "Slave driver." Casey put his hand on Georgio's shoulder as he escorted him from the apartment. "You have fun with those nice officers now."

"Oh yeah, I'm definitely looking forward to this," Georgio said as he turned onto the sidewalk waving good-bye over his head.

Casey was suddenly left with some free time on his hands. Yesterday afternoon after he and Julie made some rounds, she explained that she wasn't feeling well and needed to stay home for a couple of days. Casey asked if he could do anything for her. Julie replied, "Yes, do something about the periodic anatomical uprisings in the female species."

"Uh, I'll get back to you in a couple of days," was Casey's weak response as he exited her apartment.

It's been a while since I've eaten at home and just relaxed with a good book, Casey told himself. Of course, my cooking skills have had a lot to do with that, he recalled. He considered his options further and finally decided that he would go out for a leisurely supper. Not that there are a lot of choices, but he would go somewhere not calculated to be frequented by Resistance folks. Yes, a break would be most welcome.

CHAPTER 7

Paris, September 1942

It was early afternoon and Casey went out to the streets for a walk and to find a place to eat. This certainly was not the Paris he had read about with a restaurant on every block. His head hung a bit as he recalled: this is war. The early sunshine had vanished behind high clouds and now a bit of a fog seemed to be trying to make an appearance. Casey walked onto the rue de Lille, a street he had not been on before. This area was away from his usual haunts. The few folks he encountered all seemed to be heading somewhere and not paying attention to each other. A view of the Seine appeared. It was calming and briefly took Casey back to more peaceful times and places.

Standing up straight and throwing his shoulders back, Casey walked on. Across the street he noticed a café. Standing in the doorway he saw several empty tables and just two patrons. They were seated at a small bar in conversation with the bartender. Casey decided that this looked like an innocent enough place, so he entered and approached the bar. He and the bartender exchanged greetings and Casey ordered a glass of wine. Casey silently nodded a greeting toward the other two men, and they nodded, but quickly turned back toward each other. Casey took his glass to a table against a wall, a ways from the bar. He removed his book from under his arm and sat down.

It was quiet and peaceful here. Gradually three of the tables became occupied. Those people seemed to just quietly appear. Casey smiled to himself as he looked up from his book, scanned the room, and thought, *not a German solder among them.* His tranquility was soon interrupted as the restaurant door opened and in walked a pretty young lady. It was that lady.

Casey was almost hiding behind his book as he watched the lady scan the room. La Foyer restaurant; with Marie and Julie; dark haired beauty in the other booth. No doubt this is she. Damn she's cute, no, sexy. Is she with someone? Is she meeting someone? Lots of thoughts went through his mind in an instant, until her eyes locked onto his. She walked straight for him, not taking her eyes off his. She pulled the spare chair out and asked, "Mind if I sit here?" Casey realized that was not a question as she was sitting while she was asking. He did not respond. She looked at him, waiting for his obligatory inquiry.

"You were in the La Foyer a few days ago," was the best he could come up with.

"You must be a friend of Marie and Julie?" she asked.

Casey realized this was a question. "Yes . . . . how do you know them?"

"Oh, I've spent some time in the Firenze. Haven't you seen me there?"

Casey paused to think. How could I have missed her; seems like I would have taken notice. "No, but it does get busy." Purposefully putting his book down and leaning forward Casey asked, "My name is Denis, what's yours?"

She sat up straight, smiled and extended her hand, "I'm Maria, Denis, nice to meet you."

"Yes. I must say that I've hoped our paths would cross," Casey said. "You had such a nice friendly smile when I saw you at La Foyer. Say, may I get you a drink?" Casey thought, well that was abrupt and clumsy of me, but I would like to pursue this.

Conversation came easily as Casey and Maria engaged in small talk. Maria started to make Casey a bit uncomfortable as she turned the conversation toward more personal matters. He was torn between wanting to be very careful with such information, and not wanting to turn off a possible good thing here by being obviously evasive. "You don't sound like you come from this part of the country?"

"No, I grew up in the North. How about you, a native Paris girl?" Casey asked trying to steer the conversation away from his origins.

"Born right here; my mom was from Italy but my father was a native; killed when the War started."

Maria asked Casey about his job, where he lived, who he roomed with. Each time he would briefly answer, then immediately ask her a question to head off further inquiry. Finally she hit the big one, "How do you know Marie and Julie?"

"I met Marie at work, not long before I first saw you. We just happened to hit it off. She felt that I needed a friend, so she introduced me to Julie." He paused a moment, then, "Julie's nice and all, but I'm not really attracted to her."

Conversation stopped as Maria looked at Casey with a doubting expression. Casey could feel her asking why he is seeing so much of Julie, but no, how would she know? Maria then smiled and commented, "Oh."

Suppertime and Maria and Casey ordered a meal from the bartender turned waiter. Maria insisted on paying for hers. Casey hid his delight behind offers to pay for both. Dusk would soon descend and Maria said she doesn't like to be out after dark. She asked, "Would you walk with me a ways?" Casey was delighted at the invitation, until it soaked in that she said, "a ways." Well, who knows, he thought?

"Of course," he said, not brave enough to ask where "a ways" is.

They walked very slowly continuing their conversation at every moment. Three blocks and two turns later, Casey's mind left their conversation for a moment as he looked about to get his bearings. They were in territory unfamiliar to Casey. He was enjoying getting to know Maria, so he did not think to ask where they were going; he assumed to her apartment. At least he truly hoped that was their destination. So far they were on streets with business fronts and people walking about. Casey noticed that people on the street seemed to walk faster as dusk descends. For good reason, he thought.

Now they turned onto a street that was virtually deserted. Casey's mood and eyebrows rose as he saw that there were no business fronts, only apartment entrances off the sidewalk. Casey scanned the residences. Smiling, he wondered in which he would be spending the night. His mood and penis began to swell.

A man walking toward them from the end of the block on the opposite side of the street started to cross to their side. Casey thought he looked vaguely familiar. Probably some patron from work, he reasoned. A car drove past Casey and Maria from behind them and the man had to hustle to get across the street. Another car pulled to the curb directly beside them. Something triggered a cautionary response from Casey. He turned toward the car as two men got out, one from the front seat and the other the back. Out of the left corner of his eye, Casey caught the sight of another man running at them from behind. Casey turned toward Maria to push her and tell her to run. It was too late. The man from the rear caught him by his shoulders, and the other two grabbed his arms. The man he saw cross the street ran to them and stopped.

Casey pushed and pulled, but he soon realized that was futile. He was frisked and pushed into the car in what seemed like one fast motion. Maria swiftly walked ahead and then across the street. She appeared to be invisible to the men, as all four pushed Casey into the back seat of the car. They made no attempt to catch her. Casey caught a glimpse of Maria across the street now walking back toward the direction they had come. *What the hell!* he thought.

Casey was seated in the middle of the back seat, with a man on either side. The other two men got into the front seat and the car quickly departed. Casey looked down and thought, these guys are definitely pros. No weapons had been displayed, but Casey realized that he would be no match for four Gestapo thugs. He reasoned: look around, note details about the men, the car, where we are traveling. If they had intended to kill me, they could have easily done so and disappeared. The two in the front seat. Something about their movements; their stature. Casey thought they could be the two who followed him when he first started working. Maria . . . . sure enough she must be part of the Gestapo. She didn't know Marie and Julie; she was fishing for information about them. Did I tell her anything about Marie? Thus Casey's mind raced, accessing everything about the situation that he could.

Casey composed himself a bit. "What's this about? I have my papers."

"Ok, head down," the driver directed as he glanced into the mirror. Both men on Casey's sides put their hands on his head. "Bend down," one ordered him as they both pushed his upper body forward. They were firm but moved slowly, giving him time to adjust himself for the maneuver.

Bent over looking at the floor, Casey tried to gradually look to one side, then the next. Each time a hand moved his head back down. No more words were spoken. He was held in this position for several minutes. Casey was aware of the car making at least three turns, slowing then making another turn. It went up slightly, made two more turns, and then came to a stop. Casey imagined that they had turned into an alley or some building entrance. The men released Casey, and he slowly sat back up, looking about as he rose. They were in a rather dark room with boxes piled about. It was a small warehouse.

Quickly the front passenger and the two men next to Casey opened their doors and got out. The man on his right pulled Casey by the right arm, obviously intending that he get out with them. The other two men came quickly around and they surrounded Casey. The car backed up and departed. With a man holding each arm, and the third man in front, they proceeded to a door.

The room looked like a small lunch area. There was a counter and sink, some closed cabinets, a large wastebasket, and a wall strip with coat hooks. A couple of aprons hung from two hooks. A seven or eight foot rectangular table with bench seats on either side occupied most of he center of the room. Two other chairs were along the walls. Casey was escorted to the center of one of the bench seats, and told to sit down. Two men went around and sat on the bench across the table, and the other stood to Casey's left side. The door was to his right, and that wall had a small window looking into the warehouse. Casey looked toward the door, and the standing man moved over to Casey's right side.

"I suppose you want my papers?" Casey asked as he lifted his right hip to retrieve his wallet.

One of the men seated across stood up, answering, "No papers. You just need to listen to us." He put one foot up on the bench, leaned forward with his arm on his raised knee, and looked Casey in the eye.

"Who the hell are you, and what are you doing here?" The man had an easy manner with a rather soft, slow, deliberate voice. His words were not spoken in a harsh tone, but his eyes told Casey he was not playing games.

"My name's . . . .",

One of the seated men curtly interrupted, "You're Denis and you work as a waiter. You're new to Paris. Why are you not in the Army? Who are you and why are you here?"

The room went silent and all eyes were on Casey. He realized these men were not interested in small talk. It was time to use his head. "My family had some influence and kept me out of the Army. I was supposed to go away to a university. Then the invasion. My family's gone . . . ." Casey looked down and stopped, effectively feigning grief. Straightening up, Casey continued, "Anyway I came to Paris and found a job. I'm just trying to exist. I'm not looking for any trouble."

"So what do you think of Vercors?" the third man asked.

Casey thought, underground writer. It would be OK if I haven't heard of him. "Vercors? I don't know who that is."

"Do you have an opinion about Petain?" the man pointedly continued.

Now this I have to answer, Casey reasoned. "I don't know. I guess he feels that he's holding France together. Really, I don't try to figure things like that out."

Again, silence. Casey looked at the standing man, and looking as sheepish as he could, asked, "Are you Gestapo?"

Quickly the man sneered, "You don't know much about how the Gestapo operates, do you?"

Casey answered, "I just thought . . . ."

"It doesn't matter," the man continued. Casey had noticed that all three of these men were dressed in typical civilian garb common to working people in Paris. They certainly did not look to be akin to the Gestapo men in the train station. But he realized there were various organizations within the Nazi forces.

The men made no attempt to identify themselves. They did not address each other by name. They continued to question Casey, asking about his job, his friends, and other personal details. Casey answered their questions; most truthfully, remember his training to avoid getting trapped by making up lies when not necessary. They frequently asked Casey what he thought about the Nazi occupation, the Resistance, and the Vichy. This was a very tense twenty minutes for Casey, as he had to think hard about each question, without looking like he was thinking hard about each question. Eventually the kneeling man returned to both feet. The other two got up and they all looked at each other and shrugged. It appeared that they were through with him, so Casey carefully stood up, looking around as he did to see if there was going to be an objection.

"OK, we're going to let you go," advised the man with the easy manner. "Out this way," he commanded as he waved and walked toward the door they came in. Casey followed, followed by the other men. Turning toward the right they went through a door that opened to a dark hallway. At the end of the hallway was an outside door. As they got almost to that door, the lead man stepped aside and waved Casey toward it. "Right out there, turn left in the alley and you will be back onto the sidewalk," he calmly directed. Casey briefly looked at all three men, then stepped toward the door and opened it. Just as he started to exit, he heard a door close behind him. Slowly he turned and saw that the men were gone. Casey had hardly noticed another dark door just to the right of the one he was exiting. *Guess they're in a hurry,* he thought.

As instructed, Casey entered into an alley, turned left and walked a few yards to a narrow sidewalk and street. The least they could have done is tell me where I am. Oh well, it didn't seem that we had traveled that far in the car, Casey recalled.

He stood for a moment and looked around. Though early evening, the street was empty. To the left there appeared to be a major street intersecting. As he started to walk that way, he saw a car go by, then a person walking across the intersection and continuing on. Just about to the larger street, Casey hesitated a moment and looked down and slightly backward as he became aware of a car approaching from the rear. He was startled for a moment, then laughed, damn I'm getting jumpy. He straightened up and continued on. He stopped at the main street and scouted both directions. The left looked rather dark, though a car was heading his way. To the right there were a few more lighted areas. That's where I'll head, he reasoned. Stepping into the street he had to stop as the car that had been behind him got to the intersection. Casey cocked his head as he thought the car should have caught up to him sooner. He stepped into the street and walked around behind the car and continued on, glancing at the vehicle every couple of steps. The car then turned left and sped away.

Spirits lifted by the car departure and prospect of determining his way home, Casey picked up his pace and posture as he walked on. A few cars passed going each direction, but Casey chose to ignore them. Most looked like they had Germans in them, which he figured would stand to reason. I'll find a street I recognize, he confided to himself.

Crossing a narrow dark side street Casey heard what sounded like a cry for help. His first impulse was to ignore it. Probably nothing. Not something I want to get involved with. Could be a trap. Several thoughts quickly crossed his mind. But the one that stuck was, could be someone truly needing a hand. I'll be careful, he reminded himself.

Casey had passed the intersection when he made the decision to turn back. He turned around and very cautiously approached the nearest corner of the intersection. Stopping, he leaned against a wall where he could look down the side street sidewalk, and also back down the sidewalk he was on. He stood for a while, carefully scanning the scene. It did appear that a person was huddled in a dark spot against a building a few yards down the side street. A car coming up the main street. Casey continued walking, crossing the side street back toward the way he had originally come. As he continued the car passed, and another car going the opposite direction passed. He slowed his pace to almost stopped. As the cars got further away, he slowly turned and returned to the side street. Again he stopped at the intersection. Yes, there was a person kneeling or sitting there. Muffled weak calls seemed to be from a woman. Casey thought he saw a hand reach out toward him. He looked away, scanning the area. I've got to check it out, he decided.

Slowly and cautiously he approached the person. As he got close he determined it was a woman. She was looking at him, silent, with sad eyes and grimaced expression. Casey analyzed: She's not showing signs of injury. She could just be drunk, but she's not swaying. Even if she is drunk, she's in danger here. Again her left hand reached out toward him. Casey knelt down, careful to keep some distance. He asked her if she was hurt. She didn't answer, but appeared to be a bit more alert. I don't like this he thought as he began to stand up. I really don't like this he almost vocalized as he saw the figure of a tall man emerge from a doorway two yards behind the woman. He started to turn back but saw that a car was stopping on the main street behind him, perpendicular to the sidewalk. Casey looked back toward the man, then the car. Now two men were quickly exiting the car. Casey looked back at the first man and then looked toward his escape to the right. The man anticipated the look and moved to his left. The other two were approaching rapidly. Casey looked in several directions, but each look was responded to by a man moving to that direction. Casey stopped, stood straight up and gasped, "Shit".

The three men relaxed their posture and each continued slowly walking at Casey. All of them wore overcoats and hats. Clean-shaven and neatly dressed, Casey reasoned, now these guys look like Gestapo. One of the men from the car got to Casey first and stated, "You will come with us." Assuming that was not a request, Casey nodded his head affirmatively and turned toward the car. At that moment he noticed that the woman in distress seemed to have vanished. Now why would they be setting me up, Casey pondered as he stepped into the waiting car.

CHAPTER 8

Rome, Italy, Summer, 1938

"But you have such talent. Your art; you are smart in school. Anthony the Army will do well without you," Ginette Alberoni admonished her 20-year-old son.

"Italy will have to be defended by the Army. They won't need artists; they'll need fighters," Tony answered, not given to wordiness. "I'm the man of the family. It's my job," he added.

"But Anthony, we need you here. Your little brother Emilio needs you." she pleaded. Composing herself, Ginette directed, "Besides, you must not defile your father's death. Please, please don't join the Army."

"So tell me about my father's death. What happened that you haven't told me?" Tony pointedly asked.

Ginette looked down and paused. Slowly looking back up at Tony she said softly, "Yes, it's time for you to know. You must talk to your Uncle Pietro."

"So why don't you tell me? Why don't you talk about it?"

Again Ginette grew silent and looked away. "It's too hard for me." Waving Tony toward the door, she softly directed, "Talk to your uncle." She paused, then straightened up again and looked directly at Tony, "Do it before you do anything else."

Among his peers, Tony was tall at 5'11". His frame was large boned, which belied his trim physic. Dark haired, somewhat handsome, but with a round face. He walked with confident posture as he approached the kitchen table and pulled up a chair. "Uncle Pietro how are you?"

Sitting at the table and concentrating hard on his nephew Pietro didn't answer but motioned for Tony to sit. "A glass of wine, Tony?"

"Yes," Tony answered, reaching for the glass Pietro was already pouring.

Leaning back but staring directly at Tony, Pietro began, "So your mother thinks it's time you learned about your father? I agree."

Tony said, "Yes, I."

"Don't interrupt," Pietro ordered, "just listen." Tony leaned back, holding the glass in both hands, looked straight at Pietro.

"Your artistic talent and your way with words you got from your father. Back around 1914 or 15 he worked closely with Duce in Milan. He drew cartoons and wrote quips and articles for Benito's 'Socialist Daily' newspaper. Lucio used his French somehow with the paper. A very loyal son, Lucio was. More than anything he wanted Italy to come together and grow in strength. He ridiculed the pacifism of other Socialists and Communists. He saw them as weak and not prepared to handle the problems he felt were headed our way. Duce was a rising star, and he felt much as your father did. They became close, your father and Duce. Soon your grandpa Perrin joined them. He was through farming and moved to Milan to help your father. After pausing, "Perrin loved your father. He did since the day Lucio was born." Rejoining the story, "Then Benito went off to war. That was about 1915.

"Soon after Benito left your family moved back to Rome. But, your father and Perrin continued to work in politics. Your grandpa was always by your father's side, helping out." Pondering a sip of wine, Pietro continued, "In time your father grew tired of Duce. He was constantly changing his stripes. Once a Socialist, then a Fascist. Seems he was looking for the party that would get him into power the fastest. For sure, your father was not in line with the Squadristi. They were a bunch of thugs who did nothing for this country except harass people trying to bring order. Their tactics worked. The Fascists they supported gained a lot of power. When Duce got control of the Fascists, your father started to hate the ground he walked on. By then it was clear Mussolini wanted what was best for Mussolini, not Italy.

Tony sipped some wine and squirmed in his chair. Pietro continued, "You know the history how Falta appointed Duce as

Premiere, which caught a lot of people by surprise. But Mussolini had enough people fooled so in the election of '24, the Fascists got most of the Cabinet seats." Pausing to sit up straight, Pietro resumed, "Here's what you don't know: Remember Matteotti?" Pietro asked, but not waiting for an answer continued, "He was a tireless worker, a Socialist who truly worked for Italians, not himself. He was the main one behind the challenge of that 1924 vote. The whole thing was a fraud. At first the Fascists kind of ignored Matteotti, assuming his protests would just go away. But he continued to press, and was soon found dead. Everyone accused Duce of being involved, but then the propaganda followed that this was just the work of some thugs, who were found and tried. They're probably now living in some villa with all the food and wine . . . well that was the end of that.

"Your father and Perrin admired Matteotti and did a lot of leg work for him." Pausing for a long drink, Pietro leaned forward and looked into Tony's face. Tony thought he saw a tear well up. "Your father and grandfather were murdered in cold blood. It was brutal the way they were cut down; it was horrible," Pietro sobbed. Now almost screaming, "Their killings were hidden behind the murder of Matteotti," Pietro stood up and walked in a slow circle, rubbing his hands and looking around in a blank stare. Tony set his glass down and leaning forward rested his elbows on his knees and bowed his head.

Pietro resumed, "No one went after their killers', but of course we know who had them murdered. It was probably the same thugs who killed Matteotti. Your father's friendship and all the work he did meant nothing to that bastard." Speaking louder, "I don't believe he would have even dealt with Matteotti's murder, except I think he was pushed." Slowing down and looking at Tony, Pietro explained, "The German Socialists, you know, Hitler, were playing politics with the Government and they probably pushed Duce into at least looking into Matteotti's murder. The press was getting negative toward Mussolini."

Tony asked, "So why would the Germans get involved?"

"The Nazis are trying to rebuild Germany and they need all the friends they can get. Why they want to be friends with the Fascists,

I do not know. But, since they have formed this Rome-Berlin Axis, I guess they don't want any tarnished images."

Silence prevailed, as both men appeared to be in a trance thinking about the events relayed. As he stood up, Tony spoke first, "I need to go now, Uncle." Motioning a thank you with his empty glass, he said, "Thanks. I'll say hello to Mom." Pietro nodded his head and holding his glass with both hands watched Tony depart.

Ginette didn't say hello; she went straight to, "So did Pietro talk to you?"

"Yes mother, he did. I have a lot to think about."

"I'm so sorry, Anthony. It's so hard."

"I know, Mom," Tony concluded. Tony walked back out of the house, his mother staring after him wondering what he was thinking. She got her answer the next evening after a very quiet dinner.

"The Germans will be rescuing the Sudenten people, if they haven't already," Tony abruptly stated.

"Anthony, what do you mean?" his mother asked.

In his usual brief fashion Tony continued, "I'll be leaving tomorrow. I have to be a part of what will be going on."

"Anthony what's going on? You belong here . . . Anthony," Ginette pleaded.

"Uncle Pietro knows what I'm doing. He'll be here for you." Abruptly turning toward his brother, "And no, Emilio, you will stay here. You are not going too. You are now the head of this family. Your cousins and Mom are your responsibility."

Standing, Emilio bristled, "I'll make my own decisions, Tony."
"That's right, Emilio, you are the decision-maker. But you will make your decisions here, got it." Emilio backed down, but did not answer. He just stared at Tony.

Tony walked toward his room. He stopped and turned. "It'll be OK. Thinks are happening that are going to make this a better world. That is if that bastard Duce doesn't ruin it." Quietly he continued, "I'll say goodbye in the morning. Momma, I'll be OK. I'll be back before you know it," Tony added, feeling in his heart that that was not the truth.

CHAPTER 9

Italy to Germany, 1938

Riding his motorcycle north, a road sign broke Tony's trance. He pulled over and stopped directly in front of the sign that announced the town line of Milan. I wonder if I can find where father worked? He died so young. I was so young.

Standing up straight, straddling the bike, Tony looked intently at the sign. As though the sign was an icon, Tony pledged that he would honor his father by continuing his work to lift Italy and to bring pride to the name, Alberoni.

Tony raced through Milan as though he was leaving bad history and family memories in his dust. He had no problem getting into Switzerland. He had not been to North Italy or Switzerland before. He felt like a tourist, taking in the mountains, valleys, and pastoral countryside. But as he drew near to the German border, he slowed considerably and began to introspect.

Creeping along with his head down, hardly paying attention to the road, he tried to rehearse his next few days: They're not going to throw open the border for me. My intent to join their cause will be met with suspicion. They will try me; try my patience. I must be strong, quiet, and confident. I will not turn back.

Tony's insight proved accurate. He was thoroughly grilled at the border station. His motives were questioned. They insisted on a detailed accounting of his trip from Rome, then asked him questions designed to reveal inconsistencies in his story. Thanks to Tony's quiet direct nature, and the fact that he told no lies, the soldier in charge appeared to accept him. "You will be put on the next transport to Munich. There you will meet with some people whom, I assure you, will not be fooled if you are not telling the truth," the Captain directed. Tony shook his head in agreement, then thinking out loud, "What about my motorcycle?"

A burly sergeant answered, "If they let you join the Army, you won't need it. If they send you back, it'll be here."

Tony's mouth curled down as he reasoned that he has seen the last of his vehicle. It'll be some soldier's toy by the time I load the transport, he posited.

The back of the transport was stacked with boxes of some sort of supplies. The fold down seats offered little comfort as the truck sped along the highway. One seat was vacant, the other two occupied by two twenty something fellows. Their black hair and dark complexion led Tony to believe they were not German. Their dress and demeanor were a bit slovenly. Tony decided he didn't need to get chummy with these two. They obliged by keeping to themselves. Tony noticed that when he looked directly at either of them, they would quickly look away. Weaklings, he thought.

This can't be Munich, Tony thought, there aren't any beer halls. The fact is they did not go to the City, but directly to a military facility. The truck jerked to a stop. The soldier driver and passenger opened the back gate and speaking in German, motioned for the three men to follow them. All five entered a temporary looking structure, which appeared to be an office. Immediately inside was an open lobby. They all proceeded to a long counter that spanned most of the width.

Looking at the robust uniformed lady behind the counter, Tony thought, damn she could probably whip all of us. She spoke to the two soldiers, who soon departed. In broken Italian, the woman told the three men to stand by for a minute. Tony saw that the other two appeared to understand her, so they must be Italian. Damn disgrace he thought, as he slowly looked them over. Both stood facing the counter, obviously avoiding looking at Tony.

Within minutes two uniformed German officers entered from a room behind the counter. They wore crisp, neat uniforms, and were clean-shaven with short, light hair. Both momentarily stood just looking at the three men. Tony saw that the other two men shuffled a bit as they avoided looked directly at the officers. Both officers then looked straight at Tony. He looked straight back at them. His expression was serious but not threatening.

The shorter of the two officers gave an order to the lady soldier behind the counter. She came around and addressed the other two men. She told them to follow her. As they departed out the front door, the lady looked back at Tony and told him to follow the officers. They went back behind the counter and into a room; Tony followed.

The room had a round table in the middle with several chairs around it. One officer motioned for Tony to sit, and departed out another door. Tony pulled up a chair and sat. The other officer did the same, across the table. It was a little awkward as neither person spoke for several minutes. Obviously, they were waiting for someone else, Tony reasoned. He soon relaxed and sat back.

A young uniformed lieutenant entered the room and briefly looked around. He appeared tentative as he slowly walked over to an empty chair and sat down. He was thin, about 5'10", wearing thick glasses.

"We need to find out about you so we know where you should go," the lieutenant explained in perfect Italian. He then put a clipboard on the table and looked through some attached papers. "I will be completing a profile on you. You will answer all my questions a fully as you can," the lieutenant directed, not looking at Tony and failing to come across with the authority he was trying to project.

"Sure," Tony said, cocking his head and appearing to say, get on with it. The other officer donned a stern look and leaned forward toward Tony, sending an unmistakable message of authority.

The profile was easy for Tony. He answered all questions fully and truthfully, until they got to his parents' profile. Tony said that some thugs had killed his father. He left off the suspicion that they were Mussolini's thugs. He depicted his father as a minor journalist who did some work for Duce's campaign. Tony reasoned that since there is an alliance between Germany and Mussolini, tying his father in with the regime would be a plus. But, the fact that Mussolini probably had him killed might raise some suspicion, so he omitted that part.

Following the interview, Tony was invited to stay on the base while his information was processed. He was given a cot in a barracks, and ate in the base mess. He was summoned the next morning and informed that he was being inducted into the German Army.

Basic training was a snap for Tony. His trainers noted that he was very athletic and took orders well. He was a quick study in his conversational German classes. What particularly caught the attention of the training command was his quiet aggressiveness. It was the "duffel bag scramble" that exhibited Tony's nature. This was an exercise that tested individuals' mental posture as much, if not more, than their physical abilities.

A dozen or so recruits were instructed to line up, carrying large filled duffel bags. They were shown a dirt racecourse to run, which included some narrow passages between wall barricades. There was no finish line. At some point the instructors yelled, "halt", and the race ended. Runners in the first three places were rewarded with some privileges. The remaining field had to continue on with a hike around the compound, still carrying the loads. The catch was that an instructor, standing on a high platform, periodically yelled, "Reverse". At that point the race direction did a one eighty. Since it was not declared which direction the race would be going when stopped, it was important for the participants to always scramble to get to the front, whichever direction they were going. The point of carrying all that extra weight was to partially eliminate speed as a factor. The narrow passageways were included to make it difficult to go around others to get ahead.

Both times this race was conducted, Tony finished in the top three. Entering the passageways he forced others out of the way. He did not hesitate to run over a slower recruit in front of him. He made little noise and issued no apologies when the race was over. They liked that.

On the day his training was completed, Tony went off the base and into the nearest bar/restaurant. He was alone, as he did not gain any friends in training. He was surprised to see three of the recruit trainers seated together at a table drinking beer. Tony was more surprised when one of them partially rose, smiled, and motioned for Tony to join them. A bit apprehensive he slowly walked over to the table. One soldier scooted an empty chair up and motioned for Tony to sit.

The training demeanor was turned off, and Tony found himself being accepted as a regular soldier. The four sat, drank, and talked for the next two hours. Conversation skipped around from worldly matters to light personal thrusts and parries. At one point the conversation got somewhat serious. Tony was told that he was an outstanding recruit. He was advised that people higher up take notice when a recruit shows exceptional ability. All three laughed that someday they would each be his subordinate.

As much as this chance meeting pumped Tony up, the next year served to bring him back to earth. While the buildup to war was all around, Tony found himself assigned to one administrative office after another. First he was assigned as a clerk in a company office. Shuffling papers was not what he had imagined for himself as a soldier. But, he did his job well. He took it upon himself to learn several jobs in the office, and did them with more efficiency than the persons assigned. This was not without rewards. Tony was always assigned to man the office when the other staff endured temporary undesirable jobs, including command inspections. He soon learned that making himself indispensable had its rewards. Deep down he knew that he was destined for greater things.

CHAPTER 10

Germany, Summer, 1940

Tony enjoyed the military training he received. Basic training; infantry training update; firearms. But this, counterintelligence training, was exactly what he was most qualified for. He could not think of anything else that he would rather be doing at this time. His enthusiasm showed. As before, it was not long before he caught the eye of training supervisors.

As much as the staff watched Tony, he was watching a classmate. Gaelle was a small and shapely young lady with a strange accent. Her German was fluent enough, but her first language was French, plus she spoke English and Italian. Her German borrowed a bit from her other languages. Tony almost giggled when her accent was particularly pronounced. Tony was tough and focused, but totally out of character when with Gaelle. He was almost shy, and very sharing. He smiled a lot with her. At work and in training he virtually never smiled.

With only one week remaining in his scheduled training, Tony was excited when he got the message to go to the commander's office. This is it, my assignment, he thought with excited anticipation. However, as he walked through the cold, dark compound, he felt a very heavy weight in his heart. Gaelle; what will happen with us?

Tony reported as ordered to the unit commander. Dark eyes, high cheek bone, the tall and trim officer was a Rudolf Hess look-alike. From his seat behind his desk, the commander instructed Tony to sit. Tony's thoughts raced all over Europe as he anticipated what exciting post he would be sent to. A rare smile crept onto his face, but immediately drooped with the first words: "About this Gaelle. How do you know her? Where did you meet?" the commander asked.

"Sir?" Tony asked, at a loss for further words as his thought processes switched gears.

The commander leaned forward a bit and looked at Tony, "Do you know a lot of Gaelles?"

"Ah, no sir, I know who you mean. I met her here in this school," he answered with a distinct disappointed tone.

"You have been seeing a lot of each other in your off time. What do you know about her?" the commander asked.

"I know that she was born in France. Her father was some sort of Italian government employee working in Paris. Her mother was a Paris native, I believe." Tony paused and looked at the commander to see if he should go on. Not getting any message from the man's face, Tony continued, "We found that we enjoyed each other's company, so we have spent some time together." Again Tony looked for a signal to stop or continue.

The commander leaned back and brought his hands up together with fingertips touching. "The Army wants you two to get married," the commander directed as if he was giving out a simple weekend assignment.

"Sir?" Tony asked, sitting back and looking directly at the man.

The commander responded, "The two of you will be assigned to Abwehr. You will be undercover. Your identities will be easier to hide if you are married."

Both men looked at each other for a moment. Tony broke the silence, "Are you saying get married, or just pretend that we are?"

"No, I'm saying get married. Here's the plan," the commander said.: "You both are fluent in Italian and French. You will be transferred to somewhere in Italy and you will get married. You will do some work there, but the real job is in France. You will work undercover there and you will be most effective if you appear to be just another Parisian couple. If you are questioned about your marriage, it would look a bit suspicious if you say you were married in Germany, now wouldn't it."

Tony picked up, "Yes, and if we say we were married in Italy, that could be verified as true."

“Alberoni, after the France assignment, you can do what you want with the woman. You will probably be sent to other assignments and you won't have to be bothered with her,” the commander concluded.

Tony looked serious and nodded. Inside he was smiling. This was a good visit, Tony said to himself, I get a good assignment, and I don't have to give up seeing Gaelle. I'll deal with that “after France” business when the time comes.

Just as Tony was approaching her dorm room, Gaelle appeared approaching from the other direction. Tony quickly approached Gaelle and took her arm. He turned her around and together they briskly walked down the hallway toward the back door. Both nodded to the few people they passed as they walked. Neither said a word during this process.

Outside they abruptly turned to the right and tucked in on the back side of a large round bush at the corner of the dorm building. Gaelle started to speak, but Tony overrode her, “I just came from the commander's office and I have to talk to you.” Gaelle put a finger to his lips, looked him in the eye and offered, “I know Tony, I just came from the female superintendents office. We are to be man and wife.”

Tony looked surprised and hesitated for a moment then challenged, “What do you think?”

“What do you think?” Gaelle fired back.

Tony looked down and shuffled a bit, “I know this isn't how we figured things would happen. We've only known each other for a few weeks, but damn it Gaelle, I love you. I'm glad this is happening.” Finishing, Tony looked up and stiffened as if ready to duck if she should swing at him.

A sort of flush came over Gaelle. Very softly and kindly she looked into Tony's eyes. Running her hand slowly down the side of his face, she replied, “Tony, I love you too. You know, from the start I felt like we would be together somehow. No, this isn't how I pictured it would happen . . . . well there's a war brewing and who knows what will happen. I think we are probably very lucky.”

Silence gripped the moment as they looked at each other. Their eyes meeting provided a gateway for deep emotions to flow between them. They drew close together. Her arms folded around him as he pulled her up against his body. For several moments they stood silently together each looking out into space. Though they did not speak of it, they both developed slight feelings of apprehension. Where will this ride take us, they pondered?

Signs of war were everywhere. The base was in perpetual motion with people and equipment constantly coming and going. Graduation from counterintelligence school was in step with this activity. A quick interview with a command officer, beers with a few select classmates, early morning packing, and leaving the base. That quickly everything changed for Tony and Gaelle, and as if by magic, they found themselves on a train for Italy.

For about six hours, the newly betrothed sat together quietly, engaging in light and sporadic conversation. Their occasional friendly touches became more frequent. Touches became grasps. Both kept glancing in random directions, as if to avoid direct eye contact. But that gave way to direct eye contact, which radiated with passion from both ends. Without saying a word, they stood up, staring at each other all the time. Tony grabbed Gaelle's hand as they briskly walked through railroad cars. He had no idea where he was going; he just knew he had to find a private nook somewhere.

The men's room was just ahead. Tony headed for it, but Gaelle pulled his hand back. He looked at her as she waived her finger back and forth. "The ladies room will be nicer," she whispered, as she took the lead, still holding hands. In the ladies room, their tops came open and their pants came off, perhaps in record time. Facing Tony, Gaelle jumped up on the tiny counter and pulled Tony into her. Their passion stopped time. It could have been an hour, but probably more like four minutes when the door handle rattled. "Someone wants in," Gaelle whispered as she smiled broadly at Tony. Tony sighed in relief, smiled back, and slowly shook his head. As quickly as they came undone, they got their clothes back together. They both reached for the door handle, but simultaneously stopped and looked at each other. Soft, mutual smiles proclaimed that their love had been consummated and pledged their adoration for each other. Resuming, they both giggled as they exited the room and quickly slid by a stuffy, middle-aged lady who was looking over the rim of her glasses. The rest of the ride to Rome was spent quietly, with frequent glances at each other with faces showing telltale grins.

Rome was a fortunate choice of cities for their first assignment. For German officers, Tony and Gaelle had considerable free time. They spend most of it with Tony's family. Gaelle and Tony's mother, Ginette, became close friends.

The German Army arranged for Tony to attend classes at a trade school. His subject was banking. He was charged with learning the mechanics of bank operations. Gaelle was sent to school to learn psychology. Her professor was also an expert in interrogation. She was charged with learning how to get the most information possible from captives.

According to command instructions, Tony and Gaelle were to get married via a civil procedure. When told of this, Ginette went into a verbal rampage, accented by a multitude of hand and arm gestures. "How can you get married in a City office? That's where you go to vote or pay your taxes. Please, Tony, marry the girl like a Christian. Do the right thing", was her frequent pitch.

"You know Gaelle, I don't know why the Army would care where we get married. A church wedding would be more legitimate," Tony argued.

"You don't have to convince me, Tony. It would be nice to get married in a church, and it sure would please your mother," she added.

"OK then, I'll talk to our supervisor tomorrow," Tony volunteered.

Gaelle looked at Tony, cocked her head, and softly offered, "No, I think I should do that."

"Why you? I'm the man, remember"?

"Oh yes, I certainly remember," she said softly as she snuggled up to Tony. Looking into his eyes and with lips slightly open, she rubbed her breasts against his arm and chest. Softly she whispered, "Now don't you think I can be just a bit more persuasive?"

Tony stood silently for a moment as she rubbed her body against his. "OK, I see what you mean. But there'll be no rubbing your gorgeous breasts against him," Tony commanded.

Stepping back, Gaelle looked at her breasts, cupped her hands under them and winked at Tony. Next she saluted with her right hand and offered, "Yes sir, oh mighty one."

With that she spun around and danced out of the room. The wedding was a festive event, but no one got as much into it or out of it as Tony's mother.

Tony was surprised to be greeted by Gaelle when he got home. Usually he got home first. They kissed and hugged, but Tony quickly took her shoulders and held her at arm's length. Her serious look was unmistakable. "What is it?" Tony asked in his usual brief manner. Gaelle did not answer, but took Tony by the hand and led him over to the couch, where she prompted him to sit.

She sat sideways facing him and began, "You remember the train ride coming here?"

"Yes, so?"

"Well Tony, you are a virile man," she answered, looking down.

"You mean you got pregnant?" He figured out.

"No, you brute," she said, slapping his shoulder, "You got me pregnant."

"Well OK, yes, so are you sure"?

"Of course I'm sure," she quickly said, cocking her head. "I wouldn't guess about something like this."

"I know, I know," Tony consoled, slowly developing a smile. With a sudden broad grin Tony exclaimed, "I'm going to be a father!"

Tony and Gaelle reveled in their joy, toasting it with a glass of wine. Tony set his glass down and assumed a serious look. "You know, I'm not sure how the Army will take this news," he offered.

"Maybe we shouldn't say anything." "Tony, it's going to become pretty apparent. We just have to be up front with it. They could decide that it just adds to our cover," Gaelle reasoned.

"Yes, well, I don't know. But for sure this time I go talk to the boss," Tony insisted.

"Yes, I understand," she added, patting him on his shoulder.

It was late at night when Tony returned from the command office. He entered their apartment quietly so as not to wake Gaelle. He should have known better. She spent the afternoon and evening alternating from doing busy housework and pacing the floor. She nearly collided with Tony as she rushed to greet him. "What did they say? What did they say?" she excitedly pressed.

"Well, good evening to you too," Tony returned sarcastically. Gaelle lowered her arms spun around and started to walk away, muttering, "So it's just my life, my baby. I don't need to know what they said."

Pursuing her, Tony grasped her shoulders and kissed the back of her neck. Tony said softly, "Sit down here and I'll tell you."

"Ok, at first they were a bit irritated by the news of the baby. I think one of them was hinting that we could just give the baby to the State. But the Commander finally accepted that the child would give us more credibility and wouldn't be in the way."

Gaelle interjected, "So who was there; who did you talk to?"

"The Commander and his adjutant, and some other stodgy old man I don't know. It doesn't matter; let me finish." Tony looked sternly at Gaelle, and then continued. "We should be getting our travel orders any day now. We'll go to Paris and check in there. As you were told in your school, you will be interviewing prisoners. Basically that will be an office job. They couldn't, or wouldn't tell me what I'll be doing, but I will be working mostly in Paris. When not at our regular jobs, we are to mingle in society, so to speak, with the idea of getting involved in any anti-German movements we can get into. The nice young married couple with the cute child; that's us. OK?" Tony asked as he raised his eyebrows.

"Well, that sounds pretty straight forward. We can do that," she concluded.

"We're very lucky, really. There could be a whole bunch of things we could be assigned to that would split us up," Tony added.

"Yes," Gaelle sighed, looking up and closing her eyes.

CHAPTER 11

Paris. October 1940

The Paris air was warm for October, and a bit muggy. "I think this winter will be more pleasant than the last." Tony looked at the man sitting next to him at the bar. Recalling people talking about how bad the past winter was, Tony responded, "Well if this weather is any indication, it should be. I could do without all that cold."

"Hmm," the man answered.

Tony pushed his empty wine glass forward and got up to leave. "Pleasure meeting you, sir. In town for long?" the bartender offered.

"I live here," Tony answered, curling his brow in a suspicious expression. "I just haven't been in this part of the City long; I'll be back in."

"Good," the bartender commented as he toweled a glass and turned away.

Following a hello hug, Tony pushed away and smiled. "I just came from that restaurant around the corner."

"Restaurant or bar? Your breath gave you away," Gaelle chided waving her finger at Tony.

Not responding, Tony continued, "It's bigger than it looks from the outside. Yes, it does have a bar. I thought I better test the wine before I let you and my son drink there." Tony looked for a reaction, but just got a grimaced stare. He added, "I think it will be a good place to meet some locals and get established."

Gaelle cocked her head and looked directly at Tony. "Our son? So you've decided I'm carrying your son?" Walking away, Tony turned back toward her and stated, "That's what I said."

It turned out that Tony was not prophetic. April of 1941 featured the birth of a short but kind of plump little girl with considerable black hair, for a newborn, and very dark complexion. The delivery nurse surmised that she may have had some stress during the birthing process, but her vital signs were all good. Tony picked the name, Annetta. "A mixed breed French/Italian girl ought to have a French/ Italian name," Tony dictated.

Gaelle smiled and agreed. "Annetta is a pretty name for a pretty girl."

During the months leading up to Annetta's birth, life was relatively routine for Gaelle. She was assigned to a small camp outside Paris. Some war prisoners were brought there for interrogation. The prisoners brought to the camp were selected from regular POW institutions. Those selected were suspected of having some particular knowledge that Army Intelligence felt was important.

Gaelle's role usually involved playing the "good cop". She would ply for information by appealing to the macho nature of the prisoner. Her soft, innocent demeanor would be projected to soften the situation and put the man at ease. She could almost make it seem that she is a victim and she could be rescued if only the prisoner would give the information requested. Gaelle's supervisors did not have much faith in such interrogation methods, so they gave her only a brief time to get results. When they cued her, she was to abruptly change her stance and appear angry with the prisoner for not cooperating with her. She would cry, yell, stomp her feet, and even plead for answers. She was to always play the "pity me I'm pregnant" card.

Gaelle had limited success in gaining meaningful information. But then the same could be said for the male interrogators who typically were brutish and cruel. The camp was kept open during most of the German occupation, as the camp staff never missed an opportunity to exaggerate any limited success at intelligence gathering in order to keep their soft jobs. They were careful to ensure that the nature of the camp was kept relatively secret. Gaelle's trips to and from work took routes designed to mask her entering and leaving. She was never assigned to interrogate any local French prisoners, though few of those did make it to the camp. Her future role as an undercover operative was always kept in mind.

When Tony left the apartment for work, his appearance and demeanor completely belied his athletic Latin features and the serious almost offensive expression he wore outside of home. Dapper in his business suit, with tidy briefcase he looked more like a banker than a champion football player, which would be his choice of careers, given another time and place. And banker he was. His job followed his training as he quickly got deeply involved in finding, categorizing, and yes, stealing various forms of funds found in the captured French banks. Those funds were forwarded to Army procurement and used to fund the war.

This taking from the banks was done much like cattle graze. Cows constantly move as they pick at the grass. They don't denude any areas in order to ensure that there will be supplies upon return trips. Indeed, the larger urban banks were not robbed blind; just enough was taken to allow the bank to continue operation. Smaller suburban banks were wiped out.

Tony's role included balancing funds taken with funds retained so that the institution could continue operating. Though it appeared that he was an official of the Vichy Government, which had seized the banks, he was solely on the German payroll. He was also charged with seeing to it that the French bank managers, Vichy officials, and representatives of the Bank for International Settlement, did not interfere with his mission. Additionally, he had to contend with other German organizations trying to scavenge funds for their operations. He and other Army officials had to constantly deal with several groups which all wanted in on the scavenging action, including those from the Foreign Ministry, Goring's gang, and private German industrialists.

As always, Tony quickly became very good at what he did. But what he was doing soon became mundane and boring to him.

Signs of spring were beginning to show. The air was still brisk but some warmth was beginning to gather. Tony was standing at a desk in the bank lobby, gathering papers and placing them in his brief case. His 9MM Luger was stowed as well. His twice a week ritual of delivering accounting papers to the Army office did not involve any negotiable instruments, but he figured some thief may not know that and try to rob him.

Gerrit was a slight man from Austria. He wore his hair and mustache in imitation of Hitler. Tony referred to him as his "partner thief." Tony had little respect for the man, but made every effort to get along.

Gerrit emerged from the back office and looking at Tony pointedly asked, "Aren't you going to be late?" Tony didn't answer but snapped closed his brief case and started walking toward the front door. *Weasel,* Tony thought.

About a block and a half down the street, Tony stopped and thought. He was not going to deliver the report he was working on showing some disparities between some of his figures and overlapping ones developed by Gerrit. But if in the end there is a problem, and he hadn't kept command abreast of what he was seeing, he could have some tough explaining to do. Tony turned around and walked back to the bank.

As he approached, he saw two men entering the front door. If instinct is a virtue, Tony was blessed. Those two guys are up to something. He was sure. He was also sure that from where he was they would not have noticed him approaching before they entered the building.

Tony slowly opened the front door and thoroughly scanned the lobby. The men were not there. The door to Gerrit's office was slightly ajar. Tony quietly walked toward the office. The only other occupants were the two German women working in the lobby area. He motioned for them to remain where they are and be quiet. They had learned to respect Tony, but were still taken aback when they saw him draw the weapon from his brief case. They could only sit and stare, wide-eyed.

Standing beside the doorframe, Tony leaned toward the narrow opening in order to listen. There was shuffling going on, and soft voices. Tony could only pick up bits of conversation. It sounded like Gerrit was orchestrating some activity, but Tony wasn't sure what it was. Tony leaned a bit further into the doorway where he could pick up a bit more conversation. He understood Gerrit to tell one man that he could get more cash into his bag. Then Gerrit told one man to "also tie my legs . . . . make it look good."

There was no doubt in Tony's mind what was happening. *No wonder he wanted me to get going,* he thought.

The office door was positioned to open in. Tony leaned flat against the wall on the opposite side of the hinges. He was aware of the door opening, then one of the men walked straight out carrying a satchel. The man was looking at the front door and did not see Tony. He got two steps into the lobby when Tony put his Luger up to the back right side of his head and pulled the trigger. The fatal shot knocked the man out of one shoe as he lunged forward to the floor. Immediately Tony reached around the doorway with his left hand to the second man, who had just gotten to the opening. Tony grabbed a fist full of shirt and pulled the man forward, twisting him as he thrust the man to the floor on his back. Tony's left knee landed in the man's stomach as he pointed the Luger at his face. Groaning with pain, the man released the bag and pulled both his arms up beside his head. Tony patted the man down with his free hand. A shoulder holster held a revolver. Throwing it aside, Tony put his Luger in his waistband and taking one of the man's arms, rolled him over onto his stomach.

With his foot Tony held the man down in this position. Tony sighed a breath of relief and slowly scanned the room. One of the women, the older one, was still sitting in her chair, mouth open and in a trance. The younger lady slowly walked over toward Tony. "I called that Army number we have for emergencies," she exclaimed quietly.

"Good," Tony reassured her.

Tony pondered how he was going to restrain the man as he looked around the room. He did not need to finish the thought as two uniformed soldiers and one man in street cloths entered the bank. Tony gave them a brief description of the shooting. He told them that Gerrit was tied up in the office, but told them not to untie him; that he was part of the robbery.

Ignoring Tony's direction, one soldier emerged from the office, escorting Gerrit, whom he had untied. Gerrit got visibly agitated and started pointing toward Tony and yelling that he was in on it. That Tony was part of the robbery. The plain clothed man directed one soldier to take Gerrit back into the office, where he joined them. The other took Tony to a corner of the lobby and sat him down.

Tony could hear Gerrit ranting and making accusations. Soon the interrogator emerged from the office and talked privately with the two women. He then approached Tony. He told the soldier to go back to their office with Gerrit and the other soldier. He told Tony that he was to make a detailed report of what had occurred. Then he was to secure the bank for the day, after the dead body was removed. Tony complied. He knew Gerrit was just digging himself a hole, and that the women's account would make the events clear.

CHAPTER 12

Paris. Spring, 1941

Tony put Annetta down and then walked into the kitchen where Gaelle had just finished after-dinner chores. "What is it?" Tony asked as she turned to face him.

"What's what?" she countered, looking down and taking a seat.

Tony pulled up a chair in front of her, turned it backwards and sat facing her. "You don't exactly hide your emotions well, you know," Tony proclaimed.

Gaelle didn't answer him and started to look away in different directions. Tony leaned to the right to get back in front of her face. "I asked, what is it?"

She slowly tilted her head up and looked at Tony. "This whole interrogation business is getting to me!" she exclaimed. "They're always criticizing my methods, though their results are no better than mine." Tony knew what she was talking about. He said nothing. "I mean I understood that we would be doing undercover work. That sounds like something I could really get excited about. But all I do is talk to prisoners in hopes of getting some bit of useless information, then we go out and socialize. It all seems so meaningless," she concluded.

Tony sat looking at Gaelle for a few seconds, and then began to smile. "Well have I got good news for you." Tony said nothing more, waiting for her reaction. "Well what, what; don't just sit there with that stupid look on your face." Tony smiled and leaned back, holding onto the chair. "I got a visit today. That new Adjutant for this sector. Now he didn't say much, but he said to be prepared for a new assignment. I tried to pump him, but you know how some of those Germans can be. Anyway, he did say that we, you and me, can expect to get involved in what we came here for."

"Yes, which is?" she asked.

"I assume you will get your wish. I think we probably will be going underground someway. Anyway, he said we would be getting our orders soon."

The train ride back from bank headquarters in La Bourboule was quiet. Tony sat looking out the window, wondering if he should press the issue of his new assignment. It had been three weeks since he was told to expect orders. Anticipation always makes the time go by faster, he mused.

The man sitting in his favorite chair in the apartment had German features, dishwater-blond hair; light complexion. But he certainly didn't look like anyone from the ranks of the Army. His clothes were loose fitting, his shoes appeared well worn, and his hair was a bit unkempt.

Gaelle and the man stood up when Tony entered the room. His countenance frequently elicited that reaction, which is usually reserved for high-ranking officers and officials. "Tony, this is Georg, he's from Command."

Tony looked at the man and smiled. "So, are you here to tell us where to go?" Tony joked.

Tony watched for his reaction. Georg brought up a bit of a smile as he replied, "Yes, I guess you could say that. I understand that you both are aware that you are being assigned to covert operations." Tony nodded affirmatively but didn't speak. Georg continued, "I haven't told Gaelle much. You need to hear what I have to say together."

Tony's expression became one of suspicion as he slowly replied, "OK."

"The biggest news is that you will be split up. You will have to move out of this apartment as soon as possible." It was now Georg's turn to look for reactions. Tony and Gaelle just sat looking at each other with almost emotionless expressions. Georg continued, "Actually, you will be seeing each other quite a bit. You won't be living together, nor will you be seen in public together. You will be doing the same mission, just in different ways." Georg stopped and looked at both of them again.

Tony spoke next, asking, "OK, so what are our missions?"

"Very simple. Gaelle will be spying on the Paris Resistance, and Tony, you will be putting them away."

Gaelle straightened up and with a developing smile asked, "So we will both be working in Paris. I will be looking for members of the Resistance, and when I find them I will let Tony know and he will arrest them?"

"Well, that's very simplified, but yes, that's basically it," Georg confirmed. "Of course, Tony will be working with other people."

Gaelle leaned back and looked at Tony. He returned the look, and together they both shrugged their shoulders. She looked back at Georg and pointedly added, "There's one big matter to resolve." Georg immediately stated, "The kid."

"That's Annetta, and yes, what about her?"

"Well for right now, she will have to be placed someplace. She will not be staying with either of you. Of course, the Army can provide a place for her in one of those farm homes. But I know that you have family. There will be no problem if you have one of them take her in."

Gaelle appeared to bristle a bit and began to reply. Tony interrupted her by addressing Georg. "We knew it could come to this. Yes, we have family in Italy where we can take Annetta." Gaelle looked straight at Tony.

Her stressed expression slowly relaxed as she knew that Tony had just taken charge and effectively told her to be quiet. Time seemed to stand still as she engaged her mind in thought: "This could be much worse. Tony's mom and brother will take good care of Annetta. This is the opportunity I've been hoping for." She shuffled her position in her chair, broke a bit of a smile, looked quickly at Tony then directly at Georg. "OK, what do we need to know?"

"Excellent!" replied Georg.

The three spent over three hours discussing the assignments. Georg explained that he would be their contact. Gaelle would assume a totally new identity as she infiltrates the Resistance. Georg told them that he had some contacts that could get her started. He cautioned that she must go slowly, and that this operation could take years. In order to give her some quick training, Georg relayed a number of his experiences working undercover. As the evening progressed, Gaelle got deeper and deeper into the conversation. More and more she asked pertinent questions and picked his brain. Georg noticed that and any doubts that he may have had about her vanished.

Finally Georg turned to Tony. "You know Tony, there were plans to keep you doing whatever it is you do getting money for the war effort. Apparently you did your job well. But it was that robbery incident that got some attention at Command. I was at a meeting with the General and his staff when your assignment was discussed. What impressed them was the way you handled that first robber. You didn't have to think about what needed to be done." Tony said nothing, just nodded his head.

"Now, you'll still be in the Army, Tony. But you will be working with a Gestapo unit. That's an unusual arrangement, but again, they were impressed with your ability to take decisive action. That plus your connection with Gaelle will be good for the Gestapo's mission. Honestly, the Army is happy to have someone inside the Gestapo," Georg finished.

"You say I'm still officially in the Army?" Tony asked.

"That's right. The Gestapo will try to get you to resign your commission and join them. That shouldn't be hard to handle. Just tell them you'll think about it but first you have a job to do," Georg advised. Tony shook his head bending the corners of his mouth down.

Georg left the apartment. Gaelle got up and walked toward Annetta's bedroom. Tony walked up behind her and took her left arm. He gently turned her around until they were staring at each other. Neither spoke for a few moments. Tony broke the silence, "OK, first thing tomorrow I'll send word to Mama to expect Annetta."

Gaelle nodded, first with a concerned expression, then a bit of a smile broke her face. Tony could she her eyes looking into the future.

CHAPTER 13

Paris, Late September 1942

The car backed a few yards, and then turned right onto the side street. Casey leaned back pondering a long ride when the driver pulled to the curb and parked. It was dark by now, and this was a dark, deserted section of a small street.

The driver killed the engine and both men in the front seat turned to look at Casey. He was on the passenger side rear seat. The third man sat close to him. Casey just looked at the two in front with no real expression on his face. The front passenger addressed Casey. He introduced himself as Klaus. He did not state his occupation. Klaus explained that they know who he is, Denis, and where he lives and works. The man's demeanor was matter-of-fact, but he spoke in a pleasant, almost friendly voice.

"We have been watching you with interest. Did you know that, Denis?"

Casey shrugged and put on his most innocent face, "No. Why are you interested in me?" Casey returned.

"Well, young men who are not in the Army are a curiosity to us. And of course, when they get kidnapped off the street that really jogs our curiosity." Klaus stopped and looked into Casey's eyes.

"What organization are you with? Are you Gestapo?" Casey sheepishly asked.

Not responding directly, Klaus stated, "We are very much interested in the welfare of the French and German nations and their close relationship. But there are enemies, and we would like to know who they are." Klaus readjusted his posture. "We would very much like for you to help us."

Quickly Casey shot back, "Me, I don't know any enemies."

Klaus looked askance at Casey. "No, I suspect not. Since they had to kidnap you to find out who you are, you probably are not part of their group." Casey nodded in agreement. "But Denis, we know that you want to do what's right for your Country. In fact, we insist on it." Casey looked at each man, as they were all looking directly at him, with not so pleasant expressions. Casey lowered his eyes from direct contact, and quietly asked, "What do you want me to do?"

The man sitting next to Casey picked up the conversation. He did not identify himself. "You've been asked to join the Resistance, no?"

"Not really," Casey replied, "but there have been hints. I just tell people I don't want to get involved."

"What people?" the man asked pointedly.

"No one really. It's just whenever I'm with a group of people the idea of a Resistance group comes up. People just share their opinion, that's all. No one really asks anyone specific questions about it."

"Yes, so what is your opinion that you give?" the man continued.

"Really, I mostly just change the subject. What's the point in talking about it?"

"Indeed," the man said with some skepticism. "Well, from now on there will be a point. The point is you will be fishing for someone to get you to join."

The conversation continued for another thirty minutes. Casey was given hints on what to say and what not to say to try to make contact with the Resistance. Klaus would be his contact person. Casey would not know how to contact him, but Klaus would periodically approach Casey on the street when he walks home from work. Casey gave Klaus his work schedule.

Klaus added, "Now don't appear too anxious. You will not be invited directly to join the group. Various people who will get to know you and ask you some probing questions will contact you. Just be vigilant to listen for names, places, and remember good physical descriptions."

Casey nodded his head. He put on his best 'I'll do it but I don't particularly like it,' face.

Klaus concluded, "Denis, if you cross us; if you think you can lie or lead us on, make no mistake; we will find you and you will suffer in ways that you don't even want to think about. Is that clear?"

Casey looked directly at Klaus and in a low but distinct voice answered, "Yes, I understand."

"Good", Klaus stated as the man next to Casey patted him on the shoulder, firm enough to send the message that they meant business.

The Gestapo was nicer than the Resistance. They drove him back to within a few blocks of his apartment. Exiting the car, and walking toward home, Casey sort of smiled. Reviewing his performance, he thought that when this is all over he would go to Hollywood and try out for the movies.

It was a cool and still night. Prior to reaching home, Casey stopped walking and sat on the steps of an apartment. He leaned forward and put his head in his hands. Looking out into the night he began to ponder recent events and think through what was happening.

Georgio warned me about Peter, but Marie is confident he is OK. She would know him better then would Georgio. Maria is obviously part of the Resistance. Of course, Marie and Julie are also, yet there didn't seem to be a connection among them. But, that could be part of their tactics. That would explain why the Resistance kidnapped me rather than just contacting me directly. Besides, Marie knows I'm legitimate, but the locals are bound to be suspicious of anyone suddenly dropping in to work with them. They were probably testing me to see if I would spill my guts to the Gestapo if they grabbed me.

So where do I go from here? I need to do my job; that's where I go. Marie is my primary contact. I will tell her about what the Gestapo wants me to do.

Peter was home when Casey returned. Casey opted not to discuss anything with Peter, but he did inquire if he has seen Marie.

Peter said that he talked to her briefly today, and that she said that she was going to drop by tomorrow morning for tea.

Finishing tea, Peter excused himself. "Unlike some of you, I have work to tend to. I suppose I can leave you two alone for a while without too many bad things happening?"

"Be gone with you naïve peasant, we have important matters to tend to," Marie chided.

Peter was just out the door when Marie turned to Casey, "Denis, I've been worried about you. I haven't seen you for a while," she stated, showing a worried yet suspicious expression. Casey immediately replied, telling her how he had been taken by the Gestapo and questioned. He assured her that he played very innocent, and that he was confident they bought his story. He wanted to tell her about his experience with Maria and the Resistance, but Marie wouldn't let him get a word in.

"Good, good. Now we're getting someplace," she blurted, sitting up straight with a burst of energy appearing on her face. "OK, we need to get you out there. You need to mingle and drop some very subtle hints that you are interested in the Resistance. Of course, the Gestapo, or whoever, will be watching you as best they can. They will believe that you have made a good contact."

"Whoa, take a breath," Casey cautioned, seeing that Marie was excited about getting things going. "Yes, OK," Marie said smiling.

Marie and Casey spent the next thirty minutes plotting his next moves. He would frequent locations being in the Resistance "turf". He would be joined by Julie occasionally, but usually be by himself. That will give the appearance of business as usual, but leave Casey alone enough so that the Gestapo can secretly contact him.

Not at first, but eventually Casey would have to make them think that he is definitely on a path to being recruited by the Resistance. The Resistance will set up people for Casey to meet, ostensibly for recruitment. These will be people the Resistance suspects of being disloyal, who have limited or no information that could compromise their operation. "Throwaways," as Marie termed it. Casey will tell his Gestapo contact of the meetings, and they will later capture the person. Marie reasoned that the Gestapo will be encouraged by Casey's information, but will realize that he needs to be introduced to more deeply planted operatives. Since more and more they will come to trust Casey, they will most likely expose the mole that will accompany Casey, or at least help guide him.

After Marie left the apartment, Casey again sat quietly in contemplation. The whole business sounds simple enough from Casey's perspective. Everything that happens will be set up for him. He just has to go where he needs to go and act naturally. The most challenging task, he reasoned, would be his contacts with Klaus. He would have to be very convincing. Surely if the Gestapo thinks he is toying with them they will eliminate him in a second. And that could be the good news.

The next two weeks went as planned. Casey even had fun with it, as when he was socializing, and even at work, he made a game of trying to identify the undercover Gestapo agent who was watching him. It was a good mental exercise, but of little consequence otherwise.

Walking home late at night after work, Casey spotted a familiar figure in a recessed business front doorway. As if drawn by a rope, Casey looked around, then sidestepped into the darkness. "Klaus," Casey greeted. "It's been a while Denis, hasn't anyone talked to you about the Resistance?"

"I'm glad you're here tonight. Yes, a man who comes to the restaurant now and then talked to me tonight. He made some vague references to the Resistance, obviously looking to see what my reaction would be. I guess I came across all right. He said he would talk to me again in the next few days. I suppose he'll contact me at work."

"That's it?" Klaus asked.

"Well I don't think they will be more forward than that at first," Casey replied.

"No, of course not," Klaus agreed.

"You have your talk with him. I'll be here at the same time tomorrow night or for sure the next night."

Casey understood, nodded at Klaus, then looking about, slowly emerged from the doorway and proceeded home. Damn I'm a good liar, Casey smiled. And how dumb they must think I am to not know they will be watching me.

It was a busy dinner hour. From the conversations Casey gathered that a new batch of German troops were being garrisoned outside of town, and the officers were enjoying some time off.

Casey had no trouble spotting his "babysitter" spy in the crowd. The fellow dressed in slightly shabby street clothes hung out at the bar for several hours. His clean-shaven and neat personal appearance belied the image he was trying to project with his dress. Casey figured he better give the fellow something to report, plus screw with his mind.

Casey singled out one of the German officers dressed in plain clothes. This guy was obviously a loner, though he did briefly greet and chat with others, he spent most of his time reading a magazine. As the man exited the front door of the restaurant, Casey suddenly diverted himself from his usual activities and appeared at the door immediately behind the officer. They exited and the officer continued on his way. Casey waited a few minutes, knowing his spy would not have time to follow him out and see that he had no real contact with the officer. Casey then returned to the restaurant, and seeing that the spy was watching him, made a gesture indicating that he was situating a note in his pocket.

Later, Casey lamented that that poor officer will eventually be identified and will probably be thrown in jail, at least until they can thoroughly interrogate him. If Klaus asks me about it I'll just explain that I know nothing about the incident or the officer. The place was crowded and I may have ducked out to catch some fresh air. Casey smiled thinking, *my first shot at the Nazis.*

Casey was just finishing up his shift, and the restaurant was nearly clear. Finally, a pee break he thought as he walked down the corridor toward the restroom. As he entered, Casey was startled and rapidly stepped to one side as the door quickly closed behind him, being shut by a man who had been behind the door. Casey immediately recognized the man as one of the Resistance people who had kidnapped him. The man stood against the door, holding it closed, while signaling for Casey to remain quiet. The man made no move toward him, so Casey relaxed some. Taking a note from his pocket, the man handed it to Casey and briefly explained, "Be at this location the day after tomorrow at 1300 hours. A man will meet you to talk about the Resistance. You won't know him; he'll know you." The man looked deep into Casey's eyes.

Casey looked at the note then at the man. With his most sincere face on, Casey said, "I'll be there. This must be the throwaway, huh?" The look on the man's face told Casey he didn't understand. Casey repeated the "throwaway" concept as Marie had explained it. Shaking his head in understanding, the man turned around and quickly walked out and down the hallway.

Leaving the restaurant Casey pondered the night's events. How lucky it was that the Resistance chose tonight to set up the first meet. He had planned on telling Klaus that no one approached him, as expected. Now, he can tell the truth; that a meet will occur. He can still continue the lie about that phony contact. The Gestapo will just assume they missed the real contact with the Resistance.

Casey reminded himself that Marie was going to set up the meet with the phony agent. He assumed that she did so through that fellow in the restroom, but he decided that for sure he would verify the meeting with Marie.

As Casey started to enter his apartment, Marie opened the door and stepped out. "Oh there you are, I gave up on you and was just leaving. You must have had a long night at work?"

"Yes, seems there are some new troops in town. But I'm glad you're here. You do know about that guy from the Resistance setting up our meet?"

"Of course," Marie assured him. "I was at the meeting when they chose the throwaway. It's a person we have suspected of having a dual citizenship, if you get my drift. He's been kept out of the loop for a while, and his meet with you is supposedly his signal that he is back in good graces."

The conversation continued briefly, while Marie gave Denis some demeanor pointers regarding the meet. "Well, got to go," Marie concluded. "Oh, I got called away from that meeting before we decided where you would meet the dupe."

Casey filled her in as she started walking away. She waved good-bye over her shoulder.

The next night of work was much the same. Busy with new German faces, but this time there were no extracurricular activities.

Leaving for home, Casey's thoughts turned to how tired his legs and feet were. He was anticipating the inevitable visit with Klaus. He continued looking straight ahead, pretending not to notice the figure in the shadows of the alley he was just passing. This isn't Klaus's usual spot he thought. As anticipated, he was gently pulled into the alley. As he turned to look at his abductor, Casey recognized a familiar face. Looking straight at Casey and smiling the woman said, "Hi Denis, remember me?"

"Maria!" Casey exclaimed, half surprised and half pleased. He was still dazzled by her attractiveness, though still a bit unhappy about how she set him up with the Resistance goons. "Well yes, how could I forget our lovely evening together," he said with a half smile.

"I am sorry about that, Denis. But rough times call for rough measures."

"Indeed," Casey reluctantly agreed. "So to what do I owe this unexpected pleasure?" Casey asked, intending to sound sarcastic, but he just could not be rude to Maria.

"Denis, you know by now that I'm with the Resistance," she stated. Not waiting for a reply, "We know that you have been contacted, in fact several times by Gestapo agents."

Defensively Casey responded, "I've kept Marie informed about all of that."

"I know, I know, now just listen please," she continued abruptly but with a smile.

Maria paused, gently took hold of Casey's shirt lapels and pulled him closer. Looking him straight in the eyes, she softly stated, "Denis, you have to trust me. Your life, my life, and our cause for deliverance from our horrible enemy depend on you trusting me". Casey was taken aback a bit, but continued to look into Maria's eyes. Both people assumed very serious expressions. "What is it, what are you telling me?" Casey asked in a deliberate tone.

"Denis, have you told your German contact about the meeting that is set up."

Casey gazed at Maria. "I thought that was the whole point?" Now slowly and directly, "Denis, you must trust me, did you tell your contact about the meeting?"

Almost sheepishly, Casey responded, "No, I haven't seen him yet."

"Have you told anyone about the meeting?" she asked firmly. "I've told Marie, but . . ."

Maria interrupted, "Yes I know but I mean anyone outside of the Resistance. Anyone at all?"

"No, no one," Casey asserted. "Are you sure?"

"Yes, I'm sure."

"'What about your roommate?"

"No, I haven't spoken to Peter in several days."

Silence prevailed for a moment as both people looked intently at each other. "OK, I suppose this is one of those need-to-know situations," Casey stated.

"Denis, there is a lot going on here. It's not so much that you don't need to know. It just will work better if you trust me and do as I ask."

Once again silence prevailed, broken by, "OK, I'll do as you ask."

"Good," Maria offered, suggesting that he simply tell his contact that no firm meet was set up. "Tell him you feel you are close, but probably not yet trusted." Casey agreed to the terms.

As anticipated, before Casey got home, Klaus intercepted him. As instructed, Casey told Klaus that a meet seems to be close, but they are still feeling him out. Klaus cautioned him to be alert to who contacts him, and to pass on everything. Casey agreed, and they departed. Casey thought it was funny that Klaus did not mention the staged contact. They're probably still beating that poor officer, he surmised, smiling.

"Happy times at work?" Peter asked.

"No, just thinking about a funny incident," Casey replied. Quickly before Peter could ask about the incident, Casey asked, "What are you doing up so late? Hot date?"

"No such luck. No Marie came by to see you. I told her that it was crazy at the restaurant and you'd probably be late so she left. She said she'd come by to see you before you go to work tomorrow," Peter reported. Casey nodded acceptance and started toward bed.

"She seems to have something on her mind. Something going on with you two?" Peter added.

Casey wondered, *what is this guy's position; where is he coming from?*

"No, I'm just so irresistible women are always anxious to see me." Peter threw a wad of paper at Casey as he ducked and skipped from the room.

CHAPTER 14

Paris, October 1942

Walking toward the meeting place, Casey reviewed the situation. Certainly this meeting will be brief. If this guy wants to take me someplace else I won't go. He would have to know that I would be suspicious of that kind of move. Afterwards I will go back to the apartment before going on to work so that I can report what happened to Marie. I've got to take a lot of mental pictures here. This shouldn't be too difficult, Casey assured himself.

Casey wasn't familiar with the meeting place. He was just given an address. Turning onto the street he noted that it was typically narrow, with a rather pronounced curve. He could not see the end of the block due to the curve and the three-story buildings lining both sides. There was a narrow sidewalk on both sides. The traffic way was one-way, going the same direction as he.

Casey stopped and observed the situation for a few minutes. He saw a rather shabby older lady carrying a bag coming his way, across the street. She disappeared into a doorway about mid block. An older couple where just disappearing from view, walking away on his side of the street.

Two cars drove by. They did not appear to have German officers or really any official looking occupants. Casey thought the whole situation felt like a stretched rubber band, waiting to snap.

Here goes, Casey thought, as he started walking up the street on the left side. He checked his watch. It was 1300 hours. His target address number was 103. The numbers ascended as he walked. No number 103. Casey felt a sort of panic. He checked again. There is no number 103. It wasn't missing, the order of numbers did not allow for a 103. Wrong block, that must be it. No, Rue Pillet-Will. That's this street. Casey stopped, took a deep breath and sighed. They didn't intend for the meet to be at a legitimate address. Of course they would not want to trust that I wouldn't give the Germans the address. This location has no significance, except that from the middle of the block one cannot see another approaching until they get fairly close. I'll just stand here and wait.

Funny, Casey thought. That same old lady is sneaking a peek out her window across the street. She thinks I can't see her. He was careful not to look directly at her. *There's something familiar about her*, he thought as he glanced again toward the window. No longer there; must be the local busybody.

Casey backed up to a wall and standing on one leg bent the other foot up against the surface. Leaning there he looked both ways. There was a lady with a small kid in tow coming his way, across the street to the right. She was in a bit of a hurry as she was walking as fast as the kids little legs would carry him. Another car passed. Two middle-aged men in it could be German soldiers out of uniform. One of them looked at Casey, but the car sped by without hesitating. Seemingly appearing out of nowhere a twenty something lady was approaching Casey from his left. She was on his side of the street, and was paying some attention to him. Casey looked straight at her as she walked by. She gave him a coy smile then looked down as she passed. She needs a shave he thought, noticing some facial hair, but not much else about her.

OK, this must be it. A man in his early thirties, medium build, dressed like a laborer. He was on the same side of the street, approaching from Casey's left. He was not walking fast, but at a steady pace. It looked as though he would walk right on by. Casey's tensed shoulders relaxed, but stiffened back up when the man stopped directly in front of him.

Looking straight ahead, the man spoke softly but firmly. "This is not a recruitment meeting. Denis this is a set up and you better pay attention to what I say and do what I say without hesitation." Casey put his foot down and stood straight up, looking briefly both ways. The man continued, "We are going to stand here for a few minutes, as though we are in conversation," now looking at Casey. "They are not after you. You will be OK if you follow my directions."

Casey immediately asked, "Who are they? What's going on here?"

"Shut up and listen. Calm down and look like we are having a conversation. Nod once in a while, and look in different directions when you speak. In a bit I will hand you a folded piece of paper. Look at it and put it in your pocket. Then we will shake hands, I'll pat you on the shoulder, and you will walk away. I will stay here for a bit, but do not look back. First walk across the street, then away to the right. When you are out of sight around the bend, watch to your left. There will be a door opened. A person standing back in the doorway will motion to you to go in. Do not hesitate. Go in and that person will lead you away."

The man stopped talking and looked at Casey. Casey was sure the man was analyzing whether or not he was going to do what he is being told. Casey looked directly at the man and slowly exclaimed, "OK."

"Know this," the man continued, "things may get real hot in this street. If you have an idea about doing something different on your own, it probably will be your last idea. The Gestapo does not play games."

Getting with the scene, Casey offered, "There was an old woman in the apartment directly across from us. She's been watching me, but I don't see her now." "Could be Gestapo. Regardless, we are being watched." Casey nodded his head in agreement. "I understand," Casey affirmed, "I'll play it the way you say."

The man smiled, "Good."

With that he took a folded piece of paper out of his pocket and handed it to Casey. "Open it," he instructed. Casey opened the blank piece of paper. Playing along, Casey shook his head as if to acknowledge understanding the note, then folded it and put it in his pocket. With that they shook hands. The man patted Casey's shaking arm while their hands were clasped, and nodding his head affirmatively it appeared that they had come to an agreement. Casey started to turn to go, then looked back at the man. Instinct told Casey this man is a freedom fighter, risking his life. With just a touch of a smile Casey offered, "Good luck."

The man forced back a smile and whispered, "Go."

Casey wanted to run, but knew that that would be a bad idea. As instructed he walked across the street then down the sidewalk to the right. He fought off the temptation to look back. It seemed like he had traveled a hundred yards, but it was about a third of that when he noticed a door opening in an apartment entrance. The doorway led into a common hallway. He immediately recognized Maria standing to one side. Behind her was another familiar face. Peter. That sight caused Casey to take a sudden deep breath of surprise. He hesitated a moment, but charged forward as Maria and Peter started walking very fast down the hallway, motioning over their shoulders for him to follow.

The trio went up a stairway at the end of the hall to the second floor. They reversed the previous direction and trotted a ways down the hallway. Peter stopped and opened an apartment door. He held it open as Maria ran through, followed closely by Casey. The apartment was vacant; just bare walls and floor. Peter closed the door and they proceeded to the rear of the apartment to a window. Maria opened the lower half of the double hung window, and started to climb out.

Peter and Casey came face to face at the window. They stood a moment looking at each other. Casey said, "Peter, I . . . ."

Peter interrupted, "Come on we have to go. They will be trying to follow us." Casey smiled as he straddled the windowsill, looking back at Peter who was waiting his turn. A good feeling about Peter overcame Casey.

The three stood on a sort of platform of the fire escape. The neighboring building fire escape had a platform no more than four feet from them. Silently they looked down and both ways. There was no one in sight. Like deer silently bounding through the woods in quick succession they all crossed to the next building.

They went up one story on the escape, and if by magic, a window next to the third floor platform opened. A shadowy figure inside was just stepping back. Maria and Casey entered the apartment. Peter stopped just outside the window long enough to recheck the alley below. "It's clear," he said softly as he climbed through the window. This apartment was also vacant. Casey figured there probably are a lot of vacancies in Paris now.

The mysterious stranger motioned for them to follow him. He proceeded to a window, which looked out onto a street. Casey realized that that would be the cross street that would have been to his left when he was on the sidewalk. It was not visible from his position due to the curve of the street.

No one introduced the man, but Casey believed that he was one of his Resistance abductors. Right now, things were moving so fast that he was not sure of much of anything. The man knelt down to the side of the window. Peering out of it, he motioned for the others to look. Maria and Casey joined him. Peter took a position at another window on the same wall. All concealed themselves using drapes that did not fit the window and certainly had seen better days.

The man who had contacted Casey was just emerging from the street they had been on. He was walking very slowly and obviously paying a lot of attention to his surroundings. The entrance to the street he came from was barely visible from the window positions. But Casey could clearly see up and down the street in front of them. They watched as the man crossed the street and turned left onto the far sidewalk.

Further up the street three men appeared, walking toward him. They were dressed in over coats and projected "Gestapo." Two were on the left side of the street and another the right. The one in front on the left, dark hair, actually appeared to be Latin. His demeanor said he was in charge.

"Look to the right," whispered Peter. Down the street to the right, two more similarly clad men approaching, one on either side of the street. Looking back to the left, Maria gasped as a middle-aged man and woman emerged from an apartment. They looked about as they entered the street and quickly beat a hasty retreat back into their home. The three Gestapo men barely took notice of the couple.

"Look," Casey whispered loudly, as he pointed back toward the intersection. The old woman he had noticed watching him earlier was walking from the same street. "That old lady was watching me when I was on the street," Casey proclaimed. She was obviously following the contact man, but she did not cross the cross street. Instead she turned left so as to be walking parallel and behind him.

Again Casey exclaimed, "Look, she's signaling." The woman pointed toward the contact man across the street. The head Gestapo man nodded his head in understanding and looking to the third man across the street pointed in a waving motion toward the contact man.

Casey hunkered down as his heart dropped. That poor guy, he thought. But Casey noticed that Maria and Peter and the other man were still intently looking out the window. Looking back out, Casey saw the fleeting figure of a man run into the street behind the three Gestapo. He appeared to throw a device, which burst in the street with a low explosion, sending sparks and smoke in all directions. That man disappeared as the Gestapo men and the old lady ran to doorways for cover. Simultaneously a four-door car came speeding up the street from the other direction. A similar explosive device was tossed out of it in the vicinity of the two Gestapo men as it sped by them. Those men ran for cover also. The vehicle slowed but did not stop as it approached the contact man, who was now crouched and apparently anticipating jumping into the car. A rear door of the car was opened and an arm reached out to catch the hitchhiker. The door continued swinging back and forth as the vehicle sped off. One of the man's legs was still partially out the door as it rounded the next corner and went out of sight. Sparks were flying as gunshots were hitting the car. But the whole operation happened so quickly and with such surprise that the agents only recovered enough to get off three or four shots.

The smoke from the explosive devices dissipated quickly. The two Gestapo men on the right trotted up the street to where the other three agents were now huddled together. The old lady walked up to them. The Latin fellow was apparently addressing the group, gesturing as he spoke. Maria and Peter leaned back with smiles of satisfaction taking over their faces. Casey continued watching.

Casey's jaw relaxed as his mouth opened slightly. His eyes opened wide as he repositioned himself to get a better look. The old lady had taken off a wig and revealed that she was a much younger woman. She and the lead Gestapo agent assumed a quick but meaningful embrace.

Peter and Maria were now also looking back at the scene. With the smiles now off their faces they both looked at Casey. He looked at them and in a barely audible whisper proclaimed, "That's Marie." The three stared at each other for a moment.

"That's right," Peter stated in a matter-of-fact tone.

Maria added, "We were pretty sure she was the mole."

The unknown stranger broke their concentration with some instructions. "We're going to just sit quietly here for about an hour. They will make a sweep of these buildings but they won't look too hard as they will figure we're long gone." All four separated and assumed positions away from windows on the floor leaning against the wall. They sat silently. Casey bent his knees up and rested his chin on them. Folding his arms around his legs he sat silently in deep thought.

In about an hour the silence was broken by Peter, "We can go now." The stranger quickly walked out the door. Peter continued, "Denis your things at my apartment have been packed and taken to a safe house. When we leave here, you will go with Maria and I'll go out a different door. She'll take you to that location."

Peter responded to the puzzled look on Casey's face. "My fine roommate, your life isn't worth much in this City now. They'll figure you were in on this, and you know they would be correct."

Casey smiled a bit and nodded in agreement. "But what about you? Won't they figure you were in on it?"

"No, I'm sure Marie is still convinced that I'm not part of the Resistance. Besides if they do have some suspicions about me, they will figure that watching my activities would be of more use to them than my warm body," Peter said confidently. "Maria, on the other hand, may or may not be in jeopardy. That's why you will be departing this fair land together. She can be very useful to SOE in London."

Looking more intent, Casey started to make another comment. Peter motioned for silence and ordered, "You can talk later. Now we need to go. Come on."

Casey was lost when they arrived at their destination. The safe house was really a dingy storeroom in the back of a small market. A storeroom rendered about useless, as there were no excess products to be stored. The market shelves were mostly empty.

A small couch, chair, and cot were there for the convenience of travelers passing through. Casey's belongings were neatly packed in a non-descript duffle bag. Maria went to a small suitcase found in a corner and began an inventory of her things. The proprietor came in briefly and showed them where the bathroom was and pointed out a small gas hot plate available to them for making tea. He advised that they make themselves comfortable. He informed Casey and Maria that they may be picked up in an hour or so, or it could be several hours or even tomorrow. The two accepted their fate and paced the room for a few minutes, looking a bit like mice trying to figure out a maze.

As they settled in and sat down, Casey looked at Maria. "I know, you have a lot of questions," she blurted. "OK, first I need to correct something. We really weren't sure that Marie was the mole. But several things recently came to light that started pointing a finger at her. First, one of our group said that she was pretty sure she saw Marie go into an apartment building where we think the local Gestapo supervisor lives, or at least hangs out. We only know him as Tony. He's the one we saw her hug on the street; the Italian looking guy. He's pretty visible since he is usually in charge when the Gestapo searches places or arrests people.

"The thing is we weren't sure if he actually lived at that apartment. We would think he would be staying at their headquarters on Avenue Foch. Plus, the agent who reported seeing Marie at that apartment is a bit scatter-brained. She's OK, but we don't put too much faith in her.

"Then there's the math nut who joined our group recently. He did a chart that listed all the people we suspected were victims of the mole and their last contacts. Several names kept coming up, including Marie's. Of course, by this time we are keeping these bits of information from Marie. As much as she was trusted and admired, we could not afford to ignore any information we had.

"Finally, that bit about the throwaway agent. We don't do that. That truly made us believe that we had to look hard at Marie. It just fell together that I was able to intercept you before you told your Gestapo contact about the planned meet. Then Peter worked it so that Marie would be gone when you got home so that you couldn't tell her about your meeting with me."

"So, why didn't you just tell me what was going on?"

Maria did not respond, but threw a very stern look at Casey. "Right," he offered, "why would you risk the operation by taking a chance on me."

Pausing a moment to think, Casey finally added, "What about Julie? She must be involved with Marie and the Germans."

"Well, we don't really know that," Maria said, "she may have been duped by Marie. Anyway, she will be watched closely. She will be talked to in a way that will reveal where her loyalties are."

"OK, that brings up the fate of Marie?" Casey asked.

"Denis, she betrayed a lot of people. It's hard to say how many good people died on account of her. The Resistance probably already has her. After we snatched our man away from her and her goons she would have become suspicious as to why she wasn't part of the operation. But, it's not unusual when things happen fast not everyone is brought onboard."

"Yeah, but she was a main player in what I was doing," Casey offered.

"That's true, and sure she would have been included in the plans had there been more time. She, or they, would have immediately became suspicious, but not to the point that the Gestapo would have pulled her out. Remember she believes that Peter is a fence sitter. We planned on her contacting him first thing. I'm betting that's exactly what she did. I can just picture her coyly asking Peter if he has talked to you or if he knows when you will be home.

Casey countered, "But you know that she and Peter are related."

"Denis, there are no family ties strong enough to overcome ones hatred for the Nazis and what they are doing to us. And certainly not to forgive someone who has betrayed us." Casey pursed his lips and shook his head in understanding.

"So what will they do with her?" Casey asked, figuring he knows the answer.

"They will try to convince her that she will be spared if she tells us everything she knows."

"And she'll buy that?" Casey wondered. "Of course not. The execution will be forthwith."

Casey and Maria slouched back in their chairs and as if in meditation, both closed their eyes. Casey wondered if the fact he is feeling no real remorse for Marie is a sign he is becoming callous, or that he is just adapting to the realities of life.

The market proprietor interrupted their rest. "They're here for you. Get your things. You will be taken to a letterbox for your instructions and some papers. Then out of the country."

"Letterbox?" Casey asked no one in particular.

"That's a safe place to leave messages when we need to make contact but don't want to risk personal meetings," Maria explained.

The fog felt wet and cold as Casey and Maria, clinging to their worldly belongings, quickly and quietly walked from the market, down the sidewalk, and into an alley. Casey suddenly stopped, looked around, then at Maria. In a frantic low voice, "That's a German car," he proclaimed, nodding at a vehicle parked ahead of them in the alley. Maria smirked at Casey and nodded her head toward the car as she walked on toward it. Casey followed with a gate that spoke of reluctance.

A rather non-descript fellow in an overcoat got out of the car and opened the trunk. Maria approached and threw her bag in. Looking at the driver, "Jean," she greeted, and then got in. Casey shrugged his shoulders and did likewise. The driver did not return a greeting, as he was busy watching both ends of the alley.

Wipers were slowly clearing the windshield as they glided through the streets of Paris. Casey leaned back and stared out the window. The mist, an occasional window light, dim car headlights coming and disappearing. *Will I ever get back to this City?*

CHAPTER 15

France, Spain, England; winter, 1942

They drove for about twenty minutes. We should be near the outskirts of the City, Casey reasoned. They were in a commercial district with one and two story buildings. The car came to an abrupt halt as soon as they crossed the threshold of the garage. The door was lowered behind them. Casey became alert and started to look around and gain his bearings. That was interrupted by the driver who instructed Maria to "Pick up the mail." Glancing at Casey he instructed, "You stay here with me."

Maria walked out of the garage and onto a street. It was getting late, but there were a few people still in the pastry shop. They were scanning the nearly empty display case as if they were picturing it full of delicious choices, as it had been in the past. Their forlorn looks spoke volumes about their current hard times.

Looking at Maria, the chubby lady behind the counter was wiping her hands with her large apron. With a broad smile she would look like a jolly and content pastry chef. That smile was not there. Maria asked, "Do you have my bread?" Without answering the lady turned and went into a back room. Almost immediately she returned with a rolled paper, and handed it to Maria. Maria gave her a coin and departed.

Sitting in the back seat of the car, Maria sat quietly for several minutes reading a note that was in the package. She paused reading and an empty expression appeared. "What?" Casey asked.

"Your papers are here. There's a map and instructions. You'll avoid Switzerland; there have been some problems getting through there. Over the mountains you'll be met on the Spanish side. M19 will get you to Gibraltar, then on to England."

"Why do you keep referring to me?" Casey asked, lowering his eyebrows. "You've heard that the Nazis have moved troops in to take over the rest of France. The Resistance needs everybody here. They turned down my request."

"Your request?" Casey asked. "It was my idea that I could take over Marie's job of liaison with SOE in London."

Maria looked down, and a tear appeared on each cheek. Hardly audible she whispered, "That way I could be with you."

A lump grew in Casey's throat as he placed both hands on either side of Maria's head and gently lifted it so that they were eye to eye. A warm and gentle smile appeared on Casey's face. As if suddenly charged, they embraced pulling themselves very firmly together. They held on for what seemed like several minutes, but was actually a few seconds.

Still holding each other, they separated a bit. "I must go now," Maria said as she started to pull away. Casey held firm, still looking into her eyes. "I'll come back for you," he said with utmost conviction. Her puzzled look prompted another response. "When this war is over, I will come back here. I will look for you in our usual places. We will be together." Casey released her and sat back with a matter of fact look. A broad smile dominated Maria's face. In a happy gesture she shrugged her shoulders, continued her happy smile, and quickly disappeared.

The further he got from Paris the more relaxed he found the people who were passing him off. There were problems though and he had to use his athletic ability to avoid some conflicts. The underground network had to make quick adjustments with the Germans now controlling most of the area. Casey enjoyed the trip over the Pyrenees. The mountains were so different from the Rockies of Colorado. The villages were picturesque with their polished white walls and shy but friendly people. On occasion Casey would spend several days in one home. The people seemed so humble and almost innocent. It was easy to forget that this area and other parts of Europe were experiencing such brutality. Casey thought, how do governments get so out of hand when so many of the people are kind and industrious and peaceful? The contrast left a lasting impression on his mind.

It was early spring by the time Casey made it to south Spain and boarded the small fishing boat. After being passed off to a British war ship, Casey finally found himself being taxied back to Beaulieu in Southampton.

"Denis ole chap," Dalton nearly shouted as he reached out his hand toward Casey. "Splendid job you did in Paris."

"Thanks Dalton," Casey returned without much emotion. "I really didn't do much. The Resistance was unbelievable."

"Good, we'll want to hear all the details, but let's get you settled."

"Settled?" Casey asked.

"Yes, unless you have a better offer, we want you to work here. We can use your expertise communicating with Paris," Dalton explained.

After inspecting his new quarters, Casey returned to the Manor. With Dalton, he spent an hour with Lieutenant Sumac going over his assignment. Essentially he would return to his prior job. They stressed that his knowledge of the lay of the land in Paris and the Resistance people there would be very valuable. Afterward, Sumac retrieved a half full bottle of Irish whiskey from his desk and the trio relived Casey's Paris experience.

"I didn't see Sarah at her desk. Is she still here?" Casey asked as he was getting up to leave.

"Oh yes, we just gave her a little time off to meet her fiancé'," Dalton answered.

"Fiancé'?" Casey asked surprised, "Anyone I know?"

"Indeed, it's Jacques, or that is Kevin," Sumac chimed in. In response to Casey's puzzled look, Dalton explained, "Kevin left here not long after you did. Some Yank Army intelligence outfit was looking for someone with his language skills. We decided we could spare him, and he was bloody happy to get out of that small room he was working in. Anyway, seems he and Sarah struck up quite a thing in a short time. Next thing we heard they were planning on getting married. But then they keep shifting him around to God only knows where. Anyway, he was due back in London for a few days, so . . . ." "I'd like to see him if I can," Casey interrupted.

"I think you missed him. Sarah's due back tomorrow and I assume only his departure would free her from his clutches, if you get my drift," Dalton answered.

"Hmm, pity," Sumac added.

For his first task of this morning, Casey flipped the calendar. The new page read "August, 1944." Casey wondered where the time went. As the war started to turn against the Nazis, Resistance activities heated up, which consistently increased his workload. Communicating with Paris literally kept him in the office seven days a week.

Absence certainly made his heart grow fonder. Casey had to work at not letting thoughts of Maria interfere with his work. The most difficult job for Casey was resisting the temptation to ask about her over the radio. That would have been a huge blunder. "Damn this war!" Casey was often heard saying. No one knew his disgust had more to do with his longing for a certain female than the daily death and destruction.

CHAPTER 16

London, Paris, Colorado. 1944/46

"What are you doing Casey? You're supposed to be working," Kevin jokingly scolded as he walked into the room. Leaning back in his chair with his hands behind his head, Casey answered, "Work smirk, I think I've guided this War to a successful conclusion. You peons can take over from here."

Looking toward Sarah who was just entering the room, Kevin stated, "Would you listen to him now. This fellow won the War for us."

"Did he now," Sarah replied, "well that deserves a big round of applause." With that, Sarah and Kevin began loudly clapping. Dalton, who just appeared in the doorway, joined in.

"Thank you, thank you. Now for my next act I'll make you all disappear . . . . shoo, shoo," Casey directed as he stood and waved his arms underhanded toward the door.

"Not so fast Casey," Dalton chimed in, "Lieutenant Sumac wants to talk to you, and he's bloody pissed."

"You wanted to see me?" Casey asked as he sheepishly entered Sumac's office.

"Yes," he drawled, looking curiously at Casey.

"There's something wrong? Dalton said you're not happy?" Casey inquired.

"He said that did he? That Dalton, he's such a kidder. No Ole chap, I have good news for you. Well, I have news, you decide if it's good." Sumac explained. "Since LeClerc swept the Germans out of Paris, and most of France is back, we really don't need your services here anymore. We do enjoy your company, but I suspect you will want to move on to other things."

Casey nodded. Sumac continued, "I took the liberty of contacting Yank intelligence services. Of course, with your experience they would sign you up. But frankly they did not sound like they were recruiting very vigorously. I suspect they are cutting back on their activities as well."

Casey took a seat and pondered a few moments. "Lieutenant, I would like to stay on here for just one more quick assignment."

"And what would that be?" asked Sumac.

"How about you sending me back to Paris. You could call it a mop up or wrap up or something like that. Then I could be discharged there and I'll be out of your hair."

"This wouldn't have anything to do with a young female, now would it?" Sumac asked leaning back and looking down his nose at Casey.

Casey shrugged his shoulders but looked directly at Sumac without replying. The Lieutenant leaned forward and smiled a bit while trying to look serious. "It might be a bit tough getting to Paris as a tourist, I suspect. The fact is, you jolly well deserve this. I'm sure it can be arranged," Sumac said.

As the Lieutenant concluded, Kevin and Dalton walked into the room. Ignoring them, Casey replied to Sumac, "Thanks. I do appreciate it."

"Appreciate what?" interrupted Kevin.

"Casey will be leaving us. He's going back to Paris for a little mop up work, then he'll be discharged," Sumac explained.

"Mop up my ass," Kevin said, laughing. "He's got a skirt to chase there."

They all laughed, but the levity quickly turned to serious contemplation when Dalton offered, "I truly hope you find her Casey." They all recalled that Paris had been a real war zone with the Resistance deep in the middle of the fighting. Casey pursed his lips and nodded. Quietly he stated, "Thanks. I'm sure she made it. She can be real tough when she has to be." Forcing smiles, Dalton and Kevin patted Casey on the shoulder as the three started to depart the room.

Sumac added, "Say, Casey." As the three turned back to face the Lieutenant, he added, "You really did do a smashing job here, you know."

"I tried to tell these guys that and you know what, they just mocked me." Sumac laughed as Dalton and Kevin each pushed Casey away and walked out ahead of him.

Casey dropped his bags in the foyer as he entered the mansion. The door to Sarah's office was open and she immediately spotted Casey. Kevin was standing beside her desk. She rose and brushed by him as she quickly walked up to Casey. They embraced briefly as Kevin approached. Casey and Kevin shook hands, then they all stood facing each other. They exchanged pleasantries and good byes. Casey added, "I know a great place to raise kids. It's called Colorado."

Sarah and Kevin looked at each other, then back at Casey. "How did you know? We just found out," Sarah inquired.

"Know what?" Casey asked.

"About the baby, silly."

"You mean you two . . . . a baby . . . . oh that's great," Casey said laughing.

"You really didn't know, did you?" Kevin added.

"Hey, I know how babies are made. And you two . . . . well, enough said. But I'm serious. Colorado is a great place, the three of you would love it."

Expressions turned more serious as they stood looking at each other. Kevin broke the silence. "You know, we may just check out your Colorado someday."

With that, Casey backed out the door, waved, picked up his bags, and got into a waiting unmarked car.

Winter was essentially over but there was still a chill in the Paris night air. Casey shivered a bit in his light overcoat as he walked up to the Hotel Firenze. Well, it's still here and looking no worse for wear he thought as he surveyed the exterior. Casey took a room, but did not recognize anyone working there. It was getting late when he took a quick look into the restaurant/bar. The last of the customers were just leaving, so he retired to his room.

The next morning Casey went directly to the SOE office that had new temporary quarters in Paris. A small staff, all of which smiled and congratulated him for a job well done, greeted him. The most pleasant part was to learn that his "job" there was to sign and receive papers discharging him and giving him proper Identification. He also received a small but tidy sum of money. Though this all took only a few hours, he spent the rest of the day and into the night questioning people working there, attempting to locate Maria or Peter or anyone who might know them. Unfortunately the people in this office were brought in from various locations in Western Europe, so there were no real ties with the Paris Resistance. The officer in charge did offer that one of their missions was to find and contact Resistance members in order to locate any spies left behind by the Nazis. As they did so, they would specifically ask about Maria. Casey thanked the man, but realizing that they would be busy with other matters, decided to do his own footwork.

The next day Casey first walked to the apartment building where he shared a unit with Peter. Some bullet holes and gouges on the exterior made it clear that combat occurred here. A middle-aged woman was doing housekeeping in the hallway. Putting on his warmest and most sincere face, Casey inquired about Peter. His soft looks were wasted on this woman who exhibited a distinct, 'I don't trust you,' expression. She abruptly answered that she knew of no Peter and she said no one lived in his apartment.

OK, well that's a start he shrugged sarcastically as he planned the rest of his day. He decided to spend it looking around the old neighborhood, then in the evening return to the restaurant.

The day turned up no leads as to the whereabouts of Maria, Peter, or any others. Casey held high hopes as he entered the Firenze bar. There were a number of people in the restaurant and the bar seating was about half filled. He did decide to take a cue from the encounter with the lady in the apartment and go slow; go easy on the direct questions.

Casey sat at the bar next to a thirty-something, surly looking fellow. The bar tender was Casey's age. A handsome fellow, tall and kind of dark, with a warm smile. That fellow was properly cast Casey thought. The bar tender greeted Casey and completed his order. Though he appeared to have a friendly expression glued to his face, the bartender was reluctant to engage in much conversation. Small talk, real small talk was the most that Casey could muster with him.

Finally Casey took a breath and decided that he had to start asking questions sometime. “Say, there used to be an Italian fellow who I think was the manager here . . . . he would tend bar sometimes?” Casey stopped and gazed at the bartender. He simply wrinkled his chin, shook his head no, and stated, “Don’t know him.” He quickly picked up a glass and started wiping it with a towel as he walked away to the other end of the bar.

*That went we*ll Casey thought as he slowly turned around in his bar stool and surveyed the patrons in the restaurant. No familiar faces here. Turning back around Casey finally felt a bit of depression creeping into his heretofore optimistic outlook. He began to realize that Paris was a big city. Who knows where she might be. It’s been several years. She could be anywhere. He fought hard to suppress any appearance of the “D” word. She’s alive; I know she is, he repeated to himself.

Casey finished his drink and slowly turned around in his stool and walked slowly toward the street exit door. He needed to think and thought a slow walk in the brisk air would help. He failed to notice the surly fellow in the stool next to him had shadowed his actions.

Casey turned right onto the sidewalk and proceeded to the next corner. Walking slowly, he turned right onto the side street. He was deep in thought and nearly oblivious to his surroundings. The sound of rapidly approaching footsteps from behind quickly snapped him out of it. Casey instinctively turned 90 degrees to his left and took one step back, placing his back against a wall. He recognized the man approaching as the one who sat next to him in the bar. The man stopped walking two paces from Casey, apparently in an effort to appear not threatening. His arms were at his side and he raised both hands half way up in a halting motion. Both men stood motion and speechless for a few moments.

“Aren’t you the one who set up Marie?” the man asked.

Casey looked intently at the man. “What do you mean?”

“Rue Pillet-Will,” was his only reply. Casey realized this guy must be legitimate.

“And you are?” Casey went on, cocking his head.

“I drove the pick-up car,” the man answered while a slight smile appeared on his face. Casey thought another moment, and realizing now for sure the man could not be guessing about the incident, put out his right hand.

Without acknowledging the handshake gesture, the man asked, "Why do you want to know about Georgio?"

"I really don't. I was just hoping if I could find him he could tell me where to find Peter."

"Why do you want to find Peter?"

"Well, I would like to see him again, but I'm really hoping he can tell me where to find Maria."

Silence fell between the two men as they looked at each other. That was broken by a smile from the man and his finally offering of his hand. "Why didn't you say so? You want to find your woman," he stated while briskly shaking hands. "Come along, I think I can make you a happy man." The man turned and began walking at a fast pace toward the main street. Casey fell in step immediately behind him, skipping a couple of times to keep up, and wearing a broad smile.

It was a rather long walk to the apartment. Casey looked at every doorway ahead of them along the way, hoping that was the one. They arrived at a building and walked into an entryway. The man led Casey up one flight of stairs. They stopped at an apartment door. Without a word, the man turned back and looked Casey over from head to toe. Holding his lapels, he straightened Casey's coat, and brushed something off his right shoulder. Turning back around, the man knocked on the door, then stepped aside gesturing for Casey to step up. Casey did step directly in front of the door, just as it slowly opened. At that moment he saw the man walking away back toward the stairs. Casey turned and looked after him and raised his finger to page him, but stopped abruptly as over his shoulder he caught the sight of a woman standing in the doorway. As the man disappeared down the stairs, Casey slowly turned and faced the figure. He couldn't speak.

"I knew that one day you would be standing here," the very soft voice offered. Broad smiles slowly crept over both faces as they stood facing each other. Without further words they entered an embrace that shouted, "I love you and I have missed you for a long time"! They held that position so tightly that neither could breathe well.

Casey held Maria's shoulders as they separated to arms length, catching their breath. "It's so good to see you," were Casey's first words.

Maria smiled and cocked her head, "And you too. How have you been Denis, or should I saw Casey?"

"Well, Denis's not so good. He's gone missing. But, Casey's here at your service". With that they both turned to walk into the apartment.

As they started to walk, Maria seemed to trip slightly, and Casey reached around and caught her. "I'm sorry, did I trip you?" Casey questioned.

"No, it's my leg. My right one. It got in the way of some flying debris," she explained. As they continued walking, Casey separated from her so he could watch her steps. She had a definite limp, favoring her right leg. "What; are you all right?" Casey asked with a frown on his face.

"Sweetheart, it's now an old injury. I'm perfectly fine; it just put a crimp in my ballet aspirations," she said with a smile, softly patting Casey on the shoulder.

Light from the morning sun was just creeping into the apartment when Casey and Maria realized that they had been talking all night. Each recounted in detail all events since they had been separated. Maria told the story of her leg injury: Their small Resistance group joined others and under Colonel Rol, fought running gun battles with German troops. They would hit and run, dodging in and out of buildings and alleys. She said that at one point it seemed like they might be overwhelmed. Then the 2nd Division showed up. She did not see them much, but she was aware of heavy fighting going on. At one point, she and a few others emerged from an alley hiding spot, entering a street coming up behind some German troops who had taken cover along the sides of the street. The intent was to kill a few of them, then get back into the alley and disappear. If the Germans turned to engage them, the French troops in front of them would then have clear shots at the Germans. Of course, she and her mates would have to get out of the line of fire. Maria explained that she stumbled a bit upon turning back and running to the alley. As she regained her footing, bullets were spraying the buildings at the alley entrance, and something struck her right leg, mid thigh. She managed to take the two steps necessary to get into the alley; fear of dying trumping the terrible pain in her leg. Her comrades whisked her away from the scene. Her treating doctor dug some small chunks of concrete out of the muscle, but no bullet was found.

Though Maria told this story clearly and completely, Casey twice made her repeat it. Maria sensed that Casey was feeling some guilt about leaving her behind and her being wounded. As he started to request yet another telling of the story, Maria leaned close and closed his lips by placing her finger against them. She smiled and slightly cocked her head. “Darling, this is war. We both had a job to do. Our having to separate had nothing to do with us. It was how our roles in this effort played out. Either of us could have been wounded or killed, several times over. I’m just thrilled that my leg injury is the worst that has happened,” she said as she looked down, then back up at Casey. Continuing, she said, “Now this is behind us.” Then in a deliberate voice, “Let’s leave it there, all of it; OK?”

Casey leaned back and looked into her eyes. He smiled slightly as he replied, “You’re a wise woman, and a brave one. I think I love you very much.”

Almost whispering, “I love you too,” she affirmed. Two bodies stretching out together on the couch falling deep into blissful sleep followed a passionate hug and kiss.

The next two days could have been the picture of a perfect romantic interlude in Paris for two young lovers. It was in fact, except for the constant gnawing realization that time is of the essence here. They had to get on with their lives. Would that be together, would it be here, would it be in America? Casey could not envision a future here for him. But he realized this is Maria’s home. She fought and nearly died here. Would she want to leave, permanently? Finally Casey decided that thinking about it is not getting them anywhere. The bull must be taken by the horns, he declared to himself.

After lunch Casey took Maria’s hand and slightly pulling, declared they should go for a walk. She readily agreed. The afternoon was sunny and warm for the season. Casey was unusually quiet as they strolled westward on the Ile de la Cite’. Maria was happy with that as she looked all around as they walked, soaking in all the Spring beauty. They entered the Square du Vert-Galant and walked up to a park bench, overlooking the Seine. "Let's sit for a while," Casey offered, motioning toward the bench.

"Why Casey dear, you're not going to emulate that lusty King Henri, are you?" she asked in a coy voice.

Casey cocked his head back and replied, "What?"

She explained, "Henri the IV; a real lady's man; he favored this park."

"Oh", Casey acknowledged. Now his train of thought had been broken.

Squaring up to face Maria and taking in a deep breath, Casey started, "Now Maria, I know France is your home; you fought very hard . . . .".

"Yes," she said.

Again his head went back, "Yes what?"

"Yes, I will marry you and go home with you to America," she said with a chipper smile as if her reply should have been obvious. For a moment he looked dumbfounded, then began to smile. "You will? How did you know I . . . . ?" She stopped his words with a quick soft kiss. The tension went out of his shoulders as he slumped slightly.

Maria continued, "This has been wonderfully romantic but Casey, we have to get on with our lives."

Casey straightened up and shaking his head slightly, said, "You are definitely going to be the wise one in this family. Thanks for making this so easy."

Maria started to reply, but this time he stopped her with a short kiss. "What about leaving your home. Are you sure you're OK with that?"

She cocked her head, "Yes my dear. You are the one who will have a career. I want to go with you. But, this world will regain it senses. When it does, I would very much like to return for visits whenever possible."

"Of course," he reassured, patting her on her knees.

Thanks to friends and Resistance mates of Maria, they made their way back to London without much trouble. Kevin and Sarah enjoyed having a relatively spacious two-bedroom apartment and were happy to have Casey and Maria stay with them.

After a few days of "retirement" Casey began to realize that he needed to check in with the U.S. Military. He would have preferred to go back home first, but booking passage as a tourist was out of the question. Kevin suggested that Casey go to work with him and talk to Lt. Sumac. Kevin pointed out that he maintains liaison with American intelligence services. Recalling that Sumac had earlier offered to refer him, Casey did follow Kevin's advice.

The U.S. Army was in fact interested in Casey and Maria. After a rather quick check of their backgrounds, they were hired as interpreters and to help advise regarding identifying legitimate Resistance members. The two did get into what they were hired to do, but in less than a year, the pace got so slow that they felt that they were standing still. German and Russian language activities were now primary concerns.

Casey and Maria set their bags down on the landing outside the apartment door. Kevin stood in the doorway next to Sarah, with his arm around her shoulders. The four faced each other. "Casey you're like a bad penny, you keep coming back," Kevin quipped. Looking at Casey Sarah added, "You are going to marry this wonderful lady as soon as you hit the States, aren't you?"

Maria leaned forward and gesturing back toward Casey with her hand. "Only if he's lucky and he, how do you say, plays his cards right"? The four chuckled, then silence fell over them. They looked at each other for a moment, and then it was hugs all around.

Maria turned and picked up her bags. Casey started to pick up his, then stopped and turned toward Kevin. Pointing at him he demanded, "Now you promised to pack up your wife and young son and come see us in God's country."

Kevin countered, "You may be sorry about that offer. We may just move in with you and you can support us all."

"Hey, believe me, we'll find work for you. Boy will we find work for you," Casey threatened. They all waved as Casey and Maria walked away toward the train station.

As they were civilian employees and not sworn personnel, it was a rather seamless process for them to be transferred to the States. They had to remain technically employed so that Maria could be sent with Casey and avoid, temporarily, immigration issues.

Their Washington, D.C. apartment was roomier than they were used to. That was nice, but after just two months they were getting very bored with poring over documents and constantly going to meetings to act as interpreters.

It was after 6 p.m. and Maria was in the kitchen preparing one of her signature dinner delights. At work she had gotten done with her pile of paperwork by three and had gone home. She just paid casual attention to the apartment door shutting and hearing Casey walk in. She offered a greeting over her shoulder, but got no response. After a few minutes, she got an uneasy feeling; like someone was staring at her. She quickly turned and saw Casey standing in the kitchen doorway. He had assumed a jaunty pose, leaning on his raised left arm, with his lower legs crossed. He was smiling and waving an envelop in his right hand.

Slowly Maria set down her cooking tools. She walked toward Casey, wiping her hands in her apron. "OK, I'll bite. What have you got there, big boy?"

"Our tickets, my dear," he replied, continuing their theme.

"Tickets you say? Tickets to the theater?"

"No."

"Tickets to the President's Ball?"

"No." "Do tell, what are the tickets for?"

Casey stood up straight and holding the envelop in both hands in front of his face, "Train tickets. We're going home my love."

"Wow, wow. Back up the train here. What train to what home?" "Colorado, my sweet. Our carriage leaves the day after tomorrow to whisk us across this great nation and deposit us in the beautiful Rockies."

Maria took Casey by the arm and forcefully led him over to the couch and sat him down. "OK, mister, give me the whole story."

Casey paused a moment and looked down. "Well, the truth is they have found your work to be so unsatisfactory that they are firing you, in fact, you're so bad that they're firing me too." Maria sat up straight and wrinkled her eyebrows as she looked sternly at Casey. Immediately she slugged him on his right shoulder and blasted, "You sack of shit! I was the greatest employee they've ever had there, or even imagined! You must have gotten us fired with your devil-may-care attitude and slovenly manners."

With that they both rocked back and laughed at each other. They knew that their days at the agency were numbered as the work they were doing was steadily dwindling. The Nazis were defeated and nuclear bombs just exploded over Japan were expected to cause Japan to surrender. Everybody's mood was upbeat these days, but none more so than two young lovers in Washington, D.C. who were starting their new life together.

Maria's eyes were wide open for the entire train trip; taking in all the sights of her newly adopted country. She watched as the dense forests of the East gave way to expanses of flat farmland in the interior. The beauty of it all was highlighted by the stunning heights and sheer beauty of the Rocky Mountains that rise so dramatically from the Great Plains, and punctuated by the colorful patterns of bright golden patches of aspen groves in autumn.

The country home in the foothills just outside of Durango could only be described as bucolic. The Teels were busy with the wedding preparations. It was all happening much to quickly for Judy, Casey's mother. But she did prevail in getting Maria to live separately from Casey. Her brother's grown daughter just started renting a house in town and was happy to have a roommate. "As long as you're living under my roof you'll abide by my rules," was her usual refrain, which was always met with rolling eyes from her husband Stuart and her son Casey.

Casey and his mother were busy in the kitchen. "Who's at the door?" she shouted, as Stuart responded to the knocking.

"Give me a minute woman," he muttered under his breath. "Well?" she insisted. Walking toward the kitchen Stuart explained, "It's for Casey. Someone wants to sell you something." "Oh man, I don't have time for that," Casey snapped while holding a bowl for his mom. "Oh just get rid of him," she instructed as Stuart walked on into the kitchen. "He's really insistent; you'll need to handle this son," was the reply. "Oh, all right," Casey said in a huff as he wiped his hands on his mom's apron and walked toward the front room.

Casey pulled up short and stood motionless for a moment. "Oh my God, Oh my God," was all he could say.

"What is it dear?" his mother asked as she walked toward him. Silence prevailed as Kevin, Sarah, and Casey ran toward each other for a group embrace. Judy stood watching while a broad understanding smile filled her face. Casey turned toward his parents and started introductions, "Mom, Dad, this is . . . ."

"We know, Kevin and Sarah," Judy interrupted.

"You mean. You two. You knew about this?" Casey asked in a very accusatory tone. They all laughed and shook hands as the surprise visit was explained. It was Casey's father who first got their call, and insisted that they make this an unannounced visit. Casey put his left arm around Kevin's shoulders and his right around his dad's and led them toward the sitting room. "This calls for a drink," he insisted as they marched forward. Casey's mother gave Sarah a hug and they retreated toward the kitchen with Sarah shot gunning questions about the wedding plans.

Kevin put his arms out, palms up. Turning from side to side, he reported, "There's someone missing here."

"Yeah, she's staying in town with my cousin. But speaking of missing persons, where's the little one?" Casey asked.

Kevin didn't immediately answer, but looked at Stuart. They smiled at each other for a moment, and then Kevin admitted, "Well, actually, Michael is staying with Maria for a bit."

Kevin and Stuart chuckled as Casey looked sternly at both of them, "You mean she was in on this also?"

"Yes, well we figured there's only one person around here dull enough that we could fool," Kevin added as he ducked an ice cube that Casey launched at him.

The setting for the wedding was signature Colorado. There was a large dale with gently sloping sides, surrounded by evergreen forests pocked with aspen groves. At the far end of the valley sat a log ranch house and typical out buildings, including a swayback close-to-collapsing barn. At the near end on a bluff overlooking the valley was a log Grange hall that was used as a church on Sundays. A solid overcast did not diminish the beauty of the scene.

Little boys in their suits and small girls in flowing dresses were like tadpoles buzzing around the adults who were standing in small conversational groups. Sniffing carefully one could detect the faint odor of mothballs, owing to the infrequency that most of the folks here dressed so formally.

Aside from the brief scuffle between the ring bearer and flower girl, the well-planned wedding went off as smoothly as one could expect. The ceremony was brief, but the minister's words were potent. His advice to future couples was, "Go into your engagement with both eyes open, but go through your marriage with one eye closed."

With that, Mr. and Mrs. Casey Teel were introduced. As wedding music played, they were all smiles as they made their way down the aisle toward the back of the room. Some applause was orderly, but there were some loud hoots and hollers. This was in fact in the middle of cattle ranch country and the real cowboys, despite being dressed up, were easy to spot. Casey and Maria heard none of it. The noise of their happy smiles and beating hearts drowned out the rest of the world.

Looking like an ebb tide the crowd flowed out the back door of the hall. That door opened onto an edge of the little valley, which rolled out before them. The bride and groom were in the middle of the crowd, ducking a barrage of rice and laughing as hand in hand they made their way to the front. Stuart nudged Kevin and surveyed three of Casey's high school classmates who were standing with him. Wearing an evil smile Stuart addressed them all, "Did you get his car taken care of?"

Simultaneously the four young men shook their heads and held out their hands. "We couldn't find his car. We looked everywhere; I mean everywhere. He must have buried it or something," Kevin offered. The other three confirmed that they had conducted a thorough search but came up empty.

The crowd became quiet for a few moments. They were hypnotized as they saw that light and gentle snowflakes were just beginning to float down upon them. Casey and Maria stood with their backs to the crowd, hand in hand, as heads turned skyward as everyone took in the magnificent beauty of the total scene.

The spell was broken when a teenage girl yelled, "Look over there," as she pointed to their left. Coming from behind a large boulder situated on the crest of a nearby rise were two almost shiny black horses pulling a surrey. A driver decked out in formal clothes was urging the steeds on directly toward the crowd. People in front stepped back as Casey and Maria stepped smartly forward up to the side of the vehicle. It would have been a perfectly splendid scene, were it not for the fact that Casey slipped helping Maria up into the seat, and they both stumbled backward a step. But they quickly recovered and were on their way.

They went no more than ten yards when the driver pulled up the horses. Casey leaned around the doorpost, looking back to the crowd. He motioned for Kevin to come over. As Kevin approached, Casey loudly explained that his car is in the old barn, he pointed toward the end of the dale, and that it is under a tarp with hay bales piled around it. With that, he threw Kevin a tip of the hat wave as he sat back into the surrey. They trotted on into the valley toward the old barn. "Sneaky bastard," Kevin muttered.

Kevin, like the rest of the group, stood and watched as the ranch house and barn, and even the surrey slowly disappeared from sight as the snow began to fall in earnest. Everyone scampered back inside, shaking the snow off their sleeves and shoulders.

Maria opened the front door and held it while Casey shuffled in with a suitcase in each hand. Kevin and Sarah emerged from the kitchen and rushed to greet the newlyweds. "So how was the honeymoon?" Sarah asked sheepishly. Maria and Casey both lamented that the week went by awfully fast. "The weather turned very nice, and Casey was a perfect gentleman," Maria added looking directly at Casey.

"So what does that mean?" Kevin demanded. Maria looked at Kevin, and with a devilish grin, thumped him on the nose, then headed toward the kitchen.

"So what's for dinner?" she asked.

Not waiting for an answer, Casey asked, "Where are my folks; and what are you two doing here? I thought you'd be in L A by now."

"I'm helping Sarah with some sausage and potatoes, your parents have run away, hearing that you were actually returning, and I don't report to the Police Academy for another week, so we were asked to stay on here," Kevin declared with his hands on his hips.

Maria rejoined the other three as Sarah explained, "Your mom and dad went to town. They should be back shortly."

"Thanks Sarah, it's nice to get a straight intelligent answer," Casey uttered while casting a disgusted look toward Kevin, who shrugged his shoulders and turned his mouth down.

Sarah brought a pot of hot tea as the four sat in the living room. "You know Casey, you really should consider applying for the LAPD. With the war winding down, they will be hiring a lot of people."

"Oh sure, that's what I need, rounding up drunks and thugs from the streets."

Kevin replied, "Casey there's a lot more to it than that. There are detectives, people in communications, undercover officers. Say there's a job for you, undercover. Right Maria?" She didn't answer, but shook her head as she shot daggers at him. "Hey, you could become Chief and be the boss," Kevin concluded.

Patting the dog, Fritz, which was sitting next to Casey and seemingly paying attention to their conversation, Casey stated, "Forget it. You go play cops and robbers. The first thing I have to do is finish school."

"So it's settled. You're going to join us in L A and become a cop," Kevin concluded.

"Sarah, hit him, will you? The man's deaf." Fritz looked at Kevin for a moment then walked out of the room.

Two days later Stuart, Judy, Maria, Casey, and Fritz were standing on the front porch as Kevin and Sarah and Michael walked toward their loaded car. As Sarah loaded Michael, Kevin opened the front driver door then stood in the doorway and looked back over the car toward Casey. "Sure you won't change your mind?"

Casey walked down the stairs and up to Kevin. They embraced shortly then Casey stepped back. "This will be a great adventure for you my friend. Take care, huh."

Casey pursed his lips and shook his head. "You finish school than come see us. I'll regale you with my cop war stories," Kevin added.

The car drove off as Casey said out loud to himself, "I'll do that; I'll do that."

CHAPTER 17

Los Angeles Police Academy, 1950

Entering the bar, Casey spotted Kevin sitting at a table with three other men. "Sarah told me I would find you here," Casey declared with a broad smile and holding out his hand. Kevin stood up immediately and grabbed the offered hand.

Shaking it and patting Casey's arm with his other hand, Kevin shot back, "So you made it. I wasn't sure with all your education that you'd be able to find your way here."

A chair was brought up and placed next to Kevin as Casey joined the group. Sitting, Casey reported, "He never gives me a break; never." The group laughed and Kevin introduced Casey to the other cops.

At one point Casey surveyed the restaurant/bar. There were two single men and one older couple finishing breakfast at the bar. Casey looked around at his table mates, then offered, "I'll bet people thing you're a bunch of drunks, sitting here having beers at 9:30 in the morning." One fellow jumped in, "Yeah, people don't realized this is our after-work happy hour." "Oh the rigors of working morning watch," Kevin added while leaning back and wiping his brow with the back of his hand. "Morning watch?" Casey asked. "That's graveyard shift to you civilian types," Kevin replied.

Another fellow leaned toward Casey and asked with a smile, "So what's your excuse?" Casey leaned back and frowned, "I've not been a well man. I need this beer for medicinal purposes." Two wadded napkins bounced off Casey as Kevin's companions each scooted their chairs back in order to get up. Amidst good-byes they departed, leaving Casey and Kevin behind.

The mood turned serious. "I was real happy to get your letter that you'd be visiting, but it seemed that this is more than just a visit," Kevin offered, "something on your mind?"

Running his fingers around the rim of his glass, Casey answered, "Civil engineering is a good field, but if Syngman Rhee has his way, we'll be right back into a war. Or at least spending a lot of resources helping the Koreans. That doesn't bode well for cities and towns here doing much expansion." Casey paused as Kevin leaned back with a hand holding his chin in contemplation. "But Casey, there must be a lot of call for engineers in war time. It would seem like that would apply even to your type of engineering."

"Well there's more," Casey offered. "In your letters you've told about a lot of your police experiences."

"Yes, so?"

"Damn it Kevin, that really sounds like an interesting job. I bet every day that you go to work you run into different situations; different adventures."

Kevin smiled, "There's no doubt about that mi amigo. Plus you know what?"

Casey just looked at Kevin. "This job has benefits, including a good retirement."

They returned to the McDonough's apartment where Maria and Sarah were visiting. The rest of the morning Casey and Kevin discussed the pros and cons of a police career. Finally Sarah stepped in to cut off their conversation, and sarcastically observed, "Sweetie, you know how grumpy you get when you don't get your four hours sleep." With that Casey apologized and Kevin went off to bed.

It was true enough. LAPD recruiters were only too anxious to talk to Casey. His education, war record, and calm but confident demeanor where just what they were looking for. For him the written, physical, and psychological tests were a mere formality. He was set to enter the Police Academy on June 25th, a day of infamy on another continent.

Casey drove to Chavez Ravine early enough to be the first of his new class at the Academy. But there were others even more anxious, as a small group of young men were milling about in the parking lot. The stone buildings and fences, palm trees and other landscaping, and steep lush hillsides surrounding it made the Academy look more like a resort than a boot camp. It took only a few hours that first day though to allay any notion that this was going to be a walk in the park.

Thanks to reading material that Kevin had provided, Casey breezed through the classroom work. They studied criminal law, the organization of the Police Department and State and local governments, psychology of mobs and dealing with people, effective report writing, and even ethics. Casey was particularly interested in the aspect of criminal law having to do with judicial review and how case law has so much impact on police work. At this early stage in his career he began to realize that he very much enjoyed studying the law.

Owing to his athletic nature the physical part of the training was also no strain for Casey. The running did get to him a bit at first since he had not engaged in a training regimen since his stint at Camp X. Learning to use the baton as a defensive weapon was more like fun than training. Learning handgun nomenclature and shooting were also activities that most of the men looked forward to. And self defense; Casey could have taught the class. But he was not alone there as many of his classmates were military veterans; some having trained for various special forces type details.

One of the special days of the Academy was when the tailors came to measure them for uniforms. With so many service veterans one would think that another uniform would not generate much emotion. But this one was different. The badge that hung in the grommets on the left breast made it so. The leather belt, gun and holster, handcuff case, and baton ring all completed the ensemble that said this is something special. It said that this is not just a job. It is much much more than that.

At no time was that feeling driven home more than on the first weekend assignment. During the last two weeks of the Academy recruits were assigned to work either Friday or Saturday night in one of the fifteen LAPD Divisions. They were positioned with a senior training officer as the second officer in a radio car.

Casey carpooled to Newton Street Division with Wayne and Bill, classmates who were also assigned here for this Saturday night shift. Arriving at the Station in full uniform, they parked in the side lot and slowly walked toward the front door. They had been laughing and joking on the ride, but now with a knife you could not cut the silent tension binding them. Without thinking about it they walked close together as if that would afford them some protection from whatever perils were about to visit them.

Inside the front door were a vacant lobby and a long four-foot high counter. A lone uniformed officer manned the counter. He was black, tall and lanky, and his sincere smile immediately calmed three sets of nerves. The young recruits fully expected to be confronted by a big, grumpy sergeant who would immediately bite their heads off. No, the officer was very pleasant and did not wait for them to speak. He pointed toward a door off the lobby and instructed, "Roll call is in that room. You've got about ten minutes." All three waived at and thanked the officer as they proceeded to the door. The desk officer smiled after them and shook his head. *They're getting younger all the time,* he thought. Then it occurred to him that it's just that he's getting older. He shrugged and went back to reading his book.

Sergeant Arlin was a big man. Tall, big boned and muscular with just a bit of fat to fill out the large frame. He was an imposing man, but spoke softly and exhibited a calm demeanor. He conducted the "roll call", which was a 45-minute information session that preceded each work shift. He sat at a desk in the front of the room, while the twenty two officers, including the recruits, were seated on benches. The Watch Commander, Lieutenant Brogan walked in about mid-session and sat at the desk next to Sergeant Arlin.

When Arlin finished reading the information teletypes, the Lieutenant picked up a clipboard and read the names of the recruit officers. He instructed the others to welcome the recruits, which they did without too many undue comments. He then named the officers who would be paired up with them: "Officer Teel, you'll be working with Officer Sherman. And Bean; I mean Officer Lentil, you'll have Wayne Abare." Sherman was sitting behind Casey who turned around to face him. Casey forced a bit of a smile and a half wave. Sherman smiled back and nodded. An officer sitting next to

Casey nudged Casey with his elbow and whispered loud enough for all to hear, "Hang on kid, hang on."

Casey later learned that Sherman and Lentil were regular partners. They had a reputation for usually being the first at crime scenes, owing to their fast driving; for having the highest number of arrests; and for being the first in the thick of the action whenever there was a disturbance or brawl.

Officer Sherman was a very pleasant fellow, handsome and well groomed, with a warm smile. He welcomed Casey with his smile, but then got serious. "I drive and you keep the books." Casey knew that meant he completes the daily log. "Even when you get to your permanent Division, you'll keep the books. Your partner will let you know when you can drive. Now just stay with me. I'll handle any situation; you just watch and listen." Sherman paused and looked directly at Casey, "Above all, you have my back. If the shit hits the fan, and it surely might, I need to know that you're covering me. Dig?" Casey's eyes opened wide as he slowly nodded.

Sherman kept looking at him until Casey added, "Yes, yes I understand. You can count on me."

The cars were lined up as the Day Watch officers pulled in to end their shift. Once settled in their black and white, Sherman started to roll, but immediately pulled next to the gas pumps. "I always fill up before going out. Saturday nights are always busy here and we'll be driving from one end of the Division to the other."

As they pulled out of the Police lot onto the street, Casey settled in on the passenger side. His heart was noticeably pounding in his chest as he contemplated his circumstances: Driving in a poor section of Watts in a police vehicle with a full tank so that we can race around from one situation to another after being warned to hang on with a partner who instructed me to have his back. *What the hell have I gotten into,* he wondered

They turned south onto Central Avenue off Newton Street and traveled one and a half blocks when the car was abruptly spun around into a u-turn and came to a screeching halt facing north next to the east curb. Casey was speechless as he nearly hit his head on the door window. He braced himself against the seat by slamming his left hand against the dashboard. He looked at Sherman for a clue, but he was already exiting the car. Casey struggled a moment to find the door handle, then quickly exited onto the sidewalk. With his hand on his holstered revolver, Sherman ran up to an indented doorway of the brick commercial building running the length of the block.

As Casey ran up behind Sherman, he saw a man standing in the doorway. He was zipping up the fly of his pants and looking wide-eyed at Sherman. "Leroy, what are you doing pissing on my sidewalk?" Sherman shouted.

"No sir, Officer Sherman, I's just standing here," Leroy replied. "Don't you lie to me Leroy. Don't you lie to me."

"Oh man, I just couldn't hold it no mo." Leroy replied, looking sheepish and wrinkling his brow.

"Man if you're going to dirty my streets you better have some good information for me," Sherman instructed.

"I just got out a jail Officer. Honest I don't know nothin'. I ain't been on the street fo days."

"So you thought you'd just come out here and piss me off, is that it?" Sherman said, putting his hands on his hips.

"No sa, no sa, I wouldn't do that. I told ya, I just couldn't hold it no mo."

"OK then. You get on off the street now," Sherman instructed. Leroy quickly started walking northbound on the sidewalk, furtively glancing back at the officers. Sherman verbally stopped him with, "You better have something for me if I catch you on the street again, understood?"

"Yes sa, yes sa," Leroy replied as he turned again and walked off. Sherman stood for a moment watching his departure. Casey looked in the doorway and saw a puddle on the floor. *Damn, I didn't see that man peeing there; I didn't see him at all*, Casey thought. That worried Casey for several days, but he eventually learned that making observations on the street is a learned talent developed with experience.

"Ol Leroy. He's just one of the local drunks," Sherman began to explain. "But you know, no one pays much attention to him, which is why he sometimes comes up with some pretty good information. Usually about dope dealers or gambling activities. He'll give me what he has because he knows I let him slide instead of putting him in the B wagon when he's drunk. Sometimes I even give him a buck for a bottle of Ripple; so we're cool."

They got back into the black and white and resumed cruising the streets. The police radio had nearly constant chatter befitting a warm late summer Saturday night in the City of Angels. It seemed as though every other call transmitted from dispatch was regarding a knifing or shooting in progress. Otherwise, police units in this sector of the City were being directed to handle family disputes, 415's (any kind of disturbance), drunk 415's, major 415's, robbery just occurred, or the more urgent robbery in progress, man with a gun, woman with a gun, and other activities befitting mans propensity to find ways to be nasty to each other.

Sherman quizzed Casey regarding call priorities. "So what is the second most urgent call we can get?"

Casey thought as best he could, but his head was virtually spinning with all this unfamiliar activity. "I'm not sure," was the best he could do.

"Officer needs assistance. That's your second most urgent. An assistance call in your Division and you forget whatever else you're doing or supposed to be doing and get their Code 2 ½."

"What's that?" Casey asked.

"You know that by the book Code 2 means get there as fast as possible but observe traffic laws?"

"Yes, OK,"

"And Code 3 is emergency operation, using red light and siren."

"Yeah, and you can only go Code 3 when they assign you, and they only assign one Code 3 per incident," Casey quoted his Academy training.

Sherman looked at Casey and shook his head a bit. "Yeah, that's by the book. Anyway, Code 2 ½ is kind of in between. You go as fast as you can, and when you need to get by traffic, you use your siren." Casey caught on that this was the rule by practice, not the book.

"OK, so what is the first most urgent call?" Casey continued.

"Officer needs help!" Sherman exclaimed emphatically. "Any help call in your Division or close into a neighboring Division and you go Code 3."

Casey thought a second, then started, “You mean if dispatch . . . .”

“Fuck dispatch,” Sherman interrupted. “You go Code 3, you go through alleys, you go over roof tops, you do whatever you have to to get there as fast as you can.” Casey just looked straight ahead for a moment, then asked, “You’ve been there, haven’t you?”

“You bet your sweet ass, and when you need help you don’t want anyone going by the damn book.”

Sherman let that soak in a moment, and then continued with the street lesson. “Now get this part straight, Casey. Know when to call for what. When you get to a situation and nothing real bad is happening, but there are some people around and you get an uneasy feeling about it. At that point call for a back up. Any car in the area hearing that will swing by to check it out, even if they are doing something else. Say you get a call about a family dispute and when you park at the house you see a few people hanging around the area. They may just be curious neighbors, but if they are paying a lot of attention to you. Call for back up.

“Now, same situation except there are half a dozen guys in their twenties standing around. This time three or four people come out of the house and they’re yelling and screaming at each other and pushing and shoving. The dudes watching are standing put, and watching to see what you do. Sure, you’re going to try to talk some calm into the situation, but you just know you’re probably going to be in the middle of a fight soon. Now, now you call for assistance.

“When you try to separate the people from the house, and they are fighting you and each other, and those dudes are now seeing an opportunity to whoop on some cops, OK now you call for help. Remember, anyone or everyone there can be armed, and your badge is just a symbol, not a shield; man get some help,” Sherman concluded.

The first two radio calls they received were “415 fight”. The second had the added message, “man with a knife.” Thoughts of the Toads Wild Ride came to Casey’s mind as Sherman raced through the residential and commercial streets of Newton Division. When they arrived at the first address, which was a residential street intersection, there was nothing going on. They could see no one lingering in the vicinity.

The second call was to a side street where it intersected with a commercial street. Again, there was no activity, save for a woman walking on the sidewalk. Sherman parked at the curb near her and exited the car. Casey followed. The woman turned to look at Sherman. "Was there a fight here, ma am?" he asked.

"Yeah, but them dudes took off down the street here."

"How many were there?"

"Oh about four of em."

"Anyone get hurt?"

"Not that I could see."

"They have knives?"

"Man I don't know nuthin about no knives." Sherman turned back to the car and waved for me to get in.

"We going to see if we can find them?" Casey asked as he sat up straight in the seat and peered anxiously out the windshield.

"You kidding me?" Sherman asked with a smirk, looking at Casey. "You really want to mix it up with a bunch of drunk dudes who don't know what the hell they're fighting about anyway?"

"Gotcha," said it all for Casey.

Sherman concluded, "Trust me, we have better things to do." Casey nodded affirmatively.

Another call they received was for a "family dispute". The location was a modest size single-family residence. The grass in the front yard was sparse and obviously not attended to. Some dilapidated toys were about, and the front porch had a couple bags of trash and a broken couch. As they approached the front door, the officers could here loud adult voices. The doorbell was hanging by its wires, so Sherman pulled his baton from its ring and firmly tapped on the door. Both officers took positions on either side of the doorframe. Soon the door opened quickly and a plump, 30 something black female looked out at the officers.

"It's about time y'all got here. Now would you please do something with this man?" she nearly shouted.

"Do somethin' with *me*; do somethin' with *me*? What about you you mouthy bitch?" A tall, medium build black man was yelling as he approached the door. The two then engaged in a short, loud barrage of insults and accusations.

Both officers walked in and Sherman went straight up to the man. Holding his baton in front of his abdomen with both hands, Sherman addressed the man, “What’s your name?”

The man stood tall and formed a rather arrogant expression, “I’m Darnell.”

“Well Darnell, I want you to step back and shut the fuck up”

“Yeah, you shut the fuck up,” the woman shouted as she wagged her finger at Darnell.

Sherman quickly turned toward her and stated, “And you shut up while I tell ya’ll something.” Sherman pointed to the five-year-old boy and six-year-old girl who were squeezed into a large chair in a corner of the room. The kids were cowering a bit, but their expressions hinted at boredom. “Those kids are more mature than either of you. We don’t see them screaming and fighting over nothing.”

“Over nothin’, what you mean nothin’,” both the woman and Darnell interjected.

Sherman’s neck veins grew as he shouted, “I said shut up before we take you both to the station.” He glared at them both as they stood quietly and defiantly. “You’re supposed to be raising them kids. Look at you, all you’re doin’ is acting like a couple of fools and doing nothing but scaring the young’uns. If you can’t get along, get a damn divorce or something. We’ve got more important things to do than come here and referee your fights. So do something, but whatever it is, don’t do anything that’ll get us called back here. If we set foot in that door again we’ll be dragging the both of ya’ downtown and the kids will go to County. We don’t give a damn what you’re fighting about or who’s right or who’s wrong.” Sherman looked sternly at both of them as their expressions eased a bit. “Got it?” he asked. Both of them softly muttered affirmatively as they looked down and shuffled their feet. “I said got it?” Sherman yelled.

The woman looked over toward the children, and Darnell said, “Yes we got it.” The officers then departed.

Getting into the police car Casey couldn’t help notice that Sherman looked calm and relaxed, belying the fact that he had just been involved in an emotionally charged incident. Sherman started the car, but did not put it in gear. He leaned forward and looked over at Casey. "You'll see that some cops try to talk to the people; find out what's wrong, and try to counsel them. I've found that that takes a lot of time that could be better spent otherwise, plus you usually just get called back when they start up again. I think my approach works better." Casey looked at Sherman and for a moment there was silence as they looked at each other. Sherman put the car in gear and drove off.

Sherman spoke first, "We should see if we can eat now. If we don't it will probably get too busy later to get code 7. That OK with you?" Casey nodded and Sherman continued, "I told Rich that we'd try to meet them at Jose's. Rich has your classmate, what was it, Wayne?"

Casey answered, "Yes, Wayne, he's a good guy; a Southern boy, don't cha' know."

Sherman said, "We don't have a lot of choices of places to eat here. Hope you like Mexican. This place has good food, but it's a bit greasy."

"Well then, how can we go wrong," Casey chuckled, as did Sherman.

The restaurant was on a main street in an area where retail establishments began to give way to a warehouse district. Another black and white was already parked outside. Sherman radioed a request to take code 7; it was approved.

The place was narrow, with booths along either wall, and just a couple of small tables with chairs in the middle. The kitchen was behind closed doors in the back. Officers Lentil and Abare were sitting at a booth. As Sherman and Casey approached, Lentil got up and moved over to the bench seat next to Abare. Casey slid in first across from Abare and Lentil. Just as Sherman sat, a 5'2" Mexican lady, about 30, emerged from the back and approached their booth. She wore a half apron with numerous food smudges on it. She looked like a hooker, with short skirt and blouse open to reveal some cleavage.

Through chomping gum, she asked, "Bean and Sherm, you want the usual?"

"You bet Anna," Sherman said.

Lentil looked straight at Anna and asked, "When you gonna run away with me to some tropical island?"

Without missing a beat on her gum Anna replied, “You couldn't handle me sport. So what, the usual?”

“Well if the usual is all you're gonna give me then OK.”

“And what about you two with the new uniforms, what'll you have?”

Casey shrugged his shoulders, looked at Anna and proclaimed, “I guess I'll have what they are.”

Wayne added, “Yeah, me too.”

As Anna turned to leave, she stopped and turned back and looked straight at Casey. “Now you, honey, you're a handsome hombre. Anytime you want to go to a tropical island you let me know.”

Casey was stymied for a second, but recovered to reply as she turned to leave, “Any time you gorgeous hung of woman.” Anna chuckled and waved acknowledgement as she walked to the back.

The table conversation turned to small talk about the job and personal matters, mostly between Sherman and Lentil. Casey caught some movement out of the corner of his eye. There, again. On the wall behind the napkin holder and salsa bottle. A bug! It was a cockroach, and as he reached over toward it, it disappeared below the table. Casey looked back toward the others just in time to see Sherman whisk his hand across the bench seat. He was scooting another roach off, onto to the floor. Casey looked at Sherman, then at Lentil, who was at the moment glancing down to the floor and stomping. Casey looked back and forth between Sherman and Lentil as neither acknowledged any activity, nor did their conversation take even a small break. Casey looked at Abare, who was apparently just realizing what was happening. Another one, crawling up the wall right next to Casey. He swatted it onto the floor. He looked back to see that Sherman and Lentil were both joking about something, and paying no mind to the bug activities. Their attention was ultimately drawn to the fact Casey and Abare were staring at them. “What”, Lentil inquired.

“The bugs! They're all over here,” Casey nearly shouted.

“Yes, so?” Sherman said.

“Oh nothing,” Casey said, settling back into the seat. Save for an occasional swat or stomp, no further attention was paid to the insects.

Back in their vehicle, Casey no sooner had reported them clear via the radio than they received a call, "13A45 see the woman regarding a 415 man . . . ." The location was a large two-story house that had been turned into apartments. The officers observed another black and white parked at the curb as they approached. "That would be Sergeant A," Sherman told Casey. They had each just gotten out of their car when a man walked out the front door, followed closely by big Sergeant Arlin. The man was black, 5'9", 150 lbs, about 25 years old. He was a bit unsteady on his feet, obviously owing to the effects of alcohol, and Arlin was escorting him from behind by holding his right bicep. As they approached Sherman and Casey, Arlin released the man and explained, "Sammy here was visiting his ex-girlfriend upstairs. Seems she doesn't want to see him anymore so he was trying real hard to convince her to take him back. Isn't that right Sammy?" The man just muttered and straightened his shirt out. "Sammy's been drinking a little but he's OK. He's going home now, aren't you Sammy."

Sammy muttered and started to turn to walk away. Arlin swiftly grabbed one of his arms and forcefully turned him around. Up close and facing the man, Arlin very loudly said, "I said Sammy's going home now and he won't be back; isn't that right!"

Sammy sort of hunched his shoulders and acknowledged, "Yes sir Sergeant A, I'm going home."

"Unh huh, and I'm not coming back here!" Arlin instructed.

"And I ain't coming back here." All officers stood in silence for a minute while watching Sammy walk on down the street.

Arlin broke the silence; "I was just driving by here when your call came out. The kid was getting' into it pretty good with the girl friend, pushing and shouting. He didn't hurt her and stopped when he saw me. Anyway, onward and upward."

The next call was regarding a prowler, reported from a single-family house in a residential neighborhood. Sherman turned off the vehicle lights as they approached the address. Another police car was approaching from the other direction in a similar manner. Both pulled to the west curb one house from the target location. The officers quietly exited and converged on the front gate of the chain link fenced yard. Sherman and one of the other two officers quietly spoke. The other car earlier had gotten a similar call to a residence almost immediately behind this one. They decided that Sherman and Casey would go around the south side of the house, one of the other two would go around the north side, and one officer would stay in front. The night was dark with only partial moonlight. The medium size house was mostly dark, with a faint light visible coming from the interior.

Sherman and Casey drew their revolvers and quietly walked along the side of the house. There was about six feet of lawn between the house and the fence, which continued to the back yard. About half way to the back, Sherman's hand shot back and held Casey's arm. Sherman pointed to the dark figure of a man who was emerging from the rear, staying close to the house. Both officers crouched as Sherman holding his revolver with both hands pointed it at the figure. Casey held his gun pointed up as he stayed close to the house just behind Sherman. It became apparent that the figure was a fairly big man and that he was holding a long gun. It was either a rifle or shotgun. He was holding it with both hands across his chest.

Sherman spoke loudly and clearly, "Police officers. Drop your weapon." The man stopped and stood up from his partially crouched position. He said nothing. He didn't move. Sherman repeated, "Police officers. Drop that gun now or I'll drop you." Again, silence. The man appeared to weave back and forth a bit, as if trying to see the officers. Once more, "I said, drop that gun man. If you don't do something I'm going to shoot."

Now the man was motionless, but he slowly moved the gun to where it was almost pointed at Sherman and Casey. "Man, if you don't drop that gun now I'm firing."

Another moment of silence and no motion, then the man suddenly looked to his left, and slowly crouched in order to set the gun down. He was obviously looking at the third officer approaching from behind the house.

All three officers converged on the man who slowly stood up straight and put his hands in the air. "I'm sorry officer; I'm sorry," exclaimed the tall old white-haired man. He explained that he was the one who called the police. He reported seeing someone jump his back fence from the yard behind. After calling, he got his shotgun and started to investigate. "When I saw you all in the dark I just got scared and didn't know what to do; I couldn't move. I'm sorry, I'm sorry."

Sherman assured the man that it's OK now, but gave him a short lecture about staying inside after calling the police. "Man, I could have shot you and it would have been totally justified."

The man acknowledged, "I know, I know."

Another police vehicle had arrived at the scene, and all six officers stood together on the front sidewalk. Sherman explained what they had seen and done. One of the other officers criticized Sherman for not shooting. "I know he wasn't the suspect, but what if he was. You could see he had a gun. When you hesitated you put everyone in danger."

"Yeah, now that would be great. On the news, big bully police Officer Sherman shoots scared old black man who was just defending his house."

"That's bull shit and you know it."

Sherman shook his head, "Bull shit? You know damn good and well that's exactly how it would go down. You know what you have to do. You have to learn to read the signs. A bad guy wouldn't have stood there staring at us. He would have either pointed and started shooting, or turned and run like hell. No, there was something going on here that just said to give it a minute; hang on a bit." Judging by the pats on the shoulder by departing officers, most agreed with Sherman.

The next call was a repeat of an earlier one. "A 415 man", at the apartment house where they met Sergeant Arlin. Again, as Sherman and Casey arrived they found the Sergeant's car parked there. As they approached the building, Arlin and Sammy emerged. This time Arlin had the man by the shirt collar and belt and was half carrying, half dragging him. Sammy was trying to get his feet under him, but he was being propelled too fast. Arlin handed him to the officers, who each took one arm to hold him up. Sammy's nose was bleeding, his face was scratched, and his shirt was torn.

"Ole Sammy here decided to visit his ex again. The rug must have been loose at the top of the stairs, and he took a nasty fall," explained the Sergeant. Sammy looked at Arlin, but his eyes, one of which was starting to swell, were blurry and apparently unable to focus. He said nothing. "Take Sammy to the clinic for treatment. That should take you to end of watch, so you'll get off on time tonight." Sherman shook his head affirmatively and immediately moved to put Sammy in the car. Casey couldn't help notice that the backs of the Sergeant's hands were red and scuffed.

En route from the hospital to the Station, Casey began to quiz Sherman. "Now, do we need to make some sort of incident report about Sammy?"

"What for?" Sherman asked.

"Hey, I don't care what happened. I'm sure he got what he deserved. I just wonder what if he makes a complaint. Won't it look worse that nothing was said, rather than at least have some whitewash report?"

Sherman looked over at Casey, "OK, that shows you're thinking. Don't ever not think about covering your ass. Never ever do something that could get you into trouble without first knowing what you will say if the shit hits the fan. And yes, usually a lame report is better than no report at all. They get real testy when it appears you are covering something up. But in this case. Well, you see, Sammy will sober up by the time he gets home from the clinic. Then he will realize that he could easily have been booked, or worse, he could have been beaten to a pulp with three officers witnessing that he had an accident. No, he'll lick his wounds and be happy that that's the end of it." Casey wrinkled his chin and shook his head in agreement.

The car was quiet for the last few blocks to the station. Casey leaned back and contemplated his first day in the field. What a ride; and it's just beginning.

CHAPTER 18

The Rookie Year, 1951 and Thereafter

The banner in the gymnasium announced the banquet for the graduating class. The round tables occupied by the rookies and their wives or sweethearts had been cleared of the evidences of the supper and only beer and wine glasses remained on the tables. At one table Casey and Maria were joined by Wayne Abare and his wife Priscilla; classmate Bill, who was alone; and Kevin and Sarah, whom Casey was able to invite as guests.

Conversation was winding down as Wayne and Priscilla and Bill got up to leave. "Don't drive too slow going home or we'll run you over," Casey warned as he began to stand up.

At that moment two men, not appropriately dressed for the occasion, approached the table. Casey smiled as he motioned them over, "Hey, Sherman and Lentil, what are you guys doing here?"

Casey sat back down and the two officers took seats vacated by the departing group. He said, "You know you didn't have to get so dressed up for this occasion." Everyone chuckled, taking note of their very casual appearance.

"Hey, we're always willing to crash a party if we can get free beer," Sherman proclaimed.

Casey introduced the officers, after which, Kevin got up and looking at the group inquired, "I'll see after a couple of beers for our distinguished guests, anyone else ready for another?"

"So Casey, we're glad to see you made it through the Academy. If you hadn't you would have made us look silly," Sherman offered.

"Say what?" Kevin asked.

"Well you know don't you that your assignment to Newton Division after the Academy wasn't by accident?" Lentil offered.

"Yeah, we talked to Captain Swainert and he requested you. It's not often we see a recruit come through who seems like he'll fit in, so when we do we pull some strings," Sherman explained.

"Fit in? What does that mean?" asked Maria.

"Well Maria, let me tell you about Newton," Sherman proposed. "You see, our area is probably the poorest of the poor in LA. People arrive here from the Louisiana backcountry and they honestly don't know how to operate inside toilets. They think the commode is for washing clothes or something. Anyway, the crime rate is really high here."

Maria interjected, "Oh well, that's certainly good to hear."

"Wait, wait. You know that in recent history no policeman has been killed on duty in Newton. And you know why?"

"Something in the water?" asked Sarah.

Nodding toward Sarah and looking at Kevin, Sherman asked, "Smart aleck wife, huh?" Kevin just smiled.

"No little lady, it's not the water, it's the men. You see the area has always been kind of considered a hellhole to work in. So, whenever another Division had an officer or supervisor who was a bit of a rebel, they simply shipped him off to Newton. Now, from the Captain on down we have a bunch of non-conformists, but a really good bunch of cops. There's no place in the City you can work where guys back up each other as much as they do here. Understand what I'm saying?" Sherman concluded.

"OK, so how is it that Casey is such a non-conformist? You hardly know him?" Maria asked with a seriously curious expression.

"Fair enough," Lentil replied, "No we don't know that your husband is a rebel or anything like that, but there are other things we saw that we picked up on. Casey didn't show fear or a reluctance to get into possible bad situations, but more important he didn't just charge in either. This job's about getting into tough, even violent spots. To survive you have to proceed with enough calmness that you don't get too focused and lose site of what's going on around you. We could see that Casey sensed when something could go bad, yet he didn't shy away, but he did keep his wits about him."

Maria looked at Casey, who was sitting back with his arms crossed and holding a beer. She nodded her head in agreement.

"Another thing," Sherman began, "We could see that Casey had a sense about CYA."

"CYA?" Maria asked.

"That's cover your ass; excuse my French."

"French, that's not French," Maria scolded.

"You know what I mean," Sherman said chuckling. "You almost never hear a recruit concern himself with what the consequences of some action might be. Staying out of trouble in this job is a lot easier for the guy who thinks ahead about covering his proverbial ass."

The table went quiet for a few moments while all there contemplated what was said. "Well it does sound interesting and exciting," Maria said, breaking the silence. She then leaned forward and looking directly into Sherman's face and speaking in loud and clear French threatened: "If my man becomes the first to die in Newton, you better get your covered ass out of town, cause I'll be coming after you first, then the bastard who did him, you understand?" Everyone looked at Maria for an interpretation. She just sat back and crossed her arms, glaring alternately at Sherman and Lentil. Sherman's head lifted and went back, as if sensing a threat. Casey then chimed in with, "She said it was good to met you both and she is so happy I'll be working at Newton." Groans and heads shaking signified great doubt as to Casey's interpretation.

"I said, if anything happens to this galoot I'll be gunning for you two first."

Sherman flexed his neck muscles and sat back. Meekly he replied, "I promise, I promise, I will be ever vigilant to see that nothing bad happens to your Mr. Casey here."

"See to it", she blurted.

"Yes ma'am, yes ma'am," replied both Sherman and Lentil. "Good, then I will drink to your health and success," Maria concluded, smiling and raising her wine glass.

The next voice was a loud proclamation from Casey, who was holding up his glass of beer. "To those of us who serve and protect, and to those who threaten any who stand in our way."

"Here here!" chimed in the group in unison.

Casey was a lot more confident walking into the roll call room at the start of his first night as an official police officer then he was his first night out as a recruit. It was a Tuesday night, and there were only eight officers working. Lieutenant Brogan conducted the roll call session. "Officer Casey here has just been assigned from the last recruit class. You probably remember him as he did his weekend assignments here." Casey got a couple half waves and mumbled "welcomes". Brogan continued, "So Casey, how is it that you came to be assigned here? They usually don't assign new officers to the division where they did their weekends."

"I don't know; they said something about purgatory," Casey quipped.

With head down Brogan peered over the top of his glasses and acknowledged, "Indeed". Other officers smiled and nodded in acknowledgement.

Brogan continued, "Well you may indeed feel that you are in purgatory; you'll be working tonight with MM Connell."

A tall officer in a uniform that looked like it could use a pressing raised his hand and rotated his palm several times. He ignored a paper wad that bounced off his back. "I am the epitome of decorum and professionalism, and the lad could not be in better hands," declared Connell.

"OK, OK," Brogan loudly interjected in order to silence the boos and cat calls generated by Connell's statement.

Casey quickly realized that Connell was in fact an experienced and mature officer. It was a quiet night, and for the first two hours the only calls they handled were "family disputes." Not unlike Sherman, Connell was firm with the disputing parties, not spending time to listen to their troubles or sympathize with them.

Cruising up Broadway, the officers observed a Buick sedan slowly enter the main street from a side street, failing to stop for a stop sign. Connell was driving the police vehicle and utilizing the red lights, pulled the Buick over. Casey approached the passenger side of the car, while Connell approached the driver. Casey could see that the driver, who was an elderly, white-haired black lady, was the only occupant.

In a very sweet, subdued voice the lady asked, "I'm sorry officer, did I do something wrong?"

"Yes ma'am, you failed to stop for that stop sign when you entered from 53rd Street."

"Oh I am so sorry, Officer. I was just coming from doing some work at our church and I must have not seen the sign. It won't happen again."

Connell continued, "Yes ma'am, now may I see your license please?"

"Why sure, here it is."

"OK, you just sit tight for a few minutes and I'm going to issue you a citation."

Connell didn't get turned around before she asked, this time in a bit louder voice, "You mean you're gonna give me a ticket?"

"Yes ma'am, I am."

Now a bit louder yet, "But I told you I was sorry. Can't you just let it go?"

"No ma'am, this is my job."

Now shouting and with a lower tone, "Why you miserable mother fucker! Is that all you cocksuckers have to do is pick on old ladies?"

With that Connell quickly went back to the police car and completed the citation. He carefully approached the Buick and handed the ticket book to the lady. All the while Connell's face was expressionless. "This requires your signature, which is not an admission of guilt but a promise . . . ."

She interrupted, "I know, I know," as she signed and handed it back. With a glare that could kill, she looked at Connell and declared, "You miserable bastard, I hopes you rot in hell."

Back in the car, Casey said, "Well, that was interesting."

Still calm and apparently unfazed, Connell replied, "You know, you don't do those old folks a favor by not citing them. She could have pulled out in front of another car. At least now whenever she sees a stop sign she'll remember how mad at me she is. So, she will notice the sign."

The next radio call they received was, "See the victim of a gunshot, Adams Street Clinic." Connell drove the police car down a ramp behind the clinic and parked next to an ambulance in the emergency vehicle parking. Casey followed him inside the emergency entrance and up to a nurses' station.

"Hey MM, you got our gunshot?" asked the nurse behind the desk.

"Yeah Ann, that's us." Connell introduced Ann and Casey, and the nurse led them into the treatment room.

"Hey, doc," MM greeted.

"Hi there, MM. Well you got a lucky fellow here," the attending doctor explained, "Robert took a slug to the right side. It went in just under the rib cage, but went through and through just under the surface. Didn't hit a thing." As the doctor departed Connell walked up to the victim, who was sitting on an examining table with his shirt off and his middle wrapped with bandaging material. Robert was a middle-aged black man, 5' 9" and just a little over weight. "So Robert, how'd this happen?"

"Man, that little dude Tiny Tim he done shot me for no reason. We was just talkin and he pulled out his piece and started blasting."

Connell looked at Robert for a moment then replied, "Smells like you been partying Robert. Are you sure about what happened?"

"Yeah, man, I only had two beers."

"Uh huh," Connell answered.

"Yeah, we was having a little party at Sheila's apartment when the dude just went crazy. I don't know why he shot me; the fool," Robert said.

Connell instructed Casey to start filling out a crime report while he continued to get information. "So what's this Tim's last name?"

"That's not his name. We just calls him that cause he's so short. He's only about 5 feet tall, if that."

Connell asked again, "So what's his name?"

"Purvis something; I don't know."

"OK, so where can we find this Purvis?"

"I don't know where he lives. He may be livin' with Sheila, but this was the first time I'd been to her place." Robert went on to describe the residence as a two story flat apartment house on 47th Street, just east of Central Avenue. "I don't know which apartment it is. I just knows its one a them on the ground floor."

Connell pressed, "You don't remember which apartment it was? How did you find your way there?"

"Man I don't know. I'd had a little to drink."

"Sure, two beers, I know," Connell said, shaking his head.

On the north side of 47th street, about one-half block east of Central Avenue the officers parked just passed a flat, two-story apartment house. The area was quiet, being late on a Tuesday night. A parking area with four cars ran in front of the apartment entrances. It was very dark, with the only illumination being lights at the top of the end stairways to the second story balcony. Casey counted six ground floor apartment doors.

"This could be the place," Connell suggested. After they got out of the car, Connell opened the trunk and retrieved the shotgun. He caught Casey's questioning look. "One can't be too careful," Connell explained, "we don't know what we might run into here." Casey shook his head in agreement. "We'll just go from door to door, and see who answers our knock," Connell instructed.

Starting with the first apartment, Casey positioned himself just to the left of the door. His flashlight was in his left hand and he knocked on the doors with his right knuckles. Connell stood behind Casey, holding the shotgun across his chest. They went from door to door, until they had knocked at them all. There was no response. Three of the apartments had dim lights showing, but nothing to indicate there was anyone home, or at least awake. Casey and Connell looked at each other and shrugged their shoulders. Connell lowered his arms and the shotgun. They started walking slowly back toward the police car, but Connell detoured to look into the parked cars.

As he passed by the second apartment, Casey was sure that he heard voices inside. He approached the door, as before, and knocked. He could see that Connell was still looking around the parked cars. The door started to open very slowly. There was no noise. As the door gap was about a foot, Casey could see the figure of a man immediately behind the door. He was very short. Suddenly the man started to step back. It was dark inside, but Casey realized that the man was trying to bring his right hand around from behind the door. Quickly Casey pushed on the door with his left hand and with his right hand began pushing on the man's left shoulder. This action kept the man from getting his right hand from behind the door as Casey was pushing the door against his hand and pushing him along with the door. Casey continued this position as he followed the door, pushing the man, until the door reached the wall. The door stopped and the man's right arm emerged, holding a pistol. Casey backed up, but was helpless since he had opted to push on the man and door, rather than go for his revolver.

The little man was pointing the pistol straight at Casey, who tensed his leg muscles in order to lunge to one side. But there was no shot. The man's eyes opened wide, as he suddenly dropped the weapon. Connell, who was now behind Casey, instructed, "Cuff him." Casey was on all fours just to the right of the door. He looked up and back to see Connell standing firm with the shotgun aimed at the tiny man.

As per procedure, Casey sat in the back seat of the black and white, behind the driver, and next to the handcuffed Purvis. Casey could feel his nerves jumping inside his stomach, but he made every effort to appear calm. Connell was calm, as he spoke over his shoulder to Purvis. "So what, were you going to shoot my partner?"

Purvis looked out of the side of his eyes at Casey, then he looked down. "Yeah, I would'a shot him. But man, I don't need no part of no shot gun." Casey decided that next time he knocks on a door he'll make sure his partner is there and knows what he is doing.

After three months working nights, Casey was reassigned to the morning watch. Recruits are typically assigned three months on each watch to start their rookie year. It took him a few weeks to adjust his sleeping habits. Ultimately he found that sleeping during the day was not that difficult, once they installed bedroom window shades that blocked out most of the daylight. The first two to three days of each week, Casey would sleep only about four hours, but that was enough. Then the next day he would crash for 10 plus hours. He never could alter this routine. Another thing he could not get over: While working, just as the sun was about to come up, he would get very sleepy. That, even though he was well rested. He was told that was due to his biorhythms, and that that was true of all who worked the morning watch.

Roll call was at 2210 hours. Casey couldn't help but notice that most of the officers permanently assigned this watch were old timers. A couple of them were overweight, and several frequently looked like they had slept in their uniform. Casey couldn't help but wonder if they were assigned this watch to get them out of sight. He later learned that mostly they preferred the morning watch, since work wise it was usually quiet, except for the weekends, and around the Station there was always a shortage of command and supervisory personnel.

The first night he was assigned to work with Officer "six pack" Slovack. He was a lean man, about 5'10", in his late 50's, with graying hair. Slovack had a very pleasant nature and when they were introduced, greeted Casey with a genuine smile and gentlemanly handshake.

After roll call the officers assembled in the parking lot to take their vehicles from the night watch. Casey could not believe what transpired there.

As soon as the Sergeant who attended the vehicle swap went back into the station. a large, overweight, and rather unkempt officer named Smith took charge. He said that he and his partner would pick up the booze. He assigned another pair of officers to pick up cups and ice. Still another car was told to get some snacks. He just waved at Slovack, who seemed not to be paying attention. Casey figured they must have been planning a party for after work, which did not include Slovack.

In the car, Slovack was very pleasant toward Casey. He inquired about his background, family, hobbies, etc. His responses to Casey's responses indicated that he was genuinely interested. Casey wanted to ask Slovack about his nickname, but held off.

The first hour there were only four radio calls delivered to Newton Units. Slovack and Casey did not receive a call, but backed up another unit on a family dispute call. Slovack explained that this was typical of a Monday night.

Finally Casey could not contain his curiosity any longer. "So, they must be planning a party after work?"

"Well, no, not after work," Slovack replied without explanation.

At that moment he was driving slowly up Central Avenue and nearly stopped in front of a liquor store. Slovack looked carefully in the window, and then proceeded on. He turned right at the next intersection, then right again at the next. He then turned into an alley, which ran adjacent to the liquor store and back out onto Central.

The alley was very dark and Slovack had dowsed the lights as he slowed to a crawl. Casey sat up and intently scanned the scene. He was feeling stupid, as he just couldn't see what Slovack must have seen. Casey did not want to ask, because for sure it must have been something a good cop would have picked up on. He just stayed extra alert, confident he would soon see what was amiss.

Slovack stopped at an alley side door of the liquor store. He leaned way out of his window, and knocked twice on the door. Casey, ever alert, looked back and forth through the alley. Slovack just sat back, and appeared relaxed. After a few moments, the store door opened slightly. Sitting very high, Casey could see that a six-pack of beer was being pushed out of the doorway. The hand pushing quickly retreated and the door closed. Slovack opened the car door, leaned out and retrieved the sick pack, then brought it into the car and put it on the floor. Slovack quickly drove from the area. Casey leaned back and figured that one question tonight was just answered.

It was only about twenty minutes later that a radio message was transmitted, "Roger 13A9, Code 6 at Adams and Central." Code 6 meant that the officers in that unit were leaving their vehicle for some investigation. Casey noted that they were near that location. He inquired, "We gonna back them up?"

Slovack looked over at him. With a slight sly smile he said, "Sure kid, sure."

Southbound on Central, Slovack turned right onto Washington Blvd. Casey looked around, then at Slovack, "Isn't Adams further down?" Slovack just grinned again and muttered, "uh huh." Casey looked back forward and sat expressionless. Well, maybe he's going to approach from a different direction. Maybe he knows what's going on with that unit, Casey reasoned.

Though Adams is south of Washington, Slovack slowly turned north into an alley. Half way through, he turned right into a parking lot that was behind some commercial buildings, and thus hidden from the street. Two other police vehicles were there, and the officers were getting out. The fourth and final car on the watch pulled in behind Slovack and Casey. All officers assembled and liquor, cups, ice, and snacks suddenly appeared. Slovack joined the group, hauling his six-pack. Casey stood among them, not knowing what to say. He stroked his chin with his left hand as he contemplated his situation. Lets see, he thought, drinking on the job, that would get me fired in, oh, about two seconds.

Smith put his hand on Casey's shoulder and looking down at him advised, "Hey kid, you're welcome to join us. But, if you don't want to drink, we understand." The others nodded affirmatively and one held out a cup to Casey.

Casey declined, "I think I'll pass."

"No problem," the officer replied. Holding up the cup he added, "If you change your mind." Casey wrinkled his jaw, smiled and shook his head in acknowledgement.

Casey was soon put at ease. Several of the officers asked him about himself, and as with Slovack, they seemed genuinely interested.

Casey noticed that Smith's police vehicle front driver door was open, and the radio turned up so that any of them could hear it. The group was enjoying themselves, swapping war stories, etc., when a radio call came out. "13A11, a silent 459 alarm", and the address given. Slovack looked at Casey, "That's us, I'll get it". Slovack reached into Smith's vehicle, retrieved the radio mic, and replied, "13A11, roger." He then put away the mic, and rejoined the group. Casey started toward their police car, but stopped when he saw that Slovack was back engaged in conversation with the group. After a few seconds, Slovack looked at Casey and explained, "That's a false alarm; goes off all the time. We'll Code 4 it in 10 or 15 minutes."

Oh shit, Casey thought. Now I'm going to falsify a log. Say we responded to a call when we didn't. Slovack looked at Casey with a fatherly expression. "Don't worry, we'll drive by it before we go home." Casey nodded his head and then slowly walked back to the group. Slovack took a beer from the six-pack and handed it toward Casey. Casey looked at it for a moment, then grabbed it stating, "Ah, what the hell." Smith laughed as he observed, "Hey, you must be special kid, six-pack doesn't usually share his beer."

Casey and Slovack shared many beers after that, but primarily on fishing trips. They became friends and Slovack introduced Casey to many fishing holes in the Sierra Nevada's and nearby foothills.

Lieutenant Benton was the Morning Watch Commander. Medium height and a bit pudgy, he was always happy and eager to be friends with the officers. With some regularity Casey would pack a meal prepared by Maria to eat at the station. These were often gourmet delights, soon discovered by Benton. He got into the habit of going into the lunchroom and grabbing a fork whenever Casey showed for Code 7. Casey would just sit back and smile as Benton would scoop a forkful of his meal. Casey just couldn't complain since Benton was such a nice person and he made such a big deal complimenting Maria on her cooking prowess.

One morning Casey brought in a portion of leftovers of one of his favorite meals. As if on cue, as Casey sat down to eat, Benton showed up. He went to the silverware drawer, drew a fork, and holding it high in front of him, proceeded to march toward Casey. En route and smiling broadly he inquired, "So Casey, what are we having tonight?"

Casey smiled and with pride replied, "Stuffed lamb hearts." Benton stopped, frozen in his tracks. He stood there several moments still holding up the fork, then unceremoniously turned around, returned the fork to the drawer, and walked from the room. Casey just starred after him as two other officers in the room laughed.

Three months later and it was time to work days. This was a different world. The Station was usually a lot like a beehive. People buzzing around the Commander's office, detectives moving seemingly everywhere, clerks busy with paperwork, and uniformed officers in and out of the building at a steady rate. Casey found it interesting that each watch seemed to attract personality types. Night Watch officers were typically young, bright eyed, with type A personalities. The Morning Watch was the place for the older, laid-back officers, most of whom had little ambition toward promotions. The Day Watch had the most variety. There were philosophers, old timers who were marking time till retirement, and the ambitious fellows going to college or law school at night.

It was quiet in the locker room that morning as arriving Day Watch officers donned their uniforms. It was always quiet at that time as officers arrived, some still half asleep, some nursing hangovers, and others were quiet by nature. Such was the case with Officer D.O. Byrd. It appeared that he was somewhat introverted upon casual contact.

Teel checked the bulletin board to see whom his new Watch partners would be. There, unit 13A91, Officers Byrd, Avant, and Teel. As Casey turned and walked toward the roll call room, Officer

Connell walked up behind him and put his arm over Casey's shoulder cupping his neck. "I see they put you on 91," Connell observed. Before Casey could respond, Connell continued, "Well, you're going to learn a lot, buddy. But, not about police work," he added as he withdrew his arm and gestured with his index finger in the air. "Byrd is the Department philosopher. He will tell you how all the crime problems can be solved. Otherwise he's kind of quiet, but make no mistake. He's a good cop. You can count on him; he just doesn't exactly rush into things."

"AndAvant?" Casey inquired. "Now he too is kind of a philosopher. But, his area of expertise is in the government and law. You know he's going to law school at night don't you?"

Casey looked at Connell, "No, I didn't know that."

"Yeah, but I'm not sure how he'll do."

They stopped walking as Casey asked, "Oh?"

"Well, he has a lot of integrity. He thinks the law can be practiced with the highest of standards."

"And you don't?" Casey cocked his head.

"Well, of course, there are areas . . . . but criminal law? Criminal lawyers are first and foremost salesmen. The better you are at bull-shit, the more successful you are." Looking directly at Casey he continued, "That leaves little room for integrity."

Connell continued to the roll call room, as Casey stopped to contemplate his last statement. Catching up to Connell, who was now sitting, Casey observed, "You were working nights."

"Oh, I prefer working days, but sometimes I have to give those PM guys the benefit of my expertise."

An officer sitting behind Connell chimed in sarcastically, "Yeah, right. No one wants him so they keep kicking him from Watch to Watch." Ignoring that officer, Connell looked toward Casey, who was now seated, "Do not pay attention to the ranting of this fellow," nodding to his rear.

Officer Byrd was 6' tall, medium build, in his 50's. His uniform was neat and clean, but not "crisp" as with some younger officers. He walked slowly and seemed to almost see through, rather than look at people in his space. He welcomed Casey as his partner. His voice was soft and kind and he did look at Casey as he spoke to him.

Byrd surprised Casey by declaring that they would take turns driving, as all other senior officers reserved that task for themselves. "But there's one rule," he admonished. "We never exceed the speed limit. It is fast enough . . . . except, well you know when." Casey nodded. Byrd proved true to his instructions, as he seldom even caught up to the speed limit. The traffic during the Day Watch hours was not generally conducive to fast driving anyway.

Casey got a little bored working with Byrd. Byrd seldom initiated any investigative type action. He spent a lot of time slowly cruising residential streets, hunting for dumped stolen cars. He also wrote a lot of parking tickets, which was unusual for patrol officers. But, by the end of watch their log had a lot of entries on it, albeit none very exciting. Casey reasoned that Byrd, who was nearing retirement, was defusing any criticism that he was just coasting, doing nothing. After all, his logs were always full of entries.

One day, Casey found that Byrd had a kind of "straight-faced" humor side. It was a Saturday afternoon and they received a radio call regarding a shoplifting incident at a local convenience store. There, the owner and sole worker, a middle-aged black man, explained that a vagrant fellow who hangs around the neighborhood once in a while was just in his store. While the owner waited on a customer, the vagrant grabbed a bottle of beer and ran from the store. The owner gave chase, but soon retreated as he didn't want to leave the store unattended. He gave the officers a good description of the man, and explained that it's been about 15 minutes since it happened.

As directed by Byrd, the officers went back to their car. As they got in, Casey inquired, "Should we take a crime report?"

Byrd looked at Casey, and wearing a fatherly look, stated, "There's no sense in cluttering the system with more useless paperwork. Obviously there will be no follow-up on this. The report will just be filed and forgotten."

Casey nodded in understanding and then stared at his logbook. Byrd understanding that Casey was not sure what to do about a log entry since they didn't take a report, directed, "Just put that we received information about a possible theft suspect. You don't need to go into detail."

Byrd did not start the car while Casey wrote in the log. When finished, Casey closed the log binder and in passing asked, "So I hear you have a theory that will stop crime?"

Driving off, Byrd watched for traffic and without looking at Casey asked, "You really want to know?"

Casey thought for a moment, and then pursed his lips and nodded affirmatively, "Sure, I guess so."

Byrd turned off the main avenue onto a side street. They were now in a light industrial area running behind the commercial street they were just on. Now driving very slowly, Byrd started, "You know, way in the future when people look back on our time, this will be known as the "masochistic era."

Casey kind of chuckled and said, "The what?"

"The masochistic era, you know, the time when men allowed other men to prey on them; to rob them, to rape their women, steal their goods, all that."

Casey sat up and cocked his head back. "But we don't exactly allow this crime to happen. We spend lots of resources to combat crime. We put lots of people in jail." Byrd glanced toward Casey, "But we don't even come close to stopping it do we." Casey shrugged his shoulders. "We could, we could stop it, but we choose not to. When people choose not to stop the pain, my friend, it's called masochism." Casey braced himself to respond but was interrupted when Byrd pointed into an alleyway ahead. "He just went into that alley," Byrd stated as he pointed ahead.

"Who?" Casey asked, obviously not seeing what Byrd had.

"Our shoplifter," Byrd shot back.

Sure enough, as they pulled into the alley, a man fitting the description given them by the storeowner was walking away from them. The vagrant didn't run, which would have been futile as buildings on both sides of the alley would have kept him within the alley. Byrd stopped the car immediately behind the man and quickly got out of the vehicle and with a firm voice ordered the man to stop. Casey drew his revolver but held it to his right side as he approached. The man was just less than 6' tall, slender, with shabby clothes and a few days beard growth. With a very wide smile on his face exposing some dark and missing teeth, he greeted, "Hi officers."

"Don't hi officers me," Byrd stated. Directing Casey to the man by pointing his finger, Byrd said, "Search him and put the cuffs on."

"Why you want to do this to me officer, I didn't do nothin'," the man pleaded. Casey anticipated Byrd's question, "He doesn't have a bottle on him."

After finishing with the handcuffs, Casey proclaimed, "According to this breath, he must have emptied it into his stomach."

Byrd nodded as the man asked, "What chew talkin' bout? I don't know nuthin bout no bottle."

Casey stepped back, and Byrd stood in front of the man and just stared at him for a few moments. "So what's your name?" Byrd inquired.

"Jake, they calls me Jake but my real name is Jonathan."

"So Jake, you weren't just in the Jefferson Market, and you didn't steal a bottle of beer?"

Jake looked down a bit and shook his head, "No sir, you done gots the wrong man." He continued to look down and not at Byrd. Byrd stood quiet for another few moments.

"OK Jake, I'll tell you what. We have one of those new lie detector machines right in our car. We'll put you on it and if you're telling the truth, we'll let you go."

Jake cocked his head and looked up at Byrd. "You gots a what?"

"You know, a lie detector machine. We hook you up to it, ask you a few questions, and if nothing happens, then we know you're telling the truth." Jake just shook his head back and forth. "But Jake, if you're lying the machine will tell us and then, well we'll know we have our man." Again, Jake just shook his head and shrugged his shoulders.

Byrd directed Jake to the car and had him sit back sideways into the front passenger seat, with his legs remaining outside. The police radio, which was mounted under the middle of the dash, had two lights on its face, one red and one green. When the radio is on, the green light is always on. When the operator keys the microphone to transmit a message, the red light also illuminates. The Mic. is on the end of a coiled cord, attached to the side of the unit. Byrd directed Jake to hold out his left arm, and the officer then wrapped the coiled wire three times around Jake's forearm. While doing so Byrd palmed the Mic. so that it wasn't visible to Jake. He then held onto the Mic. out of sight. He could surreptitiously activate the red light from this position. Casey was standing nearby, watching intently. He was also holding his forehead in one hand and slowly shaking his head in disbelief.

Byrd explained to Jake, "OK now, you see that green light?" Jake, who was now rather wide-eyed, shook his head affirmatively. You see it's on. When I ask you a question and you tell the truth, it will stay on. But, if you lie, that little red light next to it will light," Byrd explained, sounding especially serious, "then we'll know you're lying." Jake was now nearly mesmerized as he stared at the radio.

"OK, here we go!" Byrd exclaimed. Looking directly at Jake, who was now looking back at Byrd with a very sheepish look, "What's your name?"

"It's Jonathan."

Jake and Byrd quickly looked at the radio. Green light only.

"Where do you live, Jonathan?"

"I lives down at the mission."

Again, both heads glared at the radio. Green light only. After a few more questions, the crucial moment came. Now Casey had his head fully buried in his hand. "Did you steel a bottle of beer at the market today?"

Beads of perspiration began to appear on Jake's forehead, but he sat up a bit and looked serious. "No sah, no sah." Slowly Jake looked back at the radio. There it was, the red light was on. "Oh man!" he exclaimed.

Byrd carefully unwrapped Jakes arm and put the Mic. back. "I don't know Jake. What are we going to do with you?" Jake just shook his head. He looked defeated. "Tell you what," Byrd offered. "You got any money on you, Jake?" Jake got up and went through his pockets. He had old candy wrappers, a couple of cigarette buts, and a few coins, totaling 18 cents. "Jake, you've caught me in a good mood," Byrd said. "We're going to take you back to that store, and let you pay for that beer."

Jake just held his head down, still holding the coins in his hand. "This ain't enough," he said softly.

"That's OK, it'll be a down payment and you can float a mortgage for the rest."

Jake looked at Byrd and with a corner of his mouth turned up asked, "Say what?"

"Never mind, just get in the car."

The officers took Jake back to the store and stood by as he gave the owner his change. As they started to drive off, Casey looked at Byrd. He smiled and shook his head, "Well, justice was done." Byrd explained, "There's no reason to put that poor guy into the system. Him spending a few days in jail to ostensibly pay for the beer wouldn't benefit anyone. No one that is except an appointed attorney who would be paid to represent him and of course the courts and judge would add another number to their justification for their existence; not to mention their next raise."

"Wow, sounds like you don't like attorneys . . . . or the courts," Casey offered.

"So how does your system for stopping crime fit into your last act?"

Byrd chuckled, "Well, more than some might expect. A little street justice for very minor crimes could be part of it."

Casey thought then resumed, "But what about all the real thieves and thugs. Street justice going to take care of them too?"

Byrd admitted that his system was more complicated then that. He invited Casey to join him after work for a beer and he would explain. Casey declined, but offered to have Byrd come to dinner one night after work.

Byrd, a bachelor, appreciated the invite. Arriving at the Teel apartment, he was greeted by Maria. "You must be Officer Byrd, but may I address you in a simpler term?"

Byrd chuckled and returned, "Please, call me Don." Seeing Casey walking toward them Byrd said to him, "But you can call me by my first name, sir."

"Yes sir, Mr. Don, step right in here." Maria took both men by an arm and walked them into the kitchen. Releasing them, she turned to Casey and pointed toward the stove. "And it's back to work for you," she directed as Casey took up a spoon and started stirring a large pot.

Looking at Casey, Byrd observed, "Well, finally found something you're good at."

"Not really," Maria interjected as she went about other preparations.

The meal was excellent, the dessert sweet, and the conversation light and pleasant. They were each finishing the last of their coffee when Byrd looked at his watch. "I should be going," he offered.

Casey started to stand up then sat back down, "Oh, you promised to share your theory on fighting crime." Looking at Maria, Casey explained, "Don has figured out how to solve the crime problem in America. He just can't get the powers that be to adopt his theory." Maria smiled and excused herself and went into the kitchen to clean up.

Casey started, "You know, hanging everyone who commits a crime just won't work."

"Oh yes it will!" shouted Maria from the kitchen.

Byrd wrinkled his chin and smiled a bit, "Oh ye of little faith. No, in fact the people who favor a hard line on crime would cringe at my proposal, thinking I'm just another bleeding heart."

"Really," Casey replied, "Now I'm curious."

"OK," Byrd began, "first of all this doesn't apply to the real psychos, the mass murderers, that kind. It does apply to 99 percent of the criminals, from petty thieves to robbers, rapists; all of them. Now when a person is convicted of a crime, petty or major felony, it doesn't matter, he'll be sentenced to 30 days in jail."

"All crooks; shoplifters as well as bank robbers?" Casey interjected.

"All of them. They'll all go to the same place for 30 days. Their routine for those 30 days will always be the same. They'll get aptitude tested to determine where they can fit in the job world. They will be given information on an appropriate trade school, college, what have you. They will be given information on how to get some financial assistance if they need it. I would even suggest that a fund could be set up with solicitations in the private sector to help finance the training. A lot of businesses, and even just plain folks would be happy to finance a plan that would mean they don't have to contend with these never-ending crime cycles.

"But the key activity these inmates will be subjected to is a simple lecture. Maybe individually, or in small groups, or both, they will attend these sessions, oh, at least six times a day. Each lecture will be very brief and very direct. They will be informed that if they are convicted again, for any crime, they will then be sentenced to 60 days in jail. Those 60 days will be just like this 30 days stint. That is, learning how they can make a living, and being told exactly what will happen if they error again. Then if they are convicted of any other crime again, they will be locked up for the rest of their lives.

"You see, over and over again they will be shown how they can make it, but told in no uncertain terms that they will be locked up for life if they commit more crimes. It could be pointed out at each session that even their immediate family will get tired of visiting them in prison when there is no hope that they will ever get out. Tell them their friends and families will eventually consider them dead and their life will basically be over.

"Imagine. Over and over, day after day, getting told the same thing. That is that society will not tolerate their criminal behavior. And of course, society would have to follow-up by ensuring that the threats are always carried out."

Byrd leaned back in anticipation of comments. Casey spoke first, "Well, I guess if you make it abundantly clear what will happen, and give people a chance to error a couple of times, it would be humane enough. But, how are we going to be able to afford the massive prisons it will take to hold all these people?"

By this time Maria had come into the room. She sat in a chair, holding a dishrag in both hands, which were rested on her knees, apparently interested in every word. "No, No," she stopped Casey. "The point is, the prisons won't be full. Oh sure, there will always be the ten per centers. Ten per centers, isn't that what you call it?" she asked with her French accent, but continued without waiting for an answer. "Anyway, those who don't get the point and continue with their behavior. But don't you see, most people will understand. Certainly the opportunist criminal will not risk going to jail for life. Anyone with half a brain will ultimately understand that they really need to not commit any more crimes."

"Sure," Byrd continued, "I know that the psychologists will say no you can't do this cause the prisons will fill up. But you know those same psychologists will teach you in Psychology 101 about learned behavior. People do learn to alter their behavior when they are confronted with negative consequences. Even dumb animals learn to anticipate when bad things will happen and avoid a situation."

All three simultaneously sat back in their chairs and quietly contemplated the matter for a moment. Maria broke the silence, "I like it. I really like it. It's hardly cruel treatment. It bends over backwards to help people assimilate into civil society. And, for the most part it would take dealing with crime virtually out of the mix of our coping activities. Yep, I like it. When they make me Queen, it shall be done," she concluded, rising smartly and walking back to the kitchen.

Byrd chuckled as he watched Maria depart. Looking at Casey he remarked, "Smart gal you got there kid. You're a lucky man."

"Ah, smart because she agrees with you?" Casey asked wryly.

"No, my son, it's because she obviously understood the superior logic of the matter. Her only shortcoming, perhaps, is that she could have married better."

With that, Casey virtually chased Byrd from the apartment. They both stopped at the door. Yelling past Casey toward the kitchen Byrd offered his thanks for the hospitality, and jokingly offered his apologies to Casey for any comments that may have offended. Casey laughed and stated, "OK buddy, see you tomorrow."

"Nope," Byrd replied. "I'm off for three."

"Lucky dog; well take care."

Byrd disappeared out the front gate of the complex. Maria was still busy in the kitchen. Casey stood silently in the doorway for a few moments. It was a quiet night. Casey's mind drifted away as he contemplated his situation. He was soon officially off probation. He will be transferred to another Division, as is Department policy. He wondered what adventures awaited; what paths his career would take. What an amazing job, he thought.

CHAPTER 19

Uniformed duty, year two and beyond

"Hollywood Division? You're going to work in Hollywood?" Maria asked.

Casey rolled over in bed to face his wife, "I told you that last night. It's just soaking in?"

"I had some dream about Hollywood. I can't remember what it was," Maria answered while lying on her back contemplating the ceiling.

Casey propped his head up with his right hand and looking down at her, "Well, was it a good dream, a bad one, what?"

Pulling the sheet away and thus exposing her trim and shapely naked body Maria looked straight at Casey and answered, "Oh, it was probably about you running away with some gorgeous movie star; blonde no doubt."

Casey surveyed her very sexy body and replied, "Not a chance, you nasty wench."

He started to roll on top of her, but Maria stopped him short as she held his left shoulder with her right hand. She was directly under him and almost nose to nose. "I think it's time we made a baby," she offered. Casey, still kind of suspended over her, cocked his head to one side in contemplation.

Looking back, he smiled, "OK, let's do it."

"Honey, I'm serious," she admonished.

Casey smiled warmly and in a soft and low voice reassured, "So am I. I have thought about it. It's time."

A calm smile filled Maria's face as she pulled Casey onto her. "Give me all you got big boy." And a baby was made.

Hollywood Station was in an old two-story brick building. Nothing glamorous about this place, Casey thought as he walked up the stairs to the roll call room. Lieutenant Parker conducting the PM roll call, introduced Casey, and assigned him to work with Officer Soto. As all officers got up to go to their cars, an officer approached Casey. He was about 5' 10", stocky and appeared Hispanic. Offering his hand, he exclaimed, "Hi, I'm John, welcome to the car."

They shook hands and Casey offered, "Thanks, I'm Casey Teel."

"So where'd you come from?" Soto asked.

"Newton. Did my probation there."

"Well I just finished my second year here. I'll be transferred to my last Division soon."

Soto was driving as they departed the Station. "I'm curious, what's it like working Hollywood?" Casey inquired.

"It's pretty busy, but not like you're used to," Soto began. "We'll get a lot of calls. There's a lot of thievery, drunk problems, that sort of thing, but not a lot of real heavy stuff. There's always a lot of traffic, so getting to calls is a bit of a hassle."

Casey thought a minute, then, "so I don't need to load my gun, is that what you're telling me?"

"No, no indeed. In fact you will encounter more bad guys here than you did in Newton, but mostly these are just lizards."

"Lizards?" Casey asked.

"Yeah, lizards are kind of the scum of the earth. They'll steal from you, swipe old lady's purses, cuss at you from a distance, but face-to-face, they're harmless. In East LA, a bad guy will stab you, or in Watts he'll challenge you straight up. But lizards, they just slink around and if confronted they'll be all smiles and cooperation."

Casey chuckled and offered, "OK, I get the picture."

Soto and Casey worked well together. They seemed to have a silent communication between them, which meant that they could anticipate each other's moves. More importantly, they knew their partner had their back.

It was a cool night and Soto was driving. They were near the end of their shift so Casey started the farewells. Soto had been given his transfer orders and this was his last night in Hollywood. "Been good working with you, John. Maybe your next Division will be more exciting." Soto smiled and nodded his head toward the radio as they were receiving a call, "Unknown trouble, possible shots fired, see the apartment manager." The address given was on a quiet residential street with intermittent residences and apartments. Casey acknowledged the call then stated, "I thought Newton was the only place where people report guns and shots fired in order to get us there quicker." Both officers chuckled, which signaled their lack of deep concern about possible gunplay.

The apartment was two two-story buildings facing each other, with a landscaped courtyard in between. As the officers walked into the courtyard, a 50 something lady approached. She pointed toward an upstairs apartment on the West side, near the South corner of the building. "Up there!" she exclaimed, "I heard some loud voices then it sounded like a gun shot."

The officers noted that it was now quiet. "Do you know who lives there?" inquired Soto.

"Yes, she's a nice single lady. She lives alone. She seldom has company there, but she does go out with a fellow once in a while."

Soto and Casey both thought, *busybody manager.* Casey warned, "OK ma'am, we'll check it out. You should go back to your office. We'll let you know what we find."

A balcony ran north and south along the front of the upstairs apartments. A broad stairway going up to the balcony was located off-center closer to the south end. The target apartment was the next to last on the south end. The last apartment was perpendicular to the others with the front door facing north.

Soto and Casey looked at each other as they slowly started up the stairs. Soto offered, "I don't think that lady would lie about hearing gun shots."

"True, but it could have been some other loud sound," Casey countered.

"I agree," Soto followed, but both officers squared up to take the call seriously.

Casey positioned himself to the right of the non-screened door, his hand on his holstered gun. Soto stood next to a picture window that was to the right of the door. Drapes were drawn on the window, but the officer could see a little bit of area inside on either side between the window and the edge of the drapes.

Casey knocked on the door with his left fist. A male voice spoke, "Yeah?"

Casey firmly replied, "Police Officers." There were a few moments of silence during which Casey and Soto looked at each other. Both officers heard footsteps from within approaching the door. They assumed a ready posture with Soto looking intently into the edge of the window.

"He's got a gun!" shouted Soto.

Casey drew his revolver and stepped slightly back. The door flew open and the figure of a man appeared. He was holding a pistol pointed at Casey. Casey quickly aimed at the man and fired, once, twice. Other gunshots cracked as flashes, smoke, and flying glass filled the area. Casey and Soto simultaneously ran the two yards back to the top of the stairway and jumping down three steps, stopped, and turned to face back toward the door. They used the stairway as cover as they were otherwise totally exposed on the balcony. Soto crouched immediately behind Casey. Casey pointed his weapon toward the door. The man exited the apartment and in one motion went to his knees and raised the pistol, again pointed toward the officers. Casey fired once more, and the man fell prone to his right.

Dead silence fell over the scene. Nobody moved. Both officers studied the man for at least a couple of minutes. There was no movement. Side-by-side and with weapons ready, Casey and Soto slowly approached the prone body. The weapon, a German Luger type pistol, was lying on the deck just beyond the outstretched arm of the gunman. He did not move as Soto slid the pistol away.

Several uniformed officers were now entering the courtyard. A voice yelled up asking if the officers were OK. Soto looked over the balcony rail at them and hollered, "It's code four here, but we need an ambulance for the suspect." Meanwhile, Casey carefully entered the apartment. A woman was sitting on a couch at the far end of the front room. She was in her thirties, tall and trim, and neatly dressed. She was holding her head with both hands; her eyes were wide open and full of tears. Casey asked her if there was anyone else there. Receiving a negative answer, Casey began reassuring the woman that everything was OK. She slowly came around and rose and hugged the officer. Tears rolled down her cheeks, but she was not crying. She pulled away and, taking a deep breath, stood up straight. "Thank you," she said, bowing and shaking her head.

As per procedure, the officers were taken off field duty following a fatal shooting. Soto's transfer was delayed and he stayed at Hollywood. He and Casey were assigned to days, working the station jail, pending the Department's investigation of the shooting.

It was about a week into that assignment, a day that both Casey and Soto were working, that they were relieved early by other officers. They were told to report to the Captain's office. There two large goon looking middle-aged men, dressed in neat suits and wearing gangster fedora hats, met them. The hat squad, Casey surmised. The homicide boys from downtown who investigate all officer involved shootings.

The first action was Captain Maloney getting up from his desk and walking out. "Thanks for the update," he offered to the detectives as he walked out. The older of the two plain-clothes detectives approached Casey and Soto, who were basically standing at attention. "Hi, I'm Detective Smith, and this is Detective Roy." Offering his hand he asked, "Who's who here?" Casey and Soto introduced themselves. Smith explained that he and Roy caught their shooting and were about finished with it. Recognizing the officers' discomfort, Smith smiled and in a fatherly manner, "Relax guys. It was a good shooting. Clean as a whistle. We wanted to tell you that in person, plus we need to go with you back to the scene and walk through the incident. That's just routine." Casey and Soto relaxed a bit and followed the detectives to their car.

Enroute to the apartment, Roy related what they had learned about the incident. The shooter, a fellow named Eugene, had a history of minor offenses. Mostly drunk and drunk driving stuff. He and the lady in the apartment had gone together, and eventually got engaged. Apparently she had enough of his drinking, so she cut off the engagement. "That night he came to the apartment with a gun and a snoot full of Old Kentucky Loudmouth," Roy quipped, "and apparently, Mr. Romeo figured he could scare her into taking him back. He did fire a shot into the ceiling, which of course prompted the manager to call you." Smith continued, "There's something interesting at the scene that we want to show you. It's a ballistics thing."

At the apartment the group walked through the incident. It just took a few minutes and the detectives found no discrepancies to linger on. While standing on the balcony in front of apartment number two, the scene of the shooting, Detective Smith took Casey's arm and led him up to the next apartment, number one. That apartment wall and front door faced north, while the others on the balcony faced east. Smith pointed out a series of tiny metal chips that were embedded in the door of number one. He then walked over to the window where Soto had been standing during the shooting. Smith explained that Soto could see Eugene at the front door by looking through the window through the narrow gap between the drape and the wall. Soto then fired two shots through the window, with one shot striking the man in the side. "Now here's where it gets scary," Smith continued." When a lead slug is fired through glass at a considerable angle, the glass shears off the outer casing of the slug, and that casing comes off in pieces and ricochets off and away from the glass. So Casey, you were in front of the door when the core of the slugs went through the window and into Eugene. The fragments bounced off the window, went behind you, and embedded in the door, there."

No one spoke as Casey slowly walked over to the position he had in front of the door. First he looked at the window, then at the door in front of him, then to his left at the pitted door. Looking at Smith, "You mean the slug basically split, passing in front and behind me?"

"That's about it."

"So the suspect was firing at me, and so was John?" Soto ducked and put his arm up for protection as Casey faked a roundhouse punch at him.

Smith laughed and admonished, "Yeah, well, I wouldn't be too hard on him. His shot was really the fatal one; it hit Eugene in the left side and pierced the heart. Your two shots at the door, and your third shot later were all in the stomach, below the heart. Oh, they would have killed him, but Soto's shot was the most effective."

"OK then," Casey offered as he grabbed Soto's left arm and ruffed up his hair, "but next time you go to the door and I'll shoot through the window."

"Deal," Soto offered, smiling.

"By the way," Casey continued, "what about the suspect's shots? Where did they go?"

"Well, he did fire that Luger three times, once inside and twice at you. We found a hole and the slug in the ceiling, and two more empty casings at the front door. Those shots probably landed in the Hollywood hills somewhere. We figure the man was pretty loaded, and instead of aiming at your middle, he tried headshots. Those are pretty tricky when you're drunk, even at that close range. Your guardian angel was watching you that night, my friend." Casey curled his lips and nodded affirmatively. Deep inside he was feeling hollowness; he felt a little weak all over. Maybe I'm just catching a cold he thought.

Casey welcomed his assignment to work days, at least for the convenience of the hours. But he did not relish contending with the traffic. It was bad enough at night; much worse during the daylight hours.

Another aspect of working days in Hollywood was the fact that the deployment is typically in one-man cars. Casey relished the opportunity to prove that he could handle matters by himself. Working without a safety net, he said to himself.

His first working day was a Friday. When he first left the station the traffic was not particularly heavy, but grew as the morning went on. At about 1050 hours he was slowly driving northbound on a quiet but major residential street. The radio had been rather quiet. He was about ½ block south of the intersection with Santa Monica Boulevard when his radio crackled. The female voice that usually delivers calls was replaced by a loud and clear male voice: "6L43, Code 3, a 211 silent at the Bank of America . . . ."

Casey had been slumped a bit in the car seat. He literally jumped to attention, as he grabbed the mike to "roger" the call. Damn, damn, he thought, a silent robbery alarm at a bank. *I'll get there and the Dillinger gang will be coming out with their machineguns. Sure glad I'm working alone.*

Casey flipped the switches for the red lights and siren, and pressed the horn ring to start the siren's wail. Accelerating he rapidly approached the intersection. He had the green light, with the red stopping traffic on the Boulevard. He almost blew quickly through the intersection but a training lecture jumped into his head. The lesson was when going code 3 to always approach a blind intersection with caution, even if you have the green light. This was a fairly blind intersection with two story commercial buildings on each corner.

Casey slowed considerably and nosed his car into the intersection, but abruptly slammed on his brakes. An eastbound ambulance going code 3 barreled through the intersection, passing just in front of Casey. He just got a glimpse of the passenger paramedic's look of horror as he threw up his arms in defense of the apparent impending crash. Casey, who was pinned flat against the steering wheel with his arms wrapped around it, shook his head in disbelief. He would have taken me out broadside, Casey gasped.

His fraught nerves made his hands shake as Casey sped on toward the bank. Before he arrived, the radio car usually assigned to that area came on the radio and declared that it was a false alarm. Casey killed his red lights and siren and quickly ducked onto a small residential street. He parked at the curb and took a few moments to compose.

Casey soon found why at lot of officers liked working Sundays. The station house was relatively quiet with little activity other than patrol officers coming and going. Particularly in the morning the streets are not busy and the police radio has little traffic.

This winter morning in Hollywood was no exception. In fact the streets were particularly quiet as it had rained last night and there was a chill in the air. A thick mist made it feel almost like it was sprinkling. Casey's first stop was the Winchell's donut shop for a cup of coffee and his favorite glazed donut. There were several patrons at the shop, so he decided to get his order to go. He had found that people finding a uniformed officer in a non-work setting were prone to strike up a conversation. This morning he was just not ready to hear about how Aunt Elsie was unjustly given a ticket. He decided to go to a small park in his area and enjoy his treat.

Casey took a route to the park that took him down several small residential streets. Enroute, the smell of the coffee and sweet treat was too much for him so he fumbled with the bag with his right hand and extracted the goodies. He had taken his first bite of the donut when he noticed a car parked on a side street. It was not parked at a residence, but next to the alley entrance. His attention was drawn to this otherwise minor anomaly by the fact that it appeared that the driver-side rear window was shattered and the driver's window open. He was not sure of exactly what he saw, so he made a U-turn and then turned onto the side street and approached the parked vehicle. He noticed two crows that were in the street, adjacent to the car, fly off for a nearby tree. He parked behind the car. The street was otherwise deserted.

Casey had his right hand on his revolver, which was still in his holster. As he cautiously approached the car, he saw that indeed the rear side window was shattered. There was glass and some organic-looking substance on the street. Casey gingerly peered into the open driver's window. The figure of a man was sitting there. There was a shotgun in his lap, with the muzzle pointing into his open mouth. His right arm extended to the trigger area. He was not moving, which Casey attributed to the fact the top of his head was ripped off. Pieces of brain and skull were scattered about on the back seat. Apparently the rear window had been closed and the blast shattered it. The broken glass was followed out onto the street by more pieces of brain and skull. Casey stood motionless for a few moments. He was dumbfounded.

Casey slowly stood up straight. "Well", he spoke audibly, as he looked all around him. That would explain the crows eating in the street, he figured. Casey returned to the police vehicle and made the mandatory radio notifications. He remained parked where he was until an ambulance crew arrived. Several times he looked at his half eaten donut, but just could not bring himself to pick it up.

"Sweetheart you need to hurry and get dressed. People will be arriving here shortly," Maria directed as Casey entered their apartment.

"Oui madame", he replied dutifully. She accompanied him to the bedroom asking, "How was your day? Anything exciting?" Casey stopped in front of his closet.

"No," he said without looking at her. "Just a routine Hollywood day?"

"That's nice, now hustle your buns." Casey drew up a half smile on his face as he shook his head.

The doorbell rang, signaling the arrival of the first guest. "So whom did you invite to my birthday party, my dear?" Casey asked as he approached the door.

"Oh, the usual, except I told DO that he could bring along any of your Newton buddies if he wanted."

Opening the door Casey exclaimed, "Well, speaking of the devil. Hey DO, how ya doin?" Officer Byrd shook Casey's hand as he looked to his left.

"You remember Jeff Avant from Days, huh?"

Casey extended his hand, "Sure, we worked together a few times. Come in, come in. What you got there?" Casey asked as Avant handed him a bottle wrapped in a plain paper bag.

Byrd said, "We went together and splurged to get you some cheap wine. Thought it would help you remember some of the good times in Newton."

Casey handed the bag to Maria, who was then greeting the guests. Pulling the bottle from the bag she exclaimed, "Ooh, Tulamore Dew. I don't think this is cheap wine."

"No indeed," chimed in Avant. "We thought some smooth Irish whiskey would smooth out some of the rough edges of the birthday boy."

Maria looked at Casey and smiled, "How appropriate."

The Continental cuisine skillfully prepared by Maria was a hit with everyone. Sarah joined Maria in clearing the table to the kitchen. Casey stood up to help, but Maria put her hand on his shoulder and gently pushed him back down. "This is your day, you fellows sit and enjoy that birthday gift; you might as well polish it off," she demanded as she produced the half full whiskey bottle she had surreptitiously retrieved from a kitchen counter.

Casey started the conversation. "So Jeff, are you still in law school?"

"This is it," he said, "this is my last semester."

Kevin chimed in, "So what are you going to do after you become a hot-shot lawyer?"

"Well, first things first. I'll be totally concentrating on passing the BAR next August. After that; I don't know."

"Hey Jeff, tell them what you found out about Sergeant Winchester. You know, that court decision," Byrd implored. Before Avant could answer, Byrd continued, "You guys know Winchester, the Sergeant on days. He made Sergeant out of vice. I think he was working downtown." Kevin and Casey both confirmed that they had worked for Winchester.

"Well," Avant started, "I was reading this Court case about a murder bust. It seems that some vice officer was hiding somehow right outside a public phone booth. Apparently he knew that a bookie used that phone to make some calls. Anyway, some poor slob goes into the phone booth and makes arrangements to buy some narcotics. The vice cop could hear every word. He gets some Narc. officers and they go to the apartment where the guy was supposed to pick up the drugs he ordered. They go in and find a couple of bad guys inside. One of them rents the apartment and has drugs on him and stashed in other places. The second guy is packing a piece. They bust 'em both. Turns out the gun they took from the second dude is linked to a recent robbery/homicide. Further checking and the guy fit the physical of the suspect in that murder. So, dead bang. Good work, right?" Avant paused and looked around. The others cocked their heads affirmatively, in unison agreeing that it was good police work.

"Now don't you know, the California Supremes reversed the convictions. Everything, from the drugs to the murder."

"What do mean reversed? What did they say?" Casey asked.

"I'll tell you," Avant began as the other three leaned forward in order to pay close attention. "Remember in the Academy learning case law. That one about the Fruit of the Poison Tree Doctrine?"

Heads bobbed but no one verbally offered remembering that lesson. "It's now called the Exclusionary Rule. Basically it says that any evidence gained illegally cannot be used against a defendant. It's more than that, though, in that any further evidence obtained as a result of that original illegal evidence is also excluded.

"So what does that have to do with this case?" Kevin asked. "It doesn't sound like the police did any *illegal* act." "Well now, you see, that's why you guys are mere mortal cops, and not supreme justices. When that officer was listening to that phone conversation, he was violating the poor chaps rights. That was the poison tree from which all the tainted fruit sprang."

"Wow, back up the train here," Casey insisted. "How was that phone caller's rights violated, and what did that have to do with the other two bastards?"

"OK. The Court said that even though that was a public phone booth, the caller had an expectation of privacy when he went in there to make his call. His right to privacy was therefore violated."

"Well, I would disagree with that, but please continue," Casey said. "The Court continued that any evidence obtained after, or as a result of that illegal act, must be excluded. It has to be thrown out. Voila, no case against the druggy or the bad ass."

"I have some serious questions here . . ."

Kevin was cut off by Casey, "Me too, but first, please do explain what all this has to do with Winchester?"

"Yeah," added Kevin. Avant leaned back and savored a long sip of his whiskey. "A little while back, several of us were enjoying some cold beer after work, and Winchester was bragging about an incident. Maybe not bragging, but he was telling us a story about an arrest he made a couple of years ago. Well don't you know, the court case I'm telling you about was virtually word for word the incident Winchester was telling us about. In fact, he was the one listening in at the phone booth."

The others looked at each other, smiling and shaking their heads. "Winchester telling us this story presents a huge issue here," Avant stated emphatically.

"Yeah, yeah, but I'm still not into this *illegal* business," Casey stated. "Illegal sounds like a violation of some criminal statute or something. Violating the asshole's right to privacy seems to come up short of that."

"That's a good point that plays into the huge issue here," said Avant.

"And if the caller had the so called illegal act perpetrated on him, how come the others also became victims?" Kevin added.

"It doesn't matter what the act was or who was involved, the Exclusionary Rule just looks at what evidence was subsequently gained from the act. That's just the way it is," Avant explained.

"Well I don't like it," Kevin said.

"That's our masochistic society," muttered Byrd.

Looking at Avant, Byrd stated, "The other day when we started to talk about this you were concerned about the import of Winchester not knowing about the Court decision. Is that what you mean by the huge issue?"

"Indeed it is, my philosophic friend, and if you can persuade our kind host to refill my empty glass, I will elucidate."

Casey did pour with his right hand while waving with his left toward empty chairs for the ladies, who were returning from the kitchen. Avant began, "OK, don your judges' hats and look at this for a moment from their point of view. That is, from the viewpoint of the judicial system. Now, you have an officer who in the course of his work violates a suspect's rights. As a result, evidence is discovered that proves the undoing of the poor miscreant. You can't just have the cops going around violating the rules and people's rights in order to make arrests." Quickly throwing up both arms, Avant added, "Now don't argue. That's just the way it is."

Kevin quickly declared, "There's no argument. Even us jack-booted thug cops wouldn't want to live in a society that allows the police to just do whatever they want. Of course we have to have standards to operate under."

Casey and Byrd both nodded in approval. "Yeah," said Sarah, "people supporting the idea of police officers making their own rules may just get bitten themselves." Everyone looked at Sarah and nodded in agreement.

Avant continued, "Right then, so how do you stop the police from running over peoples' rights?" Without waiting for an answer he added, "The courts have adopted this Exclusionary Rule ostensibly to punish the officers who violate the rules. At least, that has been offered as one justification. The truth is, the whole notion is patently absurd." Avant stopped, but there were no comments as all sat in anticipation of the rest of his comments.

"OK, up pops Winchester. The big bad cop violated that fellow's rights, so a drug dealer and murderer are excused from the prosecutorial system in order to teach the officer a lesson. Thing is, he had no clue as to the outcome of the case. After he testified, he moved on and forgot about the whole episode. So, how effective was the court's action?"

Mutters of "Yeah, not much, idiocy," etc. resonated among the group.

Downing another sip, Avant spoke, "Oh sure, the DA's office picked up on the case and passed the outcome along to the Chief, who set the wheels in motion to institute training in order to guide officers to avoid this pitfall in the future."

Casey did not let Avant continue. "But that could have been done, should always be done, but without dismissing the case against these obviously guilty slugs."

"Ah ha," Avant loudly declared in response, "my capable bar tender, you are correct. But, is training for future situations enough?" he asked pointedly, sitting back, folding his arms, and waiting for a response.

Sarah was the first to answer. "I don't want to start a war here, or a food fight, but shouldn't these cases be handled like all other legal matters?"

"Like how?" Byrd asked.

"Well, there must be something significant that could be directed toward the errant officer to ensure he doesn't do the same thing again," she offered.

"So are you saying that instead of burdening society by releasing the miscreants that we should prosecute the officers?" Avant asked, leaning toward Sarah.

Looking askance at Sarah; Casey, Kevin, and Byrd gave her an evil eye. "Well, I don't know about prosecuting them or anything. But something," Sarah stumbled. The three officers grumbled, but did not directly reply.

"No, no, guys. She's on to something here. There's just a lot to it." Avant offered as the others sat back and looked at him. "Yes, there is no point in releasing the guilty because of an officer's action. But there has to be some action taken directed at officers who violate the rules of evidence. Here's the rub on that: I don't know about the Winchester case here, but there are a lot of incidents wherein four Justices agree that the officer's actions were proper, but the majority of five Justices say that they were not. So should society require that a police officer acting quickly in the field have a better grasp of the rules of evidence than four Supreme Court Justices who have time to research the matter? Obviously that's absurd. In such cases, the officers should not be faulted in any manner."

"That makes sense," Casey said, "but what about when all the Justices agree that the officer was wrong?" he asked the group, not just Avant.

"What about that?" Avant chimed in.

"Here again," Byrd offered, "it's a matter of degree. What if a Superior Court judge and the Appellate Court side with the officer, but the Supremes disagree? Same situation."

"Right," interjected Avant, "unless there is total agreement that the officer took improper action, you can't prosecute him. But what about when there is agreement? What then?"

Avant leaned back again after stirring the pot. No one offered anything definitive to Avant's question. So he said, "How about holding the prosecution of police in these matters to the same standard as we do many criminals? That is that intent must be proved. You must prove that the officer intended to violate the suspect's rights."

Casey quickly added, "Sure, most of the time; hell, all the time, if we supposedly violate someone's rights we don't even know it. We're following some police procedure, or we're just using common sense." Kevin leaned forward and raised his right finger, "There's a popular misconception in the public that if we make an arrest, that is, a high profile one or catch a particularly notorious bad guy that we'll get promoted and the way will be paved for us to rise to Chief, or something."

"Sure," Byrd added, "that's from the movies. It's like in the military when a hero gets a battlefield commission."

"That's right," agreed Avant, "people don't realize that making a high-profile arrest gets the officer a good 'atta boy', at best. They see that putting Al Capone in prison is how we make advancement. Few realize that the police officers that truly aspire toward promotion actually avoid the high-profile incidents. Nothing will stymie promotion aspirations faster than making a high profile mistake. But you know what, there will always be some idiot out there in uniform who will take some action, knowing that it violates evidence rules, but he'll do it anyway. Well, then, that guy should go down. That would send a proper message, and it would weed out those few bad apples."

"So let me get this straight," Maria inquired, "I'll need to know what we have decided for when they make me queen."

Avant laughed. "OK, your highness, the Exclusionary Rule will be thrown out in favor of a more direct and positive way of effecting police compliance. That will be by developing training in response to court decisions, and discipline, or even prosecution, of officers who are found to be intentionally violating the rules."

"Let me just jot that down," she stated while writing in an imaginary journal.

"And don't forget that we won't try to correct errors by letting bad guys loose," Sarah added.

"Got it," Maria stated, "anything else?"

"Yes," Avant looked very serious. "Let me out of here before your husband forces me to consume any more of the devil's elixir." Casey looked surprised, "Well than be gone with you, nave. Thou tongue shall not have the privilege of tasting any more of me fine Irish whiskey. Besides, the bottle's empty." Avant shook his head up and down and grimaced, "Fine host; runs out of whiskey just as the party gets going."

With that the party broke up. As the last guest left, Maria shut the door, and then backed up against it with her arms behind her. Looking at Casey with a flirting expression she asked, "So, did you consume too much of your birthday cheer?"

He slowly approached. "Not that much," he whispered as he unbuttoned her blouse and kissed her on the side of her neck.

CHAPTER 20

Sergeant Teel

The Colorado winter air was cool and crisp. Casey emerged from the kitchen into the living room with a cup of coffee in his hand. Stuart and Judy were sitting on either side of the fireplace. A slow hardwood fire was softly flickering. Maria was sitting cross-legged in front of the hearth. Samantha was sitting in front of her holding a doll. Fritz was curled up on the floor immediately behind Maria. Samantha looked up at her daddy and smiled. Maria and Judy greeted him with "good mornings", while his father offered, "Well good afternoon."

"Yeah," Casey said, taking a seat in an old wooden chair. He continued, "Whenever we visit here my appetite is enormous and I sleep so soundly."

"Must be the altitude," Stuart observed, "You've just become a flat-land furiner, that's all." Casey shook his head in agreement as he smiled at his father, who continued, "Of course, last night's celebrating your promotion to sergeant didn't have anything to do with it."

Casey chuckled a bit and pleaded, "No, no. Really, I only had two highballs."

"Again . . . ." Casey and Stuart finished the sentence in unison, "It's the altitude."

Judy put her knitting down to her lap and addressed Casey, "So honey, are you sticking with the plans we discussed?"

"Yeah, Ma, I promised to show Maria Denver, then we'll take a day to ski the Legend. We can do all that with just three nights out."

Judy nodded in acknowledgement. Casey asked, "You're still OK with taking care of Sam? We could take her with us."

"No, no, she can stay here forever, as far as I'm concerned. It'd be pretty tough skiing with her anyway. No, you two go and have fun."

"Sure," Stuart piped up, "We'll just stay here working our fingers to the bone, taking care of the kid, and pining for your return."

"Oh poop," Judy replied, "pay no attention to him."

Casey felt that staying at the Brown Palace Hotel was a fitting splurge, befitting his new rank and pay raise. Maria tried to look nonchalant about the place, but ultimately admitted it reminded her of fine European hospitality.

The December snow was staying on the ground, but the roads were clear and the Denver weather was mostly sunny, but crisp. Maria grasped at her throat in a gesture that imitated one not getting enough air, as Casey took her picture standing on the Capital step labeled "5280 feet". That evening they strolled 16th Street, admiring the animated toy displays in department store windows. Joslins, then Neusteters, and finally Casey had to gently pull Maria away from the Daniels and Fisher window. She was almost mesmerized by that display.

The road up Loveland Pass was clear and dry, but ski traffic made the trek through the switchbacks seem endless. Pulling into the parking lot at Arapahoe Basin, Casey looked at Maria and declared, "Well here we are; the Legend."

Maria sat up straight and looked around. "This place doesn't look that big. So what's so legendary about it?"

Casey started to exit the vehicle, but looked back at Maria, "Well, for one thing, here at the base, we're at 11,000 feet."

"Mon Dieu, you mean elevation?" she gasped.

"Yes my dear, elevation. We'll be skiing up at 13,000 and some feet. That's like being at the top of Mount Geant." "Mount what?" Maria asked as she exited the car. Casey did not respond to her question as he helped her unload her skis.

At the top they got off the lift and stopped off to the side of the landing. Standing, Casey pointed ahead and directed, "We'll ski along there under the cornice. That'll be easy enough for us to get our legs. After that we can do a lot of trails. They're really fun."

Maria stood staring at a rock cliff running beside a wide ski trail ahead. Though the air was calm where they stood, powder snow was blowing off the top of the cornice. She had felt comfortable, but that sight suddenly gave her a chill. That and the realization of how high they were. "Are you sure that's safe. It looks like an avalanche could come off the top there any time?" Maria said.

"They only have one or two avalanches a week; nothing to worry about," he shouted as he skied off. She shook her head and followed his lead.

Casey proceeded slowly as it had been a number of years since either of them had skied. A couple hundred yards down the slope he pulled to the side and stopped. He could see that Maria was struggling a bit, making rather ragged, stiff turns. When she stopped by his side, he began to instruct. "Well, I see neither one of us is ready for the Olympics. We both have to remember to turn from the waist down."

He reached over from slightly behind Maria and put his hands on either side of her hip. Moving them back and forth, he directed, "Just wiggle that cute butt of yours when you turn, and keep your upper body straight."

"I know, I know," she advised, as she swatted his hands away and took off down hill ahead of him. *Feisty broad*, he thought as he hurried to catch up.

Judy approached the car as Casey and Maria were reaching in to pull out their gear. "So, how was the skiing?"

Before Casey could speak, Maria reported, "Well he's a bit of an amateur, but I gave him some good lessons."

"Sure, How to Fall Gracefully, 101 and 102," Casey countered.

"I may have fallen once or twice, I don't remember," Maria offered sporting a coy expression.

Casey looked at his mother. "You remember that girl from California, Fresno I think? She was visiting her relatives here and we all went skiing. Well that was Maria. Bat-out-of-Hell down the hill, and stop any way you can."

Maria stood looking a bit sheepish. Casey wrapped his left arm around her shoulders and facing Judy, "You got to admire the guts; you surely do. Actually, she did very well, not withstanding a few bruises on her butt."

"And ego," Maria admitted.

The orders read: Sergeant Teel, to Newton Division. Casey was pleased that he drew that assignment. He immediately went to the station and checked in with the CO. "Morning watch, Captain?" Casey asked, trying to sound pleased.

"Yes, it's a bit quieter then; give you a chance to get into the supervisory groove," Captain Swainert explained.

"Good, I'm looking forward to it," Casey said.

The Captain smiled. "The hell you are. But don't worry about it. We'll get you on better hours in a month or two."

Casey smiled back. "OK, Cap."

Casey was not a "station" supervisor. He preferred being in the field. At first he found he was a bit uneasy, driving alone in a black and white on the streets of Watts in the middle of the night. But things had changed a lot since he first worked here as a rookie cop. A lot of the older officers had retired. Younger men were now working the shift, and as far as Casey could see, they were paying attention to business and not partying on duty.

Casey soon found himself sideling up to an older black sergeant named Red Jarvis. Jarvis was a large, but not fat, man with a quick smile. His eyes spoke of a knowing wisdom gained over years of experience. Indeed, he had grown up on these very streets.

At first Casey was impressed with Jarvis because although he was a senior sergeant and of retirement age, he did not shirk his field duties. Whenever there was an incident in his area requiring a supervisor, he was always right there. Jarvis was one of those people who can calm a situation just by walking up. He had an expression that was friendly, and even smiling, but was simultaneously serious and firm. Casey was always impressed with how fast he could quiet a verbally combative situation. Angry shouting would turn to calm explanations of what was going to happen, and an agitated suspect was talked, rather than wrestled, to jail.

It became a regular routine that on the quieter mid-week nights, Casey and Jarvis would meet at an all-night donut shop during the early part of the shift. This was in the northern industrial section of the Division, just off the Santa Monica Freeway. They could park here and talk, knowing that it was unlikely that any patrol officers would be in this area. It was always very quiet at night, except for the occasional burglar alarm call, which typically proved to be false. Not a big deal, but they didn't particularly want their charges seeing them loafing and eating donuts.

One such warm summer night they were just winding up their meet. Jarvis drove off first, as Casey stayed on a bit longer while completing some paper work in his black and white. It was near midnight and a crime broadcast on the radio caught Casey's attention. It reported a robbery involving firearms. The suspects were two male and one female Negroes who just escaped in a late model dark blue Buick. A partial license number was given as "MN . . . ." The location of the incident was a place in the southern part of 77th Division. That's the area adjacent to the south of Newton. That being a fair distance away, Casey's thoughts quickly turned to other matters as he drove from the shop.

He proceeded west on a side street that was north of and parallel to the freeway. He arrived at a north/south street that passed under the freeway, and he turned onto that, southbound. Casey immediately observed that there was activity on this otherwise deserted street. About a block south of the freeway off ramp a California Highway Patrol unit had stopped a car. They were at the west curb. The patrol vehicle, with its roof lights flashing, was parked behind the car and offset a bit to the left of it.

Casey approached the cars very slowly. Two uniformed Highway Patrol officers were standing with two black men. One officer was looking at some papers while the other appeared to be engaging the men in conversation. The situation appeared calm so Casey slowly drove on by.

As he passed the lead car, Casey just got a glimpse of a female sitting in the front seat. His posture straightened up as he stopped his car. He looked back and saw that the car was a dark blue Buick. Casey slowly made a U-turn and drove back past the two vehicles again then made another U-turn and pulled up behind the CHP car. The idea that these could be the robbers in the broadcast still did not plant itself firmly in his head. The Buick was very clean, and the two men were neatly dressed and appeared to be smiling, as were the officers. Plus, this is a long way from the robbery location.

Then it hit him. The Harbor Freeway goes through 77th Division. It connects with the Santa Monica Freeway. It would not take very long to get here via these Freeways. Casey got out of his car. One of the other officers waved and smiled, as if to say that everything is OK. The two men he was talking to also looked back at Casey. As nonchalantly as possible, Casey waved back and smiled. Slowly walking forward he got to a position to see the Buick license. It began with "MN".

Casey surmised that the CHP officers were not aware of the robbery broadcast. The CHP is not on the LAPD broadcast system. Casey's thought was to handle this situation as quietly as possible. If these guys think this is more than just a routine traffic stop, they would react quicker than the officers, since they know what's happening and the officers would be taken by surprise. Casey pictured guns being drawn and the situation turning real ugly.

Smiling, Casey slowly walked around on the left side of the CHP car and approached the left side of the Buick. He observed that the two men were turned back toward the officers, with their backs to the cars. The officers were facing the cars. Casey carefully drew his service revolver and standing behind the open driver's window, leaned over and peered into it. The black female was sitting in the middle of the front bench seat. She was holding a .45 automatic pistol in her lap. She was nervously looking around to her right rear, apparently looking for Casey. Casey had calculated that she would assume that he would join the other officers.

Casey reached into the car with his pistol extended and pointed it at the woman's head. Without looking around, she froze as if sensing that she had been had. Casey quietly but firmly instructed her to push the gun onto the floor and, "Not a sound or your brains are mush." She slowly turned her head toward Casey and looked straight into the barrel of his pistol. Her eyes opened wide and her mouth dropped open as she did as instructed.

The CHP Officer who was holding the paper work was the first to notice that Casey had his weapon pointed into the Buick. Casey caught his eye, and playing charades by nodding and pointing communicated that he should follow suit and pull his weapon. That officer's eyes went back and forth between Casey and the man in front of him. Directly the officer stepped back a pace and drew his revolver and pointed it toward the men. The other officer stepped back and looked confused, but quickly pulled his weapon.

Casey then took charge. He instructed that one officer put the two men up against the fence, and the other get the female out of the car. As this was going on, Casey briefly explained that these people were wanted for a recent robbery. With that he opened the Buick door and retrieved the .45 from the floor. He held it up for all to see. The CHP Officer taking control of the woman looked at the weapon and slowly shook his head.

Back at the Station, following the booking process, the CHP Officers and Casey went to the lunchroom for a cup of coffee. Casey noticed that one of the officers, obviously the younger of the two, was having trouble with his coffee. His hand was shaking and he had to hold the cup with both hands. The older officer explained that they had gotten bored working that night, as it was so quiet. They stopped this car because of a faulty taillight. They were just going to give the driver a warning. It was something to do. "It could have been the last thing we did," the older officer offered. "Thanks Sarg, you played that really cool. I wasn't sure what all your hand signals were about, but when I saw your weapon in you hand, I figured something was happening."

"Good morning," were the words greeting Casey as he walked into the apartment. He could not see Maria, but returned the greeting anyway. Walking toward the kitchen Casey was met by Maria who was exiting the kitchen holding a can of opened beer.

Maria set the beer on the dining table and put both hands on the front of Casey's shoulders and smiled broadly. "I didn't have a chance to tell you about Samantha last night before you left for work. It was the cutest thing," she declared.

Casey took at seat at the table and sipped the beer. "What?" he asked with a smile of anticipation.

Maria sat and wiped her hands with a towel she had tucked into her waistband. "Well remember when you went to bed yesterday morning, Samantha had those three friends here?"

Casey acknowledged, shaking his head. Maria continued, "Well, I was getting ready to take them to the park to get them out of the house. I briefly heard them all talking about what their daddies did. I walked into the kitchen to pick up some snacks that I had made, and when I came out, they were gone. I assumed they had just walked out ahead of me so I went to the front door. I didn't immediately see them, but then I heard them in the house. I walked back in and they were just walking out of the hall to our bedrooms. I was about to scold Sam for taking them in there but before I could she explained. She said the girls asked what her daddy did, so she took them into the bedroom to show them. She said her daddy sleeps, and she could prove it." Maria chuckled as Casey looked down, shook his head and smiled. "Yep, that's what I do," Casey acknowledged.

Casey leaned back and wiping the smile off his face, "Yes, seems like that is all I've been doing in bed lately." Maria left her chair and stood very close to Casey.

Her breasts were right next to his face. Softly she informed him, "Well it so happens that I've farmed Sam off to Jackie. She has all the girls this morning." Casey slowly looked up toward her face. Maria continued, "Is there anything you would like to do in bed, or are you content just to sleep?"

Rising, Casey scooped her up and cradled her in his arms. "Yeah, I guess I'll just go to sleep," he said as he carried her off to the bedroom. Kicking the door closed behind them, Casey asked Maria, "So how was it again that we made that baby?"

Lieutenant Benton was still the AM Watch Commander. As usual the mid-week roll call was quiet, with all present looking half asleep. Benton raised his voice a bit as he explained that a crime pattern is emerging that needs some attention. He explained that several commercial stores along Central Avenue have been broken into recently and money stolen from vending machines, particularly juke boxes. He pointed out that few of those places could afford burglar alarms. The suspect apparently has a tool with which he pries open a door, usually the rear, and uses the same instrument to roughly pry open the machines' cash receptacles.

One officer asked, "Any suspects, Lieutenant?"

"No", Benton said with sarcasm, "that part's what you do. See if you can find him."

Another voice said, "Or her."

Benton cocked his head. "I stand corrected, him or her. Now get out of my house. I have work to do."

Still another voice, "Good night, sir."

Benton stood up, "I'll have you know that I am ever vigilant as your trusted leader. Do not mistake my meditation for inattention."

The officers uttered, "uh huh's" as they picked up their gear and headed down stairs to their cars. Staying awake at a desk through the whole morning watch was something few could accomplish.

Casey looked at his watch as he slowly cruised southbound on Hooper Avenue. One thirty he muttered to himself, too early for code 7, but damn I'm getting hungry. There hadn't been a call or radio car communication in the Division for the past 45 minutes. Casey thought he would head toward the Station. I can see if the Lieutenant needs anything done, he thought.

Before he found a place to make a U-turn, a radio call came out, "13A43, see the man, possible 459 in progress." The address given was in the 4000 block of Central Avenue. Hmmm, Casey thought, I wonder if that's our burglar?

Casey was just coming up on 41st Street, so he turned right and slowly proceeded toward Central Avenue, which was two blocks ahead. The night was dark and there was no activity on the streets at all. He turned off the vehicle lights and rolled down the window. He got just about up to the north/south alley running behind the businesses that face Central when he saw a figure. A tall man wearing an overcoat was walking briskly southbound out of the alley.

Casey pulled to the right curb and cut the engine. The man crossed the street about ten yards in front of him. It appeared the man didn't see the black and white until he got to about to the middle of 41st Street. He briefly looked toward Casey, and then continued across the street and onto the east/west sidewalk. Simultaneously Casey radioed that he had a possible suspect on foot, and gave his location. The man turned right and started to walk toward Central, but stopped as a Black and White northbound on Central passed across the intersection and then on out of sight. The man turned around and started to walk east bound away from Central. Casey exited the vehicle and quickly walked toward the man, who stopped and faced him.

"Good evening sir," Casey greeted.

"Officer," the man replied. Casey stood about two arms length distance from the man.

"Kind of late. So where you headed?"

"I'm just goin' home." Casey pointed toward the man's feet. "Now you just stay put a minute, I need to pat you down." Casey took a position immediately behind the man. "Raise you arms just a little for me, OK." The man complied, but said nothing. While patting him down, Casey could feel a long hard object under the coat and apparently stuck in his belt. Going down further, he found two large bulges in his front coat pockets. It felt like they were full of marbles, or some such loose objects. Casey guessed coins.

Both men looked to the left as a black and white pulled to the curb just short of their location and two uniformed officers quickly exited and approached. Casey took a position back in front of the man. "What's your name partner?"

"I bees Jimmy," the man said as his eyes shifted from Casey to the officers and back again.

"So Jimmy, where you been this late tonight?"

"Visiting a friend," Jimmy replied, offering nothing further.

Casey said, "OK." Looking toward the senior officer. "Ron, Jimmy here has a long hard tool of some sort under his coat. I'm sure he won't mind if you take charge of it." The officer instructed his trainee officer to handcuff the suspect. As he did so, Ron opened Jimmy's coat and removed a long, large screwdriver. He reached into one coat pocket and pulled out a handful of coins.

Casey asked, "What was the call about?" Ron asked,

"Some guy in an apartment above a business on the west side of Central happened to be looking out his window. He could see someone in the little diner across the street. It's closed and he knows the owner and knew it wasn't him, so he called dispatch. A9 also responded. They stayed there and we responded to your broadcast."

"OK'" Casey instructed, "Get on the horn and see what they have."

Ron returned from the car a few moments later. Addressing Casey but looking at Jimmy, "Seems someone pried open the back door, then pried open the juke box cash holder. Evidently someone with a strong tool, probably like a large screwdriver. All the coins are missing from the machine."

All three looked at Jimmy. Casey asked, "You know anything about that, Jimmy?"

"No sah, officer, I don't know nothin' bout that."

"That's what I thought," Casey said. "OK Ron, you know what to do. This is your felony for the night." Ron chuckled as they took the coins from Jimmy's pockets and took him to jail.

About three months later Casey stopped into the little pool hall bar in Eagle Rock where morning watch cops could sometimes be found. Anonymity for the police officers having a beer after work was a primary draw. It was one of the few places open in the morning, and the patrons were typically retired folks who kept to themselves. Casey was leaving mornings for day watch, and he felt like a cold one or two was in order.

Immediately upon entering he spotted a table in a corner where three officers were seated. They were Ron Nicholson, who was with Casey for the "Jimmy" arrest, along with two veteran officers, Lew and Sherman. Simultaneously they waived for Casey to join them. He knew all these were veteran, mature officers so he had no reluctance to join them for drinks.

The chatter started immediately with at least two conversations going on at a time. Mostly they talked about recent activities at work. But Ron quieted the group when he leaned back, beer in hand, and pointedly addressed Casey. "You know, Sarge, that court trial really pisses me off." Casey knew that he was referring to the trial of Jimmy the burglar, as he and Ron had both recently testified in it.

"So what, you got a problem with the system?" Casey asked with a smile.

"Damn straight I do," Ron shot back with a serious look. "What was that all about anyway? You'd think we committed a crime or something."

Lew and Sherman both looked at Casey. "Well, you see, we had this burglary case. You probably remember the coin-box burglar from down on Central?" All three officers nodded affirmatively. "Ron and I both had to testify two days ago in Jimmy's trial. Now, young Mr. Nicholson here has been living under the delusion criminal trials have to do with the innocence or guilt of the perpetrator. He thought because this was such a dead-bang case that we would just testify and the miscreant would be found guilty."

Ron continued to lean back and look down his nose at the group. Lew and Sherman leaned forward toward Casey. "Yeah, so? Don't tell me he was found not guilty?" Sherman asked.

"No, but we got a first hand look at the idiotic ways and workings of our illustrious criminal justice system."

The officers chuckled but continued to look at Casey for the rest of the story. Casey started to continue but Nicholson interrupted, "That defense attorney went on and on questioning Sarg. and me about what right did we have stopping his obviously innocent client. Can't a man walk home without cops picking on him? He even made a motion to suppress the screwdriver and coins as evidence obtained illegally. Illegally for Christ's sake. And you know the worst part?" Nicholson looked around but no one responded but they were now starring at him. Raising his voice Nicholson continued, "The judge took a recess while he considered that motion. Consider the motion! What a crock of shit!" Casey placed a hand on Nicholson's shoulder to settle him down, and then continued the story, "We were sitting there with the City Attorney looking at each other and thinking, that judge may just kick this case. But he didn't. He overruled the motion, citing some case that said cops on the street have a right to protect themselves by frisking suspects; as long as they have reason to suspect the person of something."

"Yeah," Nicholson continued, still raising his voice, "then that lawyer started pounding the idea that a screw driver and coins are not weapons, and we shouldn't have taken them from Jimmy."

Again Casey reached over to calm Nicholson. Casey offered, "We couldn't believe it when the judge hesitated in ruling on that. He did eventually acknowledge that given the circumstances of the case we probably, that is probably had reasonable cause to suspect that those things were evidence of the crime." Lew and Sherman sat back and shook their heads.

Casey broke the brief contemplative silence, "The real telling part of this experience is the fact that the defense attorney fought the case as he did. He wouldn't have wasted his or the court's time unless he knew he had a chance to prevail." Casey surveyed the group then asked, "Any of you have experiences in court where the central theme of the proceedings dealt with whether or not the dude committed the crime?"

Sherman said, "No, it's always been questioning whether or not we had a right to be where we were, to stop the defendant, to search where we did; that type of thing. But damn, this case was so blatant."

Nicholson picked up on that. "Yeah, late at night, eyewitness to the crime, Jimmy's the only one around and walking from the crime scene, the tool and coins bulging from his jacket."

Casey interjected, "I repeat. That attorney felt he had a chance in this court system. And the judge. He actually took a lot of time and thought deciding how to rule. Disgusting." The others verbally agreed.

Casey scooted away from the table and declared, "Welp, I'm going to get out of here, but I will leave ya'll with the thought for today. Actually I got these thoughts from Avant."

"Ah, our resident philosopher," Lew explained. "Indeed. Anyway, we all learned in the Academy that attorneys are officers of the court, right?"

All heads nodded affirmatively. "And the point of the trial is to determine innocence or guilt of the accused. So if the defense attorney has evidence that would point to the guilt, or to the innocence, of his client, shouldn't he be obliged to present that evidence?" All three officers exhibited "that's absurd" smiles. "No really. Isn't this thing supposed to be about innocence or guilt? Well?"

Sherman spoke up. "Well yeah, but the court does have to consider the defendant's constitutional rights, right?"

"Of course, but the primary mission is to determine whether or not the guy is guilty of committing the crime. All officers and anyone sworn to testify should offer whatever they can so that a proper determination can be made. That includes all attorneys involved. The dude's constitutional rights are another issue, almost an administrative matter. If the officers or prosecutors erred, then that should be discovered and appropriate corrective action taken. But that has nothing to do with whether or not this idiot is guilty of the crime. Excusing him from prosecution is not a proper remedy. That punishes society for something a police officer or prosecutor did. Where in hell is the logic in that?"

Casey stood up and leaning over scooting his chair back in added, "And with that bit of superior wisdom, I will leave you all to your humble thoughts." A folded napkin flew in his direction as he walked away, amid boos and jeers.

CHAPTER 21

Vice Supervisor

Lieutenant Brogan was tall, medium build, with a quick smile and pleasant demeanor. Casey was a bit surprised to see the lieutenant in the station with civilian clothes on. He was more surprised when Brogan walked directly up to him and extended his hand and a greeting.

"I guess you know that I'm the new vice OIC?" Brogan asked.

"Well, no sir, I didn't know that," Casey said, thinking it strange the lieutenant would ask that of him.

Brogan continued, "The reason I ask is that you've been on patrol here a while and I thought you might consider doing something different."

"You mean vice, lieutenant?" Casey asked with a smile.

Sporting his patented warm smile, Brogan replied, "I do. You've built a good reputation as a patrol supervisor, and we're particular whom we ask to be vice supervisors. I think you'd be a good fit."

Casey knew that Brogan had a great reputation as a lieutenant to work for. He was pleasant, does not get overly excited when mistakes are made, plus he was firm and fair. "Well, I'm sure it would be good for my career to get more variety of experience. Sure, put my name in the hat."

Brogan cautioned, "Good, but some guys consult with their wives before taking this kind of assignment."

Casey smiled. "Well, sir, my wife and I do consult each other on most issues, but this kind of career decision she would expect that I go ahead and make." Brogan pursed his lips and shook his head affirmatively, "That's solid Teel. I'll go ahead and start the paperwork."

"Let me get this straight," Maria started, "you're a lily-white cop and you're going to work undercover in an area that is 99.9 percent Negro?"

"Let me set you straight," Casey answered, "first I'm a cop supervisor. I will be supervising cops who are working undercover. And it's blacks, not Negroes."

Maria grabbed Casey's shoulders, leaned back and declared, "Well, my handsome stud, if that's what you want to do, then you should do it. At least now your daughter won't be telling her friends that you sleep for a living."

Casey grimaced, then quietly observed, "Yeah, now she'll tell them I chase prostitutes for a living." They both laughed, as Maria proceeded to pour two glasses of wine. Handing him one and holding up the other, "A toast to your success in your new position . . . . except the part about chasing whores."

"Thank you, my dear. But you know, there are some assignments where one must sacrifice his body for the good of the cause."

Maria assumed a serious expression and declared, "Use your body for the cause of catching prostitutes and I'll have cause to use it as a punching bag." Casey raised his eyebrows and acknowledged with a headshake.

Casey had not paid much attention to the vice unit. Their office was upstairs and he seldom saw any of the officers around. On a couple of occasions he just about accosted a man in the station who looked like a street thug, but pulled up short after realizing he was a vice cop. So it was that he felt like a real stranger when he reported for duty in the vice room. He did recognize a couple officers who had worked patrol, but most were strangers.

The unit was divided evenly between nights and days, with six offers on each. Casey was surprised that there were several Caucasian officers assigned to the unit. But they participated in most cases, as literal undercover work in bars was seldom done in this Division.

Casey was initially assigned to nights. Most of their time was spent handling gambling complaints. Most of those complaints involved wives calling to complain that their man lost his Friday pay check at a gambling game, and "when are you going to do something about that?" The tips as to where the crap games were located were usually very accurate. Casey frequently reminded the officers to make sure the game they investigate falls under one of the three 'C's". That is the Department requires that before action is taken on a gambling matter, it be commercial, conspicuous, or complained of. The latter was usually the case.

Craps was by far the game of choice during the night hours. Casey found himself doing very little. The officers on nights were all experienced and worked well together. They were very effective in taking down gambling games, plus they routinely used good back-up techniques to ensure their safety. Casey involved himself as much as possible, but typically just manned a back-up position in an undercover car, while his troops snuck up on crap games that usually located in the rear of small businesses or in alley parking lots. Casey did help with getting and loading the drunk vans used to transport the arrestees to jail. That was the most time consuming task.

It was a Wednesday night and the officers saddled up to go after a game reported to be going on in the back of a vacant business. Two officers were in one car with Casey and two others in a second vehicle. The second car, with the passenger ducked down out of sight, drove by the location. They proceeded out of sight of the business, then radioed the other car: "Looks good Sarg. The entrance is off the alley. There's a guy at the door, but he's paying total attention to the game inside. Tony will go to the side window and get the violation. I'll signal you when he's got it then we can all rush in."

"OK Washington, let's do it," Casey confirmed.

Casey turned to Dailey, who was a white officer known for his work dedication, as well as his eloquence. "So tell me how this works. When these guys get booked, they typically pay their bail and get released, right?"

Dailey looked at Casey and nodded affirmatively. "And how much is the bail?"

"Twenty-two dollars."

"So what happens if they don't have the money?"

Dailey threw a curious look toward Casey, "Well they stay overnight, or over the weekend, until the court opens. They're arraigned and then released."

Casey thought a few moments then continued. "How do these guys get back home?"

"I guess they take the bus, but maybe they get their old ladies to pick them up," Dailey said.

Casey looked sideways at Dailey. "The buses don't run this late, so what about the ones who bail out now?"

Dailey nodded his head, "Usually they get together and walk home; probably don't get there until near dawn." Casey shook his head in acknowledgement then sat quietly in contemplation.

A figure emerged from the darkness beside the building. "That's Washington," Dailey stated as he began to get out of the car. Washington motioned and Dailey, Officer Stemp, and Casey ran after him. They flowed right into an open door off the alley and stopped in a large vacant room. Ten men where lining up against one wall, with the two officers facing them. Casey noticed that no guns were drawn. The senior office, Tony, was directing the men to form a line.

There was some jive talk between the group and the officers, but basically it was not heated. Casey stepped forward and in a firm voice got everyone's' attention. "OK, we're going to do things a bit different tonight," he declared while everyone starred at him. "I want each of you men to reach into your pocket and get out your $22.00."

Everyone in the room looked around at each other, but each man did as instructed. "OK, who doesn't have $22.00?" Two men slowly raised their hands. Casey pointed to one and asked, "What's your name?"

Looking around, the man slowly answered, "James."

"So James you must be a loser." Looking up and down the line Casey continued, "Who was the big winner tonight?" There was no response, as the men looked at each other then at Casey. "Come on, don't make me frisk all of you, who was winning?" No one responded, except that most of the men looked at a fellow on the left end of the line. Casey walked up to him and looked straight into his eyes. "What's your name?"

The man backed a bit, "Lee Roy."

"Lee Roy, did you win some tonight?"

"I guess so," he said.

Looking back at James, Casey asked, "So James how much do you have?"

"Nine dollahs."

"Lee Roy, loan James thirteen, won't you?" Casey asked as he glared at Lee Roy. The money exchange was completed. Casey stepped back and looked at the second man who had raised his hand. "How much do you have?"

"I gots sixteen."

Casey looked the group over again, "Who was another winner." Getting the idea, a man in the middle stepped forward and handed $6.00 toward Casey. Casey put his hands up signaling that he wasn't taking the money, and then signaled toward the other man, who did accepted the bills.

"All of you now, count your money again. I don't want to hear about any of you coming up short." The group complied. Casey continued, "Listen up here. Who all has a car here?" This time the officers looked at each other with puzzled looks. Several men slowly raised their hands. Casey pointed to one, "What kind of wheels you got?"

"A Buick," came the slow reply from the oldest member of the group.

"Four door?" Casey asked.

"No sah, two door."

"No good," Casey said, "who else?" He found two who had four-door sedans.

Casey hiked up his pants and with all eyes glued to him, "You two drivers, pick four others who will ride with you." No one spoke as everyone continued looking at Casey with curious expressions. Casey explained, "You're going to drive those cars downtown so you have a way to get home after you bail. You drivers figure out who will ride with you and make sure you get them for the ride home, understand?" The drivers softly replied affirmatively. Looking first at one driver then the other, "Don't let me hear that you left someone downtown."

Both drivers perked up and said, "Yes sah, no sah."

"Now, just to keep everyone honest, who are the two baddest dudes among you?" Following a brief hesitation, two of the largest men were pointed out. Casey explained, "Going down, one of you will ride in one police car, and the other with me. If somehow, your two cars don't make it down there, these bad dudes will be stuck there. They like might not be too happy about that, huh?" From facial expressions it was clear that they all understood.

The caravan proceeded downtown to Central Jail. Casey and the officers stood by as each arrestee was processed. One by one they were led behind the booking counter and into the jail to complete the bail process. Two of the men looked back at Casey as they were led away. They smiled a bit as they shook their head in apparent disbelief and gratitude.

With the process completed, the officers proceeded toward their cars. Casey started to get into the back seat but stopped as he heard Tony call, "Hey Sarge."

Tony was standing in the driver side doorway, and looking at Casey. "That was a good thing you did, Casey."

Stemp joined in. "Yeah, you probably prevented some family dispute calls. But, uh, what do you think the lieutenant would say about this?"

"Brogan? He'd say good job, just don't get caught," Casey said. Dailey elaborated. "Well, we're not likely to see any brass checking up on us in the wee hours of the morning in this area. And one thing's for sure: None of those guys is going to complain." The group chuckled in agreement as they got into their cars and headed back to the station.

Thursday night and the sleepy eyed vice cops took their seats in the squad room. Lieutenant Brogan had stayed over from working days, as he did at least once a week. Casey stood against a sidewall as Brogan addressed the group. "You guys did a good job last night. In fact, one of the wives called me today to say thanks. She said her man got home earlier than usual, and with some money in his pocket." That was all Brogan said as he quietly looked about the room. The officers were silent as they looked at each other. Casey squirmed and quietly cleared his throat. He first looked down at the floor, but slowly drew his gaze back up toward the Lieutenant. Casey thought, oh he must know. That shoe's going to drop.

Brogan smiled and continued, "Anybody have anything they want to discuss? Complaints? Ideas?"

Tony cleared his throat and offered, "Uh yeah, Lieutenant, we have an idea regarding Lucy."

"That street walker you haven't been able to bust?"

"Yes. You know we even got those vice cops from North Hollywood to try, but she made them right off."

Brogan asked, "OK so what's your plan?"

"Well, if we could get one of you, uh, more senior looking supervisory types that she has never seen on the street she might go for it." Brogan interjected, "Whoa, back up the mule team here. Who you calling a senior type?"

Dailey offered, "OK, well, you guys aren't really old, but dressed in a suit and driving a nice car you would look distinguished."

"I'll distinguished you," Brogan threatened, "but go on."

Tony continued, "Friday night we can get a rental car, say a Cadillac, and if one of you were dressed in a suit and all, well she may just go for it."

Brogan asked, "That rental place still letting us borrow cars on the weekend?"

"Yes," Tony answered, "but no guarantee we could get a Cadillac, but it's worth a try. Actually, any nice sedan will work."

Brogan shook his head, "So, who you got in mind for this venture?" Slowly, all heads turned toward Casey.

Casey stood up straight, pointed toward his chest, and mouthed the word, me? Brogan smiled. "Say, weren't you involved in some sort of espionage in the military?"

"OK, OK, I suppose it's time you all get a chance to learn from the master," Casey bragged, "So tomorrow night it is."

"Let me get this straight," Maria said, "you're wearing a suit to work so that you can go undercover in Watts?"

"Yeah, that's right. Why, do you doubt my espionage abilities?"

"Honey, let me point out a few things to you. You're not in Paris, you're in Watts. You kind of stand out there."

Casey drew a serious face and looked straight at Maria, "Fie with you. A proper spy can operate anywhere."

"OK Mr. Denis, go work your magic," she said, laughing. Casey stood up tall, head back, and wrapping his right arm in front of his chest, marched out the door.

As Casey walked into the squad room he asked, "You couldn't get a car, and so we'll do something else tonight?"

"The car's in the lot downstairs Sarg," Dailey said, "but you certainly do look dapper."

Brogan, who was just leaving, observed, "Yeah, you look so good I'd go out with you." Casey threw a pencil at the Lieutenant as he scooted out the door.

Casey turned a chair around and sat in it backwards as he gathered the vice cops around him. "Actually, I've been looking forward to this. Good to get back in the field."

"Got an idea how you want to work this?" Tony asked.

"Sure. I brought a beer with me from home. I'll dribble a little on me, and then pour a little on the floor of the car. I'll loosen my tie and mess up my hair a bit. She should buy that I'm half soused. So what's the deal with her?"

Tony explained, "Lucy is about 5 feet 2, nice build, and very cute. She usually works Broadway at 42nd Place. If she's out, she'll be on the south east corner. You should go south on Broadway, turn east on 42nd, and stop at the curb a few yards down."

Casey leaned back and contemplated a moment. Then, "How will I know her? I understand your description, but that could fit several girls I've seen on the corners."

"OK. Washington and I will cruise down Broadway. You'll follow Dailey and Stemp and park several blocks north. We'll radio Dailey if she's there. He'll signal you. If she is, she will be the first to approach your car. Her pimp is always nearby, and he makes sure she gets firsts with a good John."

"Right, but what if she doesn't give me a violation right away? I may have to drive her someplace."

Tony perked up, "Oh you will have to take her someplace. She's too good. She'll screw around with you. She may give you a price, or what she'll do, but not both. You just have to go with it. Don't push her. If you're patient, eventually she'll give you the violation, but probably not till you get to a motel."

Casey acknowledged, "OK, but what about my backup?"

Washington took that up. "Tony and I will be several blocks down Broadway, out of sight. Dailey and Stemp stay north of the location. Now, make sure when you take off, make a U-turn back to Broadway. If she wants you to go straight ahead on 42nd, make the U anyway and just pretend that you didn't understand. You are drunk. Anyway, Dailey and Stemp will see you enter Broadway, and get behind you. We'll alternate tails from there so that she doesn't make us. She will look for a tail, at first anyway."

Casey seemed satisfied, but added, "Motel? You know which one she'll take me to?"

Tony shook his head. "No, we've tailed her a few times, but she always goes in a different direction. Don't worry though, with two cars we can easily stay with you."

The car was a two-year old light tan Cadillac sedan. As the group was getting ready to take off, Tony approached Casey and leaned in the passenger window. "She's going to ask you a bunch of questions about yourself; what you're doing." Casey smiled, "I got it covered. I'm a manufacturer's rep for a well-known tool company. I'm from Denver here in LA for a tool convention. I'm familiar with Denver, in case she is too and asks questions. I'm just looking for some company tonight."

Tony slapped the window seal as he stepped back. "That's perfect. Good luck."

Casey parked behind Dailey and Stemp, who were in a two-door vice car. They were three blocks north of 42nd Place. They just got stopped when Tony and Washington drove by in the other vice car. This is the shits with no radio, Casey thought. He sat motionless in anticipation, rehearsing one last time his story. It was less than a minute when the passenger, Stemp, turned around and looking out the rear window, motioned thumbs up to Casey. He immediately started the Cadillac and slowly drove south.

There was no light at 42nd Place, but a couple of northbound cars caused Casey to stop for his left turn. Quickly he scanned the scene. The southeast corner was occupied by a long, narrow walk-up café. It extended east about 40 feet, with a small parking lot in the rear. The business was open but there were no customers. Two scantily clad black ladies were in front, leaning against the west wall. Befitting the cool night they each wore a light jacket. And there she was, the very attractive Lucy, standing beside the north wall in a shaded area. The night was dark, but the corner was well lit.

Slowly Casey made his left turn, and as instructed parked at the south curb just past where she was standing. Quickly surveying he observed a lone black male sitting in a Cadillac parked at the north curb. The pimp, no doubt, Casey thought being careful not to look directly at him. He powered the passenger window down, and leaned slightly forward and to his right. Lucy came up to the open window and smiled. She initiated conversation: "Hi, are you looking for something?"

Casey smiled and said, "Sure."

With her eyes Lucy surveyed the interior of the car, and looked Casey over carefully. "You want a date?"

Casey nodded affirmatively, "Yes, I would." Casey slurred his words just a bit. He wanted to appear high, but not drunk, as she probably would not get in the car with a drunk.

With that, Lucy leaned back and appeared to be looking over the top of Casey's car. Casey figured that she was looking at her pimp. Casey turned his head only slightly to his left. Without looking directly at it he just got a glimpse of the car as it slowly drove away from the curb. In an instant, Casey's passenger door opened and Lucy sat down. Looking straight ahead, Lucy instructed, "Let's turn around and go down Broadway." *That's good*, Casey thought, as he complied.

Lucy navigated them on a bit of a circuitous route, then into a motel parking lot on Figueroa Street, only a few blocks from where they started. It was a two-story motel in a U shape, with the parking in the middle. Casey found an empty parking space in the rear. The lot was about 2/3 full.

While driving, Casey and Lucy engaged in light conversation. Casey told her about his job as a tool salesman, and about the convention downtown. Lucy smiled and at least appeared to be paying attention. Casey tried to lead the conversation to the business at hand, but she skillfully steered clear of any specific language that would be a violation. Casey thought that his troops were very proficient at tailing. The few chances he got to look into the mirror he could not see either car.

They got out of the car and Lucy instructed Casey, "This way," as she walked directly to a first floor room in the middle of the north section. Enroute Casey glanced toward the street, hoping to see one of the vice cars. He saw nothing. Lucy removed a key from her purse and opened the door. She flipped a light switch, turning on an overhead fixture. The room was clean enough. It had two nightstands with one lamp, a queen size bed, and a dresser next to the door. A door to the bathroom was closed. Casey stood and watched as Lucy opened the bathroom door, looked inside, then closed the door again. She placed her purse on a nightstand, then turned around and sat on the bed, facing Casey, who had just come a couple of steps into the room, closing the door behind him.

Casey figured that at this point any customer would want to know what he's going to get and what is the fare. He asked, "So, what about this date? What do you do?"

Lucy didn't immediately answer, but rather looked intently at Casey. Her intense look suddenly turned to a smile. Casey figured that smile was affirmation that she finally decided that he is not a cop. Sure enough, she stood up, unbuttoned her short skirt and letting it drop, saying, "You can get a half and half for fifty bucks, or a straight for forty." An offer of sex, in the street vernacular, and a stated price. Casey had his violation.

"Oh Lucy," Casey started, but immediately saw from her facial expression that she knew what was happening. Indeed, she had never given him her name. "Police Officer, you're under arrest for prostitution."

Lucy quickly pulled her skirt up, yelling, "No, no, you miserable bastard, you can't do this." She turned around, picked up her purse, and with head down walked toward Casey and the door. In range, she quickly swung the purse at Casey while bolting for the door. Casey anticipated just that action and grabbing her arm spun her around and threw her face down on the bed. He held her down with his left hand on her back while with his right he retrieved a set of handcuffs from a pouch under his jacket in the middle of his back. Firmly he took both her arms and pulling them behind her, placed the handcuffs.

Suddenly Lucy went limp, and looking at Casey and smiling stated, "OK officer, you got me. I won't give you any trouble. You don't need these cuffs on me, I'll go wit cha."

Casey just smiled as he picked up her purse, and holding her right arm led her outside and to the car. He put her purse in the back and sat her in the front passenger seat. He started to put the seat belt on when she again turned to sugar, "Please, you don't need that belt, I'm not going anywhere and it really hurts with these cuffs on." Casey thought, what the hell, she's cuffed. He closed the door and as he walked around the back of the car he looked everywhere he could see to find the vice cars. He opened the driver door and stood, scanning the area again. Nothing; no sight of the officers at all. That's not good. They must have lost me he thought as he started to sit.

Before he reached the seat, he was aware of the passenger door flinging open as he saw Lucy scrambling from the vehicle. He quickly ran around and grabbed her as she was on the ground trying to gain her footing to run. After replacing her in the seat, he angrily pushed down the door lock and slammed the door shut. He quickly returned to the driver's seat. He donned an angry face as he looked straight at her as she sat back in the seat. She pursed her lips in anger as she stared straight ahead.

Casey turned the key to start the engine while still looking at her. Lucy suddenly turned her head his way, but looking past him her expression turned to a surprised look. Casey sensed that they were not alone. He thought: Damn I hope she's looking at my troops. Slowly turning his head back to his left, he saw a very large black man leaning toward his window. He was motioning for Casey to roll the window down. Casey complied.

Placing both hands on the car for support, the man leaned close to the window and slowly but deliberately asked, "What's going on?" Casey sat up straight and putting on his most confident face answered that he was a police officer, simultaneously showing his badge. He stated that the woman was under arrest. Casey then looked into the windshield mirror and nodded, giving the appearance that he was signaling his backup. The man stood up and looked toward the street. Scanning the mirror again, Casey hoped to see the vice cars approaching. There was nothing but dead of night.

Casey figured the man would know that no cop, let alone a white one, would be out here working alone. Indeed, the man took a step back, as he alternately looked into the car and out toward the street. His facial expression was one of great suspicion, but he stood still. Casey backed out of the parking place and drove out to the street. Beads of sweat lined his forehead.

Casey drove north on Figueroa and then turned east onto a through street toward Broadway. At Broadway he started to turn north, but had to stop for a vehicle that was crossing westbound. When clear, he started to complete the left turn when the passenger door again flew open and Lucy bailed out. Casey hit the brakes and threw the gearshift into park. He got out of the car and started to run toward its rear, when he became aware that the Cadillac was starting to roll forward. For a moment he stood and looked at Lucy, who was just then running onto the sidewalk and south on Broadway. He looked back at the car that was slowly heading directly toward the northeast corner curb and the traffic light pole.

Instinctively, Casey realized that the consequences of crashing a borrowed Cadillac would be infinitely more severe than allowing a misdemeanor prisoner to escape. He ran to the car with the driver's door still open. He literally jumped into the compartment and stopped the car just short of the curb. He got turned around and drove south on Broadway, trying to locate Lucy. He did not spend much time in this endeavor as he figured she knows the area well and would quickly disappear down a rabbit hole. Indeed, he found no trace of her. That is nothing but her purse, which was still in the back seat. Well that's something, Casey acknowledged to himself.

Entering the upstairs vice room carrying the purse, Casey was greeted by Dailey, "Nice ensemble Sarge."

Without replying Casey blurted out, "What in the hell happened to you guys?"

Noting his angry tone, Dailey replied, "We're really sorry. When we saw a tan Cadillac pull onto Broadway and head south, we assumed it was you and we tailed it. We were about a half-mile down the road when Stemp saw that it was the pimp driving. We went straight back to 42nd Place but by then you were gone."

Stemp joined in, "Really Sarge, we split up and looked all over for you. Finally we decided that Tony and Washington would stay out and keep looking and Stemp and I would return to the Station in case you turned up here. We've got a call out for them to come in."

Casey stood silently for a while thinking about the sequence of events. As the irony of the situation began to soak in, his facial expression changed from anger to smiling. "You know," Casey stated, "it never dawned on me that that pimp car was so similar to mine. Well, I guess you guys are forgiven . . . . this time."

The other two officers soon returned and Casey regaled them all with a rehash of his adventure. Afterward, Stemp offered that he had read in a car magazine that some late model GM cars could pop into forward gear if they are shifted into park to abruptly. "Now he tells me!" Casey exclaimed as he gestured with an upward motion of his hand toward the officer.

Dailey dumped the purse onto a tabletop and found only a small bottle of cheap perfume, some hand lotion, and a California driver's license in a plastic case. "Typical street walker purse," he observed. "Two bits says that ain't her real name," offered Stemp as he looked at the license.

Casey ended the session with instructions for Tony and Washington to take the loaner car back to the agency and for Dailey and Stemp to leave instructions for Day Watch to follow-up on the Driver's License and to get a warrant for Lucy. He explained that he would be writing his report of the incident. Casey included with instructions for them to go home when they finished the tasks.

The next night when Casey got to work Lt. Brogan and all four p.m. officers greeted him. They all looked at Casey with smirks on their faces, but said nothing. Casey fumbled through papers on his desk as he asked to no one in particular, "Did they get the warrant for Lucy?"

"Nope," said Brogan.

Casey looked at him and asked, "Why not?"

"No need," said Brogan, as the four officers began to snicker. Casey held out his arms in a questioning manner but said nothing. Tony explained, "She already has a warrant out for her."

"OK," Casey said as he looked back down at his paperwork. "Want to know what the warrant's for?" asked Brogan with a sly tone.

"Sure, what is the warrant for," asked Casey as he was getting a bit perturbed with the guessing game.

"Murder!" Brogan exclaimed raising his voice.

Casey's head went up and his eyebrows rose. "Murder?"

"Sure, you want to know what kind of murder?" Brogan continued.

"Well, how many types of murder are there?" Casey shot back.

"Ah, in this case, it is murder of a police officer," Brogan said.

"Say what?" Casey shouted as his attention piqued

Brogan explained that there was no record of any kind attached to the license from Lucy's purse. But running that name they found that it had been cross-referenced with another alias by Las Vegas PD. They had identified her as being involved in a drug bust gone badly, in which a police officer was killed. There wasn't any information as to whether or not she was the actual shooter. Casey looked down and shaking his head back and forth commented, "Good Lord."

The Division detectives had also done some follow-up and determined that Lucy had a sister living in the Crenshaw area, and that was a good bet for where she may be staying. Brogan handed Casey the arrest warrant information and instructed, "You're the best one to identify her, so why don't you take your troops out to the sister's house and see if you can locate her."

Casey nodded affirmatively. "But don't spend too much time with this. It's no longer a vice matter, though I know you'd like to catch her."

The neighborhood consisted of rather small tract homes, but with larger lots then in some newer areas. They parked a few doors down the street and approached on foot. Casey instructed Tony and Washington to go to the rear of the house. He, Dailey and Stemp went to the front door. It was another dark night. There were lights on in the front room of the house. After giving the officers time to take positions in the rear, Casey gently knocked at the front door. It was closed, as was the screen door.

"Who is it?" came a female voice from within. Casey did not answer, but knocked softly again. Footsteps could be heard approaching the door. Again, the voice asked who was there, as the door opened slowly. Casey and the officers were standing to either side of the door not in clear view. As the door continued to open, Casey stepped in front of it and displayed his badge. He quickly identified himself. He saw a slightly heavyset black female holding the door, and simultaneously he saw Lucy get up from a couch in the room and run into a hallway leading to the rear.

Casey grabbed the screen door to open it, but it was latched. "Open the damn door," he yelled as he rattled it.

The female stood in the doorway and held up her hands. "Please officer please don't," she begged.

"We're going to rip this door open to get her if you don't open it." Again she implored, "Please don't come in, please. I'm her sister I'll bring her out; I'll bring her out."

"Lady, I'll give you one minute to get her out here," Casey demanded. He figured that the guys in back probably had her already anyway. Slowly the lady walked backward toward the hallway, all the time facing the officers and motioning for them to stop, and pleading for time. Then the scene suddenly changed. The lady stopped pleading and turned to look back. The officers stood back quietly.

Walking very slowly, Lucy reappeared in the front room. She stopped at the edge of the couch and though a bit wobbly on her feet managed to pick up a jacket folded there. With a smile on her face she continued her slow pace toward the front door while donning her jacket. She unlatched the screen and walked out, holding her hands behind her for handcuffing. She said nothing, and never broke her smile. Though she looked straight at Casey, she seemed to look through him.

Dailey handcuffed the woman then looked up at Casey and Stemp. Smiling he explained, "She had to shoot up to last her till her pimp bails her."

The two concurred as Casey looked at Lucy. Her eyes were glazed over, as she seemed to be in another place. "Lucy, it's a hell-a-va world, ain't it?" he offered. She continued to smile as they walked off.

Working days was a whole new world. Almost all of the vice enforcement in this Division involved bookmaking. Up and down Central Avenue there were numerous cash rooms. These were usually small cafes that served no food or drink, but kept rather busy during horseracing hours. They did usually supply small pitchers of milk to be used with the Scotch the patrons frequently brought with them. The proprietor may provide chitlins or some other snack on occasion.

One man or woman operated most operations. That bookie would stay near the back of the establishment next to a radio, which was tuned to a station carrying horseracing broadcasts. He or she would record bets, and collect or disburse funds as appropriate.

In order to make an arrest, the police had to catch the bookie with actual recorded bets. That provided the fodder for cat and mouse games between cops and bookies. Typically the bets would be recorded on either flash paper or dissolvo. Flash paper would virtually disappear in an instant when touched to a flame. If that was used, the bookie always had a lighted candle handy. Dissolvo was paper that would almost instantly dissolve when placed in water. For this, the operator had a bucket of water close by.

One way an officer could grab a wager sheet before it could be destroyed was to go undercover and maneuver close enough to the bookie. That was seldom successful, as the bookies typically knew their patrons, and were very leery of newcomers. Officers were occasionally successful employing various ruses they could concoct.

Just such a ruse developing session was commenced on a summer afternoon in the Vice Office. Casey had been the Day Supervisor for four months and he had thoroughly gotten into the intrigue of this type of police work. Two Administrative Vice bookmaking enforcement officers from downtown Police Headquarters were on hand, as were Lt. Brogan, the four Day Watch officers, and Casey.

Charlie and Ron, the Ad Vice officers, reminded the crew that Jake's cash room at Vernon and Central had not been touched for some time. Brogan offered that a lot of time had been spent trying to get a violation there, but that Jake was just too crafty. Officer Arlotti explained that the location is a long and narrow clothing store. To look legitimate there are a few racks of old dusty clothes hanging to the side in the front area. Four counters are set up in a staggered array so as to set up sort of a maze. One counter extended from the north wall, the next from the south, and so forth. No one can just wind his way back to Jake without him being totally aware of that person's movement.

Casey was aware of Jake's place, but had not personally been in it. He asked, "How hard would it be to get an undercover officer into the front area?"

Officer Pistoli answered, "Not too hard. We've seen people go in there who didn't appear to be regulars. Of course, they can't get into the maze. Jake has a runner handling all the money transactions, and he's the only one allowed back of the counters."

Charlie offered, "I have a plan then." All eyes focused on him.

"If we get Stemp from nights, can he get in there? He's black, and probable not seen around here much during the day."

Brogan and the Newton officers shook their heads affirmatively.

"Probably yes," opined Pistoli.

Charlie continued, "On that corner there's a gas station, and Jake's operation is on the ground floor of the building immediately north of that, right?" Arlotti affirmed that description. "So if we had a van parked in the gas station lot, parallel to Jake's south wall, a person could be in that van and out of sight. If he then opened the van side door and, say, threw out an empty aluminum trash can or two against the wall, it would make a hell-a-va noise, right?" All officers sat back in their chairs and looked around at each other with curious looks. "Uh, yeah, Charlie, it would make a lot of noise," affirmed Arlotti.

"OK, so now just prior to the trash can fling, we have a black and white chase a plain vice car up Central Avenue. They will come to a stop directly in front of Jake's. Red light and siren; screeching brakes; cops jumping out of the patrol car . . . . Got the picture?" Arlotti jumped up and smiling explained, "Sure the loud banging; all that commotion. Jake is bound to run out, along with everyone else in there, to see what's going on. Stemp just runs in behind them and grabs the sheets. I like it, I like it."

Brogan pursed his lips and shaking is head slowly, "I don't know. It just might work, but what if other traffic gets involved?"

Casey offered, "We'll do this on Saturday, about the second race at Santa Anita. There's not much traffic then, and if we pick experienced patrol guys . . . . hell there won't be any problem."

Brogan sat back in contemplation. All eyes turned to him. Raising his head and looking toward the ceiling, Brogan put his hands together in front of his face as though praying, "Oh Lord, what have I done to deserve such a crew? What?"

Slowly he lowered his head, and then with his head down, looked around the room with his eyes bent up. Suddenly, he cried "Oh hell, let's do it." And wagging his finger at Casey, "And so help me Teel if this goes wrong . . . ."

Charlie was the first to comment, "Oh I want to throw the trash cans, can I Lieutenant, can I?"

"I'm sure that can be arranged," said Brogan as he walked into his connecting office, shaking his head.

It worked like a well-oiled machine. Stemp drew little attention as he sauntered into the cash room. He picked up one of the racing forms that Jake kept in the front for his customers. He gave the appearance of seriously handicapping a race, but Jake's runner kept a wary eye on him. Then it happened. The siren, brakes screeching, uniformed cops bailing out of their car, then the loud banging. It was too much for anyone to ignore. Anyone except for officer Stemp. The front of the cash room cleared immediately. Stemp turned to face outside, but bent his gaze hard left toward the maze. In short order Jake, who was about 75 pounds over weight, ran and waddled through the maze, and past Stemp. But as he entered the front doorway, it was as though he had an epiphany. He stopped short and turned to look back at Stemp, just in time to see him vaulting the first counter and entering the maze.

Jake started to give chase, but stopped almost as soon as he started, knowing that he couldn't begin to catch the athletic young officer. Jake turned to look back out the front in time to see the car the police stopped pulling away and the uniformed officers calmly reentering their black and white. He turned back around and watching Stemp scooping up his betting markers, muttered, "You rotten bastards. You miserable rotten bastards." Jake couldn't move. He just stood in place, shaking his head and muttering.

Cigars were lit, as the mood in the squad room was one of happy achievement. Every detail was rehashed as each officer involved offered some observation unique to his position at the scene. Officer Stemp was the last to join the group, having been tied up with booking the evidence. Handed a cigar, he started to light it and muttering while puffing, "Where's the Lieutenant?"

"Meeting with the Captain about something," said Casey.

The officers were getting up and getting organized to go home when Lieutenant Brogan walked in. His facial expression was that of a whipped puppy. He stopped in the middle of the room and announced, "Listen up guys." All eyes turned toward him. "Well, the Captain chuckled and said to congratulate you on a well executed, cleaver plan. Then he got serious and said that if we pull that kind of a stunt again he'll can us all." Eyebrows raised as the men looked around at each other, raising their hands and shrugging their shoulders. They looked back at Brogan as he continued, "Seems he got a bunch of calls from several merchants in that area. They complained that a police car made a big scene about pulling a couple of guys over, and then they just took off, as though nothing had happened. Not being aware of our plan, which took the old man by surprise . . . . he couldn't give them a good explanation. He really, really doesn't like surprises."

Everyone got a serious look on their faces as they thought about what was said. As they began to gather to leave the squad room, sly smiles and snickers started to appear. Even the Lieutenant cracked his deadpan expression and had to smile as he told the departing men, "Now get the hell out a my sight, and don't ever do that again." Almost as if orchestrated, each man waived with his back turned as he walked out the door.

CHAPTER 22

The Lieutenant

"Casey, it's OK, it's your reward for making lieutenant," Maria assured Casey. They were on the couch; him sitting up and her legs were over his and her arms wrapped around his neck. Looking directly into his eyes with her brows raised, "Really, Sam is so excited about moving to Tarzana to the house with the pool, as she describes it, she won't even know you're gone."

"I know," Casey acknowledged, "but her birthday party and all."

"There again," Maria responded, "She'll not notice you're gone. She's a teenager now. Her friends are her life. You're just the one who pays the bills and tells her what to do and what not to do."

Casey smiled and nodded. "Honey, she loves you and someday she'll acknowledge you're her best friend. But now, well you're just an old parent."

"Old am I?" he joked as he pulled her close and stroked her butt in a provocative manner.

"I know, I know, you're a virile young man," she said in a sexy voice, then straightening up and gently pushing him back, "now tell me again exactly what the plans are."

"Well there are four Newton police officers going. I believe all of their wives are going, but I don't know that they all SCUBA. Anyway they're driving down tomorrow in two cars. You remember meeting Lieutenant McKinney and Sergeant Weir? They were at the last Christmas party?" Maria raised her eyebrows at Casey, "Of course I know Pat. We were with he and his wife on the Channel Islands diving trip. You big dummy, you don't remember that?"

"Oh, yeah," Casey acknowledged sporting a dumbfounded expression.

"Anyway, the three of us will go down the next day in our station wagon. That has enough room for all our gear since their wives aren't going."

Then putting his head down and looking up at Maria, he said, "We can easily make arrangements if you want to go."

Shaking her head Maria said, "No, I'm still trying to get rid of this summer cold, the other two aren't bringing their wives, and the party . . . . no I'm good here, really."

They started to stir off the couch when Casey remembered. "Oh, did you get a chance to get to the bank and get a bunch of ones for me?"

"I did. Now explain what that's for?"

"One of the policemen has been down to Guaymas before. He said that as we drive from Nogales to Hermosillo, there are several little towns. Each one has a kind of official border check station, or whatever. Anyway apparently some local yokel gets himself appointed as border agent and he checks each vehicle that passes. Checking means collecting a dollar bill."

"What?" Maria asked pointedly.

"Hey, I don't make the rules. That's just what I was told."

"Oh brother!" she muttered as she retrieved her purse to get the money.

As McKinney, Casey, and Weir loaded SCUBA gear and bags into Casey's vehicle, they paused for a moment to do some verbal inventory taking. "What about a gun?" Weir asked. "Man I hate to be without a piece down there, but I know they frown on that."

McKinney perked up and commented, "Frown on it. That's an understatement my friend. But I agree, traveling all that way unarmed . . . . just don't feel right."

Casey offered, "How about I put my off-duty Colt in the glove compartment. We all have our ID's; it shouldn't be a problem."

After a bit of discussion, they agreed to Casey's idea.

It was just a bit before noon when they drove out of Nogales, south on Mexico Route 15. McKinney commented on how the road was in better shape than he had anticipated. Weir surmised that since Hermosillo is a large town, there probably is a fair amount of commercial traffic using the road. Indeed they encountered several trucks along the route.

As they had been warned, passing through several small towns they would come upon a roadblock in the form of a vertical swing gate across the right lane. In each case a crude sign warned that that was a border crossing check point and all vehicles must stop. At each of them a lone male would appear from a crude small shack and approach the vehicle. They each wore a sloppy brown army officer cap, and a dirty old military jacket. As they approached these stops Casey would chuckle; McKinney, in the front passenger seat, would assume a serious face and hold a dollar bill out the window; and in the back seat Weir would shake his head in disgust.

Just south of Nogales they found themselves following a late model Buick with Arizona license plate. The lone male driver did not appear to be Mexican. At each checkpoint, they observed that the man would lean over to the passenger window and hold out a small plastic bag with some object in it. Without hesitation the border agent would take the bag and immediately lift the gate for the man to continue on.

After passing through several of these check points, the two-car caravan came upon a more official looking border station. It was an adobe brick building and a diversion lane forced traffic into the building's parking lot. A sign directed that all persons must check in with the agent inside and present identification. Fulfilling that directive, McKinney, Weir, and Casey exited the building. The man in the Buick was just about to enter his car when Weir approached him. The stranger had on a company shirt from a provisions company, and the name "Jeff" was over his left breast pocket.

Weir smiled and stated, "Excuse me, this is our first trip here, and we're really curious about the bag you've been handing the border guys? We were told to give them one dollar bills." Jeff smiled, chuckled, and then explained, "Yeah, that must look pretty funny. Well I drive down here from Tucson a couple times nearly every week. I sell restaurant equipment and stuff to several places in Hermosillo. That dollar bill business got to be a bit expensive, so I came up with an alternate payment plan." With that, he motioned to the front passenger seat of the Buick. There sat another plastic bag. It was sealed and contained ice and what appeared to be a can of beer. McKinney and Casey were within ear shot but not privy to the contents of the car. Weir motioned for them to come over and look. All three grew smiles and shook their heads, and then smiled at Jeff, who wore a broad grin. “One beer is cheaper than a dollar, but Poncho appreciates it more. There’s one more station down the road then it’s clear on into Hermosillo.”

The four exchanged pleasantries, then prepared to depart. As Weir started to get into the rear seat, he stopped and stood up straight, asking, “Do you suppose they’re all named Poncho?” McKinney slapped him on the back of the head, and pushed him into the car.

The two rented outboard boats were just large enough to hold the seven divers, one of the wives, who was pregnant and not diving, and their gear. At a point about 100 yards off shore, in about 40 feet of water, they anchored the boats side-by-side, with one beat up fender hanging between them. As usual, the sky was clear and bright and the water clear and warm. The divers strapped on their gear and maneuvered around in the boats so that they could drop into the water one at a time without tipping it over.

The policemen broke into two pairs, and Weir, McKinney, and Casey decided to be a threesome. With all in the water they congregated while bobbing on the surface and briefly discussed plans. McKinney, who was the most experienced diver, suggested that they all go straight to the bottom, then they would branch off in their teams from there. Agreed, each man flipped over and headed down, imitating a formation of WWII dive-bombers.

Weir didn’t immediately join the others as he was having trouble with his mask. The strap seemed to have gotten loose, so he spent a few moments making the adjustment. He got the mask on and just started to dive when he noticed a motion out of the corner of his eyes. It was the wife, kneeling in one of the boats, wildly flailing her arms and apparently pointing at something. Weir looked up and in the direction she was waving as he started his descent. “Holy shit!” he shouted into his mask. It appeared that a cloud was lying on the water, cutting off a lot of the sunlight. Must be a big boat, he reasoned as he scurried to gain depth to be well under it as it passed over.

The others had waited on the bottom for Weir to appear. They all looked at him as he approached. He did his best charades moves to point out the boat overhead. He watched in amazement as each of the divers scrambled backwards onto the bottom and facing up, each had wide-eyed, terrified expressions. Weir thought, *jeeze, you'd think they never saw the bottom of a boat before*.

Weir settled on the bottom as the light got very dim. He slowly turned around to lie back as the others had. Looking up to view the boat, his body suddenly covered with goose pimples as he grasped one of McKinney's arms. Sharks. Hammerheads. A whole school of them, milling about the surface. Seven bodies sat motionless on the bay floor amid an array of beautifully colored corral formations. Heads were slowly moving from side to side as they watched the school hovering above them. So many they were blocking the light. The warm waters felt chilly. They wished they could stop breathing, as the air bubbles ascending seemed to be attracting the large sharks. Occasionally one would leave the surface and appear to be looking around and toward the bottom, like a puma looking for a rabbit he knows is hiding nearby.

Ever so slowly the school of killers meandered off toward the north. No one moved until one of the men realized that his wife was up there in the boat. He broke from the group and rose toward the surface. Facing north all the while, and holding his abalone knife in a threatening manner, he made it to the top. The other six realized that he shouldn't have to face the danger alone, so little by little they also ascended.

At the boat, they found a frightened but unhurt pregnant woman lying flat against the bottom. Watching the surface for telltale shark fins, they got their gear and selves into the rented craft in record time. When all were in, all conversation stopped. They sat for several moments looking at each other with expressionless faces.

Casey was the first to speak. "Well, I've had enough diving for the day. How about you fellas?"

Six men and one woman looked around at each other then nearly in unison replied, "Sure, I'm good."

After packing their gear and checking out of the rented cabins, the group joined in Guaymas at a restaurant for breakfast. Over chorizo and eggs they rehashed their three-day adventure. "All in all it was a good dive, I'd say," offered McKinney. Casey remarked about how it seemed like they were swimming in a tropical fish aquarium.

Weir nodded his head toward Casey and offered, "In a few days this guy's going to come to work all black and blue." A group of curious looks shot in Weir's direction. He continued, "Teel here loaded up a bunch of nice pretty conchs. They'll look great in your wife's garden, huh?"

Casey nodded affirmatively, still curious about the prior remark. "Well he'll probably put them in a corner of the garage and forget about 'em. In a few days the meat will turn rancid and stink up the whole house, and oh is Maria going to give him a beating."

The group formed a three-car caravan and headed for home. Casey drove a bit slower than the two officers, so in 20 miles or so those two cars were out of sight. The terrain was rather desert like when the road turned from north to nearly due east, as it skirted around a small hill. Rounding the hill, the road turned back north. The three companions sat up at attention as the view of the road extended ahead as they cleared the hill. About 1/3 mile ahead they saw a medium size flatbed truck, piled high with hay, stopped at the right side of the road. It was partially surrounded by three police-type vehicles, each with roof lights flashing.

Casey slowed, but kept driving ahead. As they passed the scene, it was clear that the cars were Federal police vehicles. Nine uniformed officers were milling in the area. Some were inspecting the truckload and interior. Two were talking with the truck driver, and others were standing by. All but two of the officers were armed with short-barreled automatic weapons. The two had holstered side arms. McKinney noted, "These guys are for real. Look how sharp their uniforms and cars are."

Casey grunted affirmatively. Weir offered, "Those guys aren't traffic cops. They're looking for something. I don't think I like this."

Casey resumed his normal speed, but he and McKinney frequently monitored the rearview mirrors. Weir nervously checked out the back window just as frequently. After a few miles they were out of sight of the incident. All three took a deep breath and sat back and relaxed. Weir offered, "Hey, we have California plates and we're obviously just tourists. They wouldn't bother stopping us."

After a few moments of silence Casey stated, “Well we’ll soon find out,” as he looked in the mirror.

McKinney checked the outside passenger mirror and affirmed, “Yep, here they come.”

Weir sat back and with a look of confidence challenged, “You watch, they’ll zoom on by us.”

Casey started to slow and pull to the right, observing, “Well you’re wrong my friend. We’re getting the lights. Shall we run for it?” he added with a smile.

“No no,” shouted Weir.

As he pulled to a stop, Casey added, “Not a chance. Let’s show our badges and smile. Remember we’re brother officers; I hope.”

“What about the gun?” Weir asked with a scared tone.

“Just forget it,” Casey directed, “I doubt they’ll search the car once they see our badges.”

Several officers with the automatic rifles took positions on both sides of Casey’s car. Two others approached the passenger side door. One was medium height, trim, and well groomed. His uniform was neat and his collar was adorned with gold clusters signifying the rank of Major. The other was taller, younger, and trim. He wore captain’s bars.

With very little accent the Major spoke in English. He directed all three to exit the car and to show their ID’s. They tried to exhibit a relaxed look as they each handed their badge and police identification cards to the Captain. The Major also looked at the material then said, “You’re all LAPD officers?” McKinney acknowledged that they were.

Without further ado the Captain handed them back their ID’s. The Major told them to stand back a ways. They complied without comment, as they felt very agreeable given the presence of several officers cradling their assault weapons and watching them closely.

The Major gave a verbal order to two officers, who immediately began searching Casey’s station wagon. Casey thought that it would be a very cursory search, since they know they are dealing with police officers. But that was not to be.

An officer’s eyes opened wide and he smiled as he pulled Casey’s 3” Colt revolver from the glove compartment. The officer walked toward the Major, who was now standing back a ways, removed the gun from the holster and held it up in the air. The Major motioned for him to stand aside, then gave an order in Spanish to the others. With that three officers pulled gear from the car, and went through everything.

Finding nothing of interest, the searching officers backed off. It became apparent that the trooper with Casey's gun was trying to get the Major's permission to keep it. Instead the Major ordered him to give the weapon to the Captain. The Captain opened the cylinder and removed all six rounds. He placed them in his pocket, closed the cylinder, put the gun back into the holster and handed it back to the officer. The Major then instructed him to return it to the glove compartment. The officer developed a disgusted look, but did as he was told.

"You are going straight home now?" the Major asked.

Casey, McKinney, and Weir each eagerly acknowledged that indeed they were.

"Good," the Major said, "pick up your gear and go straight to the border."

"Yes sir," Casey replied in his most humble voice. As the three set about picking up their gear, as if by magic the whole Mexican entourage disappeared in a matter of seconds.

Silence prevailed in the car as the trio motored north. Casey finally broke the silence, "Well that was fun."

"Man, I would have bet you lost your gun," McKinney stated. "The hell with the gun, I figured we'd be using up all our sick and vacation time rotting in a Mexican jail," was Weir's assessment.

McKinney continued, "When that guy came out with your piece, I pictured us lying face down with machine guns at the backs of our heads."

Weir shook his head in agreement, but Casey surmised, "It was our attitude; I'm sure of it. If we'd been smart asses, I'm sure we'd be in that jail right now. Hell they knew we weren't bad guys and it was obvious what we were doing here."

Casey cocked his head up as in contemplation, "In fact, I wasn't worried at all."

"Yeah, right," McKinney grunted as Weir mocked in a female voice, "I wasn't afraid at all."

It was late at night when Casey finally walked in the door, having loosely stowed his gear in the garage. Maria emerged from the bedroom wearing a robe and walked into the living/dinning room, her hands in her pocket. Casey put down the mail he was scanning that was stacked on the table. "So how was it?" she asked in a genuinely sweet voice.

"Good. It was fun. Nice," he answered.

"Anything exciting happen?"

"No, it was a nice trip; the water is really pretty there; lots of colorful fish."

"Pat's wife called after you dropped him off." With that Casey got a dumbfounded look on his face, but could only say, "Oh."

Maria tromped over to a position directly in front of Casey and began wagging her right index finger at him, "You weren't going to tell me, were you?"

"Well, I."

"You almost get jailed by the Mexican Federalies, you about got killed by sharks!"

"Oh, those guys exaggerate. I'll tell you the true story in the morning."

Maria backed off and lowered her head a bit. "Well OK, I'm too tired now to give you the thrashing you deserve. Oh, and you should know. A captain somebody called from the Department Personnel Office. He said you are to be assigned to Intelligence Division. He said to call. That's what you wanted, isn't it?" Casey smiled, took Maria by the waist and drew her close and kissed her on the forehead, "Yes indeed," he answered. "This will be a whole lot more interesting than being in patrol, and could just be a fast track to Captain."

"Great to hear. Now let me go, I'm going to bed," she said. Wiggling her butt in a provocative manner while walking toward the bedroom, Maria added, "We can properly celebrate your transfer when I'm rested, and after you tell me the truth about what happened on the trip."

Casey wringing his chin and smiling stated, "You're on."

After three years Casey became disillusioned about his job in Intelligence Division. A lot of interesting information came across his desk, but he was truly a "desk jockey". The mission, as the name implied, was to gather intelligence regarding which bad guys were in town, and what they were doing. Business and friend relationships were particularly important to track. Miscreants of various natures were the targets, from organized crime figures to terrorists to militant anti-government folks. The Division was outside the regular chain of command and the Commander reported directly to the Chief of Police.

The mission was just intelligence. Any information stumbled upon about a possible plotted crime, or the whereabouts of wanted criminals, would be passed on to other Divisions for appropriate action. That is, provided that information would not compromise anyone or anything having to do with their intelligence operations. The truth is, some of the officers in this Division could not readily lay their hands on their handcuffs. Some, no doubt, did not know where the jail booking office was located.

Casey was impressed though with the ability of some of those working for him to retain information in their heads. The office files were stacked high and loaded with information on a huge number of people. They represented tens of thousands of man hours invested gaining information. Yet, many of his men could go directly to an appropriate file when asked about a certain person or organization. Frequently they could recite a list of associates of an identified individual.

But, this activity came to an abrupt end. Following the issuance of a Presidential Executive Order, nationwide intelligence gathering regarding citizens was greatly restricted. Ultimately the files were ordered destroyed. Casey heard that some officers had their own files at home, or that some men were planning to take some office files home. He surmised that that activity halted when there were threats that some Federal agency was going to issue search warrants for police investigators' homes. Nothing came of those rumors.

The Division Commander passed the word that a lot of positions in the Division would soon be eliminated, and that investigators and supervisors should start looking for "new homes". For Casey, that was a moot point. The Captain's promotional list came out, and his name was near the top.

CHAPTER 23

Captain Teel

"Daddy since this party for your promotion is such a special event, and it should be; I'm so proud of you. Anyway, I think I should be able to have some champagne, don't you?" Samantha asked, flashing her most loving and innocent green-eyed look at her father. "Well you are 19, and you are mature and responsible," Casey stated while stroking his chin in stern contemplation. Then assuming a more friendly look and smiling at her, "So the answer is no. But thank you for the kind words." Samantha knew argument was futile, so she walked off in a huff, and under her breath repeated her father's words in a mumbling, sarcastic tone.

Maria was within earshot performing pre-party chores. She straightened up and looking at Casey, remarked, "You know, I don't understand how it is that Sam loves and respects you so much; the way you tease her all the time." Casey stood tall and with an incredulous look answered, "Moi. How could she not love me? I'm so . . . ." Maria interjected, "You're so in trouble with me if you don't hurry to the store and get those things I need." Casey saluted and hurried off.

Captain Kennedy's beer bottle was empty so he excused himself from a small group in the corner of the Teel's den. He went into the kitchen and retrieved a full bottle from the styrofoam cooler on the floor. Turning he came face to face with Casey. "I haven't had a chance to talk to you and give my congrats," Kennedy exclaimed. "Thanks Tim, and I haven't had a chance to thank you for taking me into your Division."

Kennedy nodded and smiled. "I know, I know, there are better assignments than a Captain in charge of the files and clerks." "No I know. There are positions I'd rather have, but hey, being a junior Captain in a division as well run as yours? A lot of guys would fancy that," Casey replied. Kennedy continued, "Good positions, like that opening in Ad Vice?" "Well, I did put in for it, but what are the chances it would go to a rookie?" Kennedy gave a knowing smile then, "You know, as a matter of fact, with your background and record, you were seriously considered." Casey cocked his head to a side and with a surprised look, "Really, I wasn't a bit surprised that Captain Carter got it." "Look Teel, nothing's written in stone, but just between you and me, here's the plan. Commander Bock and the Chief told me when I asked for you that you would come to my command, but only temporarily. Carter is most likely going to make Commander, but he has indicated that if not, he'll retire. So, when he leaves Ad Vice, they can move you in there. You really were their first choice for that job. But, Carter will do fine, and after you have a year or two paying your dues, they can easily justify giving you those reins."

Casey thought for a few seconds then added, "Thanks for letting me in on this Tim. I assume this is totally confidential and off the record?" "See, you're way ahead of me already. That was my next statement."

Though Casey was thrilled to think that he could actually soon be commanding Administrative Vice Division, by now he knew full well how such plans have a way of not fulfilling, so it did not take too many months for him to essentially put that thought out of his mind. So in just 18 months later, he had no clue as to why he had been summoned to Commander Bock's office.

Off the elevator on the sixth floor at Parker Center, Casey turned into the north east/west hallway and almost ran into Commander Bock. "Oh Commander, you wanted to see me," Casey asked quickly in order to jump past the point where he excuses himself from almost walking into a superior officer. "Yes Casey, come with me," Bock instructed in a friendly tone while making a U-Turn. Growing a sly smile, Bock stated, "I was just going to see the Chief, but he can wait." Casey chuckled and uttered a drawn out, "OK."

"Teel, I'm sure you recall asking for Ad Vice when you were appointed captain?" Bock started. "Sure. I felt that command really fit with my background," Casey campaigned. "Indeed it is a good fit. But a new captain never gets that kind of command right out of the chute. Now you've done some time and we are considering you to take over for Carter," Bock leaned back in his chair and held his fingertips together as he studied Casey. Casey nodded his head in slow contemplation, and then asked a question that he knew the answer to, "So is Carter leaving?" "He'll be making Commander on the next list, so yes, he's leaving."

The next half hour was spent with Bock grilling Casey as to his knowledge of the mission of Ad Vice, and inquiring as to how he would handle the position. Casey felt he had handled the questions and his responses well, but then felt a giant let down. After receiving a brief phone call, Bock thanked Casey for coming by, and dismissed him. It occurred to Casey that this dismissal was just further testing him, so as he departed he stated, "Thank you Commander. I hope I do get serious consideration for the job. I assure you that I would make it my passion to be the kind of CO the Department would expect." With that Bock thanked Casey again and closed the door behind the departing Captain.

Casey walked into the kitchen and put his car keys on a hook. Maria was busy pulling a platter from the oven and did not immediately look at him. He just stood in place exhibiting a stoical look. After setting the tray on a trivet Maria turned toward him and cocking her head aside asked, "So what's with the look? Aren't you happy about getting the Ad Vice job?"

Casey pursed his lips and shook his head, "This meeting was just an interview. I suspect the command will go to a more senior captain." Maria looked from side to side than back at Casey, "So why are you supposed to report to Ad Vice Monday morning?" Casey's head went back as he studied Maria, "Say what?" "Tim Kennedy. He just called a little bit ago and said to congratulate you and to tell you to report to Ad Vice Monday morning." "He did?" "No honey, he actually said that you're fired and to come in and clean out your desk . . . . Yes, he did."

A big smile came over his face. "Monday morning huh? Ad Vice? Well how about that?" Casey pondered. Maria got in front of Casey and put her arms around his neck, "That is what you wanted, isn't it?" "It sure is. It's just that . . . . wow, Ad Vice." Casey pulled Maria against him and gave her a kiss. But his mind was elsewhere as he cut the kiss off short and stared passed her. Maria shook her head with a bit of a disgusted look, but that soon turned to a smile as she shared Casey's happiness.

The Commanding Officer's office was not large, and made even smaller by the presence of so many people. Commander Bock opened the meeting with introductions. He presented Casey to the Chief of Police, Captain Carter, Lieutenant Brogan, and Officers Ron Howard and Charlie. Bock went on, "You remember Brogan from Newton. He transferred in here about a year ago. And I think you have met Ron and Charlie." Casey responded, "Yes, good to see you Lieutenant, and trash can Charlie, good to see you again too." Brogan lowered his head and partially closed his eyes, as Charlie squirmed in his chair. "Trash can Charlie?" Bock asked. "Oh nothing, just some old vice talk," Casey assured.

"OK then," Bock continued, "Casey you'll be starting here as of now. You'll be on the next transfer, but Carter will be taking some vacation time before then, so we wanted to get you in here right away. Normally we wouldn't worry about having the CO spot open for a bit, but there's an important matter going on now and we need you up to speed and involved as soon as possible." All faces assumed serious looks as Casey leaned forward in attention.

Bock leaned back and instructed, "I'll let Brogan fill you in." "OK," Brogan started, "As you may be aware, the West side; hell the whole City, has bookmaking organizations scattered about. Some small, with just a few handbooks and a back office, and some are much larger, with numerous books and a back office with a staff of people. Well a couple of the bosses in West LA came to us; Ron and Charlie in particular, and said someone is trying to organize all the books in that area, including Inglewood, Lennox, Hawthorne; those areas. Actually organize is a soft way of putting it. As far as we can tell at this point, it is the Mob trying to muscle in. Naturally, our local bosses are happy with current arrangements. They really don't want to be dictated to by some out-of-state mobsters."

"What are we talking about; out-of-state from where," Casey interjected when Brogan paused for a breath. "As far as we can tell, so far, Detroit is where some of the muscle is coming from." "Muscle?" Casey asked. "Yeah, well, it doesn't appear that any of the local bosses has agreed to any terms. Of course, the mob isn't just going to accept that. There have been a few handbooks and a boss or two who have been approached by Tony and Luigi and told how it would be healthier for them if they were to join the organization. So far, no knees broken, but we assume that is the next move. Now I said Detroit because we have identified two of these muscle guys and they flew in from Detroit. Detroit did identify one of them as a known gangster, but the other guy appears to be under their radar."

Brogan leaned back and took a sip of coffee. Casey thought for a moment then, "So where are we now? What about those two thugs?" "Yeah Cap," Ron Howard chimed in, "we have several handbooks and even a sub-boss as registered informants. They first alerted us to this situation, and told us about the goons. We had uniforms stop them at least twice and kind of harass 'em about unrelated stuff and cited them for some nitpicking DMV crap. They must have figured they were in the Department's radar, and soon packed up and apparently went back home. Anyway, our snitches will let us know if they are approached again, but meanwhile we're watching as many bookies as we can in case they get contacted."

Commander Bock jumped in, "Probably the next wave will be real muscle who will get physical. We really want to be on top of that. We'll never stop bookmaking, but as it is now it's manageable." The Police Chief added, "I will not tolerate a Mafia presence here. This project has full priority."

"So right now nothing is happening except our vigilance?" Casey asked. "As far as we know now, nothing is happening," answered Captain Carter. Casey again, "And what about Inglewood and the others? Are the towns and Sheriff notified and in on this?" "Aaah, no," stammered Bock, "we don't know who we can trust in the other jurisdictions, and as long as the Mob doesn't know what we know we can stay ahead of them. Also, we do not want to jeopardize our sources. Now as far as the County area, the Chief has been in contact with the Sheriff. He is good with letting us handle it, and, of course, they will jump in when and if needed. But be advised that only the Sheriff is included at this point." "So far as we know," Casey offered. "So far as we know," affirmed Bock.

The Chief added, "Teel, we don't know each other. Your assignment was based on recommendations, and of course your background. Judging from your questions here, I feel confident we have the right man for the job." "Thank you sir, but I do have one more question." Looking at the group generally, Casey inquired about specifics of the current game plan. Ron offered, "Well, Charlie and I are heading a team of six officers. We split up and do surveillance on three known books or bosses. We'll stick with the same subjects for several days, and then let them go and watch three others. We're letting our snitches alone 'cause we're pretty confident they'll let us know if they are contacted. And to anticipate your next thought: to date we've seen nothing out of the ordinary." "Well thanks for reading my mind Ron," Casey chuckled, "that may come in handy sometime." The officer smiled as he leaned back in his chair.

Commander Bock asked, "Teel, do you have some other ideas on how to handle this?" "No sir, I definitely want to know more about what's going on before I attempt any changes." Getting up to depart, the Chief looked at Casey and nodded his head affirmatively, "Good for you Teel. I like that attitude." Casey formed a slight smile and nodded his head. Inside he was shouting, YES.

Casey asked to be updated on a daily basis. As requested, at least one of the surveillance team members would talk to him at the end of each day. All reports started with an open-palmed shrug followed by, "Nothing today Cap."

Monday afternoon and Ron Howard walked into Casey's office. Before either could speak, Charlie and two of the other surveillance team members walked in behind Ron. Casey stood and exclaimed, "Oh, Oh."

Ron replied, "Yeah Oh, Oh." Everyone continued standing as Ron continued, "We got a call from one of our snitches this morning. He said he had someone he wanted us to talk to. He wanted us to come to his apartment as soon as we could. Now Cap, we would have contacted you first, but you need to know this snitch. He's the only one I know that talks more than Charlie, and he's always got some big deal going that usually turns out to be nothing." Casey interrupted, “That’s OK, I’m glad that you’re thinking in terms of keeping me informed.”

Ron pulled a small notebook from his pocket and opening it continued, “Yes sir. Anyway, we went to his place, and there was a man there.” Consulting the notebook Ron continued, “He gave his name as Dante Gaetano. He’s about 35, medium height and build. He was casually dressed, but it looked like his clothes were tailored. Anyway, he looked familiar. Charlie and I both believe we’ve seen him before, but we’re sure we haven’t had any real contact. The snitch said that he’s a regular player, so he knows a lot of the books in that part of Town.” “You’re talking about the west side?” Casey asked. “Yeah, this is actually in Inglewood, but yes, West L.A.”

Charlie couldn’t keep quiet any longer, so he took over, “Dante said that he was approached by the mob.” “And he knows the mob, how?” Casey interjected. Charlie answered, “Well it seems pretty real from what they wanted. Somehow they found out that he knows a lot of the books and bosses, so they wanted to make him a deal he couldn’t refuse. Apparently they really got into his face. They wanted names, contact information, addresses, all that stuff about all the books and bosses in the area. In exchange they said they would give him a collection route when their company has all the locations organized.”

Casey showed a thoughtful look then observed, “I assume they also offered consequences if he didn’t cooperate?” “Oh yeah.” Charlie smirked, “he didn’t say exactly what they said would happen, but apparently it was made clear that his health was in jeopardy if he refused.” “And what does he want from us?” Charlie looked at Ron then answered, “He said he wants to give them the list they want, but he’ll help make it so we can set up surveillance and identify the guys. He said if we lean on ’em, rough them up a bit, they’ll decide it’s not worth the hassle since the cops are on to them. He thinks they’ll go somewhere else; maybe San Diego or Orange County.”

“Bull shit,” Casey exclaimed, which caused Ron and Charlie to stand up straight and raise their eyebrows. Casey continuing, “He knows they’d figure he fingered ’em and would probably kill him.” “That’s right,” Ron acknowledged, “but he figures that if he gets taken in and pushed around with the others, they’ll figure one of the books was responsible. In fact, he’ll tell them that he suspects one of the bosses. After that he'll take off for Florida. He's got a brother there and he figures there wouldn't be anything suspicious about him leaving town after getting harassed by the cops." "I don't know. Still sounds fish. I mean, why does he want to involve us? Why not just go along with them?"

Charlie leaned back and put his hands together in front of him. "You know Cap, I do believe him when he said his life wouldn't be worth much if he simply went along with them. He would always be a liability. He's not a sworn member of their organization. He could get scared and weasel out at any time. Then he'd be a loose end who knows too much. He's pretty sure he'd get his concrete slippers soon after things were set up." Casey thought a moment, shaking his head affirmatively, "Yeah, that does make sense. He's damned if he does, and damned if he doesn't." "That's right," Charlie added.

"Who is this guy, Gaetano?" Casey asked. Ron took over, "We checked his local record, and he has been busted; once for gambling, and once for bookmaking. A few traffic violations turned up, but that's it. The tickets were LAPD, but both arrests were by the Lennox Sheriffs. His real first name is Daniel. Apparently he sort of unofficially changed his name to Dante. Makes him sound more Italian; more like a real gangster. Well, he's no gangster, but I'd bet he's been a local player for a long time. He probably even fills in in some back offices when needed. So he's the perfect person for out-of-towners to get with to have a one-source directory for local books." "Yeah," Charlie jumped in, "plus he's expendable when he's no longer needed."

Casey motioned for the group to sit, and turned and sat on the front of his desk facing them. "So have you checked with Lennox to see if they have anything further?" Ron answered, "We have a team in Sheriff's Vice that we work with a lot. They didn't have anything more on Gaetano, past his arrest record. His address is in Hawthorne; an apartment. There's nothing significant there. We haven't had time to do much more." "Yes, well, my only concern is that the mob might place a guy like this with us just to see what we know and what we're doing. After that last guy got rousted by the uniforms, they must be a little suspicious." Casey mused.

Charlie jumped in, "I think we're good in that regard so far. We didn't say anything about what we're up to. We listened to him and told him we'd get back to him. That's what we would have done even if we knew nothing about what was going on." Casey pondered a moment then, "Yeah, OK." Charlie continued, "We assume the snitch told Gaetano that he's told us about the mob contacts, but so far we've left the snitch with the impression that we're just filing away the information, but that we're not really doing anything about it. We certainly haven't let on that the Department Command is involved." Casey stroked his chin and pursed his lips, "Good. Sounds like you're playing this just right. So now, what are your plans?"

Ron started to respond but Charlie started to override him, which drew an exasperated look from Ron, but he deferred to Charlie, "Pretty simple, actually. We've arranged to call Gaetano at a pay phone in the West LA area. It's inside an office-building lobby but out of sight. He should feel pretty secure there. Anyway, we'll tell him to make the list and to go ahead with his contact and arrange to deliver it. We'll tail him and pounce on the goons. That should send a strong message."

Casey got up and walked over to his office window. He stood looking out for a few moments. The officers looked at the Captain then at each other and shrugged their shoulders. Casey turned and spoke, "That's not good enough." "Sir?" came from Ron and Charlie simultaneously. "Gaetano will just be delivering to some runners. We need to get higher up in the organization. If we're to send a message, and be successful, we need to pounce on more than just a couple of foot soldiers."

Ron and Charlie shrugged their shoulders as they glanced at each other. Looking back at Casey Ron asked, "So what's your idea Cap?" 'Well first, let me tell you a bit about my style. I'm the newcomer here and I will not try to take over the operation. You guys know what will and what won't work. But, let me run this by ya. How about if you go ahead and set things up as you have planned. Then just before he meets with the goons, you guys pull off. Tell Gaetano that an emergency has come up and your CO needs you to do something. It needs to be something good. A kidnapping, that's it." "Sir?" Charlie inquired. "Tell him there was a kidnapping and a body exchange ready to go down any minute. The Department needs some undercover guys to be at the scene, and you're the most available."

"What about Gaetano?" Ron asked.

Casey offered, "Tell him to go ahead and meet with the mob guys. Hell, they won't be doing anything but taking the information and leaving. Tell him to hold just a few names back. He can say he's still getting some names and that he can have the rest of the list for them in a couple of days. They're not in an all-fired big hurry. I don't think they'll give him a hard time about that."

Ron acknowledged, "No, I don't think it will be a big deal for him to put them off a bit, but to what end?"

Casey got up, walked over to Ron, smiling and patting him on the shoulder, "Well now son, I'm glad you asked that." They all smiled, as Casey was thus able to stymie some of the tension that was building. Casey knelt down amidst the seated officers. "This is where your expertise will be utilized. You will in fact show up at the first meet, unbeknownst to the participants, of course. Tail the goons, get license numbers, etc. We'll want everything we can get on them. I bet the Chief will give us some extra people so that we can watch these guys day and night; even one of those new choppers. Ultimately they'll be meeting with the follow-up goons, and hopefully at least one ranking lieutenant will appear. Then. Then we pounce."

Casey got up and walked back to behind his desk. Sitting he continued, "We won't exactly be taking down the Mafia, but it'll send a loud message." "And Gaetano?" Charlie asked. "As far as Gaetano? I suggest we just string him along. He may or may not be of further use. But let's keep him close by. Buy him a couple of drinks; dinner, whatever." Ron looked at Charlie and they shrugged and nodded approvingly. But Charlie offered, "I think he's not going to want any more contact with us than necessary. He's really gun shy of the mob." "As well he should be," Casey replied. "As well he should be," agreed Charlie.

Casey looked from man to man then concluded, "You understand these are not orders. If you think something else will get the job done . . . . Even if you go with this, if you find that you need to make changes; take a different tack, you go with your gut."

All officers looked at each other for a moment, then Charlie delivered, "No, Cap. That sounds good as a general plan. Of course, we'll have to improvise along the way, depending on what we run into."

Casey looked directly at Ron, then at Charlie. "That's right. I do want to be informed as much as possible, but you will be making decisions in the field, and I've got your back. If something doesn't work; if something goes wrong, well we just jump in and fix it. We won't waste time trying to blame someone." Casey again looked directly at each officer.

Ron said, "Thanks, Cap. It's a whole lot easier to work when you know you're trusted and you can improvise without having to get every detail cleared."

"Of course," Casey remarked, rising to his feet.

Charlie added with an inquisitive smile, "You know, Captain Teel, one might think you've done this type of work before." Casey smiled but said nothing. In fact, there was an awkward silence while Casey just stared into space for a few moments. Visions of Paris, taverns, old narrow streets, yes even Marie, raced through his mind like a high-speed black and white newsreel.

Casey regained his composure and dismissed the officers. As they departed his office he thought, *Oh God I hope they don't screw up.*

Casey made an appointment and met with Commander Bock. He laid out the plans he and his crew worked up. He was not surprised that the Commander went along with everything. But Casey was surprised some time later when Bock reported back to him regarding his subsequent meeting with the Chief. Bock was given a free hand to divert undercover units to the operation, specifically the "meet", as well as the pledge of a helicopter. "That eye in the sky will really help us avoid burning a tail," Casey advised Bock.

Charlie used the cold phone in the squad room to make the call. A group, including Casey, huddled around. After shushing the group, Charlie dialed and then spoke, "One ringy dingy, two ringy dingy, three ringy . . . Yeah who's this? OK Dante do you have your names?" Charlie talked for several minutes, arranging with Gaetano for the officers to set up their tail.

Charlie concluded the conversation with, "Now where are you supposed to meet these guys . . . . We really need to know if we're going to do this right . . . . OK, well see you tomorrow."

Charlie hung up and surveying the group around him. "Smart bastard. He wouldn't tell me where he's supposed to meet the thugs. You'd think he doesn't trust us." Charlie put his open hand to his chest and donned a look of incredulity.

Casey chimed in, "He's afraid we'll take these guys down without taking him too."

Ron said, "Yeah, that would leave him hanging."

Casey and Lieutenant Brogan took a car and went to the area where the meet with Gaetano was to take place. They stayed well out of the immediate area, but monitored all activities via the tactical radio. They figured that if it became necessary for another cold car to join the tail for a few blocks, they'd be available. That didn't happen, and they returned to the office well before the operation concluded.

Casey, Brogan, and Commander Bock were in Casey's office when the first officers returned. Ron was among them, and went straight into that office. The supervisors sat quietly, but with anxiety written all over their faces. Ron kind of played with that, as he pulled up a chair and slowly got comfortable.

Ron related the events: They met with Gaetano, telling him how they had to pull off, and giving him instructions. He wasn't happy, but ultimately went along with the plan. He was subsequently tailed to a restaurant not far from Hollywood Park. A couple of undercover officers who Gaetano had not seen went inside and saw the contacts. They verified that Gaetano did pass some material to one of the men. That information was relayed to undercover units outside when one of the officers went to the restaurant pay phone and feigned an argumentative call home. Those officers stayed put long after Gaetano and his two contacts left. The two subjects appeared to be Mafia thugs right out of an Untouchables TV series. They were tailed to where they are apparently staying at a motel not far from LAX. The rental car agency where they got their wheels provided some good ID for the men. Ron advised, "We're running that down now. It's probably phony ID, but with help from Detroit, we can probably cross-reference the names. We do know they flew in from Detroit last night. We will have at least three units on them at all times, except when we're sure they're sleeping, then we'll have two units present."

Ron stood and looked around for questions. There being none, Casey thanked him and he departed. Commander Bock was the first to comment. "I'm impressed. Almost sounds like it was too easy."

Casey leaned forward and proclaimed, "You know, Commander, there's a reason these guys get assigned to this Division."

Bock smiled and nodded. "Indeed, indeed."

It was less than a week when the chips started to fall in place. Gaetano was anxious to complete the plan of getting he and the mob contacts arrested. Ron and Charlie continued to put him off, but promising, "Soon, soon."

Two bookies, one from West L.A. and one from the Crenshaw area contacted the Unit and reported that they had been contacted, visited, and leaned on by two men. Surveillance units reported at least three other bookies have had visits from apparent gangsters. Also, two more men checked into the motel, and were in constant contact with the original two subjects. Identification and background checks of these men were underway.

Casey called a squad meeting for the next morning, to which he had asked an Assistant District Attorney to attend. Commander Bock and the Chief of Police also showed up. The reason for the meeting was to identify the most probable scenarios as to how the mob would force their hand, and determine what laws will be applicable for taking them down.

To date, it appears that all books have resisted, or at least refused to join the organization. It is possible that some have joined, but there is no evidence of that. Since Mafioso's are not known for taking "No" for an answer, the consensus is that they will now start applying muscle. Roughing up a few books will send a message that can be further conveyed to others just by the presence of muscle. "Now is the time to really keep our ears to the ground," cautioned Casey.

Commander Bock was the first to query the DA. "Bill, you've been briefed on what's going down, so what do ya think; what violations can we hang our hat on?"

Bill Box, the only one in the room dressed in coat and tie, leaned back and stroked his neat graying beard with his right index finger. "OK. May I assume you know that the goons will have to do more than you should allow before we can anticipate convicting them of anything substantive?"

Not waiting for a response he continued, "I assume you want to make a legal arrest, and anticipate that they will get the message and just leave town? You're not interested in pursuing prosecutions and convictions?"

Casey's eyes opened wide as he leaned back and replied, "Wow, sounds like you've got some experience in these matters."

Box smiled and answered, "Intelligence Division. I passed the BAR, quit the Department, and went to the DA's Office a couple years before the collapse. I've had a dealing or two with these Eastern thugs."

The Chief chimed in, "Bill, for the record, we do anticipate prosecutions and convictions."

"Right", Box replied with a knowing smirk.

"Well anyway, to answer your question," Box continued, "with all your surveillance and information from established reliable informants; I assume they are so established?"

Ron said, "Not everyone we've talked to have been established, but yes, much of what we have has come from registered reliable informants."

Looking directly at Ron, Box persisted, "And you are constantly documenting your surveillance contacts, as well as the statements?"

"Of course," Ron replied firmly.

"Then we can always use good ole' conspiracy. That could be rough to prosecute, beyond a reasonable doubt, but certainly there is enough probable cause for you to be comfortable making arrests."

Appearing like bobble-head dolls in a car window, the officers looked around the room at each other and nodded affirmatively. Commander Bock spoke first. "OK then. Let's move on this. Teel, what's your plan?"

Casey stood up and leaned against a wall. He addressed all, but was looking at the Chief and the Commander. "Starting immediately, we'll give our full attention to the goons. Fortunately, they're making it rather easy, 'cause so far they're all staying at the same motel. We'll set up as many tail units as possible, so we don't get burned, and we'll not let these guys out of our sight. We're pretty confident they're ready to start some serious knee cracking. We can take 'em down as soon as they start roughing up a book." Casey paused, but no one else spoke.

Casey continued, "We've documented visits by these guys to enough books, plus we have a lot of statements, all of which should easily establish conspiracy." DA Box nodded affirmatively, his eyes on the Chief and the Commander.

The Chief wrinkled his brow and with a concerned look asked, "What about the bookie. Doesn't seem like you can show your hand before they start wailing on him?"

Casey's head was down slightly and he looked toward the Chief through his raised eyebrows, "Well, sir, there are some risks associated with breaking the law." All faces grew serious expressions, until the Chief began to nod and chuckle, then all present smiled in agreement.

Getting up to leave, the Chief offered, "Teel, I've been asked to free the helicopter from your call, but you can continue to have it. But keep me informed. If nothing happens within a few days, I'll have to consider taking it away."

"Understood," acknowledged Casey.

"Otherwise, you can have the other plain clothes units 'till this resolves."

Casey thanked the Chief, who left with a departing thought, "I do not want the Mafia setting up shop in this city." With that, the meeting broke up.

The next day, Casey was at his desk, and reached into a drawer to pull out his brown bag lunch. He was sticking close to the office for nine to ten hours everyday, which included eating lunch in. *I'm really eating better with Maria's packed lunches than I would otherwise,* he mused.

Casey was opening the lunch bag that he placed on the center of his desk when Ron and Charlie barged into the office. Keeping his right hand in the bag, Casey looked at the officers and said, "This can't be good."

Ron and Charlie started to speak simultaneously, but Charlie soon took over. "The overnight guys came in from the motel a little bit ago. They said a new guy showed up there this morning. He was about 6 feet, medium build, and dressed Capone."

"Like who?" Casey asked, now setting back into his chair.

"He looked like a boss. He had a black shirt and a black leather jacket."

"OK, and so?"

Ron picked it up, "He went into one of the guy's room, and the others joined them from their rooms. He stayed a couple of hours then left."

Casey thought a second. "So what do we have on him?"

Charlie shrugged. "Well you see Cap, that's a problem. The guy was obviously wary. He must have parked down the street and walked to the motel. When he left, our guys didn't want to leave, in case the others took off, but one of the guys did try to tail him. But he didn't want to get too close, and just saw him drive away. He was in a non-descript sedan, probably a rental."

"That's it?"

"Yes, sir, that's it."

Casey motioned for the officers to sit, then asked, "So what do ya think?"

Charlie looked at Ron then back at Casey, "The guy's good. He must have suspected the possibility of a tail so he did what he needed to avert it." Ron continued, "Yeah, we think this is the boss; some lieutenant no doubt, who's here to sign the contracts, so to speak." Casey nodded affirmatively. "Anyway, he's not here for sightseeing. They'll start moving right away so they can wrap things up and he can go back home and report to his boss."

Casey added, "I agree. So do you think he suspects we're watching them?"

Ron took this one. "Not necessarily. He'd use evasive tactics no matter what. Yeah, he may suspect that we're watching them, but he may suspect the possibility that some of the back offices have gotten together and hired some thugs."

Charlie offered, "Our tails are set up with so many units that they're not going to make us. And the chopper really seals that."

Casey paced for a few seconds while Ron and Charlie watched silently. Finally, "OK, let's mobilize. Round the clock. Let's schedule units to pick up tails of these guys whenever they move, day or night."

"Will do, Cap, but they'll probably hit during the day when the books are working. At night the bookies may have family around, friends calling, whatever."

"Agreed," Casey added, "but let's still have people on the scene all night."

All involved officers were notified that any days off were cancelled and surveillance schedules were drawn up. Sit, wait, watch, and listen were the orders of the day. All activity and radio traffic stopped as everyone took their places. Silent anticipation prevailed throughout the Unit as they waited for some movement from the motel.

CHAPTER 24

Not In My Town

Officers Rob Carter and Chuck Hurd were alternately pushing each other away from the mounted spyglass, giggling like two boys fighting over a *National Geographic* featuring photos of African tribes. They were in a motel room across the center parking lot from the rooms occupied by the Detroit men. The scope, however, was trained on another unit window with the shade opened enough to afford a view of much of the interior. A woman in her early fifties was visible and was slowly dressing, apparently unaware of the open shade, but in reality probably well aware of it. She was a bleached blond wearing too much makeup, with medically enhanced breasts, which she seemed to be proud of.

The officers' frivolous mood stopped abruptly, as Carter exclaimed, "Oh, Oh."

"What?" Hurd asked.

Carter just nodded toward the center parking lot. One of the men they were supposed to be watching was just getting into his rental car. Hurd quickly picked up the radio and opened the tactical channel.

Ron Howard had just reentered the squad room holding his newly poured first cup of coffee. Hearing the crackling of the radio, he immediately put down his drink and sat at the radio table. He acknowledged the page, then heard Hurd, "We have movement." Harter paused a moment but realized that message was incomplete, "One of the guys from unit A just got into their car and is pulling out of the driveway."

"We've got it," came a message from one of the tail units in the area. "Pete, let us know which way he goes and we'll relieve you as soon as we can catch up."

"Roger that. And what about you, ole' blue, you awake?"

A third unit chimed in, "Ain't had our coffee yet, but we're witch cha'."

Ron was about to speak when he noticed Casey standing directly behind him. "Hold it," Casey snapped, "this sounds too much like a decoy. Or, it could just be a cigarette run. Tell the first two units to give a loose tail, and the rest need to hold tight."

Ron relayed the message, then a long silence quieted the radio. Ron retrieved his coffee, and Casey was holding his as they stood next to the radio, alternately staring at it and then at each other.

Finally the silence was broken. "Hold the phone. This is Pete. The guy's in McDonalds loading up on breakfasts."

Casey picked up the radio, "OK boys and girls, this is Teel. He's going back to the motel. Do a very loose tail to get him back home. Everyone, be ready for a busy day." Four units acknowledged the broadcast. The fourth being a unit just going on duty from Parker Center.

Casey put the mike down and addressed the group that had congregated in the area. "This is it," he stated emphatically.

"Sir?" Ron questioned.

Casey recounted, "They've always gone out for breakfast. Then they've made their rounds or just gone to the track. Watch. They'll all get together for a breakfast meeting. That means final plans for making a move."

Charlie was among the group that had gathered. He said, "Sounds like it, Cap. Want me to alert the chopper?"

"No, I'll call the watch commander there. Ron and Charlie, you coordinate things from here. The rest of you on the team, saddle up and get out there. Grab some snacks; we may be a while. Lieutenant Brogan, borrow a plain car from Central Vice. We'll go out when they start moving; you drive."

Ron, Charlie, Brogan and Casey never got far from the radio in the squad room for the next several hours. The surveillance unit reported that the breakfasts arrived, and the two men from unit B joined the food and other two in unit A.

The radio crackled again. “Oh shit! You there Ron?” Came a soft voice from one of the undercover units.

“Go ahead Pete, but we can barely hear you.”

“That’s ’cause I’m holding the mike in my lap. My partner got out to take a whiz and guess who just parked across the street?” Not waiting for an answer he continued, “It’s that boss guy. I’ve got the mike in my lap, and I’m pretending to look at a map. Shit I hope Pierce doesn’t walk back now.” A few moments of silence were ended with, “OK, he got out, lit a cigarette, looked around, now he’s walking toward the motel. He looked at me, but there are a number of people in the area going to work. He didn’t give me a second look.”

Casey took the mike. “This is Teel. As soon as your partner is back, move your position so he doesn’t see you again. You need to set yourself up as a parallel tail unit. Don’t get involved in the actual tail unless you have to.”

“Roger, Cap; understand.”

A few minutes later another message: “Ron this is Harter. That boss just went into the unit with the other guys. He doesn’t change his clothes a lot. Black turtle neck, black leather jacket.”

Charlie took the mike. “He’s got an image to uphold.”

“OK Charlie, roger that.” Casey instructed Ron to have the surveillance officers get something to eat after the group leaves the motel, but to stay on there until further notice.

All those in the squad room were milling about and frequently walking by the desk with the radio. They resembled a group of expectant fathers in the hospital waiting for the announcement of their offspring’s birth. An hour before noon their anticipation was fulfilled. “This is Carter; you there base?”

“Yeah, go ahead Rob.”

“I’d say this is it. Two of the guys are getting into their two cars, and the boss guy is walking back out to the street.”

“This is base to all units. You got the message. Anybody not ready to go?” Ron assumed the few seconds of silence that followed was a group negative reply.

Casey grabbed the microphone. “This is Teel. Just pick up the two goons’ cars. Let’s not get all spread out trying to follow the boss. Just be aware that he’s still in that gray Buick rental so he doesn’t burn you. He'll probably show up at one of the places the others are going, so watch for him, and for God's sake, avoid him." A few overlapping "Rogers" convinced Casey that his message got out. He literally pulled Brogan behind him as they quickly departed the office and headed for their borrowed car. Nearly running through the hallway, Casey thought, *damn I love this*.

As Casey and Brogan drove toward West LA they monitored the now busy tactical radio channel. There was an almost steady stream of traffic with units reporting picking up the tail, leaving the tail, paralleling the suspects, etc. At one point when there were a few moments of silence, Casey chimed in with a reminder for units to watch out for the gray Buick. It was obvious from the broadcasts that the two suspect vehicles were going to the same area or destination, though they stayed apart. They did use some evasive tactics, such as doing a 360 by going around a block, and weaving around some blocks, but these maneuvers were not frequent. They seemed to be motivated more by force of habit then a real sense of being followed. No unit reported seeing the Buick.

The entourage meandered through surface streets of West LA and Inglewood, and ultimately into the Baldwin Hills area. From chatter it was apparent that the two suspect cars were closing in on each other as they left the main artery of Slauson Avenue, and entered winding residential streets in the hills.

Overriding other broadcasts, Charlie interrupted from the base unit. "They're probably heading for Percy's place."

"Percy?" Casey asked Brogan.

The Lieutenant sighed and said, "He's got a busy book at his house. His house isn't far from the big boss he works for, plus he's trusted enough to handle a lot of back office business."

Casey thought for just a moment then exclaimed, "That's got to be it!" He grabbed the Mic. and firmly broadcast, "Any unit that knows where Percy's place is peal off and get set up there, that's where they're going."

"This is Pete and Pierce Cap, we're already there."

Casey looked at his driver, Brogan, who was smiling and looking back at him out the side of his eyes. Casey formed a disgusted yet proud look, "Smart ass cops. What the hell do they need me for?" Brogan looked back at the road, chuckling out loud.

The radio got very busy again as units assumed positions in the vicinity of Percy's house while the helicopter crew, flying higher than they are used to due to orders from Casey, were nonetheless able to bring both suspect cars in to parking places within a few doors of the target house.

Chatter continued. "This is Paul and Les, we've got a good position to view the house. We're just north backed into a driveway with a lot of bush cover."

Another unit asked, "So which one of you is involved with the bush?"

From base Ron broadcast, "Knock it off. Anyone seen the boss in the Buick?"

Several "no's" were heard.

"Strange," Casey muttered, "I'd a bet he'd be here with the others."

Paul came back on. "Two of the guys are moving toward Percy's. Now here come the other two." A few moments later he reported, "Three of them went inside, but one is staying out on the front porch."

Ron came on again. "Cummins and Glenn, you ready?"

"We're about a half block away. We're enroute now."

"Cummins; Glenn?" Casey asked, throwing a puzzled look at Brogan. The Lieutenant was in the process of parking in the alley, almost a full block from the entrance to the alley that runs behind Percy's house. When stopped he answered, "Those are the guys we borrowed from Central Vice. They usually work around skid row. Cummins really makes a good bum."

"So he'll approach the front while his partner tries to get in the back," Casey recapped from earlier plans.

"That's right. Ron and Charlie figured if they were going to rough up a bookie, they'd leave a lookout outside. Cummins will act like a drunk wanting to see his bookie friend. I figure if they shoo him away, he'll at least cause a distraction so his partner can get in, or a least see enough to get a violation. Hell, Charlie figures they'll probably just take him inside just to avoid the commotion outside."

Casey shook his head in acknowledgement, and then stated, "So these are the guys we have wired."

"Yeah, both Cummins and Glenn."

An almost eerie silence fell over the radio. Brogan and Casey sat silently, but with muscles tensed. Even the area seemed quiet; there was no foot or car traffic. Tension filled the air.

From their spot, Brogan and Casey could see all the way up the northbound alley to the east/west cross street. As the alley continued north on the other side of that street, it started a broad curve to the right. Percy's house was about half a block up that section of alley. Percy's alley entrance was around the curve and out of sight. Most back yards were fenced from the alley. Vines covered some of the chain-link fences, while others were bare, but in good shape. A few had broken gates and in need of general repair. Most houses had garages in the back yard. About half of those had entrances off the alley, while the rest had driveways from the street. Trash cans and even some old concrete incinerators were ubiquitous.

The radio crackled. "What's going on?" came an anxious voice query from Ron.

A quiet voice responded, "This is Les. Cummins is talking with the lookout. There's a vice cop hidden in each of the yards beside Percy's. Can't see Glenn. He must be in the back. As big as he is, you'd think."

"Roger that," Ron added.

Casey suddenly leaned forward in the passenger seat and elbowed Brogan. "Look at that," he said in a hushed but excited tone.

Brogan leaned forward and looking toward the end of the alley confirmed, "Yeah, that's the boss. What the hell is he doing?" The lone male figure, dressed in dark pants and shirt and black leather jacket, was on the cross street sidewalk approaching the connecting alley entrance. He stopped for a moment and looked around. Tossing a cigarette into the street, he turned northbound and walked slowly into the alley.

"Shit!" Casey exclaimed, "he's going to come up behind our guys." Brogan looked at Casey with a what now expression. Casey pursed his lips and looked at Brogan. After a brief moment he directed, "I'm going up there. Work your way up the alley in the car, but stay out of that guy's sight. Work up as far as you can. The shit's going to hit the fan." With that, Casey started to exit the car, but stopped with one leg out and one still in. Turning back toward the

Lieutenant, "Radio Les and let him know what's happening, but tell them to stay put." Turning back Casey exited and began working his way northbound through the alley. Dodging in and out of cover, he carefully avoided getting too close to the suspect, but stayed close enough to catch momentary glimpses of him. Brogan thought, *this ain't captain's work, but that's Teel.*

The man stopped again at the rear gate entrance to Percy's yard. Percy's garage was on the rear south portion of his lot, with drive-in entrance off the alley. The chain link fence ran north from the garage. The gate linked the fence and the garage. Casey took a position behind an unkempt bush just in time to see the man open the gate, enter the yard, and walk toward the house.

Doing his best cat imitation Casey quickly and silently slid up to the rear of the garage. His constant running and upper body conditioning had kept him in excellent physical shape. The garage door was a lightweight metal folding type with a strip of window about 5 ½ feet up from the floor. It was obviously not the original door, and it was also not locked. Peering in from a side of the window Casey got a good view inside. It was a large single car structure. A single car was parked in it, along with several piles of stuff that often end up in a garage. It was clear that there was nobody inside, unless they were hiding.

Casey leaned down and grasped the outside handle with his right hand. With his left he pushed in on the door gently, which allowed him to lift open the door without it rattling. He brought it up just enough to duck in underneath, and then holding it as he turned around he gently lowered it back down.

Inside Casey quickly moved to the access door, which was at the northeast end. A single window in the door looked out toward the rear of the house. As he quickly and carefully approached the window Casey drew his three-inch Colt .38 revolver from his leg holster. At first he saw nothing. Slowly he moved from the side of the window to look through it more directly. The thought of suddenly looking the boss square in the face through the window prompted Casey to concentrate every bit of his consciousness on his actions. As he moved, more of the rear yard and back of the house unfolded.

Fully in the window now, Casey could see most of the back of the house and all the yard up to the house. There was nothing moving.

Then he saw it. The back door, which was without a screen, was slightly ajar. Obviously someone has recently gone in there. It must be the boss, Casey thought. Scanning carefully again he hoped to see Glenn lurking somewhere. There was nothing.

Casey just started to open the door out to enter the yard when he froze. The black leather jacket appeared. Apparently he had been out of sight near the right side of the rear of the house. He was now coming into view as he walked toward the back door, which was in the approximate middle of the house. Casey stayed frozen in his position behind the slightly opened door. He reasoned that the man probably would not look back his way unless he detected some motion.

There was a small porch with rickety handrails, covered by an unsupported awning roof. The boss took the two steps up onto the porch, and then suddenly paused as he looked directly at the door. Obviously he saw what Casey had. The door was not shut tight. Using a stealthy maneuver the man peered into the door window. Casey slithered back into the garage, bringing the door closed behind him as he saw the man suddenly straighten up and move swiftly to the left out of the back door window area. Simultaneously the man drew a revolver from a shoulder holster under his jacket. It appeared to be a large caliber Smith and Wesson. He held it down on his right side as he repositioned himself to peer back into the side of the window.

Quickly Casey gathered his thoughts. He knew that Cummins had distracted the lookout in front. That would have kept that man from checking the back of the house. Since Glenn was nowhere in sight, it's most likely he was the one who went through that door, and he didn't want to make noise by closing it. Glenn is probably hiding where he can hear what's going on inside, but is visible from the back door. This was rather simple deduction, but absolutely correct.

It is embarrassing when a police supervisor blows an operation by prematurely taking action. That thought raced through Casey's mind, but was immediately replaced with the realization that this Mafioso had his gun out and intended to use it. If Glenn saw the man coming, a sudden move for his weapon would trigger a shooting, with Glenn at a clear disadvantage.

As the boss crouched and with his free hand slowly pushed the rear door open, Casey quickly emerged from the garage and squared up about 20 feet behind him. The man was in the middle of the doorway when Casey yelled, "Police, freeze, asshole." Johnny Tesoro spun around, gun hand extended at chest level. In an instant he was facing the athletic Captain who was slightly crouched with his weapon held two handed and aimed directly at him.

Tesoro aimed at Casey and quickly squeezed the trigger. Simultaneously Casey took a half step to his left and aiming slightly to the man's left he pulled the trigger. The action of quickly pulling the triggers caused both weapons to point slightly to the shooters' left as the rounds discharged.

It seemed like half the Department was in the Ad Vice squad room for the debriefing. It was very quiet, considering all the people there, as all eyes were watching the Captain's office door. The Chief of Police, Commander Bock, and Casey were encamped in that office. Most of the conversation there involved the command officers telling Casey why it's not a captain's role to take street action. When finished, all three rose and walked toward the door. The Chief stopped just as he started to reach for the door handle. He turned and walked directly up to Casey. He took Casey's right hand in his, and grabbing Casey's right shoulder with his left hand he pulled Casey close to him. Face to face, the Chief said softly, "You know nothing more is going to be said about your actions." Casey pursed his lips and shook his head affirmatively. The Chief concluded, "You're a helluva cop, Teel. A helluva man."

As the Chief led the way out into the squad room, Bock patted Casey on the shoulder and offered, "Casey, I couldn't agree more." Casey smiled a bit but resumed a sober expression as he entered the squad room.

The Homicide detective in charge of the shooting was standing among the small crowd that was watching the three emerging from Casey's office. The Chief walked directly up to him and said, "OK Bill, give me the short version."

The detective smiled and nodded his head. "Well, the deceased was a Mafia character from back east; his ID said Detroit. His name was Johnny Tesoro, but don't know much about him yet. There were no hits on his revolver. It probably isn't hot. He died because

Captain Teel knew and followed tactical shooting procedure. Tesoro did not. One slug right in the middle of the chest. Died before the ambulance crew could cart him off. Central officer Glenn was not aware of the suspect's presence until the Captain yelled for him to freeze. Glenn drew his weapon, but by that time the man was going down. He kept his weapon pointed at Tesoro until it was clear he wasn't moving. Glenn clearly was going to be Tesoro's target."

For a moment the Chief and the Detective looked silently at each other. Then the Chief said, "OK." Then looking over toward Lieutenant Brogan he directed, "So what about the rest of the story?"

Brogan was slumping on a desk. He stood up smartly nearly coming to attention and said, "That part went as planned Sir. Glenn did hear the three goons threaten Percy, the bookie, and then they smacked him around a bit. Nothing too heavy, but they did deliver clear physical threats. They had a lookout in front, but he was apprehended without incident. We've booked all four for conspiracy, trespass, assault, stupidity; everything we could think of."

The Chief signaled for Brogan to stop, then asked, "What about this Percy guy. Is he going to be willing to testify against the mob?"

"Well, sir, we really don't know, but most likely not. The suspects are bailing out as we speak, and we assume they'll be on the first flight out of LA. They've seen that organizing these guys here won't be a cake walk." The Chief cut Brogan short as he looked around the room. "All of you guys are to be commended. You accomplished what we wanted, except of course for the actions of your trigger-happy Captain."

Silence fell on the room. The scowling Chief looked at Casey. Suddenly his look turned into a smile as he gave Casey a "good job" nod. That brought smiles and pats on the back all around, as the Chief walked from the room with a happy gait. Casey stood up and looked after the Chief. His smile turned to a serious expression. He did not speak for a few seconds, and as others in the room noticed him, they too grew quiet. Casey looked around at the group, and then started slowly toward his office. Mumbling out loud enough for all to hear, "This isn't over yet. I feel it in my bones. This isn't over."

CHAPTER 25

Repercussions

Casey rolled off Maria onto his back. She pulled the sheet part way up their bodies as she moved to snuggled her head against his chest and extend her right arm along his left side. There was silence except for some lingering panting. Casey drew his arms up and folded them behind his head. "Penny," Maria offered softly.

"Well, you know," Casey uttered slowly, "I wish I smoked."

Maria slowly rolled her head so as to face him. "You what?" she asked, assuming an incredulous expression.

"I don't know. It just seems that slowly puffing on a stogie after sex would be the perfect finale."

Maria lifted her head higher, chuckling, "You mean, sort of like blowing the smoke from your pistol barrel after the duel?"

"Yeah, sort a like that."

Looking more serious, Maria continued, "Well blow the smoke from that hot rod of yours and get your butt out of bed. Sam will be here soon and I think you need to talk to her."

Moving to the side of the bed and reaching for his pants, Casey asked, "Now what? She wants to change majors again?"

Slipping into a robe, Maria said, "No, it's more serious then that; I think. Seems she's got some issues with your shooting that idiot."

Casey stopped and looked at Maria. "Issues?"

"Yes, she has a peacenik professor who's really pounding that all violence is bad and can be avoided."

Casey continued dressing and replied, "I see. OK."

Samantha chose a college close to home. UCLA is just a half-hour freeway trip away. She did beg to stay at a campus dorm, which Casey and Maria agreed to after her freshman year. So her home visits were always happy occasions, as though she were traveling great distances to return. This visit was no exception, even though she did show up with a duffle bag full of laundry. After they all shared a snack and happy catch-up conversation, Samantha gathered up her duffle bag and headed to the laundry room. She knew her mother's lack of enthusiasm for doing laundry, so she trotted off by herself without a word.

Casey helped Maria clean up after their snacks, and then drifted into the laundry room. He said nothing while he took a relaxed position sitting on the dryer, observing Samantha sorting clothes and placing some items into the washer.

"So you might have issues with my shooting?" Casey almost whispered.

Samantha stopped her sorting and stood up. "Mom's been talking to you."

Casey looked down and smiled, "Well, yeah, that's what we do. And you and I? We've always been able to talk rationally about things."

Samantha turned to face her dad squarely, "I know, Daddy. And I know you didn't have a choice in what happened. But . . . ." Casey interrupted, "but it was still a violent act."

"Daddy, I know it was self defense and all that."

Casey put a finger up signaling it was time to pause. He continued, "This isn't really about this one incident. Your professor has some strong opinions about war, huh?"

Samantha straightened up more and answered, "Yes, and I have to agree with a lot of what he says." Samantha kept her pose and braced for a retort.

But Casey simple replied, "And so do I. War is terribly destructive in terms of human lives and resources."

Samantha cocked her head and developed a puzzled look. Casey continued, "But you know, people who publicly proclaim those obvious facts in public, as if they are the only ones bright enough to see them, are really being condescending and elitist." Samantha wrinkled her eyebrows as her looked morphed from puzzlement to disbelief. "You know what else is like war?"

"What?" Samantha asked in a dubious tone.

"Disease. Disease is like war."

Samantha dropped her shoulders and smirked, "Oh Daddy."
"No, I'm serious. Think about it. Disease causes a great amount of human misery and death. And the cost of fighting disease; it's enormous." Samantha continued her doubting look but did not reply. "Sure, and you know it's true that the effects of disease can be greatly lessened by being proactive in battling it. We go to great lengths to avoid getting sick."

Samantha now assumed a knowing look as she said, "OK now, Daddy, that's not hardly the same thing as war."

"Sure it is. Did you know that in World War II in just one battle in Russia over a million people perished? Imagine that. Just one of literally thousands of battles. And think about the totality of the resources that were squandered in the war; the big ships sunk, cities bombed."

Samantha jumped in, "That's just the point. Think of all that, and for what. What was really accomplished in the end?"

"Exactly," Casey said pointedly.

Samantha's head went back some as she looked puzzled, having expected an argument.

Slowly and calmly Casey continued, "You know that when Hitler first came to power, Germany was virtually bankrupt and had no viable military. But he knew what he wanted to do and he started to build his army. That got to the point that it was a clear violation of the Treaty of Versailles. Hitler literally tore up that document, which was the assurance that Germany would not build another war machine."

Samantha, by now, had developed a sarcastic look and offered, "I know my history."

"OK, then have you considered that if the European powers, under the authority of that treaty had joined together and taken out a then ill-equipped German Army, and their Fuhrer, what that war would have looked like, as opposed to the War that did ultimately occur?" Casey raised his eyebrows as he looked directly at Samantha.

"Hmm," she murmured, "likely it would have been a pretty short war."

"Indeed," Casey said smiling, "but of course, those people who opposed war for any reason won out." He paused and reflected, then, "And look what happened. Like I said. It's a lot like disease. We all know how terrible it can be. We all are opposed to becoming a victim, but just being against disease is hardly going to keep it away. Often times a proactive response can save one a lot of grief."

"So just being against war is pretty simplistic," she reasoned.
"Yes, and not necessarily effective in avoiding it."

Samantha pondered for a few moments, then shot back, "But not all wars are proactive prevention. Some have been just about greed or expansion; that sort of thing."

"Absolutely," Casey agreed, "and indeed your professor is right to speak out against those." Samantha took on a very introspective expression. Casey slid down from the dryer and departing the room patted his daughter on the shoulder, saying, "Nice to have you home, sweetie."

She smiled and nodded her head, though obviously still deep in thought.

After taking two days off, Casey returned to his office. He was busy emptying his in-box when Brogan and Detective Bill Johnson entered. Casey looked up, motioned for the duo to sit down, then leaned back with a disgusted look on his face. "Damn this paperwork. I thought handling traffics in patrol was bad, but look at this mess; crap."

Brogan just smiled and offered, "Well Cap, that's why you get paid the big bucks."

"Yeah, right," was his reply, though he was looking at Bill.

Bill's facial expression indicated that he was not interested in light chatter. Casey nodded at Bill and asked, "What is it Bill?"

"Well, we have a lot more information about that Tesoro character."

"OK." Bill opened a note pad and referring to it, "Johnny Tesoro was indeed a lieutenant for an organization in Detroit. But he was more than that. He was the son-in-law of the boss himself. The

Detroit investigator I talked to thinks he was being groomed for the top job there when the boss man retires."

Brogan looked at Bill and quipped, "Seems Detroit owes Captain Teel a reward, huh?"

Bill forced a slight smile, then said, "Well maybe so, but they're a bit concerned. Seems the boss, a Tony something or other has now gone missing."

"Missing?" Casey asked.

"They say he might just have gone to Vegas, or maybe Phoenix just to get over his loss."

"Or?" Casey pushed.

"Or? Well, we don't know. Those guys aren't exactly noted for their sentimental and forgiving nature."

Casey ended the conversation and directed that he was going to set up a meeting with Commander Bock, Bill, and Bill's boss, Captain Tom Dwyer. By late that afternoon, Bock, Casey, Brogan, Bill, and Dwyer were assembled in the Commander's office. Bill repeated what he had related earlier.

Bock opened with, "I know these guys aren't usually taken to attacking cops for revenge. But I want us to assume a posture that anticipates just that. What do you think Tom?" Captain Dwyer was a veteran police manager who was well past minimum retirement age. He was a gruff spoken, rugged individual. Those traits belied the fact he had a masters degree in psychology from USC. Command officers frequently solicited his advice in police matters.

Tom stroked his chin once then looked at Bock, "I agree, Rudy. We need to anticipate the worst-case scenario. The first order of business will be to see if that Tony character shows up here."

Looking then at Casey, "I'd suggest putting a couple teams of Ad Vice guys beating the bushes." Looking then at Bill, "You're not doing much are you Bill?"

The detective shook his head and simultaneously taking an inventory of his huge open caseload, said, "No, Cap. As usual, I'm completely free."

"Atta boy, you can give them a hand."

A short silence was broken by Dwyer, "Anyone that can shoot as well as Casey did under pressure probably doesn't need a bodyguard, but," he said and hesitated while looking directly at Bock.

Bock took the cue. "The Chief will be back tomorrow. I'll talk to him about getting a couple of guys assigned to Casey."

Casey sat back and took a deep breath and said, "There's just something wrong with the idea of giving cops bodyguards every time they clash with some bad guys."

All eyes looked at Bill as he raised his hand as if he was in school, "Ah, Commander, I've got a suggestion." Bock nodded at Bill, who continued, "If they were planning to hit the Captain, and that's a big if, they'd want to do it in public. They sure aren't going to do anything near a police station. If they hit him in private, say at home or while visiting friends, they know they'd be stirring up a hornets' nest among cops everywhere. My advice would be to have the Captain tailed by undercover units whenever he's out and about."

Dwyer looked at Bill. "What do you mean by a big if?"

Bill sat back and brought his hands together as if praying. "Well, hitting a cop doesn't make them any money. It doesn't win them any turf. It just buys them a lot of attention and grief, particularly when the officer is a respected manager."

For the next several minutes the group discussed the matter of Casey's security. It was decided that an undercover unit would be requested to escort the Captain to and from work, and whenever he went out. Casey did insist that he wanted them to be mostly out of sight. He offered that by always knowing where he is going they could lead, follow, or run parallel. Casey concluded that his wife would be apprised of what is going on, but his daughter would not be told. He acknowledged that she is seldom in the car with him, but if she ever were he would be most unhappy if she made the tail.

Four weeks later Casey went to Commander Bock's office. Casey got right to the point, "Rudy, you know, I think this escort service business has gone far enough." Bock thought for a moment then, "Any word on that Detroit boss's whereabouts?"

"No. Nothing here. Bill recently talked to Detroit and they still haven't seen him. He ran this whole hit business by them and they really don't think that will happen. They said that's not their MO.

Plus, these guys have the patience of loan sharks. If something was going to happen, it would have."

Bock got up and went to his coffee maker. "Cup a Joe?" Casey declined, and then repeated his request to abandon the escort.

Thinking in silence about the request, Bock poured his coffee and returned to his chair. "I just have an uneasy feeling about this Casey. Tesoro's body being picked up by that phony corporation. They're storing the body and not releasing it for burial. I don't know. It just doesn't feel right."

Casey cocked his head, but did not reply. After taking a sip from his cup, Bock relented, "OK. I guess we do need to close the book on this. I'll pull the tail immediately."

Casey smiled as he got up to leave. "Hey, after living through landing in France at night in a small plane behind German lines; how could anything bad happen now?"

Bock smiled and shook his head in acknowledgement.

When Casey returned to his office, Brogan and Bill were there waiting for him. "To what do I owe this honor?" Casey quipped.

"Bill has some more information about your victim," Brogan said. "Yeah, Cap, that Detroit detective called again. Tesoro wasn't the Boss's son-in-law. He was his son. Tony emigrated from Italy after the War, got married, and had the kid, Johnny. When he got here he changed his last name to Tesoro. Seems he had some war past that he wanted to escape."

"Interesting," Casey pondered. "So what was his real last name?"

Bill shook his head, "He didn't give me that."

"You said he got married here. That means he didn't come here with a wife?" Bill looked at his notes, "Ahh, well, he didn't say anything about that."

Casey sat back. Bill and Brogan got up to leave. They both looked back as they reached the door and noted that Casey was staring into space with a strange expression on his face. They glanced at each other as they walked out the door. Stopping in the hallway, Bill asked, "What do ya think Lieutenant?"

Brogan cocked his head and developed a curious expression, "Somethin's pulled his chain."

CHAPTER 26

Revenge

Sandor sat at the wheel of the large telephone company repair truck. He was parked on a hill a hundred feet above Summer Oak Drive, a mid-western looking residential street in Tarzana.

Sandor's three companions were garbed in baggy coveralls and all were busy working in an underground telephone cable tunnel.

"Anything yet, Sandor?" asked Ice Pick, walking up to the truck cab.

"Not yet, but its 8:15 so he should be leaving any minute now."

"I wish the son-of-a-bitch would hurry up," Ice Pick said, scowling.

Sandor's gray eyes narrowed. "Relax he-man, all we have to worry about is the gimpy broad."

Ice Pick broke eye contact, picked up a roll of cable, and strutted toward the manhole.

At 8:17 a tall man in a dark pin-stripped suit opened the front door at 18827 Summer Oak. As if on cue, his wife appeared in the doorway as he stepped out, and he turned to embrace her. They spoke for another minute. As was the case every morning for the past three days, the man seemed reluctant to leave. After another quick embrace and kiss, he got into a four-door gray ford and backed out of the driveway.

Sandor looked at his watch and added 39 minutes to 8:19. He had timed the man in the pin-stripped suit five times. Sandor knew that it takes the Captain an average of 39 minutes to drive from Sunny Oak Drive to Parker Center in Downtown Los Angeles.

At 8:58 Sandor eased his bulky frame from the truck cab, stooped down by the manhole and called quietly, "Time to go".

Ice Pick, Nickel, and Shade left tools, wire, and cable where they lay at the bottom of the tunnel. They carefully picked up cigarette butts, empty pop cans, and placed them in a plastic bag that was later dumped in a super market dumpster. The heavy gloves they all wore negated the possibility of latent prints to haunt them. Ice Pick used a pair of large wire cutters to sever nine cables that were marked with black tape.

The four men entered the truck and drove three blocks toward a hairpin turn that would bring them down to Summer Oak Drive; they parked at 18827.

Sandor walked to the rear of the truck, and in the manner of a basketball coach he quickly instructed, "O.K. Nickel, let's do it. You two know what to do."

While Nickel rang the doorbell at 18827, Shade and Ice Pick busied themselves unrolling a large spool of telephone wire on the sidewalk.

The woman seen earlier walked toward the door. Attractive, in her early 50's, she countenanced a rare blend of femininity and assertiveness, in spite of having a definite limp. Looking through the peephole in the door, the woman observed the caller to be an apparent workman dressed in blue coveralls with a telephone company insignia sewn above his left breast pocket. A smaller patch, "Bob" appeared above his right pocket. Keeping the chain on, Maria Teel opened the door and smugly asked, "Bob, what may I do for you?"

Nickel broke into a rueful grin, "I hate to trouble you, ma'am", he said, stumbling with his words, then looking at a clipboard said, "This is 18827, so you must be Mrs. Teel."

Maria said nothing, but raised her eyebrows a bit in anticipation of further explanations.

Nickel continued, "It seems that some water got into the cable tunnel up the street and we need to see which telephones were affected. Would you mind checking your phone for me? If you would just lift the receiver and see if you've got a dial tone."

Maria looked at the other repairmen unrolling telephone wire. An apparent foreman, who was half way up her entry walk, was giving directions to the other men. At that moment, Maria felt a twinge of uneasiness about the situation.

Brushing aside that feeling, she smiled and gingerly told "Bob," "Sure, I'll be glad to." Nickel heard the bolt click into place after Maria closed the door. Careful broad, he thought, as he walked toward Sandor.

"She ain't gonna open the door, she's gonna keep the goddamn chain on."

"Shit! All right, when she comes back, stick your foot or something in the door and I'll start from here and bust the bastard open." Sandor shrugged, "Why the hell couldn't she be stupid like those two in Detroit?"

Nickel nodded in agreement, turned the corner of his mouth up, and walked back to the door with his boyish, reassuring smile.

Maria checked the two downstairs phones and heard nothing. Now she felt a bit silly for having felt apprehensive before. She recalled that three days ago a telephone company truck appeared on the street above their house, and Casey had called one of his contacts at the phone company and verified that the truck and crew were legitimate. What Maria and Casey didn't know was that Ice Pick had previously sabotaged wires and switches giving legitimate repairmen a one or two day job mending the damage. On the morning of the third day, this day, Sandor and the others had waylaid the regular crewmen in the rear parking lot of their before-work breakfast spot. The telephone company employees were now bound, gagged, and drugged, and stashed under a tarpaulin in the rear of the truck. Their assailants hid their identities during the abduction by wearing ski masks and by talking with black ghetto accents.

Maria returned and opened the door, keeping the chain in place. Nickel stood in the doorway in an attempt to block her view of Sandor, who was running toward the door. The screen worked momentarily, but before Sandor reached his destination, Maria caught his charge. She immediately tried to slam the door, but Nickel quickly inserted his clipboard in front of the doorframe near the lock recess. The move worked, as the door failed to catch as it slammed against the clipboard. As if rehearsed, Sandor's bulk crashed against the door at that precise moment. The sturdy screws holding the chain were no match for the force; the door flew open.

The door caught Maria flat footed, and slammed her to the floor, stunned. Nickel and Shade dashed into the house and fanned out. Ice Pick remained outside as a lookout, pretending to work on a snarled cable. Sandor stood by Maria.

Samantha Teel was sitting at the kitchen table. She was quietly enjoying a breakfast of bacon, eggs, and a croissant. The crashing noise from the front door harshly broke the silence in the kitchen, causing Samantha to instinctively jump to her feet. Her chair fell over backward as she bolted toward the front of the house. Rounding a corner, she ran head on into Nickel. Perhaps the shock, as much as the physical force, knocked him backward to the floor. Shouting for her mom, Samantha stumbled but continued on. As though he was a defensive lineman, Nickel grabbed her ankle as she went by, sending her to the floor.

"Shade," he yelled, "help me with this bitch!"

Shade ran from the area of the master bedroom and grabbed Samantha's flailing arms. He went down to his knees, but kept a sort of bear hug around Samantha's arms and waist. His head was facing down and against her body. His grimace evidenced the extent of her struggles.

Maria regained her composure and saw the two men fighting with her daughter, who had almost gotten into the front room. Sandor, who was paying attention to the scuffle, was unable to stop Maria from bolting from the floor. He pursued her, but stopped as Maria ran past the altercation toward the rear of the house. Sandor thought, what a crazy broad, she didn't even stop to help the girl.

As if taking out his frustration, Sandor slugged Samantha on the side of her head, knocking her unconscious. Her limp body slumped over Nickel, as an exhausted shade rose from his knees beside them.

The scene seemed to slip into slow motion as Maria reappeared, charging the group. She was wielding a heavy nine-inch butcher knife. Her limp broadened her stance, making her appear larger than she was. Maria came up behind Shade, and plunged the blade into his back. She immediately jerked it out and started toward Sandor.

With unconscious vengeance, she stepped on Nickel's hands as she proceeded.

Sandor, who was back pedaling, in near shock, nervously produced a silenced .22 nine shot revolver. He pulled the trigger until all he heard were clicks.

Seven of the nine hollow-point bullets struck Maria's mid section, knocking her back against a wall. Befitting her nature, Maria called up enough energy for a last act of defiance. She rifled the knife at Sandor. The blade cut through his work shoe and severely penetrated his foot.

An eerie silence followed Sandor's scream of agony.

After an eternity, but actually only ten seconds, Nickel, blood streaming from his nose, broke the silence, "Shit!"

Sandor pulled the knife from his shoe, sat down on the floor, and surveyed the carnage before him. Maria lay next to the wall. Blood was oozing from everywhere. Shade was sitting on the floor, his back against a wall. His face was pasty gray and a band of sweat appeared on his upper lip and forehead. Several large drops of perspiration ran down into his left eye. He began blinking furiously. His breathing became labored

Nickel looked around and said to no one in particular, "I'm glad we didn't run into any real tough guys. What now, my love?"

Sandor had been thinking of that very question. His employer ordered Maria Teel kidnapped. Now all they had was a corpse. His employer is not usually enamored with failure. He thought also of the daughter. They saw her depart yesterday and assumed she had gone back to school.

Sandor looked down at the unconscious 17-year-old. "Mr. Wonder, wipe your face and tell Ice Pick to bring in the tarps those phone guys are in."

"What for?"

"Just once in your short . . . . god damn this hurts . . . . stupid life do what I tell you to do."

Nickel looked at Sandor's eyes and headed for the front door. He had Ice Pick move the truck up the driveway to the side of the house, where it was mostly out of sight of the street. Nickel then went back inside. They followed Sandor's next instruction and rolled up the kid in the canvas and carried her to the truck.

Sandor asked Shade if he could walk out OK. Shade was conscious, but appeared to be in a stupor. "I'll try," he half whispered.

Ice Pick returned and helped Shade to his feet and they proceeded outside as if in a three-legged race. Shade fell into the truck, with the help of a shove.

As the group drove off, Samantha started coming to. Sandor gave her a shot of a sleep-inducing drug. He told Ice Pick, "If she wakes up in less than eight hours, she's a better man than you."

The whole episode took seven minutes.

As they drove, Sandor ordered silence while he thought. The cops only had two samples of blood to check. The blood from his wound was still not leaking from his boot. The hollow point slugs from the revolver probably were too flattened to identify. Out loud he mumbled, "No sense crying over a screw up, once it's done, it's done."

The pain in Sandor's left foot was agonizing. That pain was not the worst of Sandor's troubles. The boss is a very difficult man to deal with. His reputation did not include compassion. Nickel warned, "Tony's got the patience of a loan shark."

CHAPTER 27

Ransom: The Setup

Casey, the Chief, Bock, Brogan, and Bill Johnson were standing around Casey's desk looking at a document there as if it were a newborn baby. Brogan broke the silence. "Apparently it was delivered here with the rest of the mail."

Casey confirmed, "Yeah, it was in my in-box with a half dozen other envelopes." He pointed to a 9" X 12" City interoffice correspondence envelop lying on the desk next to a regular mail envelop and the letter. "The letter was the only thing inside." Casey's voice and demeanor were slow and deliberate, indicative of a person who is in mourning, but driven by a quest.

Brogan explained, "There were no prints on the City envelope, the letter envelope, or the letter itself. Well, except for the mailroom lady. We questioned her. She had no particular recollection of that envelope. Hell, letters are received all the time and routinely routed from the mailroom. There's no reason to believe anyone in the process would have taken note of this envelope."

The Chief picked up the letter, as he had earlier, as if something may have changed on it; maybe he could see something he missed. Again he read it out loud, slowly, "Your daughter is alive. If she is to remain alive you will deliver $5,000. Call this number for instructions." Charlie offered, "That's a Valley number. It's disconnected. The phone company will give us a history of it, but I wouldn't expect anything from that."

Captain Tom Dwyer entered the room. Without any greetings exchanged Tom looked around at the group and began, "We've run the note by an FBI analyst who's supposed to be an organized crime expert. He says, and I agree, this isn't a ransom note. The small amount of money asked for is a message. It's an insult. There's something personal here."

All eyes in the room turned toward Casey. Bock asked, "Casey, can you think of anything beyond the obvious what would make this personal with you?"

Casey contemplated and with tears welling up in his eyes shook his head and observed, "Johnny was his son. That's pretty damn personal."

Heads nodded and several conversations ensued among all in the room. Slowly the Chief walked over to Casey. He stood face to face with the Captain and placed his hands on Casey's shoulders.

"Teel. We have our best investigators on this. You know we're family and one member's loss is a loss to all of us. It is personal, and we all feel it. Please, take some time off. Your folks are here. Be with them. Help each other through this."

Casey listened then replied, "Sir, Maria was a fighter. If the situation were reversed, she would mourn, but not until she got her daughter back."

The Chief shook his head, looked only at Casey, and in a whisper said, "I understand. You do what you need to do."

Casey's tears dried as he stood back at attention. His facial expression turned hard and deliberate. He looked at Captain Dwyer, "Tom, you're spearheading this?"

"Yeah Casey. I'll personally keep you informed every step of the way." Casey patted Tom on the shoulder as the group broke up and departed Casey's office.

An hour later Casey went into the squad room and fetched a cup of coffee. While he was in the room all chatter stopped. You could feel the sympathy flowing as everyone pretended not to notice him as they shuffled through their paperwork. As Casey passed Ron's desk, he softly asked, "Would you step into my office for a minute?" Ron did not reply, but immediately got up and followed Casey.

"Close the door please," Casey asked. Ron complied then stopped and looked at Casey. Ron had a blank expression, not having any idea what to expect.

"You going out to lunch today?" Casey asked.

"Well no, I was just going to grab a bite on the eighth floor." Casey drew a serious expression and looked squarely at Ron, "Get Charlie and meet me for lunch at the Japanese Garden. My treat. I'll be in that little back room. You be there at 1:30."

Ron stood silently for a few seconds, then, "Yeah, sure, Cap. We'll be there."

Ron turned to leave but stopped and looked up as he heard, "Ron, not a word about this meet." Without turning back, Ron nodded his head and departed.

The lunch conversation was light and infrequent. Though they wanted to, neither Ron nor Charlie asked why the meeting, and why in this secretive place. Casey was the last to finish eating. He took his napkin from his lap, wiped his mouth. Ron and Charlie just sat back and stared at him. Casey then proceeded to pour three cups of tea. While pouring he stated, "You know that interoffice envelope? It did not come through the mail room."

Ron and Charlie looked at each other, but said nothing. "Yeah, it came from inside the building, but not the mail room. Someone deposited it into the mail cart when the delivery lady wasn't looking."

Charlie spoke first. "What are you saying, Cap? Someone in the Department delivered the note?"

"That's right."

Ron started to talk, "How do . . ."

Casey interrupted. "It was the way the big envelope was sealed. I've noticed for years that these envelopes coming from the mailroom are always sealed the same way. That string on the back and the two round tabs; well the string is always, always wrapped around the tabs until the string is almost entirely buried."

Both Ron and Charlie developed doubting looks on their faces. Casey explained, "I've always been convinced that the supervisor in the mail room insists that all envelopes be sealed like that. You know, when a person supervises an innocuous function, he has to make the job seem more important than it is. He'll typically develop silly rules. It's an ego and control thing."

The officers looked at each other and shrugged in understanding.

"I also think I know who we may be dealing with." With that Ron and Charlie perked up and leaned toward Casey as if a few inches would make the difference between hearing and missing the revelation.

Casey leaned back, folding his arms while holding his cup in his right hand. "You guys have contacts in some other agencies that you've dealt with now and then. Right?"

Both nodded and mumbled affirmatively. "But if the matter turned out to involve some major mob boss; some big time organization, how would the exchange of this information be handled?"

Ron thought a moment then said, "Well, the exchange of information would be moved up to command levels."

Casey cocked his head and said, "You mean the exchange would become more formal?"

Charlie answered, "Sure, the departments aren't just going to leave it up to us grunts if it could become a big deal; something newsworthy."

Casey sat back silently and looked at both men. They looked at each other, and then simultaneously blurted softly, "Bill Johnson."

After a brief silence Casey continued, "I know, I don't want to believe it either. Indeed, I may be way off base. But I intend to look under every stone to find my princess." Casey's lower lip started to quiver as he wiped a tear from his face. The other two sat silently with their heads bowed.

"OK, I want to move on this!" Casey exclaimed as he leaned forward and looked from face to face. "If you'd rather not get involved with me outside the Department, I understand. And trust me, there will be no ill feeling on my part. No repercussions whatsoever if you want to back off." Ron and Charlie glanced at each other than looked Casey in the eye, "I'm in," came two voices as one.

"Good. Thanks," Casey replied as humbly as he could. Casey went on to explain that he has contacted the local agent in charge of the FBI. They would set up a meet and determine how to proceed. He told Ron and Charlie to act in the office as though they're involved in a new bookmaking investigation and they're out doing a lot of preliminary surveillance. Finally Casey cautioned that they each need to be aware of any possible tails.

At 8:30 the next morning Ron and Charlie arrived at the Van Nuys office of the FBI. They drove from home, but arrived within five minutes of each other. They were met by three agents, who escorted them to a small conference room. Introductions were made and pleasantries exchanged while they waited for Casey.

It was almost 9:00 when Casey arrived. He met supervising agent Boyd Jenks and field agents Bob and Richard. Before they could begin plans in earnest, Casey produced an envelope from his pocket. "It's started," he declared. Casey pulled a letter from the envelope and explained that it was delivered to his house and that it demanded that he contact a certain phone number. He is not to involve the Police Department in this if he wants to get his daughter back. He will be given instructions on setting up a meet so that he can get his daughter back. There was no ransom demand.

Boyd perused the letter then handed it to Bob and Richard, then to Ron and Charlie. Boyd asked, "What's your take on this, Teel?"

Casey explained that they are going to work on his desire to get his daughter back. That they want to get him alone somewhere so that they can kill him. Boyd agreed and added, "If this doesn't work, they'll keep working on you till you do it their way."

Casey recaptured the letter and held it for a moment. Ron then said, "Ah, captain."

Casey interrupted, "I know, this is our opportunity." With that Casey explained about his suspicions regarding Bill Johnson. He advised that he could present this new letter to the command officers, with Johnson present. Ron continued that if he is the mole, Johnson will surely relay to the mob what actions the Department would be taking.

The group spent several minutes discussion possible strategies. Finally Boyd advised, "We don't have enough here to get a tap on Johnson's phone. We can set up a tail, but he may or may not meet personally with them."

Casey observed, "Well that's the best we have for now."

Charlie entered the conversation, "But you know what boss, I bet Bill feels pretty secure here. He very well may meet with them personally, and if not, maybe he'll have occasion to meet with them for some other reason . . . . like getting paid."

It was decided. The FBI would put a tail on Johnson as soon as possible. Boyd added, "I think I'll do a little extra investigation into Johnson. That may turn up something we can use." Casey agreed. The meeting ended after Casey advised that he would set up a meet with his bosses as soon as Boyd's people were in place to get on Johnson.

Just outside the FBI building and before going their separate ways, Ron looked at Casey. "You know, Cap, I'm kind of surprised it was so quick and easy getting the Bureau to give this much support." Casey bowed his head slightly and looking out of the top of his eyes at Ron, "Hey, if they can catch a dirty LA cop, they'll drop looking for a presidential assassin in order to get him."

Ron grimaced and shook his head, muttering, "I suppose so."

The next afternoon the promised meeting took place in Commander Bock's office. Present were Casey, Ron, Charlie, Captain Tom Dwyer, Bock, Lieutenant Brogan, and of course, Bill Johnson. Bock opened, "The Chief is indisposed. I'll be meeting with him tomorrow morning. So what's this new development Casey?"

Casey produced the letter he previously reviewed with the FBI. Keeping the FBI meet secret, Casey reiterated his belief that the letter was intended to lure him to a trap. Looking up after reading the note, Bock removed his reading glasses and looked at Casey, "Have you called the number?" Casey explained that he was waiting for this meeting before acting on the instruction. Looking around the room, Casey said, "Any ideas?"

Dwyer being a firm, decisive person was the first to speak. "We should follow the usual routine. You'll make the call. We'll set up a recording device and try to trace the call. Just see what happens."

It took less than 20 minutes to get set up for the call from an outside phone line in the Ad Vice office. The same group huddled around as Casey dialed the number. Casey had a pencil and paper at his fingertips. The call went through. Casey spoke. "This is Captain Teel." Twenty seconds of silence followed, then Casey said, "Yeah, in Venice." With that Casey pulled the phone away from his ear and looked at the receiver.

Then he firmly placed it back into the cradle. "That was quick," Bock observed.

"Obviously he didn't want to be traced," Casey stated. Casey further explained that the phone was answered, but the male voice was muffled; obviously disguised. The instruction was that there is a one-day pass for him at Gold's Gym in Venice. He is to be there at 7:00 tomorrow morning, go to the locker room and change into a bathing suit. Spend fifteen minutes in the pool, then get dressed and stand by the pay phone in front of the location. He'll get a call there.

The group adjourned into Casey's office and all but Ron, Charlie, and Bill took seats. Dwyer leaned back balancing on his chair's back legs, and putting his hands behind his head smiled and proclaimed, "Smart bastards. They want you undressed and in the pool to make sure you're not wearing a wire."

"And seven o'clock," Charlie chimed in, "that's when all the guys go in for a morning workout prior to work. The place will be packed. It'll be pretty tough to spot a mole."

For the next twenty minutes Bock moderated as the group discussed strategy and options. It was decided that Casey would do as instructed. Bill would go to the Gym office later in the morning and see what information he can get regarding who paid for Casey's visit. Ron would immediately put together a team so as to have undercover officers in the Gym locker room and pool, and in cars outside. They will have units outside to tail any suspicious looking patrons as they leave. Charlie was to get a small short-range transceiver and hide it in the phone booth. After receiving the call, Casey would be able to retrieve the radio and call to an undercover van nearby with the instructions he receives. The possibility that they would try to hit Casey while he is in the phone booth was discussed. No one could see that happening since that would be such a public place, and there would be undercover officers in the immediate area.

All agreed and the group started exiting Casey's office single file. Before he got out the door, Casey caught Ron's eye. Casey used a head motion to indicate that Ron should stay back. Casey also nodded toward Charlie's back as he walked toward the door. Ron picked up on that and grabbed Charlie's arm. As all the others left the room, they both stopped just inside the door as Casey walked over and closed it.

Casey looked from Ron to Charlie and back again. "You know, there's not going to be a phone call." Charlie nodded his head in agreement and replied, "I know Cap, but we need to go through the motions."

Casey said, "No, here's what you do. Ron go ahead and put together a small group, but we won't waste manpower trying to follow anyone. Charlie, take one of the older, or even a broken transceiver to your electronic buddy downtown and have him hide a locater beacon device in it."

Charlie looked at Casey in amazement, "My electronic buddy?"

Casey looked at Charlie, then Ron, and smiled. "I know you guys have a source for some funny equipment." Charlie and Ron looked at each other then down toward their feet, looking ever so much like two boys caught with their hands in a cookie jar. Casey offered, "Hey, I won't tell if you don't. Just do it, OK?"

The two officers looked at each other again then looking back at Casey and smiling. "OK, boss, we'll see what we can come up with."

After a few moments of contemplation, Ron spoke up, "Boss, you think Bill or some goon will go get the radio and take it with him?"

"It's a long shot, which is why I don't want you to use a good unit, but it's worth a shot." Ron and Charlie wrinkled their chins as they nodded in agreement.

After his office was clear, Casey placed a call to the FBI. Boyd Jencks was filled in on the plans and affirmed that his men were in position to tail Bill Johnson.

It was Friday morning and everything went as planned. Casey went for his swim, got dressed, and then proceeded to the phone booth. He was there at five minutes past 8:00. He shuffled his feet as he slowly turned back and forth, constantly surveying the outside area. He paid particular attention to windows and rooftops of neighboring buildings. Being mentally convinced that nothing would happen here did not quash Casey's feeling of anxiety.

An elderly lady approached and stood outside the booth door. Obviously she wanted to use the phone, and quickly became annoyed that Casey was occupying the booth without using the phone. Casey ignored her for a couple of minutes, and then he slowly opened the booth door. He stood in the doorway and started breathing heavily. He contorted his face into several strange expressions, then slowly assumed a broad, salacious smile as he leered directly at the lady. She took a deep breath, looked around a moment, and then quickly walked off.

There was no call. Looking at his watch and seeing that it was now 20 minutes after 8:00, Casey looked and felt about under the phone. There was a strand of tape hanging which had been used to secure the transceiver out of sight. The unit was gone. Casey smiled and walked out. Not looking at anyone in particular, he waved his arms in a "time out" motion as he headed toward his car.

Bock, Brogan, Dwyer, and Bill Johnson were waiting for Casey when he returned to his office. Dwyer opened. "The radio chatter was that there was no phone call."

Casey affirmed and insisted that he was not surprised. "And the planted radio was gone?" Bock asked, his voice rising.

"Yes but there was some graffiti inside and out of the booth; some old, some new. Local hoods or a bum probably ripped it off. There really wasn't a decent place to hide it."

Bock and Dwyer nodded their heads. Casey added, "Charlie's completing a theft report now."

They all agreed that the next step would be to wait for the next communication from the kidnappers. Dwyer added, "I sent latent prints to the phone booth, but the chances that one of our hoods touched anything are slim and none."

They all consoled Casey by assuring him they would catch the bad guys and get his daughter back. They had no idea how far ahead of them he was. The Department was in for an awakening.

CHAPTER 28

The Pursuit

Casey left the office early and went straight home. The first thing he did there was to phone Boyd Jencks. Casey listened quietly while Jencks explained that they had tailed Bill Johnson from the moment he left Parker Center. He went to the gym as planned, then back to the office. Casey asked and Jencks agreed to call Casey with a report of Johnson's movements after work. Casey confirmed that the FBI would continue watching Johnson through the weekend. Jencks promised that he would notify Casey if anything developed over that period.

The call came from FBI agent Bob at 6:30 p.m. "Yeah, Captain, Johnson left Parker Center and then went straight home. We're there now. Our instructions are to stay with him until we're relieved later tonight."

"OK Bob, thanks for the update. One thing. You will see an old van conversion pass by Johnson's house later this evening. That'll be me. I just want to get a notion of the lay of the land there."

"We'll be watching. Oh; by the way. Johnson has a take-home car from work, right?" Casey affirmed the statement. "Well when he put it in his garage, we got a glimpse at his personal car." Casey said, "And?" "Well it looks like a late model Mercedes sedan." Casey replied, "You know the City of Angels generously takes care of its detectives."

"Yeah, right," Bob said.

Casey hung up and immediately called Charlie. "Uh Charlie, you eaten supper yet?"

"No, Cap, in California it's dinner, and I haven't decided on a culinary delight from my freezer yet."

Casey interrupted. "How about I pick you up in about 20 minutes; dinner's on me." Charlie accepted the invitation with only the tone of his voice asking why. Casey continued, "Do you know if Ron is doing anything tonight?"

"Uh, yeah, he said something about them doing something with the girls tonight."

"OK, it'll be just us. Oh Charlie. Bring that locater receiver. We're going to do a little hunting."

Charlie had just walked out onto his front porch when he saw a dingy old van conversion pull into his driveway. He ducked and peered in and was surprised to see Casey behind the wheel. Getting in he looked at Casey, "Nice wheels, sir."

"I picked this up at Rent-A-Wreck on my way home. That's the receiver?" Casey asked looking at a small but fat brief case in Charlie's lap.

"Yep. The guy said the battery in the sender is some new technology. It should last several days. This thing should pick up the signal about a half block away," Charlie explained as he looked at and patted the side of the case.

Casey backed out of the driveway and proceeded down the street. Charlie looked straight ahead but addressed Casey. "You figure if we drive through that neighborhood we'll find the punks who stole that radio?"

"You think I would do that?" Casey asked, keeping his eyes on the road.

"Nope. I figure you have some target in mind."

Casey looked at Charlie then back at the road. "As I said before, it's a long shot, but Bill or one of the mob boys may have taken the radio."

Charlie thought a moment then replied, "But that would make it appear that someone in your office that day is in on it."

Casey said, "Maybe. But you know, some of that graffiti on the phone booth looked real new. I have a hunch they put it there figuring we'd suspect some gang kids took the unit. Besides, with that thing they can listen to our tactical frequency. They would figure that would be useful."

Charlie pondered a few moments. "OK, that makes sense."

Casey continued, "Anyway, we're going to go by Johnson's house, just to see if he has it. I'm sure if he did take it, he won't be keeping it long, but the FBI said he went straight home today, so we may get lucky."

Lucky they were. As they drove slowly by Johnson's residence, the unit beeped the unmistakable reception of the signal from the hidden sender.

Casey and Charlie remained silent for several miles as they proceeded toward a restaurant Casey had chosen. As they parked in the restaurant parking lot, Charlie looked at Casey with an expression that was asking what he was going to do next. Casey understood and stated, "Let's go in and eat. I need to think about our next move." Charlie's nerves twinged a bit at his word "our."

After dinner on their way taking Charlie home, Casey outlined his thoughts. He continued to believe that Bill Johnson would deliver the radio to the mob. He further decided that he needed to involve the FBI regarding the locator device. As he stopped in Charlie's driveway, Charlie turned toward Casey and with a very serious expression offered, "Know that I've cleaned my calendar for the foreseeable future. Anytime night or day you need my help, please call. Or, just come get me."

Casey wrinkled his chin, "Thanks, I may just do that."

"And another thing," Charlie continued, "Ron has family, but he said he will do all he can to be as free as possible if you need him."

Casey looked at Charlie, and smiling a bit and shaking his head stated, "OK then."

Casey woke early the next morning. While nursing a cup of coffee he found the note with Boyd Jencks home phone number on it. He glanced at the clock every few minutes, waiting for 6:00 to appear. He decided he would wait till then to call Jencks. He reasoned, no sense pissing off the guy who's sticking his neck out for you.

The call was brief, as Casey noticed that it sounded like he woke Jencks, though he did not express any annoyance with the early hour. Casey told Jencks about the hidden transmitter and they agreed to meet at a location midway between their residences.

Jencks advised that it would take him a few minutes to get dressed before he could leave home. Casey took that time to call Charlie and Ron and arranged to pick both of them up. Just as Casey opened his back door to leave, the phone rang. His first inclination was to ignore the phone, assuming it was just another condolences call. But he got an intuitive bug and doing a double about face he went back in and answered the call.

Jencks was on the line and sounded a bit excited as he explained that he just learned that Bill Johnson was on the move. Both he and Casey reasoned that that was significant this early Saturday morning. They agreed to postpone their meet pending information as to where Johnson lands. It was decided that Jencks would stay home by his phone, and Casey would call him from Ron's house.

Casey picked up Charlie and the receiver then went to Ron's house. After a brief explanation of events, Casey asked to use Ron's phone. He was dialing it before Ron finished responding.

Boyd Jencks informed Casey that Johnson had driven to an apartment complex just off Western Avenue in the Hollywood area. Johnson was still there. Casey and Jencks agreed to meet at a bank parking lot on Western a few blocks from the location. The parade looked like a hen scurrying along followed by her running baby chicks as Casey, Charlie, and Ron quick-stepped out of the house and into Casey's rented van. All three were dressed in their Saturday morning worst.

Casey barely got stopped when Jencks hurried up to the van and entered the right rear door. Three sets of eyes glued on him as he started talking while in the motion of sitting. He explained that Johnson had left the apartment and was apparently headed back home. Jenks then offered more details. He said that Johnson did take a satchel into the apartment. It could have contained the missing radio. Further he stated that they got lucky. There is a vacant unit adjacent to the suspect's apartment. The manager is cooperating and a team is now setting up a listening device to pick up sounds from the target apartment.

Casey developed a worried expression. "Boyd, I doubt they picked this apartment from random. The manager could be in cahoots."

Johnson nodded his head in agreement, "Way ahead of ya. An agent is staying with him until; well 'till something happens and we can pull him off."

Casey's expression went from worried to relieved. Then he cocked his head and said, "How long before you hear from the listening team?"

Reaching for the door handle and getting up to exit Jencks said, "They'll be checking in regularly. I'll get to my car so I can monitor the radio. You might as well stay here. I'll keep you posted." He did not wait for a reply but went straight to his car and hunkered down in the driver's seat. Casey looked after him, thinking that he's fortunate that Jencks is taking this seriously; as though it was his own family involved. That thought gave him some peace and confidence.

For almost 30 minutes it was quiet in the van. Only occasionally Ron or Charlie would offer a few words of confidence that the rescue of Samantha was imminent. Casey only nodded. It was obvious to Ron and Charlie that Casey's mind was very busy.

All three in the van sat to attention from their slouched positions as Jencks walked quickly to the van. Again Jencks started talking before he got seated. "I don't have details of their conversations, but my men are confident your daughter is not there." Casey cocked his head a bit, and anticipating his next question, Jencks offered, "My two guys in there are as good as they come. They wouldn't have drawn that conclusion without good reason." Jencks was starring at Casey.

Casey pulled in his chin and shook his head, "OK then." After a pause, "So are you going to leave those guys in there?"

Jencks sat back and still looking directly at Casey, "Oh you bet. Anything said that might even remotely point to her whereabouts will be relayed to other units."

"And me?" Casey asked in a firm voice.

"Of course. And you."

Charlie gave Jencks the receiver, and he stated that he would get it up close to the apartment to verify the radio is there. The four agreed that they would sit tight in case someone from the apartment, or even Johnson, goes to another location; hopefully where Samantha is being held. As he departed the van Jencks advised, "I'll call you at home with any updates."

Casey told him, "OK, I'll be there."

As they departed the parking lot, Casey snarled, "Bull shit!" Charlie and Ron cocked their heads back and looked at Casey. Driving slowly and hunkering around the steering wheel, Casey explained. "Again I say to you two. I totally understand if at any time here you want to step aside. I'll do everything I can to minimize your involvement, but things could get hairy."

Charlie replied first, "In the words of one of my elders, bull shit. I know I speak for Ron. We're in this for the long haul. We're family, and that certainly includes Samantha."

A slight smile crept onto Casey's face, as did a small tear. "Thanks. I appreciate that."

With a bit of a dubious tone, Ron asked, "So, ah, what's the plan?"

Casey began to answer with a question, "Johnson doesn't have a family, does he?"

Ron answered, "Supposedly he has two or three, but I understand that he lives alone now."

"Well I'm tired of screwing around. I'm going to have a little chat with Mr. Johnson." Charlie and Ron looked at each other out of the sides of their eyes, but said nothing. Casey continued with directions. He said they were going to Johnson's house. Ron was to use what cover he could find to surreptitiously cover the back door. Charlie would stay in the van, out of sight, but would watch the front of the house. Casey concluded with, "I'll go to the front door and go in and have a talk with Johnson. Charlie, you have my back. You've got to divert any visitors who might show up. Ron, you just make sure there aren't any surprises from the rear, and give Charlie a hand if he needs it."

Charlie said, "Sure, OK." But both thought, *oh shit*.

Bill Johnson was wearing a plaid sport shirt and jeans. He opened the door and appeared startled for a moment. Then smiling explained, "Oh hi, Captain. I didn't recognize you."

Casey smiled back and said, "Yeah, I look pretty rough around the edges these days."

Johnson didn't move to open the screen door but asked, "So what brings you here?"

"Bill there are some developments and I really would like to get your expertise. Can I come in?"

Johnson opened the screen and stepping back and still smiling, "Oh sure, come in."

Casey said, "I know Dwyer and Bock mean well, but it's not their family." Casey assumed a sort of pitiful expression. "I just have to get my daughter back."

Johnson nodded in understanding and with a sympathetic expression asked, "So what can I do to help?"

Looking at Johnson Casey offered, "Well I'm trying to get together a few good officers to help; off duty of course. I'm willing to hire on a part time basis. We'd do a lot more surveillance. You know, go to some of the bookie joints. Try to pick up on any thing; any thing that might show some unusual activity."

Johnson nodded his head and said, "That sounds reasonable. Sure, I can give you some time. And Cap, you really don't need to pay me."

"Thanks Bill. I appreciate that. So do you have your service weapon here?"

Bill looked at Casey with a bit of a curious expression, "Well sure, why?"

Casey smiled and patted him on the shoulder assuring him, "I just want to see what you carry. I'm pretty sure I can furnish you with something a little more formidable."

Bill smiled and walked a few steps over to an end table next to his couch. He opened the top drawer and withdrew a shoulder holster. Smiling again Casey said, "Let me see that pea shooter." Johnson again looked a bit dubious, but he smiled and looking down at the holster he unsnapped the holding strap and withdrew the .38 revolver. Looking back at Casey he found himself staring into the barrel of Casey's .45 automatic. Casey was squared up and holding his weapon with both hands.

Without expression, Casey firmly ordered Johnson to place his revolver on the floor. Also without expression, Johnson complied and slowly stood back up, bringing his hands up in front of him in the surrender position. Both men looked into each other's eyes. There was silence for a moment.

Casey broke the silence, "Have you ever seen a man gut shot?" Johnson maintained a dumbfounded look and said nothing, but did slowly shake his head to express a negative reply as he could see Casey was now aiming the weapon at his belly. Casey's eyes were wide open and his eyebrows were cocked in a tense expression, a truly psychotic expression. He bent his knees slightly and continued a firm grip with both hands on his weapon, looking so much like a person about to fire. Casey continued, "I've seen it in the war. It's horrible. The pain is excruciating, and for some reason you don't lose consciousness. If you get immediate medical attention, you may live. But with all those internal organs messed up, just living is painful and nothing works right." Johnson just stared at Casey. "That's of course if you get treated right away. If you have to wait long for an ambulance, you'll probably just drown in your own vomit and belly bleeding."

Johnson was mindful that Casey continually referred to "you". While looking straight at Casey, Johnson's expressions went from surprise, to fear, and finally to realization that his involvement had been exposed.

Slowly lowering his hands he cocked his head a bit and raised his eyebrows, "You know Captain it won't take a genius to figure out who shot me? Then your daughter won't have any parent."

Casey glared at him, "No shit head, you don't understand. I came here to plead with you to tell me where my daughter is and you pulled that weapon there," nodding toward the floor and his revolver. "And you pulled it after I pleaded oh so nicely with you to please help me find her and after I assured you I wouldn't implicate you. Oh your own mother will be glad I shot you after I finish my sob story."

Johnson straightened up and raised his hands back up. His expression went back to one of terror and sweat beads started to appear on his forehead. He began to plead, "Look Captain, I had nothing to do with what happened at your house. I had no idea they were going to do that." His body was quivering and his knees buckling a bit, but he continued standing and holding his hands high.

Still looking intense but with a bit of a smirk Casey replied, "Sure, so that's why you immediately came forward and offered to help."

Backing away a couple of steps Johnson pleaded, "Captain I couldn't. I couldn't. You know those guys. They'd kill me."

Now aiming his weapon intently at Johnson's stomach, Casey said, "The difference, asshole, is they'd kill you quick. They wouldn't get any pleasure watching you die a slow, agonizing death." Casey's expression developed into a wicked smile. He appeared to start pulling the trigger, "Either you know where my daughter is and you're going to tell me right now, or you're just a worthless piece of shit to me and, well, you should just kiss your ass goodbye."

Before Casey finished Johnson shouted, "I'll tell you, I'll tell you," with voice tone rising, "Captain, please." Lowering his head and now softly he whimpered, "Please."

Casey spoke calmly, "You know where they have her?" Johnson explained that he has had two occasions to deliver messages to the abandoned building where they have Samantha. He described it as an old gym that went out of business when the new Golds opened nearby in Venice. He detailed the location, which is on a side street just off Lincoln Boulevard.

Casey demanded, "How do I get in?"

"It's all locked and boarded up. They go in and out through a side door just into the alley. You probably can force it. It's not a heavy door."

Casey pondered a second, then, "Yeah, likely I'd catch a quick bullet going in that door."

Johnson shook his head, "Yeah, likely you would."

Casey continued, "If I show up with uniforms you think they'd stand and fight?" Johnson shrugged his shoulders and answered, "There's usually three or four men there. I've heard them say something about an escape route. They might just open fire, figuring they can slow you down then boogie." After a pause, Johnson with bowed head turned his eyes up toward Casey, "They're probably not the smartest people you've ever dealt with."

"Yeah, that makes them more dangerous," Casey observed. Johnson nodded.

Johnson looked at Casey with a pleading look. It was an expression that shouted, "Oh please believe me." Casey thought that that's a lot of detail to be making up under the circumstances. "OK, Bill, I believe you. Obviously you know that if you're lying to me it'll be my life's passion to hunt you down and finish what I started here."

Johnson shook his head and as humbly as he could he acknowledged, "I know that, Cap."

Casey backed up to Johnson's front door, continuing to point his weapon at him. Casey reached behind and opened the door. As he backed into the doorway, Johnson got a strange look on his face and looking intently at Casey and rolling his palms open asked, "So what are you going to do?"

Casey looked at Johnson with a matter-of-fact expression, "I'm going to get my daughter. Well, that's after we yank your phone line out of the box. 'Course I know you won't have time to make any phone calls. Very soon Tony will know that you sold him out." Casey stopped and took a step back into the house. Placing his right index finger up to his mouth, then pointing it at Johnson, "If you foolishly take the time to get to a phone and warn them, then you will add me to the list of folks wanting you dead." Now waving his finger back and forth, "And turning yourself in? That would mean prison and you'd be a sitting duck for the mob. Plus, remember that the guards are part of our family." Casey's eyebrows rose as he looked intently at Johnson.

Johnson's shoulders drooped as his head bowed again. He looked forlorn. Casey again started exiting the house. He paused for a moment to advise, "If you move fast and often, you may just be able to keep ahead of the hit men."

Casey looked away as if in thought and shaking his head, "Yeah, but I'd move pretty damn fast and soon if I were you." With that, Casey exited and firmly closed the door behind him.

Casey moved quickly to the van after a quick detour to the outside phone box. Charlie and Ron came running up behind him like a couple of well-trained puppies. The officers held on as the van quickly accelerated and due to poor shocks rocked to nearly the point of overturning. Casey had a very intense expression, and looking straight ahead at the road: "I know where Sam is. We're going after her."

CHAPTER 29

The Siege

Commander Bock looked a bit irritated at the ringing phone. He put down the butter knife and wiped his hands on a towel. His sandwich was almost finished but his hands were greasy from handling the deli meat. "Yeah, Bock." Lieutenant Brogan was on the line. He explained that Boyd Jencks had called him looking for Captain Casey. Brogan explained that Casey had met with Jencks earlier and that he was supposed to be home waiting for Jenck's call. Bock wiped his hands more, then took down Jencks phone number and told the Lieutenant he would talk to him

Jencks briefly explained again that Casey was to be home waiting for word from Jencks. The FBI agent went on to unravel a tale for Bock about an undercover FBI agent from Detroit who just arrived in LA. That agent has shadowed Tony and others in their organization for several years. He's on the trail of Casey's daughter, and will be checking in when he gets a good location for her.

Jencks and Bock discussed strategy for a few minutes, and then Bock signed off with the plan that he would have Brogan and others look for Casey. Bock would remain by his phone for any follow-up from Jencks.

Casey informed Charlie and Ron about what he had been told by Johnson. He drove straight to Venice Division Station and went in to talk to the Watch Commander. Again, Charlie and Ron walked fast and skipped along trying to keep up with Casey. They all entered the Watch Commander's office and after identifying themselves,

Casey and the WC, Sergeant Wessell, walked from that office to the empty Commanding Officer's office.

Charlie and Ron stood by in the WC office, looking around and backing toward the wall, trying to look invisible. Two uniformed offices came in, looked them over, and then placed reports in an incoming box. No words were spoken as the uniformed men walked out, constantly peering suspiciously at the very casually dressed men.

In a few minutes Casey and Sergeant Wessell reappeared. Wessell produced a hand-held radio from his desk and handed it to Casey. Casey waived it in thanks as he quickly walked from the office, signaling for his charges to follow.

As they entered the van Charlie and Ron looked at each other with puzzled looks, but said nothing, knowing that Casey will fill them in. Casey did just that as they motored toward that old closed gym.

Casey explained that they have a black and white at their disposal. Sergeant Wessell will be the second man in that patrol car. They will be in touch via the hand-held radio on a tactical frequency. Casey concluded, "I don't know what we're going to do exactly, but we'll check out the location and figure it out. I really don't want the cavalry there yet, but having a uniformed unit standing by may come in handy." Charlie squirmed a bit as he thought, there's that "we'll" again.

They found the deserted gym just as Johnson said they would. It faced south toward an east/west side street just off Lincoln Boulevard. The front had several windows, which had been painted black, and had a large boarded up doorway. The left side of the two-story building, which had several windows but no doors, faced east toward Lincoln. There was lightly painted over lettering that was not legible. The opposite side faced west and was along a north/south alley. That side had no windows, but did have a first floor door off the alley.

The area was all commercial locations. All that were within a block were closed for the weekend with about 50% permanently closed. There was medium traffic on Lincoln, but the side street was virtually deserted. There was no pedestrian traffic, except for three

20 something year old males hanging out on the north sidewalk, just west of the alley entrance.

As they turned right off Lincoln onto that side street, Casey instructed Charlie and Ron to quickly duck down out of sight. Casey drove past the location slowly, but not so slow as to look conspicuous. He looked up the alley and saw a dumpster against the gym wall just north of the alley door. The three young men stayed put, hardly noticing the van. As they turned right again at the next block, Casey told his men to get up from their hidden positions. Well out of sight of the target location, Casey pulled over and stopped.

The officers did not comment while Casey slumped over the wheel, obviously in deep thought. Suddenly Casey sat back and a slight smile appeared. He looked first at Ron, then at Charlie. "Charlie, you're a genius!" he exclaimed.

Charlie looked at Ron, shrugged, and then looked back at Casey. "Of course I am. What did I do?" Casey recalled the incident when they drew a bookmaker out of his cash room by creating a phony police incident in the street. Charlie and Ron looked at each other and then back at Casey.

Casey went on to explain his new plan in detail. He told of seeing the dumpster just past the gym door. Casey would take a position behind it. Charlie would drive the van. Ron would man the radio. Coordinating with the patrol unit they would engage in a chase that would culminate on the side street, near to the alley. The approach would be on the side street, coming from the west back toward Lincoln. It would stop short of the boulevard, so as to attract minimum attention. With the siren going and brakes screeching, Casey would find some object to throw to generate extra noise.

Casey paused and all looked at each other. Ron opened, "What if these guys think the uniforms are after them? That could be disastrous."

Casey said, "Yeah, I thought of that. For sure, they're not just going to rush out like that bookie did. They must have a way of looking out without being seen. Once they see it's just some cops stopping you loathsome dope heads, they'll relax and hopefully walk out to watch. All they have to do is just step outside the door a bit; then they're mine. Thing is, the clock is ticking. We've got to get in there for Sam. At least with the uniform backup if this doesn't work they can get a bunch of troops here in a hurry and contain the situation."

Charlie chimed in. "OK, Cap. We can make it work. Let's do it." Ron offered his vote in favor of the plan and also encouraging words.

Casey cocked his head then declared, "Well, there's one order of business first." They looked at each other. "We have to get those scum bags on the street out of there. They could really screw up the whole thing."

"Yep," Ron said, nodding.

Casey turned back to face the front and started the van. He explained his plan as they drove. They proceeded north, and then turned east onto the next east/west Street that returns to Lincoln. Just as they passed the north/south alley that lies next to the side of the gym, Casey suddenly stopped in the traffic lane. Slowly, he backed to a position in full view of the alley. Six eyes scanned the alley way as Casey explained, "I could've sworn I just saw a man in the alley; down a ways there against the east side."

All were silent for a moment while they continued to peruse the alley. Then Charlie commented, "I don't remember that blue sedan being there."

Ron stated, "Yeah, it seems to me I did notice it before. But I don't know." Casey concluded as he moved the van forward, "Maybe I just saw someone dumping his trash. No one's in the car. We ain't gonna have perfect conditions here. Let's just get on with it." Casey was speaking out loud but basically just convincing himself.

Casey parked the van virtually in front of the three men, who had not moved. Charlie and Ron were again ducking out of sight. The men watched intently as Casey slowly got out of the van on the driver's side. He had a sweater draped over his right hand and arm, which he held up in front of his waist. He faked being drunk. He was holding his sweater covered arm as though it was injured. The three men chuckled as they watched Casey stagger away from them on the sidewalk. He just went a few steps then turned around. Looking sort of confused he walked back toward the men. One of them demanded, "What are you old man, confused?"

Another asked, "Hey, you got any money for us?"

Casey hung his head down as he approached them. He walked very close to the adjacent building front appearing to be trying to avoid eye contact. The tallest man in the group slowly turned, watching Casey as he walked between him and the building. Still smiling, but stated firmly the man said, "Hey, you didn't answer. You got any money?" Casey was now between the man and the building front. The other two were standing, laughing, behind the big man, with their backs toward the van.

Casey looked up and sheepishly replied, "Yes, I have some money." With that he quickly raised his right hand, revealing the pistol that had been hidden by the garment. Just as quickly, the muzzle of the gun went up and stuck directly under the tall man's throat, pointing up toward his brain. Casey simultaneously grabbed the man's collar and held tight. The man with the gun in his throat dropped his hands by his side and stood straight up cocking his head back. But Casey had a firm hold of him. The other two saw what was happening but turned around as they heard the door of the van open. They saw two men, one just stepping outside the van side door and the other in the doorway. Both were shielded from side view by the open van doors and both were pointing revolvers directly at them. In these positions, only a person close by could see what was happening.

Casey spoke clearly and loudly, "You dirt bags look a little pale. I think you ought to head right down to the beach and get some sun."

The tall man could barely shake his head, what with the pistol under his chin and Casey's iron grip on his collar. He mumbled something. "What did you say?" Casey demanded in a commanding voice. "Yes sir. Yes sir. We're leaving," the man said as he forced the words, almost choking.

Casey stepped back and while lowering his pistol, motioned with it for the men to go. All three ran, walked, and stumbled along west bound. Casey and company quickly hid their weapons as they watched the men depart.

They looked back at the gym, which was about thirty yards to their east. There was no sign of activity. There were no west side windows on the building, and the angle to where they were from the front windows would make it difficult for anyone inside to see them.

"Let's go," Casey quickly directed as they all entered the van and departed.

Casey drove the van slowly to the next corner and after turning right, stopped briefly while Charlie got behind the wheel and Casey squatted next to the right-side double door. As they drove on, Casey reiterated the plan as before, and then got on the tactical radio. He called for Sergeant Wessell and the uniformed officer to meet the van a couple of blocks away after Casey is dropped off.

Casey did exit the van at the north end of the alley where they had stopped before. Casey paused momentarily while he scanned the alley. Seeing no activity, he quickly moved south through the alley. He furtively peered into the blue sedan that was parked about twenty yards into the alley, then proceeded on and took a hidden position behind the trash dumpster just north of the alley door of the gym.

The plan worked flawlessly. Charlie drove the old van to a screeching halt directly in front of the alley entrance. Apparently having some fun with the situation, the officer driving the patrol car stayed further away from the van then he would have had it been an actual pursuit. That way with red lights flashing and siren screaming he was able to lock the brakes so as to come to a sliding halt, rather than just stopping, shy of the stopped van. While moving down the alley, Casey had collected two metal trashcan lids, which he hurled at a building wall directly across from the gym door. Casey thought, it sounded like World War III had just begun.

From behind the dumpster Casey had a side view of the doorway, but he could view enough to see that the door was moving. Damn, he thought, as there was no one exiting the door. The uniformed officers with weapons drawn and in loud voices commanded Charlie and Ron to get to the back of the van and, "assume the position". They both faced the vehicle and with arms spread leaned forward, placing their hands on it. Sergeant Wessell kicked at both of their legs, causing them to spread.

Wessell glanced toward the alley. He could see Casey peering out from behind the dumpster. Casey exposed his right hand and put it into a rolling motion, signaling Wessell to continue. The Sergeant looked back at Charlie and Ron and began loudly barking at them.

Then it happened. Two men slowly emerged from the gym door. They were paying strict attention to the activities in the street. One began chuckling and elbowing his partner.

Suddenly both men felt a great weight slam against their backs. Casey had emerged from behind the dumpster and quietly and forcefully charged, throwing his body into both of them as if slamming two forwards against the hockey rink wall. The two men quickly scrambled to get up, but at about half way, they suddenly realized that the uniformed officers were now charging toward them with revolvers pointed. Behind the uniformed officers Charlie and Ron were gathering themselves and pulling their weapons. With two quick large steps Casey got to the gym door and swiftly but quietly closed it.

Almost whispering Casey instructed the uniformed officers to quickly get the men into the van. Without words, Wessell and the officer nearly took the men's shirts off as they pulled them by their collars, running them to the vehicle. The whole event unraveled so quickly and firmly that the two kidnappers were initially confused and did not gain the presence of mind to call out until they were virtually thrown into the van.

Casey, Charlie, and Ron took positions beside the closed gym door. Casey went to the dumpster, looked around inside and then reached in and pulled out a ten by twelve inch white cardboard box. He returned to the doorway and in a loud whisper instructed, "OK, back me up, but this is my show. If there are goons in there they'll be aiming at this doorway." He flipped the box to Ron and continued, "Charlie you push the door open." Now raising his voice a bit, "You two stay out of the opening. Ron push the box into the opening, about head high. Keep your hands back." Ron looked down and nodded as Casey was taking a prone position on the ground in the doorway with his weapon firm in hand. Casey snapped, "OK, now."

Charlie took the doorknob, slowly turned it, then with a jerk pushed the door wide open. He immediately backed up against the wall, gritting his teeth. Ron pushed the box into the opening as instructed. His neck and shoulder muscles tensed and he closed his eyes and ducked his head between his arms in anticipation of gunfire. Casey aimed his weapon inside, holding it with both hands.

There was not a sound, but one could almost hear the tension twang.

Sergeant Wessell was now standing against the building wall next to Ron. His weapon was drawn and held in both hands pointing up; his facial expression was intense. As the silence continued, taut muscles slowly relaxed. Casey got up by backing up onto his feet, thus rising while continuing to face toward the opening.

Still clutching his pistol with both hands, Casey quickly but very softly directed, “Fan out when we get inside, but don’t get too far apart. I’ll stay in the lead. Pay attention to our perimeters and our backs.” Casey was peering inside and did not look at anyone as he gave the directions. Had he looked at the Officers and the Sergeant, he would have seen that all their tense expressions had melted into looks of serious determination. Looking straight ahead and gingerly entering the building, Casey whispered, “Let’s go.”

CHAPTER 30

Face To Face

A short entry way opened into a large room with a high ceiling. In the center there was a boxing ring with some good and some broken, hanging ropes. The canvas floor was tattered and torn. Open space circled the ring, with several doorways leading to rooms around the perimeter. There was a balcony that was a running track circling overhead. Off that track there were other doors. Several skylights offered some light. There were many light fixtures scattered about, but only a few were lit. Overall there was light, albeit a bit dim.

The four rescuers proceeded slowly and silently. They peered and poked into and around all objects. Constantly scanning before them, they were bound to instantly pick up on any movement. And that they did.

All eyes, and weapons, turned toward one of the perimeter doors. It had a sign on it that was loose at one end and thus hanging down. It appeared to read, "MEN". A man was backed against the other side of the door and pushing it open. He turned half way to his left, revealing that he was holding two rolls of paper towels, which explained his method of exit. He was 5'9", a bit pudgy, with dark hair.

The man was speaking as he rolled through the doorway, "What the hell's with all the noise. You idiots . . . ." Cut off in mid sentence he dropped the towels but kept his hands in the holding position. Without moving his head his beady dark eyes scanned the string of pistols aimed at him. "What the hell is this?" he demanded, keeping his hands raised. Casey lowered his weapon and stepped up to within three feet of the man.

With his eyes wide open and starring directly at the man, Casey explained, "I'm here for my daughter. Can you help me out?" The man's expression started to turn from confident anger to a trace of fear as the Captain's sarcasm and wild look in his eyes got through to him.

"You're way off base; she ain't here," the man stated, but without a lot of conviction as Casey continued to stare wide-eyed straight at him.

Softly Casey asked, "Well than, perhaps you'll be good enough to tell me where she is?" The man kept his hands up but backed a step and began to show beads of sweat.

"I told you, she's not here."

Casey cocked his head, drew an angry look, and aiming his pistol toward the man's crotch, "You tell me that one more time and I'll shoot your balls off." The man kept his hands up and slowly backed to gain separation from Casey. He said nothing. His eyes bulged with fear but his expression and actions were bound in the tradition of omerta. Silence.

Casey lowered his weapon and eased his angry expression. The man kept his hands in the air, as only Casey's pistol was lowered. Calmly Casey asked, "What's your name?"

The man looked from side to side then back at Casey, "Tony. Tony Tesoro."

Tony and Casey looked straight at each other for a moment. Though not said, both knew that Casey had killed Tony's son.

Casey looked back at Sergeant Wessell and told him to cuff Tony. With his back now toward the boxing ring, Casey faced the officers. Wessell searched and then handcuffed Tony by one arm to an exposed water pipe. Stepping away from Tony, Wessell looked at Casey and exclaimed, "He's clean."

Casey, Charlie, Ron, and Wessell were now standing together as Casey directed that they would search each room one by one. He was concluding when two quick gunshots rang out. The blasts were amplified by the fact they originated within the large room. The unmistakable sound of a shell ricocheting around the room caused all four officers to wildly spin their heads around as they all ducked and scrambled for cover against the base of the boxing ring. Tony, who was sitting on the floor, ducked his head as he covered it with his free hand. His feet flew up in the air. There was pandemonium as bodies scrambled to improve their cover as they frantically looked around anticipating the next shots.

A moment of silence prevailed. Casey then looked to his left and saw that one of the doors off the main room was open and a man's body was lying in the doorway. Casey stared for a few moments, and convinced the man was dead, or at least out, looked back at the others. They were all scanning the balcony with weapons held up.

While still looking up, Ron quietly stated, "The shot seemed to come from that balcony."

In the same tone, Casey directed, "Look over there." He was motioning with his pistol toward the man down.

Puzzled looks appeared on all faces as they looked at the body, then back toward the balcony, then back again. The quiet was penetrated by a lone voice from above, "FBI. I'm FBI." With that, two hands slowly appeared, coming from the balcony floor. The right thumb held a pistol, which was dangling loose. A person lying on the balcony floor would be out of sight of the men below.

Casey barked, "Put that piece down and stand up."

His caution alert went up as he had detected a Latin accent in the man's voice. The voice repeated, "FBI, don't shoot."

Casey confirmed, "We won't shoot. Stand . . . ." Casey quickly glanced back toward the opened door. There was a high-pitched whimper. Casey listened intently. There it was again.

Casey stood partway up while backing up. On the balcony the figure of a man slowly appeared. Loudly now Casey instructed, "Keep him covered." Casey sprinted toward the man down and the open door.

Casey knelt next to the man's body and while peering through the doorway into the room, he felt the mans neck. There was no pulse. Casey glanced down at the man as he stepped over him and then took a crouched position just inside the room. He held the pistol in both hands and his index finger was poised to pull the trigger. Slowly he lowered the weapon and stood erect.

The room was lit by one lamp that was on a table against a sidewall. Two chairs were at the table. Directly opposite the doorway and about fifteen feet away was a metal frame bed. A young lady was sitting upright on the bed. Her right wrist was handcuffed to the bed frame and her mouth was covered with a crudely tied bandana. Her eyes were wide open in terror, but those wide eyes developed a beaming smile as she recognized the man running toward her.

Casey threw his pistol on the bed as he quickly untied the bandana and without words drew his handcuff key and freed her wrist. Both father and daughter were silent as they stood together and embraced with an all out bear hug. Their bodies rolled back and forth as tears filled their eyes.

Ron and Charlie stood quietly just inside the doorway as they observed Casey pull back from Samantha a bit as he held her arms. He leaned his head forward and started whispering in her ear. With tears continuing to well up, she gently shook her head in acknowledgment, as she was the only one who could hear the words spoken by her father.

In a few moments Casey leaned back, but continued to hold Samantha. They both smiled softly into each other's eyes. Charlie and Ron approached the couple, one on each side. They both patted her shoulders as they looked at her face. Samantha smiled as she looked from one to the other, seeing tears slowly marking their cheeks as well.

The foursome slowly walked from the room, amid assurances from Samantha that she was "OK." She threw a brief disgusted look toward the body on the floor as they stepped over him and entered the main room. Casey continued to hold his daughter in one arm as they approached the other men.

The stranger from the balcony was standing with Sergeant Wessell and two other uniformed officers. Two more uniformed officers had entered the gym and were walking toward the group.

Wessell addressed Casey with a recap. Motioning toward the stranger, "His FBI credentials are good, but I did send my partner out to the car to summon a Bureau supervisor." The Sergeant continued with the story that the man was working undercover. He was targeting the organization in which Tony Tesoro was a regional boss. He heard about Tony's son being killed and about the kidnapping. He felt he could help find the victim because he was in tight with one of Tony's main underlings. But, since he was working on the larger organization, his bosses wouldn't send him here for fear that would blow his cover. He decided to take personal time off and come anyway. "His gun has been fired. He did shoot that guy. He saw the man easing the door open and taking a bead on us."

Casey looked deep into the man's eyes. "Likely your bosses aren't going to be very happy with you." The man nodded his head while grimacing a bit. Casey released his daughter and stepped directly in front him. "Whatever it takes. From me and from brass from our Department. We'll talk to anyone in the Bureau to make this right for you. Hell we'll beat up Hoover if that'll help." Casey and the man smiled at each other.

"Well thanks, but that won't be necessary," the man offered, "the fact is I've been considering retiring anyway."

Casey smiled and patted him on the shoulder, "OK, but I mean it. Anything we can do, please contact me personally."

They started to turn away, but turned back towards each other as the man continued, "I need to tell you. This was a bit of a personal thing for me as well." Casey cocked his head, as others close by tuned in. Motioning with his head toward Tony, who was being escorted out by two uniformed officers, "Tesoro here is a total bastard. We grew up in the same area of Italy. A lot of us, including him, were in the war with the Nazis. When it was done, most of us went home and worked to make things better. Him? No, he wanted to continue being a damn Nazi. A tough guy taking advantage of people. Years later I was recruited by the FBI. When I found out he was with the Mafia here, I did all I could to work against him."

Casey cocked his head and observed, "Well, seems like you've succeeded. His role here makes him guilty of capital murder in California. They probably won't hang him, but I bet he'll spend the rest of his miserable life in prison."

Detectives were beginning to arrive on the scene. Casey, again holding Samantha by his side, and the others began making their way toward the exit. The FBI man again addressed Casey, "I'm really happy you have your daughter. My daughter's grown now too, but she'll always be my baby girl." Casey looked at Samantha and they threw each other a quirky smile.

Just outside the door, Casey shook the man's hand and stated, "You know, I didn't get your name."

"I'm another Tony. Tony Alberoni." Casey's facial expression became blank as he looked at Tony. His expression also went away as they looked at each other. In a moment they released their hands and as they started to part in a far away voice that sounded like he was thinking of something else, Casey offered, "Thanks again, Tony." Tony waved in acknowledgement as he walked away. Both men maintained strange, sober expressions as once more they glanced back at each other

Samantha stepped slightly in front of her father as she looked around at him, "What is it, Daddy?"

Still expressionless he said, "I don't know. Let's get you to the clinic for a checkup."

THE END